THE ROOK

GENTLEMEN ROGUES
BOOK 4

NANA MALONE

COPYRIGHT

This is a work of fiction. Names, characters, places, and incidents either are the product of the author's imagination or are used fictitiously, and any resemblance to actual persons living or dead, business establishments, events, or locales, is entirely coincidental.

The Rook, Book 4 in the Gentlemen Rogues Series

COPYRIGHT © 2023 by Nana Malone

Cover Art by Najla Qambar

Alpha Reading: Suzi Vanderham

Edited by Angie Ramey

Proof Editing: Michele Ficht

Published in the United States of America

FREE READ

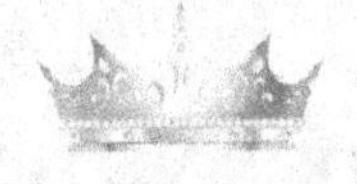

PROLOGUE

NISSA

I thrashed as I grabbed for my sister. "Lenora. Lenora, I don't want to go."

Even though she was stronger than me, my sister's hands were too slick to hold on to.

Miss Theresa and Miss Mary tried to pull us apart, but Miss Mary earned an elbow in the gut for her efforts. Miss Theresa kept trying, but I was wiggly and small. I didn't want to go with the man, but Miss Theresa said there was paperwork that proved he was my father.

I didn't know what it meant. All I knew was that they expected me to leave Lenora behind. *My sister.*

The only person on earth I had left. I wasn't going to do it.

Miss Theresa had always been nice. She would sneak me extra cookies for dessert sometimes. But she was not as nice to Lenora. She always said Lenora was *difficult*, and I was the easy one. I hated being called the easy one.

I didn't care what they said, I was not leaving her. Not today. Not ever.

My head thrashed against Miss Theresa's hold, and my braids flew around my face. "Let me go. I want my sister."

Miss Theresa crooned in my ear. "Hush now, Nissa. Mr. Montgomery is waiting."

"He has to take us both. We're sisters. He can't split us up. You said we wouldn't be split up."

Finally, Miss Theresa realized that trying to pull me back and wrapping her arms around me was just a recipe for disaster. So she secured my arms against my side, and knelt in front of me, blocking out Lenora, who was pounding her back with her fists. But then Miss Mary had Lenora again, and this time, she had her in a bear hug so my sister couldn't break free. "Listen to me, Nissa. I'm so sorry. He said that he'll arrange for you to still see Lenora, okay? But he's got the blood and paternity tests. There's nothing I can do."

I shook my head. "I will run away. Every single day, I will run away."

A deep voice rang from the hallway. "Well, you can try. But you're my daughter, Nissa. I'll find you and bring you back home because I want to keep you safe. I didn't know about you before, but now that I do, I can't leave you here."

A chill ran up my spine, and I glowered at him, sending him a mutinous look. In Miss Mary's arms, Lenora howled and screeched, bucked and fought. And instead of lunging at Miss Theresa, she lunged at the man, kicking and wailing. He held her off easily and then knelt, keeping a firm hold on her. "I'm so sorry. I wouldn't split you up, but she's my daughter. I need her with me."

I was still glowering at him. "You let my sister go. I hate you."

His expression was soft when he looked at me with icy blue eyes. There was no warmth in them. But his voice was low, and at least it was kind. "I'm sorry this hurts you. I'm sorry your mother didn't explain. And I'm sorry I have to split you up. But get your things, Nissa. You're coming home with me."

When he released Lenora, I could see the defeat in the slump of her shoulders, and my suddenly larger-than-life sister broke. "Lenora, no. Don't cry, Lenora."

She lifted her gaze to me, her eyes filled with tears. "You have to go with him, Nissa."

I shook my head. "I'll run away every single day."

And then my sister crawled over to me. Miss Theresa moved aside, giving her room to talk to me. Lenora sniffled, her hands still slick with sweat, tears tracking down her brown face over her cheeks. "I love you. Don't run away, okay? He said that he will let us see each other. He's your dad."

"No, our dad died with mum."

She squared her shoulders. "You heard him. My dad isn't your dad. You have to go."

I shook my head. "I'm not leaving you."

"You have to. I love you. I'll see you soon, okay?"

Julian Montgomery took my hand firmly and tugged me behind him. And all I could do was turn back and watch my sister, her image getting smaller and smaller until the door was finally closed.

1

WESTIN

"I need you to go undercover."

That was the last thing I expected my Ops Commander, Gabe Webb to say when he summoned me into his office. I was a junior agent. Still too green for a solo undercover mission. "Something tells me there's a reason I'm here all by my lonesome."

He nodded. "We have intel that number one on our most-wanted list, Antonio Igno, is having a meeting with someone you know."

Before he said the words, I could feel it in my bones. I knew who it was.

The man who had stripped me of everything. My life, my inheritance, my name... my love.

I started shaking my head before he could even finish. "No, I'm not doing it. I'm not going back there. You and I had a deal. You said I never had to go back."

"I know. And if it wasn't Igno, I wouldn't ask you to. But rumor is they had a meeting at the Winston Gala the other night. Our sources tell us that Montgomery took something from Igno. A ledger and the cipher that goes with it."

I blinked rapidly. "Wait, Igno's ledger? That thing is legendary. Supposedly, there's a physical copy and a digital copy. That digital copy is all over the dark web with hackers trying to access it. No one knows where the cipher is. No one's ever seen it. That ledger is more secure than the NSA."

Not that the NSA was that secure because I had hacked it once. Only for a few seconds, and I had to get out before they caught me. But I had done it.

"That's the one. He has a physical version of it and a cipher that only comes out for his meetings. The cipher, it seems, has gone missing. We think Julian Montgomery stole it from him."

I shook my head again. "There's no way. Montgomery is greedy and ambitious, but he's not a fool. He knows Igno would kill him."

"In which case, we're down one cockroach. But the point is, we want the cipher, and we think you can get it."

I swallowed hard and squared my shoulders. "*You* think I can get it, or Oversight thinks I can get it?"

The Rogues Division was a secret *if I tell you, I'll have to kill you* type of organization that was an arm of the British government. King, Queen, and country and all that. We went after the worst of the worst. The ones that the government couldn't touch and keep their hands clean. We still had a code; we just had less red tape.

Gabe Webb was the Rogues ops command. He reported to Oversight. Oversight was basically the pencil pushers who made the big game decisions, the master chess players. The problem was each of them had their own agenda. Agendas we weren't privy to. Hell, even Gabe wasn't privy to them. And now he was about to send me back to dance with the devil, so I had to know if it was his call or theirs.

"I know I gave you my word. If there was any other way to do this, I would."

I listened to what he *wasn't* saying. This hadn't been his choice. Oversight had commanded him, and regardless of what Gabe said or did, or what I said or did, I was getting sent back. Julian Montgomery was technically my godfather. He'd been best mates with my dad, and when my parents died, he'd taken me in. I'd thought I at least had someone who loved me left in the world.

That was my mistake. Julian was harsh and exacting. He made me live with his housekeeper on the edge of the property. At best, I was a beloved servant of sorts. It was all very *Great Expectations*. But Mrs. Pembry was delightful. She and her husband looked after me until he died when I was sixteen, and then I was all she had left. She treated me like her son. And in so many ways, I finally had that love that I'd been missing. Love that Julian would not have been able to give me simply because he was a narcissist and uncapable of it.

When I turned eighteen, instead of going off to uni, Julien forced me into his business. And for a kid with no prospects, nowhere to go, and no access to his trust fund, I had no other choice. The choices I made when I was with him were ones I couldn't take back. The things I had been asked to do still haunted me to this day.

Once I broke free, I'd been hell bent and determined to live the life I should have. Cambridge, a real life, all of it. So I'd created Westin Rourke. And that was where the Rogues found me.

"How do you expect me to pull this off?"

"Obviously, he's been looking for you since you disappeared. You know that."

"I do know that. And I told you I wasn't ever going back."

"I know. But if Igno's involved, that means Montgomery's daughter is also in danger."

That was when my stomach went into freefall. Nissa Montgomery had been the only bright spot in my childhood. "There's no way Montgomery would allow her to be hurt."

"From what you've told me about Montgomery, he would risk her for his own ambition without a second thought."

I clenched my jaw. "Fuck."

"I need your yes."

"And if I say no?"

He shrugged. "I'll send you back involuntarily."

"So one way or another, I'm going in?"

Gabe sighed. "It's better if it's your choice. And we both know that if Nissa Montgomery is in trouble, you're going to go get her."

I hated that he knew me so well, but he had almost psychic powers. Nissa Montgomery was essentially the only reason I would return to hell.

Unfortunately, I was certain that after the way I'd left she hated me.

WESTIN

A few weeks later, the biting chill of the wind sliced through my tactical gear. Everything would change in less than twenty minutes.

The only visual the sliver of moonlight offered was my puff of breath in the night air.

Sweat beating on my forehead, heart hammering against my ribs, I knew I had the training to survive this. But knowing you knew how to survive and believing in your actual survival were two different things. I forced a deep breath and tried to find my focus.

In less than twenty minutes, life as I knew it would be over.

I was going back into the fray, to the place I promised myself I would never return.

Well, promises were made to be broken.

Not this kind of promise.

I wasn't sure which was worse, that I was going in for an indeterminate amount of time, that I was going at all, or the way I was going to have to do it.

My team was going to worry.

Stop talking as if you're not coming back. You're coming back.

The plan was simple. Or at least it had seemed simple when Gabe sat me down and told me what was going to happen.

It was like a scene from that movie, *Taken*. 'You're going to be taken.' As if that was some shit I would take lying down.

But you have to take it lying down. The mission is to get in and not kill Julian Montgomery on sight.

Julian Montgomery, my godfather and all-around psychopath, was supposedly in league with the number-one arsehole on our Rogues most-wanted list.

Honestly, the news didn't surprise me at all. The only thing that surprised me was that he hadn't been in league with Antonio Igno before. Igno was a drug runner, arms dealer, human trafficker, and terrorist, and the Rogues had been trying to take him off the board for nearly a decade.

During the past year, we'd come close several times. But each time he just squeaked out of our grasp.

But not this time. This time you're going to get him.

Four years ago, I'd escaped out of my godfather's grasp. It hadn't been easy, and I'd had to leave everything I cared about behind. But I'd done it. Made a clean break. And now I was going back.

Gabe had leaked information about my location. We knew Julian was looking for me, even though I'd made it look like I'd fallen off the face of the earth. And if you asked the right people, they would have told you I was dead. But the old man knew what kind of skills I had. He was stubborn and didn't like to lose, so he'd kept looking.

But his obsession was going to come back and bite him in the arse. Over the course of the last month, we'd been building a profile that made it look as though I'd fallen in with criminals. Since the Rogues division was so clandestine, only the highest levels of government knew how we operated. Since some of our activities couldn't be broadcasted, we often had to mask them as something else.

During the last few missions I'd been sent out on, we made it appear as if our fake criminal syndicate, the Tique Collective, had stolen weapons. We'd even gone so far as to leak a partial of my face. We figured sooner or later one of his little spies was going to find me.

Once I was in, I was to get as close to Montgomery as I could. Find out what his business with Igno was. Once we had them both in the same location, we'd snatch them both up.

It all seemed so simple, except the one snag I hadn't told Gabe about. But with any luck, I wouldn't have to involve her. With any luck, I wouldn't even *see* her again.

Tonight's actual mission was simple. Retrieve Niall Marks and then follow the intel to the Keely Cartel. Then my teammates would apply pressure on Marks and infiltrate the cartel. Nothing we hadn't done dozens of times.

Except this time there was going to be a snag in the plan. I was going to go missing midway through.

I just hoped none of my teammates got in the way. Our team consisted of myself, Lachlan King, code name: The King; Jasper

Saint, code name: The Saint; Kaya Reynolds, code name: The Dove; and Saffron Abbott, code name: The Heir.

Kaya, our latest recruit, and Antonio Igno's illegitimate daughter, was on comms. She was in less danger there. King and Saint would be on the other side of the building, too late to actually get involved and do anything. But Saff would absolutely try to engage with whoever came for me. She had trained all of us and was one of the best hand-to-hand combat specialists I'd seen since being in Rogues. She also had a hell of a way with weapons, but when Saff came for you, she preferred to use her bare hands. And in this case, I worried it would get her killed.

Gabe had thought it best that none of the team know what was going to go down so it felt really authentic. After all, when the mission was reviewed by Oversight, it needed to look on the up-and-up.

I didn't know all the details of Oversight. I just knew that Rogues, and Gabe specifically, were not autonomous. When things went wrong, we answered to somebody.

And this time, Gabe wanted a win before Oversight interfered. The last time they had tried to assert themselves, one of our operatives had almost died. I still shuddered when I thought how close Kaya had been to danger.

Over the comms, I heard Lock's voice. "All right, Rook, go to position two. Dove, confirm comms."

I made my move toward position two, keeping myself low, disarming my weapons as I went. Unfortunately for my team, I would *not* be an asset on this mission. And I'd be damned if I gave Montgomery any of our tech.

Kaya's voice came over the line, and I smiled. "I hear you loud and clear, King. Heir, comms check?"

Saffron's voice was low since she was at the bar watching her target. "Roger, loud and clear."

"All right, Heir, you're on."

"Perfect. Now, sweetheart," Saffron added, "I don't want you to come over and break his nose, but I do want you to get a *little* jealous."

I laughed under my breath when Saint said, "King, don't break anything."

All I heard on the line was Lock's chuckle and the background noise from the bar. "Dove, can you reduce the noise for me?"

Kaya didn't respond.

Saint tried again. "Dove, do you copy?"

All we got back was static.

Shit. Montgomery's team was here.

I moved as far away from my team as possible. If they saw what was happening... The blood rushed through my veins, and my stomach twisted. I tossed my two weapons to the side, knowing my team would find them and take them back.

Saint tried his comm again. "Dove, do you—"

"Copy," she answered. "I just... interference."

Saff's voice came over the line again. "Copy... position..."

Kaya's voice was back. "Interference... jamming... fix..."

I kept my comms in for as long as I could, but when Montgomery's team came for me, I would ditch them. Rogues would be able to track me with them, and for now, we didn't want that. I needed in with Montgomery first.

Saint's voice came back. "Team A, come in. Switch channels. Do you copy? Switch channels."

When Kaya's voice was back, she was loud and clear. "I got it. One of our antennae looks frayed."

If I was going to do this, I'd better do it well and keep my team safe.

Saint sounded perplexed. "What do you mean, frayed?"

"I got out of the van and climbed on top of it to check."

"You did what?" Saint's voice was all growl.

Kaya sounded exasperated. "Saint, we don't have time for this. Heir, do you copy?"

Saff's replied, "Yes, now I copy. I'm in position and making my approach. Rook, do you copy?"

And that was my signal. I took out my comm, put it in the mud, and stomped at it with the heel of my boot.

Just as I reached my position, I could hear the rumbling of a van.

I acted as if I was going toward the bar, and I could almost time the darkness falling over me to the second.

Three, two, one. Two big men grabbed me. I heard rustling, and suddenly all illumination vanished. Nothing but darkness surrounded me.

I was on my way back to hell.

WESTIN

I woke from my stupor bleary-eyed and with a mouth that felt like sandpaper. My kidnappers must have drugged me after they black-bagged me because I was groggy and disoriented with no sense of direction or where I was.

"You know, you are a hard man to find."

I heard the voice before the black bag was yanked off my head.

When I was finally relieved from the darkness and stench of the bag, I shook my head, careful to peel my eyes open slowly.

To my surprise, I was in an office, brightly lit with a gorgeous view of the South Bank. I could have easily been here for a meeting except for the fact that my godfather knew me well and left me restrained.

I lifted my head and snarled at him, trying to shake off some of the exhaustion. "Still a twat I see."

He chuckled low. "What was that again? I didn't quite hear you."

"I called you a twat. Wish I could say it was good to see you again."

He chuckled low. "Even though you have given me a merry chase, let there not be acrimony between us. I'm just so happy to have you back in the fold."

I struggled against the restraints. "You say that like I'm here voluntarily."

He sat in a massive leather chair that looked like it was artfully worn in certain places to look older than it was. Nevertheless, his seating position looked much like a throne. Which was probably how he wanted it. His opportunity to exude power and strike fear in the hearts of his enemies. I knew him for what he was though, nothing more than a common thug. He just had a nicer veneer.

There was a time when I'd adored my godfather. I loved when he would come and visit me and my parents. But I had only seen him through a child's eyes at that time. When he took me in after my parents died, I saw the real man.

Hell, I'd even seen him dangle a man over a balcony. The difference was that back then I was afraid. Now I was determined to take him down or die trying.

He owed me blood.

"You know what I find interesting Westin? You left here hating everything about me, but you still found yourself in the hands of criminals. Not so smart after all, were you, kid? All that time playing chess and winning against me, and I *still* beat you."

"That's the difference between us. This kid kicked your arse, and you, a grown adult man, couldn't let it go." We used to play all the time. And more often than not, I won. At first he'd taken my winning in stride, but as I got older and continued to win, it irritated him. Eventually he stopped playing against me.

He glowered at me. "I took you in, boy."

"Yeah, sure, if that's what you want to call it. What happened to my trust fund?"

He pushed to his feet and strolled over to me casually. Automatically, I worked against my restraints, the plastic of the zip ties cutting into my flesh.

"I never laid a hand on you." He leaned forward then, bringing his face close to mine. "After your parents died, I watched over you, Westin. I'm disappointed in you."

"Why am I here?"

"We'll get to that. I do want to know though, why you would ever leave all of this?" He spread his arms.

"You forced me to do your bidding, and I'd had enough. You wouldn't give me my trust fund. I'm not sure what part you don't understand."

He scoffed. "Your trust fund is in safe hands. You're telling me that we argued over money?"

"An argument? Is that what you'd call it? I told you I no longer wanted to do your bidding, and you sold me off."

Julian clasped a hand to his chest. "I did no such thing. You are being dramatic. I merely made other arrangements for you because you were inappropriately close to your charge."

I clamped my jaw tight. I was not going to say anything about her.

"See? Even now, you can't deny it."

"I'm not talking to you about Nissa."

He *tsked*. "You know, I've always admired young people for their ability to just throw caution to the wind. It's admirable. But you forgot your place. You thought you were allowed to think for yourself."

"You wanted to make me a killer."

He rolled his eyes. "You were always so dramatic. You were my property and should have done as you were told. Instead, you turned my daughter against me. And you dared to put your hands on her."

I shook my head vehemently. Had he hurt her because of me? Because in a moment of weakness I'd let my control slip? "I didn't touch her."

"If you say so. But it's all water under the bridge now." He straightened. "You managed to successfully evade me for four years. Where have you been, Westin?"

"It doesn't matter."

"It matters if there are enemies that we need to clear."

"I don't have any enemies... except for you."

My godfather chuckled low this time, sitting on the corner of his desk while tugging up the leg of his Tom Ford trousers, just so. "You're home now, Westin. Let's not talk again about you leaving or escaping, or anything like that. What's mine is yours. Except for my fucking daughter."

"I told you I'm not talking about Nissa."

"Oh, we'll talk about Nissa because she is the whole reason you're here."

I swallowed hard. Photos of her were all over his office. Nissa on horseback. Nissa at a school swim meet. Her swim cap was off, and her blond-tipped afro was dripping wet. She looked thrilled. Her brown skin and the silver medal she clutched gleamed in the sunlight.

Every photo in the office was of her.

"I'm not doing this anymore. If you want to kill me, kill me."

My godfather scoffed. "Why would I kill you? You're my godson. I just got you home. And I'm glad you still have such strong feelings for Nissa because you're about to do something for me."

"If you think I'm going to help you in any way, you haven't been paying attention."

He chuckled. "Yes, yes, I hear you. You're angry and rebellious. It's a shame, too, because you and I really would have made an excellent team. But you've made your choices, and here we are at an impasse. Except, not really. Because I know something that you don't know."

I frowned at that. "I'm not a twelve-year-old boy anymore. You can't lure me in with secrets. You can't pretend to confide them in me. That doesn't work anymore."

"I've only ever had your best interest at heart."

I fought against the restraints again. "What the fuck do you really want?"

I knew that this was not the way Gabe wanted me to handle things. He wanted me to come in apologetic, begging and pleading. Gabe wanted me to secure his trust, but I knew Julian would never believe it. Nor should he. After all, I'd escaped under the cover of night and stayed hidden for four years.

"You black-bagged me and dragged me here. What is so urgent?"

"Someone is trying to kill Nissa. You are going to keep her safe."

The bottom fell out of my world. Someone was coming after Nissa? "What? Who?" I couldn't keep the anger out of my voice.

"See, I knew I had the right man. We'll get to the whos and the whys later. Don't run from me again, Westin. You leave and she's exposed. And let's not forget Mrs. Pembry. You won't leave her behind again will you? Right now, you need to consider your prospects. I'll be back." He signaled to one of his men. "Uncuff him. He won't go anywhere now. I trust you can take care of your own leg restraints, Westin?"

I loathed him. He was right. But not for the reasons he thought. And then they left me alone in his office with only one way out, which told me there were guards posted on the door. How many was the real question?

I was no fool. I knew for a fact I was being watched, so I was extra careful as I rubbed my wrists together and untied the leg restraints on my right foot. I activated the tracker on my boot and then pulled out the sliding compartment with my secondary comm unit inside.

As I reached over to untie my other foot, I slipped the comm inside my ear before whispering, "I'm in."

2

NISSA

I SAT in the waiting room, my heart pounding in my chest. I fidgeted in my seat as I waited for my interview.

As a general rule, I made it a point to never want anything. That way I couldn't be disappointed. I had spent so much time telling myself I was fine with never getting what I wanted. But this time it was different; this time I wanted the job.

Quinly Global was a renowned company with translation opportunities in sixteen countries, and I was fluent in six of those languages. The Mandarin and Russian were what made me attractive to companies.

Government service was always an option, but staying in London was not something I wanted to do. There were other private options, but Quinly was my best hope for getting out of this city. What if I failed? How low would I sink if I couldn't get the job? My heart pounded harder as fear took hold. What if I did get it? Would this position be worth all I had sacrificed? Would it fulfill my dreams of freedom?

After what felt like hours of sitting with nothing but the turmoil of my own thoughts, Jason Connor's assistant called me in. I stood and smoothed my hands down over my pencil skirt.

The sweat from my palms transferred to the slippery material of my skirt, causing me to tug at it anxiously. I didn't want to look unprofessional by having wrinkles in my clothing.

Shit.

I covered the mark with the folio I was carrying and stepped forward with a smile. "Thank you."

The assistant's smile was warm as she noticed my nervousness. "You'll be great," she said kindly.

I smiled my thanks and followed her down the hallway to Mr. Connor's office. He was the COO of Quinly Global and a wunderkind. The youngest C-level executive in the company's history at only thirty-three years old.

My heart raced as I stepped into his office. He was already seated behind his desk, but he rose when I entered.

He was quite handsome and well dressed, a far cry from the pictures on the internet and in magazines. We shook hands and then he asked me to take a seat across from him.

All of this tension was for nothing. I had this, I could do this. All I needed to do was focus on getting out from under my father's thumb, one way or another.

Taking a deep breath, I looked across the desk at Mr. Connor and smiled confidently. It was time to show him what I could do.

He began by asking me why I wanted to work for them and what made me stand out from other applicants. I took a deep breath and then launched into my prepared list of qualifications. Fluency in six languages, experience working with international firms, familiarity with global markets, etc.

And as he listened intently to every word I said, he seemed impressed by not only my knowledge but also my passion for this opportunity.

Finally, we got onto the topic of incentives. Salary expectations, vacation policies, and so on, which was something that had been stirring anxiety inside me all day long.

But as it turned out there were no surprises. Quinly offered competitive wages plus a benefits package comparable to similar positions elsewhere. The only thing left now was an offer.

When all questions had been asked and answered, Jason smiled warmly at me across his desk before standing up again to shake my hand one more time.

My heart hammered as I offered my best smile. I'd killed this interview. I'd done everything I could do. This job was the thing that would finally get me out of here.

But as electricity hummed in my blood and I stepped onto the lift, my phone buzzed and I pulled it out.

Evil Father: *Come to the house.*

I HAD BEEN SUMMONED.

Which, knowing my father, could be good or bad. I never knew with Julian. But as I wasn't due for one of our forced, awkward dinners for another two weeks, my heart couldn't help the excited uptick. *Maybe he finally has some news.*

Julian and I were the epitome of oil and water. We'd never learned to work together. The more he tried to control me, the more I tried to buck the system, within parameters of course. But it was like I was speaking binary and he was speaking Latin.

Not to mention, I had a few thoughts on what he did for a living. Nothing like learning your father is a glorified criminal from your schoolmates to really color your feelings about him.

Mostly it was rumor and conjecture. At least that's what I told myself. After all, how would he still be walking around free? At the same time, I knew enough to know he worked with shady characters and I wanted nothing to do with any of that.

That was one of our biggest points of contention. He wanted me to take over a part of his business. I, having no desire to be controlled, refused. It was just one of the points we constantly argued about.

But the one area we agreed on was my sister. He'd been trying to help me find her for years. I sometimes worried that if a man with all of his connections couldn't find her that something had happened to her. But I couldn't let myself think that way.

She was out there, somewhere trying to find her way back to me too.

Because of our legendary arguments, we'd come up with our arrangement. Julian, for the most part, didn't interfere with school and my personal life, and once a month I was forced to show up for dinner or an event with him.

For the most part it worked.

Does it though? You weren't allowed to study at Edinburgh like you wanted. You couldn't study photography like you wanted. And he still vets all your mates.

Okay, so he still very much had his thumb on me. But that would change soon. With graduation looming I'd soon be free.

Today, I knew declining the summons wasn't an option. Julian's personal bodyguard and driver, Felix, had been outside my door when my roommate, Jamila, and I left the flat this morning.

I did my best to tamp down my nerves as I stepped out of the Bentley when Felix opened my door. I politely took the umbrella from him and jogged up the stone steps in front of my father's house. On either side of the stairs sat massive stone lions. Behind them were several potted plants leading up to the glass front doors. A massive portrait of my father hung in the foyer above a sitting area. I had grown up at Montgomery Manor, at least for part of my childhood. I hated everything about the place. I couldn't wait to leave it.

But of course, no matter what I did, my father kept yanking

my strings, tugging me back into the fold, and all I wanted to do was escape.

If you play your cards right, you will finally be free of Julian Montgomery.

All I needed to do was finish school and I was out of here. For years, I'd been squireling away money. Hiding it. Getting ready for my grand escape. Somewhere he couldn't reach me.

There is nowhere he won't look for you.

My father's butler, Dennis, opened the door with a tight smile. In the nearly ten years I'd known him, I had never known the man to show a genuine smile. "Jeeves, you're as uptight as ever, I see."

"Madam."

"Jeeves, you've known me for years, yet you still call me madam. Maybe you should try my name."

The man never showed emotion beyond pressing his lips firmly together. "Madam, you insist on calling me Jeeves. My name is Dennis."

I give him a smirk and a tap on the shoulder. "Touché, Jeeves. Touché."

I took a left toward my father's study, but I was surprised to find him in the massive living room. "Oh good, Nissa, you're here."

"Well, you did summon me. We had a deal, Julian. Can I assume that I'm here because you have good news for me?" I knew better than to get my hopes up too high, but it couldn't be helped. Just the kernel of hope was enough to keep me going.

As always, my father was dressed impeccably. He wore an Italian silk tie that brought out the blue of his eyes, and his bespoke suit was expertly tailored. He made an imposing picture.

And that was just how he liked it.

He frowned. "Good news?"

"About Lenora. Why else would you summon me outside of our monthly dinners?"

"Sorry to break it to you, but I have more important things to discuss than your wild goose chase."

"My what? You're the one who has always said you wanted to help me. This wild goose chase was your idea."

He blew out an exasperated breath then folded his hands into his lap. "This is important, Nissa. If we could set aside the theatrics for one day, that would be preferable."

I crossed my arms and prepared to do battle. I had a meeting today, and thanks to him I might miss it, depending on what bullshit this was and how much of my time would be required.

"Theatrics?" I ground my teeth. The longer I argued with him, the longer I would be forced to be here. Better to get this show on the road. "What do you want, Julian?"

His smile was beatific as he glanced up at me. "Did you have a good day yesterday? Everything all right with your flat mate, Jamila?"

Why the hell was he asking about Jamila? He never asked about anyone unless it served his purposes somehow. "She's fine. Why?"

"Things are about to change. Your lovely flat mate will be moving in with her boyfriend, Adam. He just got a bigger flat for less rent in one of my buildings, and he's going to ask her to move in with him."

"What? Why?"

"Don't bother fighting it, Nissa. It's already a done deal. They discussed the move yesterday, and he's already signed the lease."

My gut twisted. This was *his* version of theatrics. The bait and switch. Hoping to get my attention on the smaller thing before he dropped something much larger and more painful in my lap.

My stomach fell. Every time I turned around, he was infiltrating a part of my life.

I still didn't budge though. "Say what you have to say so I can go."

He chuckled. "This is why I know you're the right person to take over for me. It's why I'm preparing you."

For a year he had been insisting that I needed to take over the family's 'property management' business. What he didn't realize was that I knew who he *really* was. My father was controlling and not much better than a criminal.

"You know full well that I've already said to stick your offer where the sun doesn't shine."

"Why must you always do this, Nissa? This could have been so easy. You come over, and we have a pleasant breakfast. It could be a lovely morning between a father and his daughter."

"Yeah, well, most daughters don't have a father who's a criminal and wants them to take over the family business like in some mobster movie. I have no interest in that ever being my life."

He sighed, almost looking regretful. "I've had a deal go a little backward. So for the time being, I've determined that you are in need of a bodyguard."

Was this just another way to control me? I could feel the invisible walls pressing me on all sides. "Do you even hear yourself? Why do I need a bodyguard?"

"Sometimes business can get sticky. Don't make this a big deal, Nissa. These men are looking for someone to blame for a deal gone wrong, and I'm on that list. So now I need to take precautions."

All I could do was stare and shake my head at him. "What the hell did you do?"

"That's not for you to worry about, Nissa. What you need to be concerned about is your new bodyguard."

"I don't want this."

"Well, it's this, or you move back home. Which will it be?"

I clenched my jaw so tight I was worried about my molars. I had no power here. If I wanted some modicum of pretend freedom, there was no way I could say no.

"There are moments when I wish I'd never met you."

That didn't even phase him. "I know, but deep down inside you still love me. And you know I love you. Whether you believe that or not, you're still getting a bodyguard. I underestimated Antonio Igno. So I want to make sure you're protected."

"Good job looking after me. Exposing me to dangerous men who want to hurt me to get to you."

"I'm trying to take care of you and our future. I will not always be here. This business will accommodate you in the lifestyle to which you've become accustomed. Do you think that there aren't people who know about you? People who will come after you whether I'm dead or alive because they'll assume you have taken over anyway. I'm trying to teach you to protect yourself."

"I wouldn't need protection if it wasn't for you."

"I've chosen a bodyguard for you. Accept it or move home."

I shook my head. "This is not happening."

"Try me. I'll just leave the two of you to get reacquainted." He stood up, unfolding his long legs as he pinned me with a glower. "You have your freedom because I allow it. Don't forget that, Nissa. I'll leave you two to get reacquainted."

My heart slammed against my ribs. There had to be a way out, because I could not live like this anymore. Constantly in fear of what he might be capable of and of what that would mean for me. And then of course the constant fear of who he might hurt to get exactly what he wanted.

I heard footsteps behind me and whirled around, my heart and my belly doing a free fall, my blood pressure dropping so suddenly I started to feel dizzy. I couldn't believe what I was seeing, and I shook my head. "No."

There he was in all his sharp-jawed glory. His face had gotten more angular. Like he had turned from a boy into a man. He'd filled out too. Though lean, he'd clearly found a weight room wherever he'd gone.

He wore his hair shorter now, just barely an inch longer than a buzz cut in the front. His strong nose looked like it had maybe been broken before.

His eyes, though, they were the same. Bright clear aquamarine.

He approached slowly, as if approaching a dangerous wild animal. And just like always, the gravitational pull to Westin St. James was one I couldn't ignore.

"Hey, Nissa, you look good."

Hearing the low timbre of his voice made me tingle. Every nerve ending stood at attention. When he was within a foot of me, close enough to touch, close enough to hug, close enough to taste that forbidden kiss, I drew my hand back and slammed it straight into his nose.

<hr>

WESTIN

The blood tasted acrid on my tongue, and pain bloomed along my cheekbones, up into my forehead, and down to my mouth.

She'd learned well. I had taught her that punch.

And now she's using it against you.

I knew better than to toss my head back and pinch. Instead, I grabbed a napkin from Julian's tea setting and quickly applied pressure. "This doesn't feel like happiness to see me."

"I swear to God, I will kill you."

"I encourage you to try. But Nissa, this is not going to go how you think."

To be fair, I had completely underestimated her. That sweet girl I'd left behind was gone. Instead, she was replaced by this woman who knew how to throw a punch. And a kick. Oh, and look, there came an elbow.

I blocked them all easily. And when she roared and launched herself at me, I knew that she wouldn't stop until she did damage, most likely to herself.

I threw the napkin aside and wrapped my arms around her, tucking my face into her neck so I could avoid a bite coming for anything major. I encased both of her hands in one of mine, pinning them behind her.

When I had her secured, I backed her up against the wall, towering over her, making sure she knew that I was stronger and that, for now at least, she was beat. The wall had the benefit of the shadows and a camera blind spot.

Maybe you don't underestimate her this time?

I leaned over until my lips were against the shell of her ear. "Stop it. You *will* behave, do you understand?"

The sound of her breath coming out in short, shallow pants was kicking my blood into high gear. Nissa had changed. She wasn't much taller, but she'd certainly filled out more. She was also stronger. More agile. And her face was more sculpted. When I'd left her behind she was sixteen. Now, with her twenty-first birthday on the horizon, she was the kind of woman you couldn't forget.

She lifted her gaze and met mine, and the two of us stood locked in that embrace for what could have been minutes or hours. I had no idea, because with her, time stood still.

With my body pressed up against hers, all I could think about was every moment I had spent wanting her and not being able to have her the last time. Needing her, knowing full well there would be repercussions for her and for me, until finally my control had snapped. It had been the best damn night of my life.

And then you left her behind with that psychopath.

For four years, I had told myself that I hadn't had a choice. That I had needed to survive. That one day I would go back for her.

But the more distance I put between myself and Julian Montgomery, the more I started to feel like I was a free man. And that guilt, that clawing need to go back for her, I'd buried it deep. Because if I gave into it, I would have come back. And we both would have been worse off for it.

But you still ended up right back here, didn't you?

When Nissa spoke, her voice was low but strong and firm. "If you like your bollocks where they are, I highly suggest you release me."

I realized then that while I had been taking that happy little stroll down memory lane, my cock was thickening against her belly, and she had eased one of her thighs between my legs. One swift jerk up, and I would be forced to release her. She was giving me a warning.

"Like it or not, Beauty, this is happening. You know your father. He always gets what he wants."

"Not this time. I'm not the same person. I'm not the moon-eyed girl who thought she was in love. I had no idea what that word even meant. The only thing I feel for you now is disdain and pity."

"Good. You *should* feel that. Because I don't feel anything for you anymore." *Liar.*

A smiling Nissa Montgomery was a sight to behold. There was a time when I had lived for that smile. The sheer delight in her face and playfulness of her spirit.

But now I recognized it for what it was too late. The crispness of her movement was a thing to be admired. And I would admire it... just as soon as the spreading ache in my groin dissipated.

I had no choice. I released her and sank down. Her move had brought me right to my knees as if I was worshipping her.

Don't you wish you could?

Nissa leaned forward. "If I see you again, I'll put a bullet in you. Don't you ever come near me again."

3

NISSA

Nine & a Half Years Ago...

Julian was going to kill me. I knew I wasn't supposed to be out on this part of the property. At least not without someone watching.

But I'd heard the water, and I wanted to see it. I liked to go outside when I was upset.

Usually I went to the gardens, but today I had needed to run. Unfortunately, I'd worn my flipflops instead of my trainers, and I'd rolled my ankle on a slick spot near the brook. I sat still, wrapping my arms around my legs, afraid to look down at the ankle because something warm and sticky was sliding down my foot.

Well done, Nissa. Now stop crying and get up.

I could almost hear my father berating me.

Your fake father.

I tried to shove aside the thought. He had documentation and everything. He was my father and I had to deal with it.

Except at times like this when I was sad, or upset, or worried, I thought about my other father. The one who smiled all the time and tickled me and my sister Lenora. He'd chase us around the house, pretending that he was a monster coming to eat children.

When he caught us, he would snuffle our necks and tickle us until we squealed. Or until my mum got in on the fun and insisted that we were her children to eat. And then the chase would be on again.

If I was being honest with myself, my tears were for them. The more I asked Julian to see my sister, the angrier he got. But that had been our deal. He'd said if I'd come along with him without a fuss that I could see her as often as I wanted. But I hadn't seen her. Not once. I'd written lots of letters. And at first, she had written me too. And then the letters stopped. Just like that, and I had no idea why.

Two months ago, I'd tried to go and find out what happened to her and why she'd stopped writing. I'd made it as far as the northern boundary of the property before one of Julian Montgomery's men found me.

Two months later, I actually made it all the way to London before he caught me. My third attempt was made a couple of weeks ago. And to be fair, it wasn't really my fault. Julian had taken me in for a doctor's appointment, and I had simply wandered away on the Tube toward the group home in North London. I'd almost gotten there too. But three roads away, a car had pulled up and out stepped my supposed father.

He'd stuck an Apple watch on me then and told me if I took it off I wouldn't be allowed to leave the property. And every time I took it off, I was sequestered. I'd stopped running then.

A voice startled me. "Are you okay?"

There was a boy standing above me on one of the boulders, looking down. He was lanky, with light sandy brown hair. It probably went blond in the summertime. He came a little closer, and self-preservation made me scooch back. "Who are you? My father has men watching this whole property."

He smirked down at me. "Ah, you must be Nissa."

I frowned. "Who are you? And why do you know my name?"

"I know your name because your father told me. And he told me to stay away from you."

"Why would he tell you to stay away from me? I'm the innocent one."

"I'm pretty sure that's why I'm supposed to stay away from you."

"What's your name?" I asked.

"I'm Westin St. James."

"What kind of name is Westin?"

"What kind of name is Nissa?"

I shrugged and shielded my gaze from the sun. Which was odd because, well, we were just west of London. It was always gray. "Well, Westin, are you here alone? Do you have a phone? I twisted my ankle. Julian's going to kill me."

He lifted a brow. "Why is he going to kill you? Just because you twisted your ankle?"

I nodded. "I'm not supposed to be all the way out here by myself. We have 'trust issues,' as he says."

He smirked then, and the expression was quite pleasant on his face. He was cute as boys went, with his pale blue eyes and his curly mop of hair. I had been studying the topic all year. Okay, if I was being honest, it was Lenora who got me into it before Julian Montgomery had shown up. Any spare money she'd earned was spent on teen magazines like *Hello!*

The ones she liked were old though. Movie stars. My personal favorite, was Tom Hardy. He was very cute. I also like the guy who played Loki, and all the superheroes, and sure, Tom Holland was cute too. This guy reminded me of Loki. Not his hair though.

"Are you going to stare at me all day, or are you going to take my hand?"

I blinked rapidly and realized he was holding his hand out to me. "Can't you go get someone, like an adult?"

"No, the way back down by the brook is too far, and by the time I come back, it'll likely start raining or something. Mrs. Pembry would be upset if I leave you here all by yourself."

My brows lifted then. "The housekeeper?"

He nodded. "I live with her."

"Are you her son or something?"

He shook his head. "No. My parents died."

At that moment, my heart broke for him. "I'm sorry. My parents died too."

He cocked his head then. "I thought Uncle Julian was your dad."

I shrugged. "I had other parents. When they died, he turned up. He had paperwork showing that I was his daughter. And then I came to live here. I had to leave my sister behind though."

His brows dropped. "Julian didn't take your sister?"

I shook my head. "No. He said we'd see each other, but I haven't seen her once since we left her. It's been nearly a year, and..." I let my voice trail off. I was rambling to a stranger.

He offered me both hands then as he knelt in front of me. "I'm sorry. That sucks."

"Thanks." I took both his hands and using my good foot and his body as leverage, he helped me to my feet.

He wrapped an arm around me. "You rolled it pretty bad, and you've got a cut too. I just want to get you up there to the clearing. It'll be easier to pick you up from there."

"Pick me up? I think I outweigh you."

He frowned down at me. "Hardly. I'm stronger than you are."

"You are not. And I'm tall."

He nodded. "But I think most of that is afro."

He indicated the massive afro puff on top of my head. "No, under the afro, I'm also tall."

He chuckled under his breath. "Come on then, tall girl."

When it became apparent I couldn't walk, we stopped and he frowned. "Okay, looks like I have to give you a piggyback ride."

"Are you sure you can do that?"

"Oh my God, are you always so annoying?"

I huffed. "I'm not annoying. I'm just asking a question. If you feel insulted, that's on you."

"Yes, of course, I can carry you. Come on."

He carried me then, up the incline, around the rocks, and up into the clearing near the massive oak tree. "Here. You can use my shirt, okay? We'll tie it up so that cut stops bleeding."

He sat back, reached behind his head, and pulled his T-shirt off in that way so many boys did. I found the motion goofy, but endearing. And then I watched as his scrawny arms tore his shirt into a nice long strip.

I put my hand out to take it so I could wrap my own ankle, but he shook his head. Gently, he lifted my foot and eased off my flipflop. "You shouldn't have worn these down there."

"I know. I was just upset that Julian wouldn't let me call my sister, and I took off."

"He's a dick. But just because he's a dick doesn't mean you have to be stupid. You have to be careful, okay?"

I didn't like being admonished. But still, he was right. Who knew how long I could have been down there?

"Come on." He tore another strip off the bottom of his T-shirt before slipping it back on, giving him a half tee. My ankle was wrapped, not too tightly but firmly enough that I could put some pressure on it. "Thanks."

"Yeah, no problem. Mrs. Pembry's cottage isn't far from here. It's about four hundred meters or so. You'll see it right there between the trees. I'm sure she can drive you back up to the house."

"You're not going to tell her where you found me, are you?"

He shook his head. "Just that I found you under the trees and you rolled your ankle. How's that?"

I didn't know this boy, but he was already willing to protect me. And he'd already shown that he was gallant. Who knew boys could be gallant?

"Thanks, Westin."

He shrugged. "I mean, you're just a girl. I think Mrs. Pembry would want me to look after you."

I could see the pride in his face. He thought he was really doing something special, but I was focused on the part where he said I was 'just a girl.'

"Just a girl?"

He shrugged. "Aren't you a girl?"

"Yeah, I am. But you said it like it meant I was somehow less than you."

He had that adorable furrow again. "Well, I mean, I'm stronger. I'm probably faster too."

"How dare you? That sounds like a challenge. But I'm injured, so I can't run."

He laughed. "You're going to challenge me?"

"Yes, of course, I am."

"Okay, when you're better, we'll race."

I nodded shortly. "All right, what are we playing for?"

He frowned. "Playing for?"

"Yeah, if we're going to have a race, there has to be stakes."

He considered that as he carried me to the trees along the road to the cottage. "All right, I have my Coldplay T-shirt. I love that thing. If you win, you can have it."

"A band T-shirt?"

"Oh yeah, they're cool. You don't know this yet, because you're just in primary, but bands are awesome."

"I know bands. I like One Direction."

He rolled his eyes. "As if One Direction is cool."

"Coldplay *is* cool. And so is One Direction."

He audibly gagged. "Oh no. Tell me you're not one of them."

"You leave my One Direction alone."

"I almost want to lose just to give you the T-shirt so you'll have something cool. You can't go into secondary liking One Direction."

"I think they're awesome," I said mutinously.

"If you say so."

And as I pondered what was wrong with him, a little part of me fell in love with Westin St. James.

4

WESTIN

Okay, so Nissa was going to take some convincing.

What did you expect?

Honestly, I'd come out none too worse for wear, though my nose hurt. She packed a hell of a punch, and she was just as stubborn as I remembered.

Just as beautiful too. Her hair was in two space buns. She looked cute. Fun. I wondered who she'd become in the four years I'd been gone.

Julian had a two-man rotation going on her right now, and I would take over during the week. We would rotate on the weekends unless that couldn't be managed. I'd be staying with Nissa around the clock though. He knew I wouldn't run. Not with the threat looming over me.

I'd been given one of their phones, but I'd already made modifications to allow me to access encrypted lines to the Rogues. When I typed in my passcode, Gabe's voice came on immediately after the first ring, clear and tight. "Status."

"I'm on the primary target now. No access for a search. I'll be on the secondary target by this afternoon."

"Any problems?"

I tenderly touched my nose. "No, everything went as expected."

"All right. And you're good? You've had no issues?"

"None that will currently get in the way of the mission, so I'm fine."

"This is one of those things you're going to have to communicate clearly, Rook."

"There's nothing to do. Right now, I play their game. And when I can't, I call you in. Isn't that the plan?"

He sighed. "You're sure I shouldn't put someone else in as well?"

I knew what he was asking, but I kept my shit together. "I'm fine. I got this. I'm in. No problems. I'll have to stay on secondary per Montgomery's orders. I'm being watched."

"Fine. If you can turn secondary, do it. We'll make her an asset. It'll make things easier."

My stomach flipped. "What? You're looking to make her an asset?"

Gabe sighed. "No, but if she *can* be one, then we'll make her one. She's not the target; he is. And we'll use whatever means necessary to get to him."

Some days it was easy enough to pretend that the things I did were for the good of the world. I could feel that I was doing the right thing, making a difference. But at other times, when I could feel the manipulation from Gabe, I wondered how much of this was really making a difference.

"Whatever you think I'm going to do, I'm not. So get that idea out of your head."

"All I'm saying is if the girl is an asset, or can be, we need to utilize that. But don't get your knickers in a twist. You know the target. We'll make it work."

"Is the team aware where I am now?"

Gabe chuckled. "Yeah. Saff isn't too pleased, but she knows how the game is played."

I'd heard that before. "Don't you ever get tired of saying that? Don't you ever get exhausted of having to come up with reasons for us do things that make us uncomfortable?"

"I do, but I know what the mission calls for. Check in again when you're with the girl. Igno's got a deal going in six weeks. We have that long to find out what it is, where it is, who the players are, and stop it. Get your shit together."

Was I up for this? I didn't really have a choice. Nissa Montgomery was going to make my life difficult. It didn't matter though. And Gabe knew I wouldn't back down from the mission. "I got it."

"Stay safe and stay careful."

"Roger that." And then I hung up with him, wondering how on earth I was going to get Nissa to comply.

Nissa

I hadn't seen Westin since he announced his reentry back into my life. Maybe for once my father had listened to me. Unlikely, since I still had a guard, but at least it wasn't the one I had vowed to kill.

After leaving Julian's house, I spent the rest of the morning in the library. I had an economics project to do and a foreign policy test to study for. Every now and again I would look up and around half expecting to see Westin at the door.

But he wasn't there. Just one of the hulking forms in suits. I think today's was called Charlie? Whatever. I had to keep my eyes on the prize. My freedom loomed if I could just finish school and get a job far away from here.

When my eyes were starting to feel like I had sandpaper in

them and my mind started to fog out, I decided it was time for a break. Glancing around the library, making sure nobody was watching me, I did what I always did after I finished studying. I used the time to dig into my research on my sister.

I looked for every variation I could think of on our last name. Lenora Crane, Lenora Crandall, Lenora Crain. I hunted LinkedIn and Instagram. Still, it came out blank. No social media. Nothing easily identifiable. Nowhere to be found.

I had tried all the avenues I could think of. When I was eighteen, I started going through the care system trying to see if I could find her. But she'd aged out and I had nothing to go on. And unless she'd put her DNA on one of those sites, I wasn't going to find her, not without help. Not to mention my father had taken great pains to keep us apart.

That was the thought that always haunted me. After, all these years where had she gone? It was like she was a literal ghost. It was entirely possible I'd never find her, but I couldn't stop trying.

I rooted one of the photos of us I always carried out of my bag. It was the two of us in matching princess flowery costumes. We looked so happy, as if right around the corner, someone hadn't been waiting to ruin everything. It was the last photo I had of the two of us together.

As I was packing my bag to head back home, my flat mate Jamila called. "Hey, Nissa, you might want to come back to the flat."

"I was just on my way. Why? What's up?"

"A bloke named Westin St. James is here. Claims he's your bodyguard."

Oh hell no. The bloody audacity. I muttered under my breath, "Oh, for the love of fucking God."

I was home in less than fifteen minutes, barging through the door, ready to do battle. And sure enough, Westin was at the bloody stove, cooking something that smelled garlicky and divine. Jamila saw me and gave me a sheepish smile. "Well, he said he could cook. And it sounded appealing."

"Get out," I shouted.

He laughed. "I'm not going anywhere, Beauty. You and I, we're about to become bosom buddies."

"I don't want to become your bosom buddy. I want you gone."

He pushed away from the stove, putting a perfectly made omelet onto Jamila's plate. "Sorry, love, take that up with your father. Right now, I'm making brunch for your mate."

"You can't just take over my life. You don't know me anymore."

Jamila piped up, taking her plate with her. "I'll just leave you two alone."

I stopped her. "Don't you dare leave me with this Neanderthal."

Westin smirked at me. "Name calling, Nissa? You know how this goes. Neither one of us has a choice right now."

I *did* know how it went. But this time I refused to lie down and just take it. I wasn't letting Westin St. James back in my life or my heart.

"I love you. I'll be back later." Jamila already had her jumper on and was halfway out the door... still holding her plate.

"Jamila!" I called. But she was gone.

"Looks like it's just you and me."

"You can't just walk into my life like you know anything about me." I frowned as I took in the suitcases by the guest room. When dawning set in, I started laughing and shook my head. "No way in hell are you moving in here." It was one thing to have a bodyguard, but a live-in one? Hell no.

"Not much you can do about it except get on board."

"You don't know me at all do you?"

"Don't I? I know everything there is to know about you."

"No, you don't," I huffed. "You only think you do. I'm a different person than I was four years ago. You are arrogant and self-important. Which is disappointing, because if you had any sort of brain, you would have used it and stayed the hell away. This isn't going to work out."

He laughed. "I don't know what to tell you, but you're stuck with me. And did you ever stop for one moment to think that I came back for you?"

"Do you even believe the bullshit coming out of your mouth? If you think I'm the same naive girl I was when you left me here, you have another think coming."

He shrugged. "Game on, then."

5

NISSA

AN HOUR LATER, Westin was busy moving his things into the guest room. I was busy sulking in my room. I called my father three times but got no response. This was happening. I was stuck with him. Why would my father do this to me?

It had to be punishment of some sort. He could have given me anyone else on staff. But instead, he gave me Westin. He knew how devastated I'd been when he left without a trace. Westin St. James was nothing more than a punishment.

And I could choose to endure it, or I could choose to fight back.

There was a knock at my door, and I braced myself for battle again. But instead of Westin, it was Jamila. "I'm back. Before we even got to talk about everything you and Westin were going toe to toe."

"I heard about you moving in with Adam."

She threw up her hands. "How did you even know?"

I didn't want to scare her. One of us worried was enough. "I saw some paperwork lying around. I figured you'd tell me when you were ready."

"So, you're not mad about this?" she asked chewing her bottom lip.

What I was mad about was my father's manipulation.

He is never ever, ever going to let you go.

I shook my head slightly to clear it and focused on Jamila. "No, of course, I'm not mad. Why would I be? You and Adam are great together, and this is a real opportunity for you guys to live happily ever after. I will be okay."

"I know you will."

"It's okay. Don't worry about it. And if I'm being honest, I sort of expected this eventually, you know. You guys are so cute and in love."

"I know. I just don't want you to be alone."

"I'm not alone. You see the new bodyguard I have. He'll make sure I'm very much not alone."

Jamila snorted a laugh. "Oh, I bet he will. Your chemistry is crazy."

My gut cramped at that. There had been a time in my life when I would have killed for someone to notice chemistry with me and Westin. Not anymore though.

"Your dad is so weird. Who does he think is going to kidnap you? I mean, he's just like a basic business guy. Property management or something, right?"

"Yes, but you know how it is. Rich people think they're so important."

"Good point. And let's face it, the more money he has the more crazy people will do things like go through you to get access to him and his wallet. Maybe someone found out that you're a student here? Could be a good thing that he's sent someone to keep you safe."

"That's just the thing, though. I'm not safe from Westin."

Her brows furrowed as she flopped back on my bed. "What

is it with you two anyway? This is more than you not wanting a bodyguard. This is something else."

I wondered how much to tell her without endangering her. "Let's just say that this is not my first rodeo needing a bodyguard. And not my first rodeo with Westin."

"Ooh! I love a good second-chance romance opportunity." She grabbed my pillow and hugged it to her tight. "I give you guys two weeks before you're banging. Oh my God, this is the best day ever. This is wicked."

"Mate, it's not going to be as fun as you think it is. And we are *not* going to bang. If I have my way, I'll get someone else assigned to me."

"He's well fit. What's wrong with him?"

"Besides abandoning me, I'm sure he's fine at his job. But he walked away and left me four years ago."

She winced. "But maybe he had a good reason. Have you spoken to him since?"

"No, I haven't."

"So you don't know where he went. He could have had a good reason."

"Whatever it is, I don't want to know. When he left, he broke me. I was completely alone with no one who understood me. He doesn't get to just walk back into my life. Not to mention, my father has a hold on him and something very bad would happen if he ever found out we hooked up."

"It's not like you're going to tell him."

"You don't know my father. He has a way of finding things out."

She sat up in the bed. "Well, I don't want to think about you hiding out in your room just to avoid him. Come out tonight. And before you tell me you have to study, I know for a fact you don't have an exam until next week. Besides, this way you get to torture your bodyguard. Imagine him having to tell dear old dad that you took someone home."

I started to laugh. "But I never bring anyone home."

"He doesn't need to know that."

WESTIN

I should've expected to hear from Saff. Honestly, Gabe was the hammer and Saff was the soft touch.

"She's cute."

I groaned and turned around. "What are you doing here, Saff?"

We were currently at the pub, and I was watching Nissa watch her mate's drink. Nissa was nursing a pint, the same one she'd been holding for the last thirty minutes. She did not seem in the same kind of jovial mood as her mates.

"You know how it is. Being undercover can be difficult."

"Bullshit. Gabe didn't like how I sounded, so he sent you to assess."

"You're getting smarter, Rook."

"I've always been smart."

"If you say so." She swiped my pint, took a sip, and frowned at it. "What's wrong with it?"

I laughed. "It's not alcoholic. You know, I'm on duty."

She groaned. "Oh no. While you might be on duty, we can still have fun."

"No, I can't. I promise you, this one is a handful. And she's hellbent on making me pay for existing."

"What did you do to her?"

"Nothing."

"Go on, tell me."

"I left in a way that probably made her think I left her."

Saff *tsked* and shook her head, her braids cascading down her back. "Naughty, naughty."

"I know. That wasn't the plan. I didn't really have a choice when Montgomery asked me to do something, and I did it without knowing the consequences. Once I found out what I'd done, I told him I wasn't going to do it anymore."

"That's the problem. Sometimes we take these gigs, and we think we're doing the right thing, but we're not. You couldn't come back and tell her what was going on?"

I shook my head. "No, it wasn't possible."

"Let me guess, she blamed you?"

"How did you know?"

"Well, I've been there before. Maybe she will forgive you eventually."

I shook my head. "I doubt it. She's holding a grudge."

"Maybe. But usually, I find that when people hold that kind of grudge, it's because they're hurt. They just want to be told that the other person cares about them. That they understand that they caused them pain. I'm pretty sure if you explain that it'll be okay."

"You don't get it, Saff. She's going to hold a grudge *forever*."

"Maybe she will for a time. But you've got to do your job one way or the other. If she's hindering that, you need to find out why and resolve it. You know the deal. Human beings are unpredictable."

"I know. We are difficult. And we make irrational decisions."

"Yes, because we're hurt. So it's up to you. You decide what you want to do. But if you ask me, a good apology will go a long way."

"And if I can't find a proper way to apologize?"

"Well, keep doing this. See how well that works out for you."

I sighed. "All right, I'll try."

"Yeah, you do that. In the meantime, don't let her hit you again."

I scowled. "Those were lucky hits."

"If you say so. But I trained you, didn't I?"

"Yeah, you did."

"Right. So next time, keep your hands up. Sounds like she's a feisty one. I think I like her already, and I see why you do, too."

I rolled my eyes. "Really, Saff?"

She giggled, took another sip of my pint, and then murmured under her breath. "Incoming."

A blonde who'd been eyeing me earlier sauntered up to me. "Is this seat taken?"

I kept my scowl in place and nodded my head. "Yup, it's taken."

"Are you sure? Because I haven't seen anyone sit here."

Next to me, Saff chuckled as she swung her long legs around on the stool and scooted off. From my periphery, I could see her head out the door in seconds. She was leaving me to deal with this. "You seem lovely, but I'm waiting for someone."

"What if you end up waiting for that person your whole life and they never show up? Meanwhile, I'm here and you'll be missing out."

I gave her a tight smile. "Sorry, not interested."

She scooted off with a huff. "You don't know what you're missing."

"So I've heard. Now, if you don't mind, the woman I'm staring at is over there."

And sure enough, Nissa was about to get herself in a hell of a lot of trouble.

⁂

Nissa

I watched from my spot on the bar stool as Jamila and Adam did shots.

Not that I begrudged their happiness, I just was going to miss my mate. Not to mention, she was leaving me with *the bodyguard*.

As per our agreement, he left me alone. Well, mostly anyway. He lurked in the corner at the end of the bar, and I could feel his eyes on me. And honestly, was that the way you were even supposed to bodyguard? Weren't you supposed to be watching the surroundings?

But no, Westin was watching me, as if I was the one who needed watching. Which was just bullshit. He was the one working for the devil incarnate.

And the devil incarnate is your father.

Well, he obviously knew that, and he'd made his choices. I'd had no choice. I hadn't asked for any of this.

All night I'd seen women approaching him, and he just kept shaking his head. The aura around him screamed *powerful*. With a simple look, he'd managed to deter ninety-nine percent of all comers. Only one had been brave enough to actually speak to him, and he'd politely declined her. She tried again, and he'd less than politely declined her with a lifted brow and a cocked head.

He'd still turned her down with his gaze pinned on me.

Jamila came bouncing over. "Oh, come on, Nissa, cheer up. I'll still see you all the time."

I forced my melancholy away. "I am cheered up. I am so excited for you. You guys are going to be so happy. Besides, I still have plans for us this year. Much drinking. Much fussing about who's going to become my new *Bachelor* buddy?"

Jamila guffawed. "Gosh, I really can't imagine the bodyguard watching *The Bachelor* with you."

"Neither can I. I think he'd be annoying and sulking the entire time if he did that."

Jamila pondered and lifted a brow. "Although, you could force him to watch with you. I feel like that would bring great satisfaction."

"You're right! I could tell him it's part of the job. He would completely beg out of here. It would be perfect."

"See, your mood is already lifted." She smiled. "You're welcome."

"Ugh, I just wish I wasn't stuck with Lurch over there."

"I'm sorry. But maybe it'll be okay."

"No, don't be sorry. I really am very happy for you. You'll be happy, and Adam loves you. Not to mention, you guys are completely aligned career wise. This makes sense. I just need to give Adam the speech. You know, the one where I tell him to look after you or face my wrath. Because my mate is a complete and utter badarse."

"So is my mate. She's fantastic, brilliant, and she's going to become a captain of industry. All those business magazines are going to put *you* on the cover."

I knew what she was getting at, and still my brain viscerally rejected the very idea of it. The idea of me in a business setting, caring about the corporate ladder. The problem was, other than knowing I wanted to do something that actually helped people instead of making money for people who didn't need it or deserve it, I didn't really know what I wanted. I just wanted it to mean something. Which was why I gravitated toward translations and interpreting. I could really help people that way.

I'd even had a few interviews over the last couple of weeks, though none I was as hopeful about as the one with Quinly Global.

I wanted to be passionate and excited about something. Anything. But I didn't tell Jamila that because tonight wasn't the night for introspection. This was a happy *I'm moving in with my boyfriend* shindig.

"Honestly, you are going to be amazing at whatever you do, Nissa. Cheers, mate!" Jamila toasted me with her beer bottle. "To us."

The pub had started to fill up. There was a giggling group of freshers, straight from an exam; the second years, who also looked dazed from an exam and far less jovial; some graduate students, and some locals who looked like maybe they'd been dragged out to a spot they didn't normally frequent. The Totem was a college hangout. While it was nestled smack dab in the middle of London, it was still mostly students.

In the front part of the pub there were tables and a bar where you could sit around the corner before it opened. That's where Jamila had currently dragged Adam.

A gaggle of blonde freshers ran to the floor, screaming at the top of their lungs, "Come on, Eileen," and the rest of the tune that I didn't even understand how I knew the words to even though I was certain I had never heard the song in its entirety.

I finished my pint and decided to hit the loo before the place got really crowded. Normally, I loved being out. It was like my inner me was always searching for excitement and fun. But I wasn't feeling it tonight.

On the way, one of the fresher lads decided to try his luck and stepped directly in front of me.

"Excuse me," I muttered.

"I saw you sitting at the bar by yourself. I was working up the courage, then you started coming over. So I thought I'd introduce myself."

I sighed. "Look, whatever your name is, you seem nice, but—"

"My name is Douglas, and I am *very* nice. I'm also well fit, if I do say so myself."

And there it was, the ick immediately crawling up my spine. Even if I had initially thought, 'Oh, nice smile, good lad.' Now, I just really wanted to toss him out of my way.

"Aw, come on, just give me a chance."

From several feet behind him, his mates were laughing and shaking their heads as they watched the two of us. "A dare from your mates, was it?"

He smiled sheepishly. "A little, but you are fit, so... What do you say? Dance?"

I shook my head. "No. There are lots of fresher girls here who haven't heard all the bullshit before."

I tried to sidestep him, but he grabbed my elbow. "Look, you are clearly by yourself. You could use the company, right?"

I glowered at him and then glanced down at my elbow. I balked at him and then opened my mouth, ready to eviscerate him with my tongue. But suddenly, he released me. It almost appeared as if he'd started to float. It was only when I lifted my gaze behind him that I realized Westin was right there, lifting him off his feet with one hand. "Mate, the lady, and I use that term loosely, said she's not interested. So sod off."

Douglas had apparently had one too many, because he did not know what was good for him. Westin was six foot three, and while lean, he was clearly solid muscle, and he wore that *I'm really not fucking with you* look on his face.

God, the arrogance. Yes, his face was beautiful, but he was also a complete wanker.

But at that moment, every woman in the place and half the men were staring at him. Douglas scrambled. "Mate, what the fuck?"

Westin's gaze met mine. "Am I wrong? You don't want to dance with this knobhead, do you?"

"No, I don't. But I—"

Westin placed Douglas down on his feet and glowered at

him. "Don't touch. Matter of fact, stay very far away from her, understand?"

Douglas did not understand, and he tried to shove at Westin, who didn't budge at all. Douglas shoved again, and he ended up stumbling backward onto his arse, which sent half the pub into uproarious laughter. Westin glanced at the table of Douglas's mates and cocked his head. "He yours?"

The two lads who'd been laughing at Douglas nodded and came jogging over. "Yeah, mate, we'll take him."

"Yeah, don't let me see him here again; otherwise, I won't be so pleasant."

Both of them widened their eyes and nodded profusely. They could sense the threat even if Douglas couldn't.

"Oh my God, did you have to make a scene?" I whispered harshly.

Even Jamila and Adam were glancing over the crowd from their spot in the middle of the dance floor.

Westin glowered. "Maybe you forgot what my job is."

He picked up the beer he'd apparently sat on a nearby table, and then someone jostled him from behind and it all happened in slow motion. The surprise expression on his face, the beer sloshing out of his mug, and my subsequent alarm as the ice cold liquid poured out in my direction.

His beer spilled all over me. Liquid slid down the front of my top, between my breasts into my bra, and oh joy, there it went down to my belly button. I wondered if maybe it hadn't been on purpose.

"Damn it!"

He whirled around, and it was a drunken girl who held up both hands in apology. "Sorry, not so steady on my heels now."

Westin rolled his eyes. When his gaze met mine, he frowned and then let his eyes rove down.

His eyes darkened, and his lips pressed into a thin line.

When his gaze snapped back up to my eyes, he growled. "Jesus, cover up, would you?"

"Me? You were the one who just spilled beer on me, what the hell?"

All he did was sigh and then proceeded to start unbuttoning his shirt.

I blinked at him, glancing around rapidly. "What are you doing?"

"I can't let you walk around like that. Everyone can see your nipples."

I gasped then quickly wrapped my arms around my front and middle. "How the hell was I supposed to know that I couldn't wear a demi-cupped bra? I didn't expect to be in a wet T-shirt contest."

He just cleared his throat. "Put this on."

The problem was, as he handed me his shirt, all I could do was stare at the epic display of muscles. London was having unseasonably warm weather still into September, which was shocking. And I wasn't mad at it at all, except, what the hell was he going to wear home?

I must have stood there gawking for several seconds because he cleared his throat and said, "If you've looked your fill, put the bloody shirt on."

I glowered at him. "And what are you going to wear?"

"Me shirtless might get some stares, but it's not going to stop fucking traffic. So cover the fuck up."

"You're the one who spilled on me."

"Put it on. We're leaving."

"This is Jamila and Adam's night. I'm not leaving."

"Yes you are," he said calmly.

I glowered at him. "You can't make me."

Instead of backing down, he smirked and took a step toward me. "Are you sure I can't make you?"

Heat ballooned in my belly, spreading outward, coiling and uncoiling into every nook and cranny of my body, making my nerve endings hum. "The last time I checked, you're not supposed to handle the merchandise."

"If it means your safety, I am. Now put on the goddamn shirt."

I didn't do as I was told because he was threatening me. I did as I was told because, well, I was cold. And to my chagrin, one of the bartenders came around the corner and tossed a T-shirt to Westin, which he caught with one hand and then threw it on. The T-shirt was clearly made for someone smaller because it looked like he was trying to bust out the seams like the Hulk. But still, he put it on and grinned at me. "I'm so glad we're in agreement. And now, you can enjoy the evening with your mates."

"I loathe you."

"You've said so before. Maybe try and say something different next time. It's getting boring."

And as he marched back to his position at the end of the bar, every female gaze followed him. I didn't know what I was going to do yet, but one way or another, I was getting rid of him.

6

WESTIN

AFTER THE BAR, I knew Nissa was going to be a problem. Especially with her tits pointing at me like that.

Going to the pub was an exercise in torture. Sure, there were the usual concerns of crowd control, covering the exits, lines of sight, all that. But there was also the fact that all eyes had been on her the moment she walked in. It was all made worse by the fact that she didn't even know. She was completely oblivious to the attention she was getting, the leering hungry eyes on her.

The beer was an accident. And had I known what was going to happen, no way I would have allowed her to wear that white tank. Not with that bra anyway. Because the moment I'd seen her pert nipples peeking out behind lace and cotton all blood had rushed straight to my dick. It had taken a full thirty seconds for all my brain cells to come back online.

She was an issue that I was going to have to find a way to resolve, one way or another. I had told Gabe that I could handle this. That she wasn't going to be a problem. That I could do my job, find out about the ledger, and be out of there before anyone was the wiser. The problem was, I had a feeling that was complete and utter bullshit.

If Montgomery had Igno's cipher, or even the ledger itself, I needed to get access to the house to get it, and obviously, he and I had a trust problem. Without Nissa in tow, I'd have no excuse to get back into that house. Once in the house, I had my ways. But getting there was going to be the issue. And right now, Nissa had zero interest in going anywhere with me. If I knew her well, she was working on a plan to get rid of me right now.

I needed her to forgive me. I needed her on my side; and quickly.

My cock had an idea of how to do that. But I knew from history that his way wasn't going to solve our problem. The only way to get her to trust me and forgive me was the truth. But neither of us was ready for that yet. Especially now that I'd seen the tips of her pert dark nipples peeking out at me.

Fucking hell. What business did she have wearing a bra like that?

Why does her bra matter?

I knew I was being irrational. Fuck. Why did I think I could do this?

My dick had an opinion on that.

You can't. Let's go fuck her now.

Yeah, that was his solution to everything. But that was not happening. Not Nissa. Too many buried feelings under that bridge. She hated me, but the feeling wasn't exactly mutual. But wanting her pissed me off. I'd been tortured by her for longer than I cared to admit. I wanted no more of it. I just wanted freedom.

After a cold shower and with a still-hard dick, I shoved on sweatpants and towel-dried my hair as I picked up my phone and typed in my code.

It was a combination of my codename and my fake birthday. The year was correct, but the birthdate was actually my initiation into Rogues date. Within thirty seconds, Lachlan called me. "All right, mate?"

"Yeah, I'm fine. I'm still on the secondary target."

"Anything with the primary target yet?"

I sighed in frustration. "No, not since he forced her to accept my assignment. Other than that, he's been quiet."

"All right, well, stay on him. How are you?"

"I'm fine, mate."

Lachlan's sigh said a lot. We had been in the same training class, and unfortunately, he could read me like a book. Just like when we were sparring. And while he couldn't see me, I could still feel the weight of his judgment.

"What's going on?"

"Nothing. This target is a pain in the arse."

Lock laughed. "Oh, I know lots about pains in the arse. And I have seen this particular pain in the arse. She's fit."

"I hadn't noticed." *Liar*.

He just chuckled under his breath. "Sure, you haven't. You know her from before, don't you?"

I'd been honestly waiting for this question. Waiting for someone to notice. "Yeah, she hasn't changed."

Lock whistled under his breath. "Is she a problem for you?"

I sighed. "No, I can do the assignment." Because at the end of the day, what choice did I have? Westin Rourke was someone I'd created to protect myself. And if I did this right, I could let Westin St. James out and finally put this behind me.

"It's not a problem. *She* is not a problem."

"I'm your handler on this case, unless you prefer Saff."

I considered Saff asking these questions, knowing full well that I might have a thing for Nissa, and heat brushed up my neck. "Nah, you're fine."

"Okay, whatever you say, mate. Just remember, whatever it takes to get to the target, whatever you have to do."

A flare of fury worked its way up my spine. I knew he was saying I might have to use Nissa to get to Montgomery. But that wasn't me. I wasn't that person anymore. At the same time, I might need to be, and that didn't sit well. "I hear you, but that won't be necessary. I'll do the job, gain his trust, and get in."

"You can do this."

"Oh, I know." As pep talks went, this one needed work.

"Excellent, then you don't have any problems, do you?"

"Nope. I've got this."

"So what was that thing at the bar tonight? With the beer? You have quick hands, Rook. Good for sparring. I've never seen you slip. Not once. But somehow that lager just slipped on out and poured all over her."

I swallowed hard. "Shut it." His laugh was a guffaw, ringing in my ears. "I hate you. Put Saff on."

Lock laughed. "Wait'll I tell Saint."

"You're not fucking telling Saint anything." The two of them loved to take the piss out of me.

"Oh, he's going to love it. Should I start singing like we're back at primary? Westin and Nissa, sitting in a—"

I hung up on him. Why the hell was I so desperate to stay with a family that I wanted to shoot half the time? Lock and Saint were the big brothers I never asked for.

He has a point though. You don't slip. That was intentional.

I smirked to myself. It backfired on me though. Because now, the mental image of her tits was going to haunt me forever. On the internal scoreboard, she was winning, and she wasn't even trying.

I knew what I had to do. Stay the hell away from her, or it was going to cost me everything.

WESTIN

I turned on the shower. I didn't like wasting the water, but it was at least going to keep my voice muffled. I actually even planned on taking a shower afterward. I had the towel slung around my waist and everything. I just needed to do a quick check-in for the briefing meeting.

I typed in my code and called in. "Rook here."

I kept an ear out just in case Nissa was up and moving about.

Everyone else was on camera, but I stayed off. They likely would understand why.

Although, Saint and Lock decided to give me shit for it.

"What's the matter, pretty boy? Afraid to show your face?"

Over their guffaws, Saff reprimanded Lock. "Gentlemen, can we focus please? Besides, Rook probably has an ice pack on his black eye."

"It's not a black eye, damn it. She got one lucky hit."

I was never going to live that down To prove that it wasn't that bad and merely some bruising around the outside of my eye, I turned the camera on. That elicited whistles from Saint and Lock. And, if I was being honest, from Saff and Kaya too.

I sighed. "Are you lot done?"

Kaya grinned. "I feel like the blokes are just getting started, but Saff and I just had to make a bit of fuss there."

"Well, if you've seen your fill, can we get this going so I can keep an eye on the princess?"

Saff rolled her eyes. "Princess she is not."

"I know, but her father treats her like one, so that's the nickname."

That was not the nickname. Her nickname had always been Beauty, mostly because of her obsession with those horse books in the library, especially *Black Beauty*. She loved that damn book. She used to watch all these horse shows, and on those afternoons that she would come to Mrs. Pembry's to look for a play-mate and I was busy, she would end up watching them for hours. I'd started calling her Beauty out of habit. But none of them needed to know that.

"All right, I'll make this easy for you. I've some quick and dirty bugs placed and I've tapped into the security feed. I haven't had access to the study, so that will have to be on the next round. As for the manor, as far as I can tell from my last trip into it, there has been some construction, but not to the interior tunnels. I haven't explored all of them yet though, so next time I'm at the house, I'll have another look-see and make sure every-thing is as it should be. But for now, the map you have is enough to study."

Saff sat forward. "What about the exterior? Are we still going to be able to use that tunnel by the brook?"

I nodded. "From my surveillance from the day I was captured, yes, you will still be able to use it. But there is a clearing nearby, so when you exit that tunnel, you will have to be very careful to remain unseen unless you want to go to the perimeter. It's a long way around and more heavily guarded, but it's up to you."

Saint, all business tone, frowned at the maps. "I don't see a great place for egress. We're going to have to run back across the clearing?"

I shook my head and pointed at the cellar. "I need to confirm this, but that cellar should be open. That one was an escape route that Montgomery put in himself. As far as I can tell, maybe right before I moved in, so just a little over a decade ago. It should be intact, but I will confirm it for you."

Lock twirled his pen around his fingers and back again. "And you're sure he doesn't suspect you?"

"Oh, he suspects me of something. But right now, he's more concerned with me watching Nissa. He's making sure that I will guard her with my life. But to think I'm not being watched is ridiculous. Someone is paying attention. They're not doing it with cameras though, because I've got control over those. He's got to have someone watching me externally, so I'll just be careful when I'm on-site. Like I said, this is all the information I have for now."

Gabe nodded. "This is good work, Rook. Do we need a secondary on Nissa?"

"For now, no. Montgomery has got a rotation schedule. On weekends when I'm off, I'll do my best to come in. No more visits from the team, please. They're distracting."

Saff pouted. "I was just checking on you. You didn't seem like yourself."

"I have it handled. Are we done here?"

I heard movement in the living room, and I needed to see what that was about.

"Yeah," Gabe said. "We will review the data and get back to you with more questions. And Rook?"

"Yeah?"

"Be careful."

"Always."

Nissa

Yesterday hadn't exactly been the unmitigated success I had hoped it would be. I still had a bodyguard I very much did not want, my flat mate was moving out, and I still wasn't any closer to finding my sister.

But today was a new day, and I was just a little bit closer on that last point. I had a lead that I had completely overlooked before. The problem was that I couldn't easily go about unencumbered.

I didn't exactly try to *sneak* out of the flat. I was just in a hurry. I had stayed in my room until the last possible second.

After last night, I decided it was better if Westin and I avoided each other for a while. And if I was being honest, he was going to ruin my little recon trip with all his 'safety this and safety that' bullshit.

There was a group home that had taken older kids when they aged out of the one that my sister and I had been in.

I'd hoped to take the day and head out there. I wanted to get there when the administrator would be there. When I called yesterday, she said she'd be there this morning. So I had to hustle, and I had to wait until Westin was done working out. Apparently, he was a morning workout person. And well, his workouts sounded an awful lot like sex. Not that I had listened at the door or anything, because that would just be creepy. He was just very loud and enthusiastic with his grunting. And he liked to mutter things like, "One more, you can do one more." And, "Ah, there it goes." And, "Fucking hell, that's so tight."

It was hardly my fault that my brain went straight into the gutter. The moment I heard the shower going, I rushed to get my things.

Yes, I knew what it looked like. I knew it appeared as if I was *sneaking* out, but it was more of a calculated departure.

God, I was so close. Backpack on, coffee cup in hand, when that voice, a low deep baritone, called out from the corner of the kitchen. "Just where the fuck do you think you're going?"

I whipped around, causing my bag to fall off my shoulder. "Jesus fucking Christ, why do you keep doing that?"

"Nissa, where the hell are you going?"

"Nowhere."

"It looks like you're going somewhere *without* me."

"I just was going to grab some coffee."

"Then why is there a to-go cup in your hand?"

I frowned. "I thought you were in the shower."

"Wow, so you really waited until I was in the shower before trying to run out?"

I sighed. "Well, it was worth a try." *Sonofabitch.* I wasn't going anywhere without him today.

It was then that I realized he was shirtless and in a towel. Oh, for fuck's sake.

He marched toward me, and instinctively, I backed up against the door. "What?"

"Hand them over."

"What?"

"Your phone, and your keys."

I shook my head. "No."

I watched as his left hand tightened on his towel as if it had started to loosen. My gaze traveled down his body, and I couldn't help slightly licking my lips as they hit his belly button and just a little bit of... Oh my God. There's no way that was his dick. The imprint looked like an anaconda. Jesus.

Don't you remember?

That was the problem. I did remember.

He cleared his throat. "Again, you can take a picture. It'll last longer. Keys. Phone."

"No, I'm not giving them to you."

"Don't you dare for a moment think that I will not drop this towel and forcibly take them from you if it means you being in this flat when I finish my shower."

"If you put your hands on me, I swear to God, my father will end you."

"I think you misunderstand. I'm here to protect you, not be your babysitter. Your father isn't going to do that to me when I'm protecting you from your own stupid decisions."

He stuck his hand out and waved impatiently. I glowered at him. "No one is after me. Damn it."

"It doesn't matter. Your father wants you protected, and that's why I'm here. I can't do my job if you keep doubting the authority I have. And besides, you wouldn't have made it past the elevators. The cameras would have gotten you, alerting the secondary guard outside."

My eyes went wide. "There's a secondary guard?"

"Have you met your father?"

That was accurate. That was just like my father.

Fuck.

"So, I suggest you get used to me, love. You're stuck with me."

Pouting, I put my to-go cup down. "Fuck." Then I handed him my phone and my keys. Because he was right. What choice did I have?

"Now that's a good girl. Do me a favor and wait right here until I get back."

All I could do was fume and scowl as I watched him march back into his room. If I ever wanted to be able to search for my sister, I would have to make sure Westin St. James wasn't my guard. Which meant I was going to have to talk to my father whether I liked it or not. I just had no idea what angle I was going to take. Because the question was, under what circumstances would my father have Westin replaced?

You know what circumstances.

I *did* know the exact circumstances, but I wasn't sure whether or not I was willing to play hardball.

7

———

WESTIN

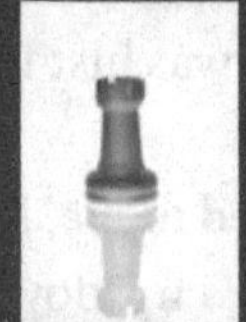

9 YEARS AGO...

I wasn't *hiding* from her.

Sure, you're not. That's why you're in the wardrobe, hoping that she'll give up looking.

It was my birthday. I didn't want to celebrate my birthday, but I knew there was no way Nissa was going to let it go. She'd taken to coming down from the house when looking for a playmate. I wasn't always available because I had chores and, well, video games. And I had mates. School things as well. But whenever I was around, she liked to tag along. And she knew my birthday was coming.

I'd been waiting for her to finish looking through the house. Mrs. Pembry was up in the main house, and she wouldn't be home until this evening. She always liked to do a cake and some presents. Some, she claimed, were from my godfather.

I knew better.

My godfather would wish me a happy birthday, but it would be some stodgy, formal affair up at the house. I'd be expected to dress appropriately and comport myself properly, and then there would be a whole discussion about business, legacy, and all of that bullshit. It wasn't for me; it was for him. The last one had been so boring I almost fell asleep. Mrs. Pembry had snuck me a Coca-Cola in my glass.

My uncle always insisted on wine, but I didn't like wine. Luckily, he was all the way at the other end of the table, which he thought made him appear powerful. And he couldn't tell that the dark liquid in my glass was Coca-Cola. I loved Mrs. Pembry for that.

My birthdays never included Nissa. I had asked about her the year she came to live with him, but he said that she was always busy. I didn't think he knew about her little excursions. I didn't think he knew that she played with me. He wouldn't like it. It was almost as if he kept her clean and sterile, and I was the workhorse. The distinction didn't actually bother me, but I did worry about her. Which was odd. Because I was accustomed to worrying about no one.

Every day, she would sneak out of the house and come running down to the cottage. I promised I would show her the tunnels and the secret hiding places, but I never did. She didn't seem to know about the tunnels inside the house either, and I never told her. I kept them to myself because I liked having something that was just mine. It felt like a terrible secret I was holding, but I still couldn't tell her.

"You might as well come out of the wardrobe, Westin. I know you're in there."

I sighed and groaned as I opened the wardrobe door and stepped out. "How did you know?"

"Your shoes were by the door, so I knew you were in the house somewhere. Which meant you were hiding. Why are you hiding? It's your birthday. I'm here to celebrate."

"Look, I'm thirteen now. I don't want to play hide and seek. I want to go play video games."

She sighed. "Then the new PlayStation I got is of zero interest to you?"

I blinked slowly. "What?"

"Let me tell you, it was difficult sneaking it out of the house."

"You brought a PlayStation here?"

She nodded slowly. "Well yeah, it's your birthday. And since I get the impression Julian wouldn't want us playing inside the house, I came here and brought the fun. Besides, I never use this thing."

"You have a PlayStation?"

"Yeah, in my room. I don't even know how to play, so you have to teach me. But first, we eat cake."

Nissa was still so little, though she still wore her afro piled high above her head, making her look taller. She had slight shoulders, and slight body. I had this instant feeling of warmth and protectiveness over her. She was going to need to toughen up. Maybe I would show her how to fight.

You don't know how to fight yourself.

I didn't, but I was pretty sure I knew more than she did. And she was little. People picked on little girls and took advantage. I wouldn't want anyone trying to hurt her.

"Earth to Westin." She snapped her fingers in front of my face. "Are you ready, or not?"

"I guess so." I said mutinously. I wanted to pout. I hated my birthday. But here she was insisting on cheering me up. And much to my annoyance it was working,

Nissa was hard to ignore in that annoying-little-sister kind of way.

She took my hand, the warmth of her small one seeping through my body, making me feel lighter and putting me at ease. Wasn't that my job?

"Westin?"

"Yeah, Nissa?"

"Why were you hiding in the wardrobe?"

Lying to her was never easy, so I opted for the truth. "I don't want to celebrate today."

"Okay, why not?"

"My parents died on my birthday."

She stopped tugging me along and stood in front of me, her eyes brimming with tears. "I'm so sorry."

I shrugged and averted my gaze, rapidly blinking the tears that threatened to pool there. "Yeah, I mean, whatever."

"That's terrible. But if your mum and dad were here, I'm sure they would want you to celebrate because they loved you very much."

"How do you know? You didn't even know them."

She didn't hesitate in her conviction. "I know because you're nice."

I frowned, and she took my hand again, tugging me along. "Because I'm nice?"

"Yes. You're nice, and you take care of me, even when I'm annoying. Which you think is often, but it's really rarely. And people are only nice when they've had people being nice to them. We usually get that from our parents, so I know they were nice. And if they loved you, that means that they wouldn't want you to be sad, especially not on your birthday."

I could only laugh at the eleven-year-old who marched me into Mrs. Pembry's ancient living room and right to the PlayStation that she'd managed to hookup to the TV herself.

"Now, since you're nice, I'm going to let you go first. Oh, wait, but first, we have to have cake." Nissa reached into her backpack and pulled out a chocolate cupcake with vanilla frosting, my favorite, and placed it on the table along with some candles she planted directly into the icing. "I had to be careful transporting that." She'd used a glass jar for the cupcake, and then she pulled out some matches and lit the candles. She then treated me to a rendition of a happy birthday song, which sounded much like a screeching badger who'd lost its tongue.

"Oh my God, Nissa please, save me from your voice."

"Hey, all that matters is the love behind it, not how good it sounds."

When she increased the volume, I playfully tapped her with a pillow. All it did was make her sing louder.

"We can do a pillow fight later, but first you have to make a wish, okay?"

I sat down, my eyes still brimming at this eleven-year-old kid who never seemed to leave me alone but always seemed to know exactly what I needed to hear, and I smiled at her. "This is the best birthday I've had in a while."

"Good. Now, blow out the candles. I made that cupcake myself. Okay, Mrs. Pembry helped me. You'll get the rest tonight. But still, I iced it and everything. It's made with love. Now make a wish."

I would never tell her my wish. Not ever. But in that moment, I wished that I'd never have to leave Nissa Montgomery behind.

8

NISSA

"Nissa, what a surprise to see you at home."

My father's happiness to see me made me want to grind my teeth. He knew that by assigning Westin to me, I would be forced to come and plead my case.

The man in question was not three feet behind me. Sticking by me like glue, just like he had all damn day. Every class, he'd sat in the back. My father had already worked it out with my professors, which was another problem. At some point I needed to be able to take charge of my own life without his constant interference.

But that was an argument for another day. Today's argument was getting rid of Westin.

My father's gaze flickered to him. "Any problems?"

Westin's voice was a low rumbling timbre behind me. "No, sir."

"Good. Leave me with my daughter. Don't go too far though. I expect she won't be able to stomach my presence for too long before she's ready to go."

He gave my father a sharp nod before turning to leave, and I scowled at his back. "Replace him, Julian. I get what you're trying to do. You wanted to teach me a lesson that I have to do exactly as you say. I understand. Now call off your dog."

Julian sat back in the chair in his massive study. The worn leather chair matched the one in his office. He folded his arms across his chest. "Now what lesson would you have learned? Please, illuminate me. I'm curious."

"You wanted to show me that you control my life. That there isn't a move I make that you won't know about. Okay, fine. But give me someone else. *Anyone* but him."

"Is there a reason you don't want him specifically?"

His dark gaze bored into mine. This was it. I could say it. I could have pointed out to dear old dad that before he left, Westin and I were closer than we should have been. I could have said that I trusted Westin with my life. I could have mentioned that we'd crossed that untouchable line.

And then he'd vanished and never come back. Just like everyone else in my life that I loved, he had abandoned me.

Instead, I just lifted my chin and said, "It's a bad fit. "

"You need to explain yourself. If he's hurt you or touched you in any way, I will have him killed."

My stomach fell. I might not want Westin following my every move, but I didn't want him dead. It was one thing to want him to pay for leaving me, but another thing entirely to murder him. "What? No. That's not something you'll ever have to worry about. But he's still a bad fit, and I want him gone."

My father's smirk was all too knowing. "If he hasn't given any cause other than annoying you, then he stays. Unless you *do* have cause. In which case, like I said, I will have him killed and find a replacement."

I swallowed hard. It didn't matter how I felt. It didn't matter that he'd hurt me. What did matter was that I couldn't have his life on my conscience. "Wouldn't you consider replacing him just because it would make me happy?"

"In this case, no. There is simply too much danger."

I'd known all along my father was unlikely to remove Westin from my duty, but I'd still had to try.

It was when I turned to leave that I saw something interesting on his desk. Some sort of binder with etchings on the outside. "What is that?"

He frowned at me and shook his head. "This is not something you want to touch. Whatever little impulsive part of your nature tells you that you want to know about this thing right here, shut it down and kill it dead. Because I might be a monster, but I am your father. It is my job to protect you. You don't need to know what this is. You don't need to know how I got it. Just know that this ledger could one day save your life."

WESTIN

I didn't know how much time I had. No doubt, Nissa was doing the whole *my bodyguard is mean to me* deal. Which was fine. I didn't care because I had a job to do.

I knew my way around the house. I'd grown up on the property, after all. Right off the foyer was a butler's pantry, and next to that was a little panel.

I was in a camera blind spot, and I gently pushed around the top of the panel and hit both top corners at once, which activated the panel and it slid sideways, allowing me to step through. Once inside, I used my phone light to find the button to depress and close it back before moving as quickly as I dared.

The tunnels were smaller than I remembered.

No, you're just bigger.

If Nissa was with her father in the study, that meant his office was empty. Or at least it should be.

Up ahead to the right was the curvature of the tunnel and the stairs. I knew the third one up had a creak that could be heard in the hallway, so I skipped it. Taking the stairs two at a time, I went to the second floor and turned left, depressing the next panel that led me straight into Julian's bedroom.

I paused, listening for anyone in the bedroom, and then breathed a sigh of relief when I opened the panel to find the room empty.

To the right was a massive walk-in closet, then the main chamber, and to the left of that, the office. Montgomery didn't do much work in here, but what was important was the safe.

I'd programmed a little decryption device. It was crude, but in the field it worked. Quick and simple. In less than a minute, I had the safe open and searched. Nothing that looked like a ledger. I took quick photos of everything else.

I was careful to put everything back exactly where I found it and closed the safe.

In less than ten minutes I was back downstairs and roaming the halls. At one point, I passed by the kitchen and heard familiar humming.

Memories hit me square in the chest. "Mrs. Pembry?"

The elderly woman whirled around. "As I live and breathe, Westin, is that you?"

I gave her a small nod. With a sob she stepped forward, her hands white with flour and dough, and embraced me tightly. "You've looked after me all this time, but I never thought I would see you again."

After I left, I'd sent money back, depositing it straight into her rainy-day account. She'd thought I didn't know, but she had a separate bank account under her maiden name, and I'd found the bank records when I was a kid. Every few months I would send her something. Nothing that would alarm the tax man, just a little so she'd have something for herself.

"I don't know what you're talking about Mrs. Pembry. That wasn't me."

She wiped her hands on the towel stuffed in her apron and waved a dismissive hand at me. "You and I both know it was. But if you need to pretend, that's fine. Honestly, I'm disappointed to see you back here."

"It was unavoidable, Mrs. Pembry." In retrospect, I knew he'd done me a favor when he settled me in her cottage. And least I'd had love in those years. Mrs. Pembry brooked no nonsense, but she was full of love and it was exactly what I had needed. So despite himself, my godfather actually did me a favor.

She went back to her pie and kneading her dough. "So why are you here?"

I told her as much of the truth as I dared. "I'm back for Nissa. Julian needed me to watch out for her again."

She pressed her lips firmly together. "If you ask me, he's the one she needs protection from. She's been terribly unhappy since you left. That bright beautiful girl. Something broke in her the night you went away."

It was the last thing I wanted to hear.

Maybe it's the one thing you need to hear.

I knew she wouldn't forgive me. It didn't matter how well I explained. There were so many things that I couldn't even begin to apologize for.

I heard Julian's voice in the hallway, and Mrs. Pembry stood taller and slid her mask of indifference back into place. When Julian walked in with his daughter behind him, he nodded at me. "Nissa is ready to go."

Judging by the look on Nissa's face, she did not get her wish. For the time being, I was still assigned to her.

As we left the manor, I asked her, "So what happened? I thought you were going to get him to fire me."

"Turns out, you're not worth the effort. Besides, I can make you leave all on my own."

"I dare you to try."

9

NISSA

AS IT TURNED OUT, Jamila was a traitor if her laughter was any indication. We were headed to our economics exam, and I had just told her about how Westin had caught me trying to sneak out.

The bodyguard in question was about ten feet in front of us.

"Wait, how did he catch you?"

"I don't know. He went to get something in the kitchen. I was dumb enough to think he was actually in the shower. And there I was, caught."

She clutched her side and giggled. "Oh my God, that's just priceless."

"That's not helpful, Jamila."

As we crossed the street, I narrowly missed one of the messenger people in the bike lane. He was the one who almost ran into me, but he had the nerve to curse me out.

Rude.

Westin glanced back to see if he needed to reassess the threat, but I shook my head, my father's warning still ringing in my head. My father would kill him if he knew what had happened between us.

It was a long time ago.

It was, and it had no bearing on anything now. Checking to make sure there weren't any cars coming, we moved through the traffic and students heading for class, and I asked Jamila, "Am I going to see you before my International Law Class?"

"Sorry, love, but no. I've got a meeting with Professor Henelle, to make sure we have all the things we need for the research equipment. But I will come by for dinner tonight, and you can finish filling me in."

"I don't know if I will because you clearly are taking his side."

"No, I'm not. I'm always on your side. I just find it hilarious."

"It's not funny, Jamila."

"I know. He's the worst. We hate him."

I winked at her. "That's more like it."

She laughed. "Next time though, don't get caught."

"It just happened."

"You know, would it be the end of the world if he went with you?" she asked.

"Anywhere I go, he'll tell my dad about it. I feel like I have a human ankle monitor."

Jamila clapped her hands. "What you need to do is be the picture of cold disdain. Right now, he's having all the fun. He's enjoying this."

I rolled my eyes. "How can you tell? He never smiles."

"Oh, I get that, but have you seen yourself? You're well fit. And he's a man, presumably straight, although maybe not. If not, you're fucked."

"Thanks for that."

"I mean, if he's straight, you know what to do. Be the picture of cold disdain, and eventually he'll crack. Or you could do the whole bit where you walk around in a towel and see how that goes. Those are my two best pieces of advice."

"I'm not sure that's actually advice."

"I'm just saying I think you should play along."

"Play along with him? Just accept this?"

"Maybe if you play along, he'll think you're giving in. And then he'll let his guard down. He'll be gone in no time."

I considered that. "You know, I don't mind that idea, and it might actually work."

"See? I do have some good ideas." She put her arm through mine conspiratorially. "This could actually be fun, you know. Torturing him incessantly. You know how to do this. It's like a cold war. You make him rue the day that he turned up on your doorstep."

Maybe I'd always underestimated Jamila. "You know, I've always loved you."

She laughed. "Oh, I know."

As we settled into our economics lecture hall, I started thinking of all the ways that I could make Westin St. James pay. Or at least make his life so miserable that he wanted to quit.

Jamila was right. This could actually be fun.

Nissa

Several days after my vow to boot my human ankle monitor, I hadn't managed to make him quit yet. Not that I was trying too hard. I had a full class schedule, and I was using any available free time to chase leads on my sister. I'd gotten lucky seeing the article mentioning Sister Mary's retirement. I'd been able to make some calls but so far no one would give me answers. My next step was to go there.

Today.

I was trying to motivate myself to get up when I heard the low grunting from the living room.

He was doing this on purpose. He had to be. Who else woke

up at five a.m.? Only the truly wicked. I knew he wanted to work out, which was okay with me, but did he have to make those sounds? I couldn't take it anymore.

Another low and throaty sound came from the living room and made my whole body pulse. It sounded... dirty.

There was no other way to describe it. It sounded like somebody was getting a proper dicking in the kind of way that would make an old lady blush and a college student lament her current lack of a boyfriend.

Who are you kidding? You've never had a boyfriend who made you groan like that, ever.

None of them had compared to Westin.

Not once. I'd had exactly three boyfriends. The first real one when I was seventeen. He thought my boobs were squishy toys, so no groaning there. Mostly irritation and pain, and I refused to ever go out with him again.

Then there had been Ned Williams at eighteen. He was better and a very good kisser. Solid marks. But he'd only ever seemed to want to *kiss*. The one time I did put his hands on my boobs, he recoiled as if they'd burned him. So no groaning there, either.

And then there had been Matthew Leroy a year ago. Much better about the kissing and also with the boobs. We hadn't made it very far though. The moment he stuck his hand down my trousers, he'd started rubbing at my left flap and pulled back and watched me, asking me if that was how you did it. I was so shocked and surprised all I did was blink at him for a moment, and then I said, "No, a little to the right, actually."

He did not appreciate the directions, so no groaning for me.

It was fine. I was twenty years old, and to date, only one person had ever made me moan. And unfortunately for me, he was currently grunting through a workout in my living room.

The problem was, I needed to like someone as a person in

order to sleep with them. And after what had happened with Westin, I couldn't bring myself to trust anyone again.

Jamila kept telling me that I was odd. That nobody cared who they shagged.

Except, *I* did. Not that I had ideas of something flowery and romantic. I didn't need rose petals on a bed or anything like that. I just needed to like the person.

Like is the wrong word. You mean love.

Well that was a problem because I certainly didn't love Westin anymore.

All I needed to know was if they were decent, kind, good. Did they kiss like a dream? And did they have any idea how to make me moan without actual sex first? Basically, were they skilled in the art of foreplay?

Not too much to ask for.

Maybe it was me. I had no idea. My point was, at 5:05 this morning, Westin had me remembering exactly what it would be like to make him moan and that *he* could make *me* moan.

I clamped my thighs together, trying to block out the imagery of him over me. Okay, there had been one teeny-tiny sex dream.

Honestly, it wasn't my fault. I was clearly overtired, and well, he was hot. Very hot. And to be fair, I have functioning eyeballs. I might not like him or the fact that he worked for my father, and I was stuck with him, but for some reason, there was a very primal part of me that responded to him. Every accidental brush, every touch, every slide of his gaze over my body, pulled something low in my belly. I wasn't immune, and honestly, it wasn't my fault. Who would be immune to that?

Maybe someone who doesn't have a death wish?

He was that kind of bloke. The kind that was all trouble.

Stop thinking about him. Get up. You could use a workout your-

self. Maybe if you go run you won't have inappropriate dreams about your bodyguard.

Fine. There was no way I could go back to sleep anyway, not with Mr. Groanypants out there moaning. He did it again, and I dragged the duvet over my head.

Ah, goddamn it. I could almost picture him, his hair wet, his body damp with sweat, his muscles bunching as he moved over me with a cocky smirk on his face as he looked down at our bodies to watch himself fucking me. Fuck, that was hot.

With a curse, I dragged the duvet and pillow off my face. "Bollocks."

Obviously, I wasn't getting any more sleep, thanks to him. I stood and went over to use the bathroom, brushed my teeth, and washed the sleep out of my eyes. If I was up, I might as well do something useful with the early-arse hour.

I dragged my favorite workout top on. It was screen-printed with *I know how to drive a stick* and a picture of a woman on a broomstick riding off into the sunset. It was cropped and hung over one shoulder. It was also threadbare, but I loved it and was not giving it up no matter how worn out it was getting. I'd thrown on a pair of capri-length workout pants, socks, and my trainers. It was embarrassing how long it took to find them at the back of my closet, but find them I did. I tugged off my satin scarf before pulling my workout headband over my straightened hair. If I was lucky with the rain, I might be able to go another few days before I had to straighten it again.

Once my headband was in place, I pulled my ponytail high up on top of my head and made it into a bun. I wanted to make sure not a drop of moisture snuck through.

The weather was definitely about to turn rainy, so eventually I would have to go back to braids. But I liked my hair loose. I rarely wore it straight. It was usually either natural or in some kind of protective style.

When I was dressed, I gave myself a once-over in my full-length mirror and shrugged. The capris were arse-huggers, and well, I had arse in spades. If he was going to insist on following me, at least I could torture him a little.

I yanked open my bedroom door, and the onslaught of water was gasp-inducingly frigid. "What the fuck?"

I was pelted with massive sprays of water, until finally it stopped, but not before I was drenched from head to bloody knees. My trainers were spared, but the rest of me was not, including my hair. When I peeled my eyes open, all I could do was stand there as my heart galloped, trying to break free from my chest, sure that there was some kind of water-propelling monster or burglar in my flat.

All I heard was Westin's low chuckle coming from the living room to the right of my door.

When I blinked the water out of my eyes, I saw some kind of water gun rig, complete with a catapult device for water balloons. "What the fuck? Are you responsible for this?" I stomped out into the living room to find him doing a plank. He lifted his head slowly and flashed a grin at me. When his gaze met mine, his eyes went wide and he fell out of his plank onto the ground and rolled over guffawing. "You look like a drowned rat."

"I swear to God, I will kill you." I launched myself at him, not caring if we both got hurt. He was going to die today. "What the bloody hell did you do that for?"

To my chagrin, he caught me easily, rolling me over and pinning me down with his weight.

Unable to budge him, I still fought, my hands balled up into fists. I managed one whack on his face. Then with a growl, he snatched both my fists with one of his massive hands and drew my arms up over my head.

Not to be thwarted, I tried to buck him off me, and I could

feel... Oh God, he was hard. The thick length of his erection pressed like steel against my stomach, and I knew I should stop moving. I fucking knew, but I was just so angry.

His command was a sharp bark. "Enough."

"Fuck you."

He grinned. "I know you'd like that, but that's not why I'm here."

Which only made me fight harder. The one thing that his words couldn't do was accomplished by his chuckle.

If I hadn't been so angry, I would have noted that it was mellow, like a really good brandy with a hint of sweetness on the edges. I stopped struggling then. "Let me go."

"Not until you understand that if you want to sneak around and play, we can. I play to win though, as you can see. And look, I made you wet."

My mouth hung open. I couldn't believe he just said that. "What?" My question sounded throaty and breathy, like I was turned on.

Well, you are.

The point was, he did not need to know that.

"You are wet. Soaked, actually. I can feel it."

Heat suffused my body, embarrassment taking over until I realized he meant with water. I was soaked in water.

My brows snapped down. "Get off me."

"If you insist, Beauty. But let this be a lesson next time you want to make a quick escape from me. You won't make it. I play to win, there's no escaping, and I hold a grudge. So, you might as well get used to this little arrangement."

I scowled up at him as he released me and eased off me gently. One way or another, I was going to get him back, and payback would be a bitch.

10

—————

NISSA

THANKS TO THE WESTIN, Julian combo, sleep was getting harder and harder to come by. Every time I closed my eyes. The dreams started again, and I was powerless to stop them. It didn't matter that I knew it was stress. It didn't matter that I understood that Westin coming back was another control trigger for me. None of that mattered.

Because it seemed my subconscious gave zero shits about how aware I was of my stress.

I thrashed as I grabbed for my sister. "Lenora. Lenora, I don't want to go."

Sweat poured from my pores, and my hands were slick and my hair matted to my face. I screamed again. "Lenora." But the more I reached for my sister, the further away something pulled her. Or maybe I was the one being pulled.

The arms around me tightened like a vice. Keeping me close, pulling me in. Drowning me. The edges of darkness crept up my arms trying to envelop me, submerging me in It. And I thrashed and fought. "I want my sister. I want my sister."

The voice that responded was smooth, cultured, almost kind. A tease. A lure. Designed to make me complacent.

I had left my sister in that place for a whole new life. One I didn't want, One I didn't ask for. I managed to kick out, free from the darkness, and once the oily dark material slipped off my skin, I screamed.

But then I could no longer see my sister. I ran in one direction, the streets becoming thicker and thicker with people. I was no longer in the care home. I ran through the streets of London, and I could feel the footsteps behind me like a herd of elephants, or a group of men that worked for my father.

They were determined to bring me back. Determined to lock me in that house. Determined to never see me free.

So I kept running, my lungs burning, my breath coming in short pants. My legs and arms on fire from the effort it was taking to keep moving. And just when I saw her profile, part of her mischievous smile, someone stepped in front of her, blocking my view. The dark hair, the two big guys, the thin-lipped smile.

I stopped short. Julian.

"Nissa, time to come home. You'll never see your sister again."

"You promised. You promised I would see her again. You're a liar. And I hate you. I will never love you."

My father loomed bigger and bigger as he walked toward me, his visage appearing more and more sinister. "You belong to me. You will never be free. And you will never see her again."

When he grabbed me up, I screamed again. This time he started shaking me. Shaking me so hard. I fought, my arms thrashing. He wasn't going to get me again.

Suddenly something jerked me from out of the dream, and I was back in darkness. But this time the strong firm hands on my shoulders, shaking me weren't hurting me. "Nissa, wake up."

I blinked rapidly as light poured in, so bright that I had to shut my eyes immediately. "What the hell's going on?" I asked.

"You tell us. The two of us were convinced that you were being murdered."

I peeked my eyes open again and frowned when I saw Jamila

in the doorway by the light switch holding her cricket bat. Westin was on the bed and had been shaking me. On the nightstand was a gun.

I immediately scooted away from It. "What are you doing?"

He sighed. "You were having a nightmare."

I swallowed hard. That much I could ascertain for myself. I was slick with sweat. And that panicked feeling hadn't dissipated. I could still feel Julian shaking me. Telling me I would never be free. I wouldn't meet Westin's gaze because he knew what this was. I'd been having these dreams for years.

"I'm sorry you both thought I was being murdered. I'm fine. Just a bad dream."

Jamila lifted a brow. "That was a hell of a dream. You're sure no one's in here?"

I nodded and shook myself from Westin's hold. I dragged the duvet off, needing to change my clothes. Maybe a quick shower would help me calm down. Westin's gaze roved over me. Flicking down to my breasts, and then quickly back up to my eyes and away again.

I glanced down and realized my white tank top was now see through thanks to my sweat. Crossing my arms over my chest, I muttered, "Yeah, I'm fine. I'm sorry to wake and worry you."

Westin stood, took the gun off my nightstand, and shoved it into the waistband of his gray joggers. It was my turn to pretend that I hadn't caught a quick peek at the imprint in the gray material as he stood.

"If you don't mind, I'm going to do a quick check of the room okay?"

"Knock yourself out, I'm going to grab a shower."

He nodded and proceeded to the loo. When he came out, his gaze drifted to mine, and I could see the worry and concern in his expression. Worse was the knowledge. That intimate knowledge that he had of who I was. And the fact that I was still having this very bad dream.

There was a time when I would have talked to him about it, a time when he would have held me close and asked me to tell him stories about my sister so I could remember her well. There was a time when he would have told me that when he was old enough, he would help me find my sister.

That time was long past.

I had to remember that version of Westin no longer existed.

The problem with that was, he had the knowledge. It was still embedded somewhere in that robot mind of his. And I hated that he knew me that well. I hated that tiny part of me that longed for understanding.

When he was done with the loo, the closets, and under the bed, he checked to make sure the fire escape was locked, even though we were on the fourth floor. "To be safe I'll check the rest of the flat, but I think no one's here."

I nodded. At the end of the day, he was just doing his job It wasn't his fault the dreams had started again.

Just as he left, Jamila came over to give me a squeeze, still holding her cricket bat. "Honey, who the hell is Lenora?"

My heart squeezed. "What?"

"Lenora. You were screaming her name in your dream."

"I—" I shook my head. "I don't know. It was just a dream."

Her brow furrowed as she watched me, but then she stepped back and took her bat with her as she left. "Okay, get some sleep."

I knew for a fact that was never going to happen.

Nissa

Exhaustion tried to pull me down. It was like walking

through sludge. I was busy pouring my coffee into my to-go cup when Westin came out of his room. "Are you almost ready to go?"

I nodded. "I have an exam this morning."

He cleared his throat as he watched me, and I sighed. "What? What is it?"

"I know I probably shouldn't ask this, but are you okay?"

I knew why he was asking, and my gaze flickered over to Jamila's bedroom. "I'm fine."

"Jamila's gone already. She said she'd see you after your first class for coffee."

I sighed. "Oh, right. I forgot."

"So you don't have to pretend with me."

I didn't have to pretend with him? What the hell?

After everything we'd been through, he had the nerve to say that to me? "Wait, just so I understand. You're telling me that I can talk to you, that you are trustworthy, and that I can tell you my deepest, darkest secrets and you are here for me. Is that what you're telling me?"

He sighed. "Yes, essentially. I know. I shouldn't say it, but I'm worried."

When in doubt, deny, deny, deny. "Why are you worried? I'm fine, Westin. I certainly don't need you."

He sighed. "Look, all I'm saying is, given our history, I know a little bit about why you were screaming for Lenora. I just want to help."

I lifted my brow. "You want to help? Where were you four years ago when I woke up alone?"

He winced as if I'd hit him. My pride tried to strangle the questions down, but it was too late, because they were bubbling up whether I wanted them to or not.

"Where were you over the last four years when my father tried to squelch every inch of rebellion and freedom I tried to carve out for myself? Where were you when I had to sit there and listen to him as he picked my school, picked my courses, told me exactly what I was going to do? Where were you when I was fighting for a mate, fighting for freedom, fighting to make sense of my world without the one person I could trust?"

"Nissa, if I could have come back—"

I shook my head. "Don't do that. Don't tell me that if you could have come back for me you would have, because I know that's not true. You didn't come back then, but you're back now, right? I don't need to know the whys or wheres or hows. I just know that I wasn't important enough for you to come back. Or is that not the truth?"

Steely blue eyes met mine. "I can't tell you where I've been."

"Sure you can't. Don't worry about it. I turned out just fine. I don't need you. I don't need your help."

I tried to brush past him, but he reached out and took my elbow. "I know you don't want to hear this. And trust me, I understand. You never expected to see me again, and I know I hurt you. Believe me or don't, but every day, I thought about you."

I turned, forcing him to release me. "You recognize that's bullshit guys tell girls, right? Don't gaslight me, okay? I'm stuck with you for the time being, so let's just figure out a way to live with each other. Jamila is going to be gone soon. I just want to get a routine down for the rest of the year, and then I'll be free of you, okay?"

His brows furrowed. "What do you mean, free of me?"

I rolled my eyes. "I don't have to talk to you. I don't have to tell you anything. I don't have to confide in you. Matter of fact it is probably better for me if I don't do any of those things."

"I know you think you can't trust me, but you can, Nissa. I'm sorry I haven't been here for you. I am well aware I don't have any right to ask you to trust me. It is kind of bullshit. I get it. But if you do want to talk, I am absolutely here. You and I have history. It's probably better if we don't pretend that's not true."

"We do have history. And that history has taught me a lot. It's taught me to be wary of men bearing gifts of their hearts and those kinds of things. I'm not buying it. I've been fine since you left, and I will continue to be fine."

He nodded slowly. "Okay, if you say so. Just know that if at any point you're not fine, I'm here. You can talk to me or not. It's really up to you. I'm just worried about you."

I shook my head. "No need to worry about me. I survived you walking out. I will survive a couple of bad dreams." I stepped out into the living room and grabbed my backpack. "Are you ready? I have to go to class."

He followed behind dutifully, and I knew from the look on his face, we weren't done with this line of questioning.

11

WESTIN

So much for getting Nissa to trust me again. This morning had been a disaster. And she'd spent the day freezing me out.

It was one thing to spend every single day with her, not being able to touch her. It was another thing to feel like I never knew her.

What did you expect? It's been four years. Maybe she is a different person, not the girl you left behind.

I hadn't expected anything less, but fuck, it still burned.

Don't you have other things to focus on anyway?

Wasn't that the truth. I had a mission. And that mission was covering Nissa Montgomery and finding out what her father was hiding. That mission did not include getting my feelings twisted up over her again.

Focus on what you're supposed to be doing.

And that was the plan. Keep my focus. I knew what my priorities were.

Well, you have another priority.

That, I did. While I was keeping an eye on Nissa, and trying to find a way in with Julian, I intended to get my life back. No, it wasn't the primary objective, but if I had a way back to reclaiming my life, I was going to take it.

Nissa hadn't come out of her room since Jamila left. She'd grabbed snacks, her books, water, and closed herself in to her room.

The old me would have at least felt a little bit bad that she was withdrawn and hiding from me. But even as the twinge of feelings flared up, I shut it down. Not the plan.

Besides, Nissa wasn't letting us get close ever again, so I didn't have to worry.

It's your feelings that are the problem, not hers.

Fucking hell. Instead of worrying about her, I poured my energy into the one thing I could control. What I was doing was illegal in several countries. And considering that Rogues sent me in to spy on Julian, this was beyond risky.

But still, the rush of adrenaline called me. My fingers buzzed with the energy. I could do this. *This* I understood. *This* made sense. Besides, Julian had stolen from me. He owed me blood and a whole lot more.

I setup my proxy servers and relays, careful to bounce them over forty points, and then I set a timer. The thing with most hackers was sometimes we got cocky. Sometimes we wanted to poke around things longer than we should. They were people with skills. The kind of skills you see in movies that seemed fantastical, ones that could break into anything.

The truth of it was most hacking required time, patience, and an understanding of your fucking limits. Nine times out of ten, your ego could get you in trouble, looking for just a little too long, wanting just a little bit more, meaning to leave your stamp all over whatever the fuck you were looking at. But that wasn't me.

Oh, really?

To be fair, that was how Rogues had found me. I'd gotten a

little too curious about one of my mates at Cambridge. Rogues had been keeping an eye on him in connection to his father, who did a nasty bit of work for a Russian oligarch. Weapons, trafficking, the whole nine. But still, men like Antonio Igno made that look like child's play. Anyway, I'd poked along a set of assets. It was the lure I shouldn't have gone through, and I got busted. The worst thing was, I hadn't even known Rogues was a thing I needed to look out for. I'd been bloody worried about British Intelligence, which was what Rogues were, in a way. But British Intelligence didn't have the manpower to fuck with someone like me. Besides, I wasn't stealing anything.

Just the same, I'd stayed just a little too long and my relays had gone bad. Truth be told, they just had a damn good hacker. The next morning, as I'd headed out to class, fifteen Rogues agents were waiting outside of my fucking dorm room, strapped and ready to party. They'd known exactly who the fuck I was. They'd cracked the Westin Rourke identity in an embarrassingly short amount of time. Gabe had let me keep the name though once he understood why I bothered with it. And it was the best decision that I ever made.

So why are you going to cock it all up by poking your nose where it doesn't belong?

That was just the thing, my nose did belong here. It was my money, after all. My legacy.

I set my timer, flicked my gaze over to Nissa's door, and cracked my knuckles. I was just going to have a quick look. Besides, Gabe would want me to have a look. I might find something interesting.

Excuses, excuses. If you're going to have a poke about, look. Just be quick about it.

It took longer than I had anticipated. In four years, Julian had learned a little bit about asset projection. Diversify more. He'd gotten better at hiding the money.

Three minutes in, with two minutes left on my timer, and I found what I was looking for.

The money trails. And I was buried in it. Files upon files, upon files. Accounts upon accounts. Julian had been skimming off the top of his legitimate businesses for years. That wasn't a surprise. He'd been using legitimate businesses to wash his money for years. But there was an influx of cash twelve years ago when I'd come to live with him, then another around ten years ago. He'd been put in charge of my trust as well around the time Nissa came to live with him. He'd taken a massive payment from the trust to pay himself. The five million pound fee was enough to make me wince.

But the dribs and drabs of payments over the years made me frown. And then on my eighteenth birthday, there was a massive transfer of the remaining balance into a separate numbered account.

I'd known he had stolen from me. I had known part of the reason he'd taken me in was to take charge of my trust fund. But knowing it and seeing how he'd done it were two different things. My one minute timer went off, and I frowned, looking back at the first date. What was that date? And why was that account separated from the others?

The thirty-second timer went off. I knew I should back out, have a poke around another day, but I couldn't help myself. I searched some more of his other reference files and found another massive payment to a medical lab. Two hundred thousand quid. Synergics Genetics? What the hell was that?

Ten seconds. Fuck. I didn't have time to look anymore. I'd have to come back.

It was only as I shut down that the date stuck out in my mind and my gut clenched. That was the same year Nissa had come to live with him.

WESTIN
Four years ago...

I KNEW THERE WERE RULES. And I understood them.

It was an awkward thing when you were assigned to be your best mate's bodyguard. A part of me thought it wouldn't be that bad. After all, I already cared about her. She was my *best* mate.

She's more than that.

I'd never admit it to her, but my whole life had changed when she'd come to live with her father.

I saw her less now that she went to boarding school during the week and only came home on the weekends. But she always found time to see me if I was around and wasn't working for my godfather.

Uncle Julian had made working for him sound like it was a summer internship. Like it was only temporary. But now that the time was coming for Nissa to head to sixth form next year for her final two years of secondary, I got the impression he was thinking something more permanent. Which I couldn't do.

I'd agreed to work for him for a year, but I wanted to go to uni. I'd gotten in at my top choices and had deferred. But I didn't want to work for my godfather for the rest of my life.

Then why did you say yes?

I knew the uncomfortable answer. Sure, Uncle Julian hadn't really made it a choice. But the truth was, I stayed for her. *Because* of her.

She may have been my best mate, but she'd become so much more than that.

And when Julian finds out, he's going to cut off your balls.

Which was why I was never going to tell a living soul. As part of this internship, most of my job was watching Nissa. On Fridays I would pick her up from campus and bring her home. If she wanted to see her mates, I was to drive her, survey her activities, watch her.

For the most part it was an easy gig. Except for her one mate Casey who always looked at me like I was a Christmas goose and she hadn't eaten in months. Nissa teased me mercilessly about it, prodding me about how I should just give in and ask Casey out because then maybe she wouldn't have to hear about me nonstop.

I didn't though. Casey wasn't really my type.

Then who is your type?

That question played at the edges of my consciousness that I didn't dare touch. The rules hadn't needed to be spoken out loud. I understood them. My godfather understood them. Hell, even Nissa understood them. As soon as she went off to school, our relationship had instantly changed.

While we still talked and texted, it was a very big brother-little sister kind of thing and less emotional sharing. I certainly never divulged anything I was really thinking, and Nissa had stopped poking and prodding so much, almost as if she could tell that there was this line that we were sometimes crossing.

Besides, I was eighteen, and she was still sixteen. She and Mrs. Pembry were the only two people that I actually loved in the world, so I kept those niggling feelings to myself when I caught some of her schoolmates staring at her arse. That wasn't her shit to deal with; it was mine.

Some of my mates has started to notice her too, which made things awkward. A month ago, Bill Sykes came round the cottage. Nissa was home from school, and she popped by to say hello. The rest of the night, Bill wouldn't stop hitting on her. Finally, I had to tell him to back the fuck off with a reminder that she was only sixteen.

Nissa had been well ticked off with me, reminding me that at sixteen, by law she could shag whoever she wanted. Age of consent in the UK was sixteen but she knew nothing about blokes and was going to get herself in trouble.

I'd never been angry at Nissa. Not in any real way. Sure, she was a pain in the arse, and her constantly sunny disposition could really grate on the nerves, but I couldn't ever stay mad at her.

But when she'd said she could shag anyone she wanted, the flash of fury in my blood had me wanting to throttle her and lock her up somewhere far away until she could see sense.

Blokes like Sykes were man-whores. As a mate he was all right, but with girls, they always ended up crying. And the eejit didn't believe in condoms. He literally thought he didn't need them.

There was no way I was letting someone like him anywhere near Nissa. Not ever.

Apparently, she hadn't taken well to me telling her who she could and couldn't go out with.

Thankfully, she'd left the Sykes thing alone, but now she was on a bloody date. She'd said yes to some twat from her school.

I'd wanted to separate his body from his spine. But Julian had said no. That the twat was from an influential family so killing him was ill advised.

Not that I would have left any evidence of his corpse.

But I'd been outvoted. And now she was on this bloody date... that I had to watch. She and Julian had an arrangement. There were to be no bodyguards in the car with her, so I was in the follow car. All night as I watched, that tosser had been leering at her. Frank Michelin. What the hell kind of name was that?

I still didn't understand why Nissa had said yes. She didn't even like the bloke. His lips were too big for his face, his eyes were too far apart, and he made a steady stream of *that's what she said* jokes. I never would understand why on earth she had said yes when he had asked her out... with me standing right there, mind you.

He'd strolled up, happy as you please to ignore me, and asked if she wanted to go out on Saturday. Nissa had gotten all flustered and fumbled her words. I was convinced she was looking for a kind way to say no, and I almost stepped in and did it for her. But then she'd said, "Yeah sure, why not?"

I had the quite irrational urge to pick him up and throw him a mile away. Why would she say yes to that goat?

And now I was being tortured by his fumbling at basic conversation. Yes, I had bugged her car. That was the safest route. And no, she didn't exactly know she was bugged.

Everything was fine until they rounded the lane that would lead to the house. There was an outcropping where you could park and watch the stars, and he pulled in. I gave him some space, staying about a hundred meters or so back as the rain pelted my windows.

This is too much space. Go and get her.

I shoved down that thought. That was irrational. Nissa was like my sister. This was her first date. I knew how important she thought it was, and I had to just sit back and let it happen.

Good job of that. Is that why your hands are gripping the steering wheel so hard?

My breathing was harsh, and all I wanted to do was go and rip that guy's lips off before they could get anywhere near her.

But I had to follow orders.

Frank said, "This is a great place. Do you come here often?"

If those were his pickup lines, I probably had nothing to worry about. But then I wasn't a sixteen-year-old girl out on her first date, looking to impress her mates.

"Oh, I live here, remember? That's my house up there. I've walked all of these grounds."

I couldn't help but smile at her obliviousness.

Good old Frank tried another tactic. "So, when am I going to see you again?"

I found myself holding my breath. What the hell was she going to tell him? There was no way she liked him and wanted to go out again. None. I could read body language. Besides, she was too young for any of that. She could get up to all of that shit at uni.

"Oh, Frank, you're sweet. Honestly, you are, and I like you. I just... I'm not really feeling any chemistry, you know?"

His voice went lower. "I've been nice to you all night. You acted like you liked me."

Bloody hell, he was one of those.

Nissa's sigh was heavy. "Please, don't be that bloke."

"What bloke?" he said, his voice getting much louder. "The kind who hates feeling led on?"

"Jesus Christ, you are that guy," Nissa said.

"You know what?" he said angrily. "You can just get out here."

What the hell? There was no way he was going to kick her out of the car and not take her all the way home. Julian might be a prick, but he had rules. And the appearance of geniality was one of them. That kid was going to earn himself an enemy tonight.

Just the one?

Well, I hated him on sight, but I had different reasons.

Nissa squinted up at the rain as she shoved the door open and climbed out of his car. "Thanks for nothing."

"Next time don't be such a cock tease."

She rounded on him. "Are you out of your mind? Just because we hung out and I let you win at darts—because honestly, no one is comically that bad—I mean, couldn't you even tell I was faking it? That doesn't mean in any way that I owe you anything, just for the record."

"Jesus, do you have to be such a—"

Before he could finish, I pulled the car up directly behind his, making sure my brights were on and my tires screeched as I threw the car into park.

Nissa's eyes went wide with panic as I climbed out of the car. "What are you doing Westin?"

I barely heard her though. I just jerked open the driver's side door, pulling Frank out of his car. "Mate, I'm going to say this once. If I ever see you near her again, you're not walking away unscathed. Do you understand me?"

Frank tried to look hard, popping his chest out a little and squaring his shoulders. "Just who the fuck are you?"

"I'm her mate. She's a pain in the arse, but I have a vested interest in making sure she stays alive. Nod if you understand."

Frank struggled in my grip, and Nissa tried to make me let him go, "Westin, you don't have to—"

I didn't spare her a glance. "If you put your hands on her again, if you even get on her bad side, you will have to deal with me. Do you understand?"

Frank tried to shove me off, but I had his arm behind his back at a sharp angle and his face was planted on the boot of the car in seconds as rage coursed through my veins.

"Make sure I hear you because I really don't want to break this arm. The sound reverberates in your consciousness for days. I really hate that loud pop sound that it makes. But I swear to God, I will dislocate it, so let me hear you."

I applied a little more pressure, and Frank screamed, "Fuck, yes. Understood."

"Now, fucking apologize."

Frank sputtered. "What?"

"I said, fucking apologize. Did I stutter?"

I held Frank up and shoved him toward Nissa, who stumbled back several steps as Frank mumbled, "Sorry."

"Right. Apology not accepted. Please get the hell out of my face," Nissa said with a bite.

I shoved him back in his car, and Frank was more than happy to go, cursing under his breath as he went.

She wrapped her arms around herself. "What the fuck was that?"

"That was my mate nearly getting herself in trouble. Some of these blokes are twats. You have to be careful."

"What? So it was my fault?"

"No, that was *his* fault. We're not going to argue about this. Get in the fucking car."

"No, I can walk home from here."

I prowled toward her and wrapped my fingers around her elbow. They were firm but gentle. "Get in the car, Nissa. At least let me get you home. If you want to ignore me after that, go ahead."

"I-I'm fine."

"I know you are. But on the off chance you're not, just get in the car, okay?"

"Yeah, okay."

I opened the passenger door for her, settling her in the car.

When I was seated back in the driver's seat, her scent wrapped around me, taking me over. She smelled fruity and sweet but also with a hint of spice.

I recognized in that moment that we weren't just mates anymore. I wanted her, and I was likely to kill any man who put his hands on her.

12

NISSA

"So basically, what you're telling me is, this is war?"

I was sitting along the corner of the couch, my weighted blanket wrapped around my knees and covering my legs as we caught up on episodes of *The Bachelor*.

Yes, it was misogynistic. Yes, watching women fight over men was terrible. However, it was highly entertaining. Especially when you were waiting for one of the women to tell the Bachelor he wasn't shit. Although that never happened.

"It is war. But right now, he's not budging, and Julian is adamant that he stays."

"Is there something you want to tell me, babes?" Jamila studied me, her gaze a little too knowing.

"No, nothing to tell you."

"Oh, come on, hot bodyguard shows up. You hate him on sight. You took one look at him and you're ready to shoot first? What gives? Not to mention that screaming nightmare you had. That sounds like plenty to talk about."

I shook my head. I didn't want to get into it. How was I supposed to explain anyway? Just go with, 'There was a time when I would have told you that Westin St. James was the start and the end of my world. That I loved him. That he would protect me always.' No I couldn't say that. Besides, that girl was a fool. I was no longer a fool.

"Let's just say it's a long, complicated story. We grew up together."

Jamila grinned and sat up, then snatched the bowl of popcorn from my lap. "Oh my God, I knew it. I *knew* it. That tension that I saw in the kitchen that day, it's unparalleled. And the fact that you guys are running around trying to one-up each other, it is every enemies-to-lovers romance come to life. Tell me everything."

I rolled my eyes. "You know what, like I said, there's nothing to tell. I don't want to get into it. That was so long ago."

"Uh-huh, sure. Spill." Jamila was not buying it.

And she shouldn't buy it because even though it was a long time ago, you are still holding on to the anger.

I was. I had a right to be angry. He'd promised to love me. But then he walked away. And I hadn't seen him again up until he walked into my father's house as if nothing had happened.

I worked my hand as I remembered hitting him straight in the face.

Nothing had felt quite so satisfying in years.

"Look, Nissa, I get it. You've got your walls up. You're trying to pretend that this doesn't faze you. You're doing that thing that you do where you erect a shell around yourself. It's not a cement shell, because it's permeable in places. You're empathetic, and sweet, and kind, and people love you. But when it comes to your heart, dear God. And this is me, your bestie. I love you. And I'm watching you as you erect this structure around your heart when it comes to him, so something has to be going on."

I knew Jamila. She wasn't going to let this go. I lowered my voice in case he was listening outside the door. "He was my first."

Jamila caught the direction of my gaze and whipped around to stare at the door, and she, being the bestie that she was, lowered her voice too. But that did not stop her from mouthing, "Oh. My. God."

I placed a finger against my lips telling her to shush. "It's not a big deal. It was years ago."

"And here I thought that you were a prude."

"Well, that's a fair assessment. I won't touch just any dick."

"But apparently, you will touch bodyguard dick."

"No, I will not. Not ever again."

"Oh no, was he terrible?" She scowled at the door, shoving off her blankets. "Did he hurt you?"

I knew Jamila. She would march straight over there and jump on him if she thought he hurt me in any way.

"No, he didn't hurt me. It was actually..." my voice trailed off as I try to think of the right word. "It was exactly what it should have been. All the stuff you see in movies and read about in books. It was perfect. And then in the morning, he was gone, and I never saw him again."

Jamila's mouth fell open. "What?"

"Yeah."

"No, there's no way." She shook her head, clearly in denial.

"I'm telling you, Jamila, that's what happened. He just walked away from me as if I never mattered. And now he's back, working for my dad, yet again."

"Fucking hell, Nissa, I'm so sorry."

"Yeah, so you see why I'm less than pleased."

"I mean, does that even make sense though?" She talked around a mouthful of popcorn.

"Oh my God, Jamila, stop. I know you. I see that look on your face. You want to dissect every possibility of why he left. Don't do it. Do not, because you will make yourself crazy."

Jamila was notorious. She could find anything on anyone. It

was actually terrifying. A new boyfriend that seemed shady, Jamila would be all over social media, and she would find him and find all the dirt needed to drop the motherfucker.

"Please, please, please. I'm just going to do a quick search."

I shook my head. "Oh my God, please don't, Jamila."

"I mean, look, it's just a tiny little peek. Besides, don't you want to know what he's been up to all this time?"

Before I could even answer her, she had her laptop in her lap, handed me the popcorn bowl, and was scooting even closer so we could share the blanket. *The Bachelor* was long forgotten.

She pulled open Instagram, doing all the usual searches on his name. And while he did have social media, it was mostly bare. Lots of beautiful landscapes with photos of him jumping off some kind of ledge, looking every bit a carefree playboy twat. The thing is, there weren't many. Less than twenty. But the last one being of some cafe in London. The caption just read, "Time to go home." It gave us zero information. "This has nothing. Less than nothing. This isn't even personal. Do you think he has a Finsta?"

I rolled my eyes. "Jamila, I told you, this was a waste of time. He works for my dad, and yes, he's really good with computers. If he doesn't want you to find information, you won't."

She lifted a brow. "Challenge accepted."

I laughed and shook my head. She clicked through some of his pictures, clicking on some of the locations, and starting some basic reverse engineering, saying she could find what the locations were and see other people who might have gone there, to see if she could connect him to anyone. "Look, it's just a basic—"

I stopped her. In one of the photos of a bar was a face I recognized. A face I hadn't seen in a long time. And my stomach cramped. *Finn Wesley.*

I hadn't thought of Finn in years. He'd been at the care home with us. And he and Lenora had been thick as thieves. She'd had a massive crush on him. Why hadn't I ever thought of trying to find some of the other kids to see if they knew where Lenora had gone?

My heart started to beat wildly in my chest as my stomach fluttered. Finn Wesley. Holy shit. I wasn't at a dead end. I had places to go. I just hadn't ever thought of them.

Next to me, Jamila studied me carefully. "Are you okay? You're staring off into space, love."

"Sorry. Sorry, Jamila. I, um, I just thought I saw someone I knew."

She hyper-focused on the photo. "Is it him? Is he in here? I don't see him."

"No, not him. Someone else."

"Someone cute?"

I shook my head. "No. I was wrong. It isn't someone I know."

Why don't you just tell her?

I could spill all about my sister and everything we'd gone through, but no one knew. The only person I'd ever told was Westin. And I just really didn't want to get into it with Jamila. But the moment she went home to Adam, I was going to look up Finn Wesley. Maybe if I could track him down, he might have something to tell me about Lenora.

How are you going to track him down? Jamila is the only one you know who is this good at cyberstalking.

That wasn't true. At least I had a lead now. And that was more than I'd had yesterday.

Okay, we have a lead on Lenora, but that begs the question, what are you going to do about your current problem?

I had no idea. But I wasn't going to focus on that. If I could keep the focus on Lenora, I just might survive my bodyguard.

WESTIN

A few nights after finding Julian's accounts, I still had no idea what to do with the information. I'd have to dig more before I felt comfortable going to Gabe.

Or you want to give him something so good, he won't lose his shit over the protocol breach.

My brain had still been working it all through when I'd finally fallen asleep only to be woken not an hour later by a text.

It was two in the bloody morning when it came through. For the last couple years now, I'd slept light. You never knew when you were going to get called on a mission. So when I got the text from Gabe, I frowned. It took my brain a moment or two to do the check-in procedures. But once I got him on the phone, I grumbled. "What?"

"Interpol. They're chasing Igno too. And they have the same idea that we do to go through Montgomery."

I cursed under my breath. "Fucking hell, Gabe, aren't you supposed to play nice with the other agencies?"

"In theory, yes. But since we're after him for terrorism, we get primary. But that's only if we can get our hands on him first. If we can't, we have to go on piecing, and you know how it's going to go. If they get him first, he'll lawyer up, and Interpol is required to do things by the book. We don't want that."

I cursed under my breath. "Yup, got it. So, what you're telling me is I need to be on alert?"

"Yeah. They're going to go through Nissa. We're out of time. Whatever situation you need to resolve with her needs to be resolved post haste, because you don't have any more time to do it."

I cursed. "Fuck me."

"I would never tell you to do this, but I am not beneath you banging the girl to get information."

"She doesn't know anything, Gabe, and I'm not going to do that."

Are you sure about that?

There was a long pause on the line. "If you say so. Where are we on Julian?"

"I'm still stuck on secondary. I did manage to plant the two bugs I came in with. One in front hall, the other in the morning room. Have we been able to get anything off them?"

Gabe sighed. "Not really. We're shifting now. I'm going to need bugs in his office, study, den, somewhere he takes meetings."

"That's going to require me to get into the house."

"Nissa doesn't go home?"

"No. She goes home once a month upon arrangement with him. So, unless I get summoned, we need to give him a reason to call her home."

I could hear the frustration in Gabe's voice. "Damn it."

"So, how do you want to do this?"

"Hang tight. I'll figure something out."

"Why do I get the impression that you figuring something out, is not something I'm going to like?"

"I've already told you, the fastest way to access Julian is through the girl. You, apparently, are squeamish."

"I'm not squeamish. I'm just against lying to her."

"You and I both know that you went back on this mission for more reasons than your inheritance or your legacy. You're back for the girl." I could almost hear the shrug in his voice, his nonchalance. I wondered about his complete ability to use people for whatever angle he needed. "It is what it is. You went back for her, so *be* back for her. I'll pull some strings to see what I can make happen."

"Fine, anything to get me in that house. Because without anything concrete, Interpol might beat us to it."

"I know. In the meantime, you keep them the fuck away from that girl. I don't care if you have to actually plaster your body to hers, but you do what you have to do."

"Copy. I won't let them get close."

"Good, because if Interpol gets a hold of Montgomery first, Oversight is going to have a lot to say about it. And I would rather not answer any more questions from them."

"Do they not know I'm under?"

"They don't exactly know, but they will eventually."

I sighed. "More games with Oversight."

"That's the game we play. You're in the field, and I do the dancing."

"What's it like being a spy?"

It wasn't in Gabe's nature to answer that kind of question. "It's exhausting. If I'm being honest, it's really fucking exhausting."

It occurred to me that while Gabe had been entrusted with the position of ops command, the one who had to play the games with Oversight, the one who had to pull the strings, the one who saw the big picture, he might not actually enjoy it.

He'd been grooming and training Saff for some time, prepping her to take over. But what happened to him when she did? Would he just... what? Go back to being an agent? I had no idea, and I had no idea what that meant for us. Because while Saff was amazing, she was still my age. There were still a few years yet before she would be ready to take over that kind of responsibility.

"I'll play the Nissa situation how I see fit."

Gabe sighed. "All right, that's on you. You've been warned. We are not the only kids in the sandbox anymore. You just watch that they don't come and steal your toys."

"Copy that." I hung up with him and ran a hand through my hair. I was up now and opted for a drink of water. I didn't bother to put a shirt on. It was only because of Nissa that I threw on my gray sweatpants. When I padded out into the living room, I found her already in the kitchen with a mug down as she gingerly poured milk from a pan.

Her gaze lifted when she saw me, and I didn't miss the flicker of her eyes over my skin. How could I not notice? That little flickered gaze had left scorch marks across my chest. "You're up?"

She shrugged. "I couldn't sleep," she said as she grabbed another mug.

I frowned at her. "I just need water."

She scoffed. "Please, I know for a fact you're not going to turn down hot chocolate."

She had a point. "Do you have marshmallows?"

She just rolled her eyes at me as if I was the idiot for asking her questions. When she put the pan back down on the stove, she walked over to the pantry and grabbed the mini marshmallows. "Everyone knows it's not hot cocoa without the mini marshmallows."

She added a generous heap into her mug, but only a few for me. I had to chuckle. She added a little whipped cream to both of our mugs and then stirred. "Come get it while it's still warm."

The flick of her tongue over her lips had me mesmerized for just a moment. "Thanks."

She shrugged. "You're welcome, I guess."

She washed the pan quickly in the sink. And when she put it on the rack, I murmured, "You don't have to stay in your room, you know?"

She hesitated. "What choice do I have?"

"This is your home. I'm honestly just here to keep you safe."

"We're not friends, remember, Westin?"

I nodded slowly. "Okay, maybe we're not friends. But truce?"

To show her I meant it, I stuck my hand out, and she frowned studying it. "Do you actually mean it?"

"I do. I have to be here. I know you don't want me here. I know I'm encroaching on your space and your freedom. I don't want to, okay? This is not the way I wanted to come back at all. But it is what it is. So, if we can work together, that would be amazing. And I promise to lay off a little bit."

"Can I go to class by myself?"

I laughed. "You do know what bodyguard means, right?"

"It was worth a try." She tentatively stepped forward, still clutching her mug with both hands. When she took my hand, I realized my whole display of us burying the hatchet was a rookie mistake. Her soft hand gliding into mine and the electrical current zapped me straight to my bones. I had to grit my teeth against the feel of it. "Fine, truce."

I wished I could tell her the truth, honestly. But my voice was caught somewhere in my throat, and the softness of her hand, so delicate in mine as I ran my thumb over her skin, made me speechless. When she lifted her hand and shook, I followed along, but I couldn't let go.

She lifted a brow, and then I remembered what I was doing, so I released her. "Truce. We don't have to be enemies, Nissa. This all will be smoother if we can at least have some common ground."

"I agree. I'm stuck with you, so I might as well make the best of it."

"That's one way of looking at it." I raised my mug in salute and took a sip. It was just how I liked it.

She shrugged and handed me the small bag of marshmallows. "You can have a few more."

I grinned at her. "Ah, you're warming to me."

"Don't hold your breath. Good night, Westin. I still don't like you."

I grinned after her. "That's what they all say. And they all come around eventually."

She flipped me off as she walked into her room, and I had to grin. She might not have exactly been thrilled, but like Gabe said, my mission depended on her. It would make things a lot easier if we were working together. Or at least, not at each other's throats.

13

NISSA

I'D WOKEN up early again ready to do some more work. I had several interview requests, and I made a note to deal with them after my statistics class. I also had a response from a Finn Wesley on Instagram. As it turned out, he was not the Finn I was looking for. But he did want me to send nudes.

Ew.

Despite this, nothing was going to put a damper on my mood. I had a lead. For the first time in ages, I had something concrete I could hold onto when it came to my sister.

Hell, I was so preoccupied that Westin's workout activities didn't even bother me. I'd woken up hunting for images of Finn on Instagram. I found a few. Several actually, but nothing that told me where he was, or what he was up to. I was definitely going to need some help.

I was still so preoccupied, I didn't even hear the soft knock on my door until the door opened and Jamila stuck her head inside. "Hey, beautiful girl, I'm heading out in a minute."

And just like that, my world crashed down. I'd completely forgotten that today was the day Jamila was leaving for good.

Because of your father.

I forced myself to grin at her. "No. No, no."

She stepped into my room and climbed on the bed with me, wrapping me in a tight hug as she smothered me. "Oh, come on, love, Adam's here. He's already loading my boxes into a lorry downstairs. I'm just a few blocks away. Just the other side of campus, honestly. We'll still see each other every day."

"Yeah, but we won't walk to class together anymore, and who's going to bring me coffee when I forget?"

"You forget, I cross paths with you on the way to my Astronomy class. I'll still bring you coffee. All you have to do is text me."

"But it's a whole other setup," I winged.

"You're going to be okay, love."

I stopped teasing her. "Yes, Jamila, I will be fine. I'm just giving you shit. And I'll miss you. We've been flat mates since freshers."

"Yes, I walked in on you trying to braid the back of your hair because you refused to pay the braid shop prices."

"Do you know how expensive they are?"

"Yes, I do. And I will tell you what I told you then. Make your father pay for it."

"Well, I'm still on the *I don't want anything from him* vibe, so there's that."

She rolled her eyes. "I get it. I do. But if he's going to meddle anyway..." She hitched her thumb toward the door and presumably toward Westin. "You might as well enjoy it."

I groaned. "Please don't leave me."

"I'm not leaving you. At least not very far."

She clamored out of the bed and helped me up. I grabbed my robe and tugged off my satin cap before following her out into the main living area.

Westin was helping Adam with the boxes. His gaze flickered over me quickly but then flickered away. We were trying to find a way to live together. It had been okay for a couple of days with our truce, but how would things change without Jamila as a buffer?

You have to figure something out because, without Jamila here, it's going to get very, very tense.

We were going to have to find some common ground somehow, but I just was in no place mentally to deal with that. I needed to mourn the departure of my bestie, and then I would deal with the bodyguard I didn't want.

When Adam and Westin were done, Adam walked over and gave me a hug. "You're not mad, are you?"

I shrugged. "You owe me several pints. I do hold a grudge, you know."

He grinned as he let me go. "Well, how about if I have something better than several pints?"

"Jamila can stay?" I asked hopefully.

He shook his head. "No, she's mine now. But I have Larkin tickets."

My eyes went wide. "Larkin?"

Jamila bounced up and down on her tippy-toes. "I know. I've been keeping that secret for three weeks."

Larkin was a hot pop band. Their songs had dominated the charts in the UK for months. And rumor was they were excellent in concert.

"What? This is amazing. How did you get Larkin tickets?"

Adam grinned. "My old flat mate. He got an internship and had to travel, so he had to get rid of these tickets. I have four."

"I can have one?"

And then Westin rode in like the killjoy he was. "You can't go to a concert."

"What? What do you mean I can't go to a concert?" I asked lifting a brow.

"Security risk."

"Bullshit. I'm going." I turned my attention to Adam. "I'm going."

Adam looked from me back to Westin, back to me again, and then down at Jamila. "How about this, I will leave you two Larkin tickets, and you can determine what you want to do with them. If you want to give them to some mates or come with, that's up to you. I got them for free anyway. I can't tell you how good the seats are, but Larkin, right?"

I gave him a solid nod. "Larkin."

Over his shoulder, I could see Westin frowning and shaking his head at me.

In a few minutes, I would be left alone with him and no longer have Jamila there as a buffer. I was going to enjoy the time that I did have because I wanted to get to say goodbye properly and worry about him later.

"You know what, we'll figure it out." I wrapped my arms around Jamila, and she squeezed me so tightly.

"Love, I'm going to see you for classes tomorrow."

"I know. I'm just... I'm going to miss you."

My eyes stung with unshed tears, and I rapidly blinked them away. I wanted Jamila to enjoy her triumph. I didn't want her feeling bad about leaving me behind with my arsehole bodyguard. And well, I didn't want him to see me crying. Adam gave me another squeeze and left the tickets on the counter. "Honestly, no pressure, but I'd love to have you there. Obviously, it would make Jamila more than happy. So just let me know, yeah?"

"Yeah, I'll let you know. Thank you for this."

"Cheers." Then he shook Westin's hand. Jamila scowled at him, bestie solidarity and all that, and then they were gone. I could feel the chasm and void that she left behind. Her larger-than-life, sometimes frenetic energy was completely sucked out of the room, and I felt alone. And empty.

Westin was watching me. "It's not happening. You can forget about those tickets."

I slipped them off the counter, holding them in my fingers, and rubbing them together between my thumb and forefinger. "We'll see about that."

"We will see. No concerts for you. With Jamila gone, we're going to be a lot more security-focused. We were slightly lax with her, but I put some extra men on the elevators, and one downstairs. But now that she's gone and we don't have to deal with the extra security of a person coming back and forth, we'll pull down to me and the driver downstairs, okay?"

I watched him as he was attempting to lay down the new law, and I wondered how on earth I ever thought I could have loved him.

The problem is this version of Westin is very different from the one that you fell in love with.

Wasn't that the truth? There was no hint of the old Westin. He was completely gone. And good thing for me, there was no hint of the old Nissa either, because this version of me knew better. I was never, ever going there with Westin St. James again.

———

Nissa

Later that night, I stared at my email.

Due to recent developments, we are saddened to say that we can no longer offer you employment at Quinly Global. We do wish you luck in your search, and we hope at a later date, we'll be able to work together. We find your ideas truly interesting and wish you the best of luck.

My stomach turned. This was the second email like this today.

I didn't know what was going on, but two companies I'd

interviewed with in Toronto had turned me down for jobs. One *had* offered me a job, the other one had consultant positions wide open. I knew for a fact they were still looking for someone because the job was still open when I looked. So what the hell was going on? Why had they offered me the job then taken it away now?

In the library, I slammed my computer shut and ran my hands through my curls. Westin looked up from his phone. "Everything okay?"

"I'm fine. Let's go."

His brow furrowed while he searched my gaze. "Sure, we can play that game, you're completely fine, nothing is wrong, but I thought we had agreed that we'd reached a truce."

"If you must know, I didn't get the job I applied for."

His brows snapped down. "What?"

"Yeah, second one this week."

His gaze narrowed. "Did they say why?"

"Who knows? They said, 'due to recent developments,' and the other one said something about budget concerns. All I know is, I don't yet have a job."

"I'm sure you'll get one soon."

"Yeah, I should get something. But these were great interpreting jobs. One of them with the Canadian government, and one for an international media company. I really wanted that one. Great job, great pay, an opportunity to travel, and..."

He leaned forward. "And what?"

"Freedom. Just a chance to do what I want to do, what feels good for me."

"Toronto, huh?"

I nodded. "That's the plan. There's also Australia, and that feels nice and far away. But maybe a little *too* far. I don't know. I still want to come back, of course. I have friends here. And obviously, if I can find Lenora, I have family."

"So, you plan to leave?"

"I plan to get as far away from Julian as I possibly can. The farther, the better. Even better if he can't find me."

"How exactly do you plan to do that, Nissa?"

"Well, how did *you* do it?"

He sat back, put his phone away, and crossed his arms. "We're not doing that."

"What do you mean, we're not doing that?"

"I'm not talking about the years I was gone, Nissa."

Of course he wasn't. "Okay, if you say so." I grabbed my backpack and slung it over my shoulder then shoved my seat back.

He stood immediately to follow me. "Don't be mad."

I held a deep breath. "I'm not mad, Westin. You do what you want to do, and you say what you want to say. You go about it however you want to go about it. It's none of my business. You were the one who asked for this truce and for us to find a common ground, to at least not be so mad with each other all the time. You're in my space. I don't want you here. I don't need you here. You've been here for weeks, and nothing's happened."

"I am a good deterrent, you know."

"If you say so. The point is that it doesn't matter if it's all talk."

He sighed. "Look, when I left, I knew your dad wasn't going to let me go easily. I changed my name, and I very deliberately stayed off his radar. It wasn't easy. There were a lot of things I didn't get to do. There's a way to do this without having to resort to complicated schemes."

"Oh, I'd love to hear that. If you have some methods, please do share them with me. Right now, all I need is a job. A job that will take me away from here if I can make it happen."

He was quiet for a moment. When he spoke, his voice was soft. "You can. I have complete faith in you."

"Sure, you do."

"I do. You'd be surprised."

"And what about you? Are you going to tell me why you came back?"

"I already told you why I came back."

"No, you just told me that you did come back. Not the whys. I mean, you could have stayed away, kept running. Why didn't you?"

He shrugged then eyed me up and down. "I can't tell you that, Nissa. Just know that I am back for you and Mrs. Pembry." More softly, he added, "I missed you."

My stupid heart leaped because, like a fool, I wanted to believe him. "Sure you did. Does that work for you, by the way?"

"What?"

"I'm sure many women have fallen for it, wanted to believe you."

He chuckled low. "I have yet to meet a single woman it worked on."

"And yet you still try."

"And still yet, I try." He laughed.

While I couldn't ask him questions about himself, he peppered me with inquiries about what I was studying, what I wanted to do, and where I wanted to go. I realized that if I'd just let him ask the questions, I could almost forget that he had abandoned me. I could almost forget that he had left me to my own devices.

That wasn't an easy thing to forget though. "Just tell me one thing, Westin. One thing about your life, and I'll stop asking. This feels very one-sided."

He thought about it. His gaze searched mine. "You mean besides that I missed you?"

The chill of the London wind zinged through my peacoat. It wasn't raining, but there was moistness in the air that was causing my hair to puff up.

"All right," he said. "I did get to go to Cambridge."

My eyes went wide. "You did?"

He nodded with a happy smile. "Yeah, I did."

"I knew you wanted to go to school, but I didn't know you were going somewhere so fancy. How did Julian never find you?"

"Well, it turns out when you hack the system, and change your name, create a whole new persona, people looking for you won't find you."

"Jesus. Is that what it takes to run from him?"

"Yes, but I don't think you have to run. I think you just maybe have to talk to him and let him know how important it is for you to have your own life."

"You know him. As far as he is concerned, I will never be free."

And that was true. I should talk to him if he was a rational human being, but he wasn't. And I thought about my job rejection. I had no idea what to do. I was trapped and cornered, and all I wanted was a little piece of freedom.

I waited by the door as Westin searched the flat, then he gave me an all-clear nod. I came in and hung my bag on the hook by the door like I always did. I wanted to scream. I just wanted some fucking freedom. A chance to live like a normal person. But was this how it was going to be? Every job I applied for, every interview I took, had my father gotten to them? Was he the one keeping me from my life?

No. It's not possible. How did he even know?

I eyed Westin. To be fair, I'd interviewed at both places before he'd come on as my bodyguard, so there was no way he could have known.

He was very good with computers though. It's not like he couldn't find out.

Fuck. I frowned and stared at him. He lifted his gaze toward me as he put on the kettle. "What, you don't want tea?"

"Did you tell my father about my interviews?"

His brow furrowed. "Excuse me?"

"My interviews, did you tell my father?"

"When would I have told your father? And also, I didn't know you had interviews."

I searched his gaze, and something told me he was telling the truth, but God, the feeling of it. It felt like this had my father written all over it, and Westin was the only person close enough to have access to that information. "You're his plant, aren't you?'

"You think I had access to information about you before I came here and only just now used it?"

I realized I was being a bit hasty. "I don't know. Do you know how badly I wanted this?"

"I'm sorry, Nissa. But look, I'm sure something else will come along."

I shook my head. "No, nothing else is coming along this. I know what he does."

"I'm sorry." I could hear the sincerity in his voice. I could feel it in my bones. He was sorry. "What can I do? Is there any way I can help?"

I eyed the tickets on the counter for the concert that he'd told me I couldn't go to. "Let me go to the concert."

He coughed. "No, absolutely not. I know you're upset and looking for some way to lash out, but no, I can't let you do that."

"Well, you can't stop me, Westin."

"On the contrary, that is precisely the reason I'm here. That's a security risk. I can't let you go to that."

"You can't keep me trapped. My whole life, I've been stuck. I just want to be free."

"And I'm sorry. I am, but you can't go."

I stared at the tickets for a long moment as I leaned on the counter, rocking from foot to foot, watching him. "You're here to protect me, right?"

"Yes, and you have to understand I would give my whole life to keep you safe."

"So you said. You can only keep me safe from people that hurt me, right?"

He frowned. "I don't know where this is going, but I don't like it."

"All I'm asking is, are you my jailer, or are you my bodyguard?"

He sighed. "I'm your bodyguard, that's it."

"Excellent. Then you can't actually stop me from going. If I tell you I'm going, I'm going. And it's your job to keep me safe there."

He straightened then. "Nissa, you wouldn't dare."

I grinned at him, the little flare of rebellion taking root. "You can't actually stop me from going. What are you going to do, tell my father? Sure, tell him. I don't care. If he's going to control me, I'm at least going to take the opportunity for a night of fun, and you're not going to stop me."

14

NISSA

Maybe this wasn't the best idea.

But no one would never, ever, ever hear me tell Westin that. I'd never actually been to a festival before. There were some things that I loved, the energy, people everywhere, and everyone having a fantastic time. We had the tickets for the Larkin portion of the concert because they were on the back half. The front half included acts like Kelly Rowland and Harry Styles. And that was a different ticket altogether. Could I have gotten that ticket? Sure. But that would have required my father's influence, and like hell was I going to call him. So I was going to be happy with these tickets.

Westin was a statue next to me. He was so tense it rolled off him in waves. Everything from the rigidity of his jaw to the stiff way he held his shoulders. He was on alert. Constantly watching. Jamila and Adam were already pissed to the winds and having a grand time. Jamila was extra bubbly.

Once Westin realized that I had every intention of going to the concert, he'd backed down. Though yesterday, I really thought he would tell my father and get the plug pulled. But for some reason he hadn't.

Maybe the old Westin was in there somewhere.

There were several opening acts that came on, and the crowd wasn't too bad. We still had an hour before the Larkin show started. Westin had gotten additional guards who turned up. I didn't know what he'd told my father. Hell, I almost didn't care. I was going to relish the fact that I was being allowed out for a little bit of freedom. All day, all night, for as long as I was allowed. We'd all been driven here, which was probably for the best considering that Jamila and Adam were already pissed to the wind. Jamila grabbed my hand and twirled me around. I couldn't help but smile and giggle. She started singing the lyrics to one of the songs.

I joined in and wondered when was the last time that I'd genuinely had fun without worrying constantly and thinking about what was hovering around the corner. This concert was just what I needed, and I was going to enjoy myself. I would let Westin worry about the safety and security of it all, and I was going to have bloody fun.

Adam clapped Westin on the shoulder, but Westin just scowled at him, trying to corral us to the front of the main stadium where we were supposed to be. More and more people filed in over the next hour. And with each new person, Westin looked more stressed and more hyper-vigilant.

It was only after we heard the gong and we took our positions in the cordoned-off VIP section that he relaxed just a little. "Nothing bad is going to happen. I keep telling you, you're a hundred percent unnecessary."

He glanced around and then pressed his earpiece. "You let me worry about that."

I rolled my eyes and turned my attention to the stage. Briston Aker, lead singer of Larkin, was gorgeous with shaggy sandy-blond hair, green eyes, the kind of whip-cord lean body that rock stars were apparently required to have, complete with six-pack abs, and he looked just a little bit dirty.

Jamila and I started to scream, singing along and dancing. It was then that I looked over at Westin, and he had on a half-smirk as he watched me. I smiled at him, and he blinked in surprise, as he was completely not expecting that. When he grinned back, I noticed he'd started to mouth the words as well, and I could see the old him in there somewhere, lurking, trying to peek out instead of being locked away.

By the time the third song came on, we were all feeling looser, having fun, and enjoying the experience. Adam had Jamila wrapped in his arms. Westin's hand brushed with mine, and I was sort of surprised by the contact. I lost my footing, pushing into the rail. He immediately wrapped his arm around my waist and pulled me in tight to steady me. "All right?"

"Yeah, I'm fine."

He nodded and went to release me, but I glanced up at him. "You know all these words, don't you?"

His brow furrowed. "No, I don't."

"Yes, you do. I heard you listening to this last night."

"There's no fucking way."

"I could hear you in your room. You were playing the album."

He lifted a brow. "Eavesdropping, Beauty?"

"Well, you were playing it loudly enough for me to hear."

I couldn't for the life of me understand why I did it. If you asked me later, I would deny it entirely. But I started moving in time with the music, letting the deep base of the beat infiltrate my lungs and my soul, and my muscles, and I started dancing against him. I twirled in his arms, singing loudly along to the music, relaxing because I knew that with him, I was safe. Wasn't I?

I could pretend for one night that I was the girl at a concert with her mates, having a good time, and I opted to relax and enjoy myself.

What was interesting was that he didn't move away. Instead, he placed his hands on my hips and let me move.

There were all manner of reasons to hate and despise him, to never trust him again. There were reasons to worry about my heart in his presence, but in that moment, I wanted to pretend that I was someone else and he was someone else, and we were just there in the moment.

I swayed my hips seductively, and song after song played on with Westin's hands on my hips, occasionally tightening and loosening. Jamila bumped into me causing Westin to have to catch me again, and then my arse bumped his hips, and I could feel every single fucking inch of him. I gasped and held perfectly still. Westin didn't move either. I could feel the tension in his body.

When I swiveled again, his hands tightened on my hips. His breath teased the shell of my ear. "Don't play with me, Beauty. Not a good idea."

I didn't care though. Tonight, tonight I was carefree. Tonight, I had my freedom, and I was going to enjoy every moment of it. I swiveled my hips again, deliberately grinding against him. His fingers dug into my flesh, and he groaned low. "You are playing with fire. This isn't a game we can win."

I turned in his arms. "Who says I'm playing?"

I danced in front of him, working my hips in time to the music. Westin stared down at me, his eyes growing dark. He licked his bottom lip as we danced together. Feeling naughty, I kept my gaze locked on his, as I moved my body in time to the beat. Larkin helped me out and added a reggae influence to the beat of their song. I dropped a little bit, winding my hips a little. Westin's hands slid on my arse and tightened. "Fuck, Nissa."

"Yeah, Westin?"

"I—"

Behind us, there was a loud bang and a sudden crush of people. Even in the VIP section, people automatically moved forward away from the sound, tossing us up against the stage.

Westin released me and immediately pressed his finger to his ear. "Coming your way."

"What's going on?"

He took my hand. "We've got a problem."

WESTIN

Nissa was a fucking tease, and it was the sweetest form of torture.

With every swing of her hips, with every grind to the thumping, pounding music, I had slowly been losing my mind, and she had been doing it on purpose, trying to drive me mad.

But that bang behind us reminded me of why I was there, reminded me of what I was supposed to be doing, not getting caught up in her and in that burning emptiness where my heart should be.

You're slipping.

I immediately grabbed her hand, and when she tugged it back, I scowled down at her. "We don't have time for you to argue. Move it, now."

I already had her halfway toward the exit of our section, then she shook her head. "Adam, Jamila."

I realized that she wasn't leaving without them, and the panic was getting worse. The band kept singing, but it was clear that something was wrong. Several men were pointing to some-place I couldn't see at the back of the field.

I knew she wasn't going to go without her mates, so I

reached back for Adam's collar and helped to get a grip on Jamila, then tugged him along.

When he realized that we were going somewhere and that there was a problem, he wrapped his arms around Jamila and followed behind, his hand on my shoulder.

I managed to tug them through the VIP section to a side stage. But in my comms, there was nothing but static. I couldn't hear the other guards. Which meant they couldn't fucking hear me, so it was my responsibility to get her out down to the garages and to safety.

Motherfucker. And this was why I didn't want her going to a bloody concert.

Lucky for me I had an ace in the hole. But even when I switched to the other channel, I still couldn't hear Saff. Fuck. It was getting too crowded because something was happening. Something I couldn't see. Adam frowned as he looked down at his phone. "It's a little slow, but it's all over Instagram and TikTok. There are some people that can't get out."

"What the fuck?"

Without thinking about it. I reached down and scooped up Nissa, swinging her over my shoulder.

"Stay with me. If we get separated, head down to the garage."

The VIP area for parking was a quarter of a mile away from the fields and from where everyone else had to park. We had special passes. We'd get through easily if the crowd wasn't a problem.

Adam nodded and tugged Jamila along. The problem was that Jamila was very inebriated and not steady on her feet.

Before I knew it, I lost them in the crowd and couldn't find them again. Nissa was screaming and struggling in my arms. I realized I was going to have to find another way to get her out. There were too many people the way we were going, too many opportunities for danger. Fucking hell. I'd mapped several exits, but I needed to look at my phone to catch them.

I paused against a pillar by one of the men's bathrooms. When I put Nissa down, I met her gaze. "All right?"

"I looked for Adam and Jamila in the crowd, but I can't find them."

"Four minutes and we'll be at the car. And so will Adam and Jamila."

"How are you sure? What if something is really wrong?"

"Two seconds, Nissa. Let me focus on getting you out of here safely, and I'll figure out how to find Adam and Jamila, okay?"

"I can't just leave her. She's my best—"

We were jostled again and then I saw him. A bloke who looked out of place. He was a little too neat. Not quite the concert-goer vibe. He had on the right clothes. Ripped jeans. Concert tee. Average. But there was something about him that was just wrong. He looked staged.

He met my gaze and then immediately started to make his way toward us. Fuck me. Interpol. Gabe had said he would try to hold them off, but if they wanted Nissa, they could attempt to take her. A quick look at my watch gave me the best route. We needed to get back the other way into the crowd.

Fuck.

I reached for her again and she shook her head. "I can walk."

"Nissa, we don't have time to—" Someone bumped me, but it was deliberate because they gave me a kidney shot as they went past. The pain had me hissing, but I stayed on my feet, my body caged around Nissa and the pillar. One look at my face and her brows lifted. "Westin, are you okay?"

I coughed aloud in pain. "Let's go, Nissa."

This time she didn't argue, didn't fight the hold I had on her wrist as I tugged her behind me. One glance over my shoulder told me Mr. All Wrong was following us.

Finally, my comms started to work again. "Rook, where are you?" Saff's voice came through the comms.

"Section S, making my way back to the car along the south route."

"Roger that, I'm on my way to meet you."

I don't know where she was, but I hoped she was close. As we fought our way through the crowd, Nissa finally gave up and tugged on my hand. "It's too hard to wade our way through."

I nodded and then scooped her against me, lifting her over my shoulder again. I could have sworn I heard a mumble, something along the lines of, 'This is humiliating.'

But it was faster this way. I prayed to God that Adam and Jamila made their way through the crowd too, or Nissa would never forgive me.

When we reached Section Q, I saw Saff through the crowd and I signaled to her that I had a shadow. She nodded and headed for him straight away. But what I didn't account for was the shadow behind Saff.

I had to make it all the way down to Section M, and while the crowd had thinned, I was going to have to put Nissa down. "Sorry Nissa, you have to walk. When I tell you, duck, okay?"

"What do you—"

I didn't have time to argue. There was a woman, a brunette, a little older than the average concert goer, maybe about thirty. Stunning. Leanly built. Her gaze was on Nissa, not on me.

She stepped forward, and I stepped in her path, shaking my head. I frowned as she assessed me.

She pulled her Taser out of nowhere, which I blocked easily, and before I knew it, someone behind me hit me with something hard.

A man. My height. Lean like myself.

I blocked his next shot, gave him an uppercut, and sent him sagging down. Nissa, to my surprise, wasn't screaming, wasn't getting hysterical. Instead, she kicked him. "What the fuck is wrong with you?"

I couldn't help but grin as I turned back to the woman, whose eyes had widened at Nissa.

Another man tried to grab Nissa, and I blocked the woman's next shot and turned to fight him, but Nissa was already doing my job for me. He had a hand on her wrist, which she stepped into and took her elbow to his elbow, forcing him to release her. And then she gave him a backward hammer fist straight to his nose, which made it crunch.

Blood spattered, and he cursed. He grabbed for her hair, but I was there with a gut punch and then another uppercut. He cursed again as he swiveled out of the way and then Saff... Oh boy, Saff. Before the brunette knew what was happening, Saff had her in a chokehold and knocked the Taser out of her hand.

The man I had just put on his knees reached for her, and the woman shook her head. Saff was calm, deadly. She didn't let go of the chokehold and just pulled the woman into the dark. A part of me almost felt sorry for her, but she had tried to Tase me, so there was that.

The man reached out and tried to grab me around the waist, and I got him with an elbow to the back of the neck, which dropped him on the ground. I wasted no time after that, grabbing Nissa and tossing her on my shoulder and prowling through the crowd.

This time she didn't fight me at all. Her hold on me was loose, but I could feel her shaking. "Are you okay?" I shouted over the din of the crowd. All she did was hold on to me tighter as if to signal that she was fine. In my comm, I heard Saff's voice. "She's down."

"Copy. Alive?"

"I make it a point not to kill Interpol agents."

"She's Interpol?"

"Affirmative. I got a list of Interpol agents that might make a play for Nissa. She's one of them. Agent Nyla Kincade. Do you have it from here?"

"Yeah. I've just got to make it to the cars."

"Roger. I'll have the follow detail ready to go."

Why had this turned into such a bloody mess? This was supposed to be easy. She wanted to go to a concert. She wanted to be free for one fucking night, and it had all blown up in my face.

I reached Section N, and finally the crowd had dissipated enough to put Nissa down. She was right there with me. Walking alongside, not saying a word, not fighting, not arguing, not going hysterical. She was deadly calm. And for some reason, that worried me even more. It would be easier if she was asking a lot of questions if she was crying, but no, none of that.

At Section N, we took a hard left and followed the emergency exit signs to the private garage where we'd parked. Julian's men were waiting, as were Adam and Jamila. Nissa ran to her mate. "Oh my God, are you guys okay?"

Adam nodded. "Yeah. What took you guys so long?"

Nissa slid her gaze to me but answered him quietly. "The crowd, that's all."

And once we had everyone tucked in, she looked at me. "You were right."

"I didn't want to be."

"I'm never going to be free from this, am I?"

15

NISSA

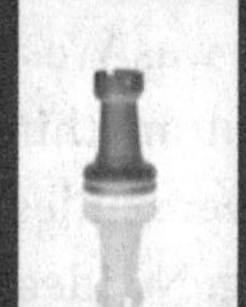

Back at Mrs. Pembry's cottage I followed him, taking note of the tension in his shoulders. "Why are you so mad?"

"Are you seriously asking that? That was careless, Nissa."

"You do recognize you're mad at me and I didn't do anything wrong? He's the arsehole here."

Westin leaned close and growled, the sound sending a shiver over my skin. "Yes, he is the one who is wrong. But he could have hurt you, Nissa. You need to be more careful. Not everyone is good or kindhearted. Especially blokes. You need to be really fucking careful about the kind of guys you choose."

I whirled around on him. "There you go, saying it's my fault again."

He ran his hands through his hair. "Fuck, that's not what I'm saying, Nissa. I'm saying I didn't like seeing him paw at you. I'm saying I fucking hated it. I'm saying I never wanted you to go out with him. I'm saying I never want to see you go out with anyone like that again."

I squared my shoulders and leveled a narrow glare at him. "Well, if you have so much to say about who I go out with and what I do, maybe you should pluck up the card and ask me out yourself."

His brows furrowed for a moment even as his lips parted. "Nissa, we can't have that conversation."

"Why not? Why can't we have that conversation? It seems like maybe it's an important conversation for us to have."

He was so close now. I could feel his breath on my skin, but he still felt so far away. This was Westin. My best mate. The only person I could talk to about anything. And for the last several months it just felt like we were miles apart on everything. I had no idea what I'd done wrong. No idea why it was like this now.

He cleared his throat and took a step back, too furious to even process it properly. I took a step toward him. "Why do you do that? Why do you walk away from me when I'm trying to talk to you? Why do you act like you don't want to talk to me anymore? Why do you act like I've done something wrong?"

He grabbed my shoulders, backing me up several steps until my shoulder blades were against the wall. "Don't you fucking get it? I love you, Nissa. You are my best mate. The person I worry about. The person I think about all the time. I've always got you on the brain. I'm only worried about you. That you have what you need, that you're happy, that you're safe. And then you just go out with someone like that."

"Well, maybe I was trying to get your goddamn attention. Because sometimes I feel like you don't see me."

I could feel the growl that emanated from his chest all over my skin. "I see you, Nissa. You are all I fucking see. Why don't you know that?"

"Why have you never said anything?"

His gaze was hot and fiery on mine. Anger, and frustration, and something else I didn't recognize. "Nissa, I could tell you that I want you. I could tell you that I crave you. I could tell you that I need you in my blood, and I still wouldn't be able to do a goddamn thing about it. So it is probably for the best if I just keep my goddamn mouth shut. It's better if I don't tell you those things so I don't feel like I have my heart ripped out. You are literally my best mate. But I know what Julian would do if we cross that line. You might not, but I do."

"I don't care about Julian. I just want you."

He swallowed hard even as he shook his head, but he didn't release me. "You don't know what you're saying, Nissa. You should go out with blokes like that twat tonight, but ones who are more respectful, obviously. You should go out with blokes that spoil you and know to open doors, know exactly what to say, and have been to the same schools. I'm not that bloke. I don't have any of that right now, and you deserve better."

He released me then, and I could see it in his eyes, the resignation, the way he was moving away from me. The way he backed away. I didn't even know what I wanted exactly. All I knew was I wanted him, and he was going to stop this. I didn't know what I was doing. I just reached for him with my hand on his chest, over his heart.

Westin closed his eyes, putting a hand over mine and holding me in place. "Nissa, I'm not strong enough to walk away from you. I don't want to. This is wrong. If Julian finds out, he—"

"I don't care about Julian. I care about you. I only went out with Frank because I thought maybe I could forget you. And I thought maybe I wouldn't think about you all the time. But I do, and it sucks."

He swallowed hard and took a step back. "Nissa, you deserve the best."

I took a step toward him. "I think I've already got it. I think I've had it all my life. From the moment you picked me up by the creek, I think I have had the best."

He took another step back. "Nissa, the things I have done... You don't deserve—"

"Westin?"

"Yeah?" His voice was hoarse, a scratchy whisper, so husky it was barely intelligible.

"Why don't you let me decide what I want?" He swallowed hard. This time, he was the one pressed up against the wall. "Unless you don't want me."

"I've wanted you in some capacity every single day since the moment I saw you. You have always been the first person I thought about every morning and the last every single night before I sleep. You are more than just my best mate. You are literally everything to me. I know I don't deserve you."

"Shut up. I know what I deserve. And I know what I want. Westin, it's you."

For a long moment, I thought he wouldn't kiss me. I thought that he would continue to hold back. I thought that he would push me away, again. But his tongue peeked out and moistened his bottom lip, and his hands shook as he raised them to cup my face. "Nissa, tell me if there's something you don't like, okay?"

I nodded vehemently, tilting my head up so that he would kiss me. And I expected a harsh claiming, like I'd seen in the movies. I didn't want to tell him, but Frank had been my first kiss and it was awful. Too much saliva and far too much tongue, and God, way too many hands. I didn't want him. I wanted Westin. But Westin only always looked at me like a little sister. But right now, the way he looked at me and held my face so gently, it's like he took the control away from me.

When he brushed his lips over mine, they were soft, explorative, and oh so gentle. It was like melting into a kiss. It was the perfect kind of kiss. One where a flash of heat was immediate, blazing hot, and difficult to ignore. I was too hot, but all I could do was latch onto the flame. The kind of kiss where my insides were turned into molten lava with a simple flick of his tongue. When he pulled back, I whimpered, trying to pull him closer to me. He groaned low, dropping his forehead to mine. "I am going to be so addicted to this."

I knew exactly what he meant because at that moment, Westin St. James was ruining kissing with anyone else ever again. When he laced his fingertips in mine, letting our breaths co-mingle, I came down to earth ever so slightly, lifting my gaze to his. "I really, really like your kisses."

"I really, really like yours too, Nissa."

"Are you going to kiss me again?"

He nodded again. "Yeah, I am. Except, I'm going to give you the chance to say no, a chance to walk away. You have already given me more than I could ever hope to have."

I shook my head. "Westin, I want *everything* with you."

His teeth scraped over his bottom lip and his bright blue eyes scanned mine, assessing, gauging me. He kept my hand in his and pulled me down the hall to his room. I thought there would be this flurried motion of arms and legs and lips and teeth. Every brush of his lips on mine was like kissing live wire. It was coursing through my skin, and Westin took his time. Whether it was a soft kiss to my cheek or the way he gently pressed his fingers under my shirt, he was being careful.

I was more desperate. I clawed his back, his biceps, trying to get closer, desperate to have more. I knew something fantastic was waiting under the layer of cloth between us. I knew that something precious yet so tenuous was right there. I could feel it. And Westin was holding back. It wasn't until I finally reached forward and placed my hand on his face like he did with me earlier and whispered, "I love you," that he finally knew I really wanted this.

His gaze searched mine, then he started blinking rapidly as if trying to clear the tears from his eyes. When he kissed me again, there was no more hesitation.

It was still a gentle seduction, a brush of his lips, his hands skimming up on my skin, his lips kissing down my body. A gentle peeling away of my clothing, and my frantic tugging of his. And when he finally made love to me, finally made me his, all I could think was that I never, ever, ever wanted to leave his arms. His lips were tucked into the crook of my neck as he kissed me, his body molded to mine, pulsing inside me, and he whispered against my lips. "I love you too. I have always loved you."

Those little words had me breaking apart around him, holding on tight, praying to God that I would be able to hold on to him. Because without him, I might not be able to survive.

WESTIN

I woke up to the light streaming in and the scent of Nissa all around me. I waited for the remorse. I did. Just none of it came. I had loved her for so long, and she was mine, in my arms, and I wasn't ever going to let her go.

On my nightstand, my phone rang and I frowned. All I wanted was more time with her, more chance, more opportunity. Just another five minutes. But the phone incessantly rang, and I sighed. When I checked who it was, I sat up in bed, careful not to disturb her. "Yes, Julian, what do you need?"

"Come back to the house."

"Yeah, in a minute."

"Not in a minute, bloody fucking now."

My gut knotted. How the fuck did he already know?

I knew I had to keep her safe and keep her out of this. I'd just go up for now. I set the alarm for her. By the time I came back, she'd be ready to go, and I could walk her home.

If you can still walk after Julian is done with you.

He might be pissed off, but there wasn't much he could do. Nissa had made her choice.

Yes, she did, and you did, too. Now you have to pay the piper.

I took a five-minute shower and threw on the usual black cargoes. I wasn't like his other security that I had to wear suits yet. I took my bag up to the house, and true to all the rules I had learned to follow, I didn't dare go into the front, but to the servant's entrance. After all, that's where Mrs. Pembry entered, so that's where I should enter.

When I met him in his study, he sat back and said, "Westin."

"Sir."

He grinned at me. "I do like it when you call me sir."

"What do you need, Uncle Julian?"

"How was Nissa's date last night?"

My jaw clicked shut, and I had to work on soothing the muscle there. "He got a bit handsy. I dealt with him."

Julian lifted a brow. "He got handsy with my daughter?"

"Yes, but truth be told, she didn't need me to deal with it. She was handling it on her own. Still though, I made it perfectly clear he was to go nowhere near her ever again."

"I will have to make sure I make an example of him."

If I'd been a better person, I might have begged for the kid, but he was stupid and dumb, and I wasn't a better person. Whatever the fuck Julian did to him, he deserved.

"I have another matter for you."

I could tell from his demeanor, he knew something was going on. "Yes, what is it?"

"It's about Nissa."

Fuck. Last night, I'd known the risk I was taking with her, with myself. But still, her big dark eyes told me it was worth it, telling me that she loved me, and my control just fucking snapped. I shouldn't have done it, I knew that. But still, I couldn't help myself. She was mine. I'd always felt that way. And now she was *really* mine.

"What do you need me to do?"

"It's time for you to take a more active role in the business."

I blinked at him slowly. "What kind of active role? I'm already guarding Nissa."

"Yes, but I'm going to make some changes and additions to that. I need you to do a job."

A flicker of warning and awareness made the hairs on my neck stand up. "What kind of job?"

He slid a folder to me. "You're going to eliminate a target."

My mouth went dry. I knew what Julian did. I wasn't stupid. I knew the kind of people he had working for him. But he didn't really expect me to work for him doing that, did he?

"I-I never killed anyone before. This is not usually what you have me do."

"Well, look at it like a promotion. If you do well on this one, you'll get others."

"And if I don't want to do this?"

"You are part of this family. You will follow my orders, Westin St. James. This is the job. You're going to do it for me, and you're going to keep your mouth shut. The secrecy is really for your benefit, honestly, because once Nissa finds out what you've done, she'll never forgive you."

I shook my head. "What?"

"Open the folder."

My heart started to race and my hands started to shake. What the fuck was this?

I opened the folder and there was an older version of Nissa staring back at me. She looked exactly like her sister. There were some differences. There was an upturn to Nissa's lips that always made it look like she was on the verge of a smile. Hell, the woman in the photograph was missing a smile completely. But they had the same dark eyes. The same massive thick curls. "What? You want me to kill her?"

Julian nodded. "Yes. I had hoped it wouldn't come to this, but she's shockingly persistent. She wants her sister. She'd been writing to her every month for six bloody years. I've got the letters locked away in the safe, so they're secure. But it needs to stop because Nissa is starting to push back and ask questions about why we haven't found her sister yet. You're going to eliminate my little problem, because with her sister in play, Nissa will be a whole lot more difficult to control."

"Why don't you just send her away?"

"You think I haven't already thought of that? Taking care of her is a nice permanent solution. I need Nissa here. She's my family. She's my daughter."

I closed the folder and pushed it back at him. "I can't do this."

"You will do this. Mrs. Pembry has about outlived her usefulness, and I will kill her if you don't. But before I do that, I'll boot her from the only home she's known for the past twenty years. I will wait until she's destitute and desperate, and then I will have someone that you know go and kill her, in a painful, slow kind of way. So, son, you want to do this job and make this headache go away. If you think of running, don't bother. I will find you. But if you take care of Lenora and then come on back to the fold, any indiscretions you've had before now, I'll overlook. You're doing this."

I shook my head. "No, I'm not."

He shrugged. "That's fine. I can send someone else. I'll just tell Nissa that you did it anyway. And I'll make sure it's very, very public."

"I'll tell her I didn't."

"Oh, you misunderstand. If you don't do this, Mrs. Pembry dies, and you die. And you'll die with Lenora, with Nissa thinking that you killed her sister. So those are your choices. Choose wisely."

Last night had been the most important night of my life. One that would never be matched. But Julian was shattering it. No matter what I chose to do, it was going to hurt Nissa. Not just hurt her, it would break her.

I stared at the photo of the girl, knowing that Nissa had been searching for her for the past six years. Knowing that Nissa needed her sister, needed her family. And I made my decision. The problem was I had no idea how on earth I was going to pull it off.

16

WESTIN

I had been summoned...again.

Something was going on. Julian had requested that I come to the house. Not Nissa, *just* me.

Last time you did this, things went bad.

He'd assigned another two-man team to accompany her during her classes and had me come here. The good news was I was getting access to the house. The bad news was I didn't know what the fuck was going on, and I hated surprises.

"I'm here. What do you want?"

"Your attitude needs an adjustment."

"Sorry that I'm not happy to see you. You do recognize that you're forcing me to be here, right?"

He studied me for a long moment. "What's happening with Nissa?"

"Nothing, she's going to school. Zero problems."

You aren't discussing the whole Interpol trying to get close to her last night situation.

It was a calculated risk not telling him about that, but it was one I had to take. There would be too many questions about why I had that knowledge. Not to mention how much it would spook him.

"You were hired to take care of her."

"And I'm doing my job. So what's the problem?"

He scowled at me. "This. This is my bloody problem." And then he slapped down a stack of papers.

I frowned. "What is that?"

"This is my daughter who thinks she's leaving. She has been fucking going on interviews."

"Not on my watch. She goes to school, and she comes home."

"Phone interviews. You haven't been doing your fucking job."

"My job, as you defined it to me, was to make sure no one hurts her. Not to make her a prisoner. That wasn't our arrangement. If she's been interviewing, it has nothing to do with me."

"Nothing to do with you?" He stepped toward me as if he intended to put his hands on me, which would not end well for him. Good God, would I welcome it.

"What's the problem, Julian?"

"My problem is you. She watched you run and thrive, and she thinks she can do the same. She is not leaving me."

"This sounds like a conversation you need to have with Nissa."

"If I discover that you've been enabling my daughter in any way, shape, or form, I'll kill you. Actually, I'll kill Mrs. Pembry, and then I'll kill you. Do you understand?"

I sighed and then slipped my hands into my pockets. "And that's your favorite threat. Just so you're aware, it's getting old and repetitive." Not that I was going to let him anywhere near Mrs. Pembry. I already had plans for that scenario. If ever he went near her, I had a failsafe in play. I'd rather not employ it if I didn't have to, though.

"What do you want me to do about Nissa?"

"She hasn't been on any in-person interviews?"

"No. Like I said, she goes to class, then comes home. Occasionally, she sees a mate. That's it."

"Well, you make sure she doesn't. In the meantime, I will deal with my daughter."

"What are you going to do? Because you did hire me to take care of her. Even against you."

He laughed then. "I would never harm my own daughter. Besides, I very much need her alive. But she's not leaving."

My gut knotted. I knew that the one thing Nissa wanted was her freedom. Well, and her sister. And Julian had no intention of ever letting her have either one. Just what was she up to? And how much trouble was she going to get into?

The question is, do you do what Julian suggested and keep her away or do the one thing that you want to do?

It was a no-brainer. If Nissa wanted her freedom, then I was bound and determined to help her get it. The question was how we were going to get around her father.

Nissa

What had happened at the festival was my fault. There was no other way around it. I shouldn't have gone. I had known I shouldn't go, but I had been so relentless about my freedom. I should be able to do simple things like enjoying a night out.

But there had almost been a stampede at the goddamn festival. Westin had been worried. I could tell in the way his shoulders had been tense when we'd finally made it home. He'd checked the flat but hadn't even been able to look me in the face.

Just apologize and get it over with.

I knocked on his bedroom door. He dragged it open, frowning down at me. "What's up, Nissa?"

Why was it so hard? It should be easy to say, 'I'm sorry. You were right, I shouldn't have been there. Thank you for saving my arse.' Except I couldn't quite bring myself to say the words. Instead, I scowled back up at him. "You looked pissed off."

"I'm not pissed off, Nissa. What do you need? Why do you look ready to go out?"

I glanced at myself. I had put on a V-neck long-sleeved T-shirt and a hoodie with jeans, and I did have my boots on. "I was planning to go out."

He shook his head. "I swear to God, you never learn. If you want to go out, you need to let me know in advance, so I can scout and look for potential trouble spots. Instead, you just want to take risks."

"I know. I'm sorry, okay? I'm sorry about yesterday. I don't know what else to say. I shouldn't have been there. You were right. I just want to be able to live like a normal person for once in my life. I know everyone else would just be dying to be extraordinary in some way. But not me. I just want to be average. Completely, totally, average. And I just feel like that's impossible."

He sighed. "It's not impossible, Nissa. You just have to be more careful than most. I checked the news reports. There was a small explosion of one of the propane tanks by the makeshift kitchens. It should have been easy to manage, but with the crowd, they had a hard time controlling everyone, so there was a bit of a stampede. Some kids got hurt."

"I recognize that you are doing your job and I appreciate it."

He sighed and let his head hang. "Do you want to talk about the other thing?"

I frowned. "What?"

He crossed his arms and then leaned in the door jam, the motion making his biceps stand out. And I could see them under the tight black Henley he had on. Practically taunting me.

Not that it mattered, because I wasn't intimidated. "What are you asking?"

"That thing you were doing. The dance, the tease. We're not going to talk about it?"

I swallowed hard. "I have no recollection of that."

He flashed a grin then, looking every bit the Westin I once knew.

"Can we just maybe pretend that I didn't do anything?"

His gaze met mine steadily. "Absolutely not. You know exactly what you did. I just want to remind you of one thing."

"Oh yeah? What's that?"

"You and I, we have a lot of history. And while you want to pretend like it's over, I know for a fact it's not. I can feel it in your body. Last night, you were teasing me deliberately. I just want to make you very, very aware that if you keep teasing me, one of these days, you're going to get caught."

My insides turned to jelly. Why the fuck was that so hot?

"And if I don't want to get caught?"

There was that cocky grin again. The one that had my stomach in knots. "Then don't tease me. It's really that easy. We can have the kind of relationship where I'm your bodyguard, and nothing else. Maybe your mate. Or you can keep playing with fire. And if you do, you and I are going to take a little jump down memory lane. This time, I will be there when you wake up, and I will make sure every single inch of you is sore enough that you can't walk in the morning. There isn't an inch of your skin that I will not lick, and kiss, and fuck. I just wanted to be very, very clear so that you know what's going on now."

Holy. Fucking. Shit.

There was something just a little bit edgier about Westin now. A little bit tempting, a little bit dangerous. And like the girl who always loves to play with fire, I lifted my chin. "A, I'm not afraid of you. B, if I feel like teasing you, I will. C, I think you talk a big game. Now, can you get your shit so we can go? I have an appointment."

I turned on my heel then, heading for the door to grab my coat, and all I heard was the low rumble of his chuckle that made electricity dance over my skin.

Yes, I was absolutely, positively, playing with fire. Because while I might be calling his bluff, I knew that he was one hundred percent serious.

I found Kevin Smith easily enough. He was on campus. We'd had a computer class together last year, and I remembered how good he was, specifically in geo-tracking. He talked endlessly about it why it was important, what you could tell from a photo. He knew all about the use of deep fakes. He knew it all.

When I knocked, I could hear him running to the door. He tugged it open with a grin. "Nissa, hey. Glad you could come by."

I smiled up at him. "Thanks for trying to help me."

"Sure thing. I—" He frowned when he spotted Westin.

I glanced back at Westin, who looked every bit as brooding and intimidating as he was. Except, I knew the boy in that face. The one with the quick smile, the patience. I knew he was still in there. Kevin just kept frowning. Westin grinned then. "I guess Nissa didn't mention I was coming."

Kevin cleared his throat. "Sure, any mate of Nissa's is a mate of mine, I guess. I just didn't know she was coming with her boyfriend."

I quickly interjected. "Oh no, he's not my boyfriend."

The tension around Kevin's shoulders eased. "Okay."

Westin lifted a brow, and I turned away from him so that I couldn't see the sardonic smile on his face. "I'm her bodyguard."

Kevin stuttered then. "Uh, is there a reason you need a bodyguard?"

"Yes, my father is slightly overprotective. Westin is just a deterrent. Ignore him. I can't wait to see what you have to say about the pictures I sent you."

He nodded. "All right. Come on in."

Kevin's flat was what I imagined a lot of computer science students' flats were like. Lots of monitors. A couple of computers. Lots of things for what I assumed was needed for processing power.

He took me to the main computer on his desk. "I've got the file pulled up here."

When I stood next to him, he smiled down, and I noticed the quick flicker of his gaze to my cleavage and then quickly away. "Um, I should have asked, sorry. Do you want like something to drink? Wine or something?"

It was then that I noticed the chilled white wine and glasses on the counter. I smiled and ignored him. Yes, I knew Kevin had a crush on me. Was I going to exploit that crush? A hundred percent. Did I feel bad about it? Yes, I did. But I needed help.

Could I have asked Westin for help?

Absolutely not. Westin was a wild card, and I didn't know what to do with that.

"Right. Okay, I guess we just look at that account then."

"Yeah, if you don't mind. I'm trying to find someone."

His brow lifted. "What? Like an ex?"

"Well, my childhood was complicated, but I just need to know about my sister. I'm trying to find her, and I can't do it on my own, so I'm hoping you will help me locate where she is."

This was the most personal Kevin and I had ever gotten, and his brows lifted. "What happened to your sister?"

Westin interjected then. "Oi, mate, can you help the girl or not?"

"Oh yeah, yeah of course. I'm just curious."

I shot Westin a withering glare. "No, it's fine. We used to be in a care home, and we got separated. I was looking for her, but since, you know, the record's sealed and all that..."

"Oh shit, I'm sorry."

"It's fine. But I want to do this right, you know? Find her and all that. So, can you help me?"

He nodded. "Yeah, yeah, of course. I wish you'd told me. It would be nice to know something more about you than, you know, what I learned from class."

I smiled and hoped what I gave was a dazzling smile and not a grimace. There was nothing wrong with Kevin. He was sweet. Maybe not my type exactly, but he was really nice. "I don't really talk about it. You know, it makes me sad."

He was flustered then. "Oh shit, sorry. I uh, didn't mean to make you feel sad. You know, just if ever you want to talk or anything. Like, my sister is adopted."

I gave him a smile. "Oh, you must be a great brother."

"I hope so. I mean, she was adopted as a baby, and she knows both her birth parents and stuff, so it's not the same."

I placed a hand over his, squeezing gently. I could feel the heat of Westin's gaze on the back of my neck, as if he'd put a hand there, squeezing gently, telling me to stop touching this motherfucker.

Well, I needed this motherfucker to help me find Finn, so I was going to do what I needed to do.

"Um, right." He cleared his throat and made a series of taps. "Um, if you look here, there are some clues in this background, the decor. A simple Google reverse search helped with that. Then over here, the DJ. He's kind of famous. And the time stamp is a definite clue. That was New Year's Eve last year. So that told me where the party was. A lot of these parties have some kind of a guest list, especially for something like New Year's Eve, and usually, promoters want your email address so that they can find you again, you know. The name of the bloke we're looking for?"

"Finn Wesley."

Kevin nodded. Another few quick taps and... "Yup, it's right here. His email, and he put his address in too."

I blinked in shock. "That easy?"

Kevin shrugged. "Well, I mean the hacking wasn't exactly easy, and it was kind of illegal. But it's a bar, so they didn't have the strongest security."

Still, I could feel Westin's glower.

"Thank you so much, Kevin. I-I don't know how to repay you."

He smiled down nervously at me, sliding his gaze over to Westin and then back. "Actually, I was thinking that you and I could maybe—"

I reached for my wallet. "I remembered you had a fee the last time you helped Ariella in class."

His face fell. "Oh, I wasn't going to charge you."

"Oh no, I insist. You charged her a hundred, right? I pulled together a hundred and fifty if that's okay. I figured the price has gone up since last year."

His brow furrowed. "No, I'm not going to charge friends."

"Oh, come on. You're friends with Ariella too, right?"

"I—guess."

Westin was by my side then. "Time to go Nissa."

"This has been great. Thank you. I appreciate it." I took a photo of the address with my phone. "I wouldn't have been able to find him without you."

He flushed then. "Oh sure, you would have figured it out."

As we left, Westin's grip on my elbow was tight all the way down the hallway until I shook him free. "What is your problem?"

"Did you need to flirt with him?"

"I don't know what you mean."

He leaned then, crowding me. "Don't fuck with me, Nissa. The flirtation, holding his hand, giving him a nice peek of your tits, high and firm. He took several peeks, or didn't you notice?"

"You've taken more than several."

"Well, you had your arse grinding on my crotch last night, so there is that."

I swallowed hard. "I needed the help, and I knew he had a crush on me. I felt bad about it, which is why I insisted on paying him."

"Looks like he wanted more than a payment."

I lifted a brow. "What's wrong with you? Are you jealous?"

He growled at me. "*I* could have fucking helped you."

I kept my gaze level with his. "Are you sure you're willing to go against Julian? Because you turned up and every interview opportunity I have has dried up. So you can see why I wasn't exactly wanting to have you help me with anything."

"I already told you, I had nothing to do with that."

"I know. It's just I made the appointment with Kevin before I knew that, so it is what it is."

He aggressively pushed the lift button. "Next time you need fucking help with something, you come to me. Do you understand?"

His grip on my elbow was not painful, but it was firm enough to clarify his point. There was also something in his gaze that looked almost hurt.

"I'm looking for my sister. And right now, for the first time, in a long time, I have a lead, and I do need your help. But more importantly, I need you to not tell my father. Can you do that?"

Nissa

Westin was in a hell of a mood. When we stopped at the cafe near the library for a snack, he was still scowling. "Oh come on, you're not seriously mad at me, are you?"

"I would have helped you, Nissa."

"Aren't you happy I have learned to solve my own problems? You haven't always been around, Westin."

"Don't you think I fucking know that? Now that I am, it pisses me off that the one thing I could have helped you with, you didn't even come to me with. Who is this Wesley kid anyway?"

I sighed, waving at the waitress to order tea. "Just some kid who knew Lenora and me at the care home. I don't even know if he'll know where she is, but it's something to go on."

He frowned. "You never gave up, did you?"

I shook my head slowly. "No. I didn't. Nor do I ever intend to. I've run into a lot of dead ends over the years, but I know she's out there. And knowing she's out there keeps me going. Julian claims that he has tried to find her, obviously. But with all his resources, how is it that he was never able to find her? I personally don't think he's looked hard enough. And that's okay. I don't need anything from him. I can do it myself. She's out there. And that's all I need to know."

Westin's eyes were grave as he nodded slowly. "Let me help you."

I shrugged. "You are helping me, in a way. You're guarding me, and watching me, making sure no nefarious twathole tries to take me or kill me or something."

He licked his lips. "You know I won't let anyone hurt you, right?"

The way he said it, with seriousness in his voice, I believed him. "I know. I just... You probably don't understand, but she's my sister."

"I understand better than anyone. You love her. You will do anything to see her safe."

I lifted my gaze to meet his, and we held it for a long time, watching each other. Aware of each other. And then as if to cut the tension he said, "Can I trust you to stay put?"

"Yes. I'll stay put. Besides, the car and driver are right outside. I wouldn't make it far."

Westin nodded. "Yeah. You're not going to go anywhere."

I sighed. "The trust goes both ways."

"I know, which is why I'm saying it. You're not going to go anywhere, right?"

I sighed. "No, I'm not. I promise."

"Excellent." Then he stood up and proceeded to go to the loo.

The waitress brought me my tea, peppermint and chocolate. The woman on my right murmured. "Gosh, that smells divine. What is that?"

I grinned at her and I had to blink twice at her beauty. Long braids, medium brown skin. Wide dark eyes.

"Peppermint and chocolate. Though I wish it tasted more like chocolate."

I kept perusing the food menu and decided I would have some scones.

I found banana and oat scones and smiled happily. Ah, I loved those. We had those scones in St. Andrews at the little cafe that Wills and Kate met at. They were to die for. The waitress approached. "What can I get for you, love?"

I glanced up with a smile. "I'm going to have the banana and oat scones."

"Of course. And what about your mate?"

"Right. Him. I guess we'll share a scone. Scratch that, he can get his own."

She smiled. "You two close?"

I glanced toward the bathroom door. "Once. We were close once."

"Yeah, I know about that."

The woman to my right took a sip of her tea and moaned. "You were right. This is delightful, but I wish it had more chocolate."

"Right? It's a total missed opportunity."

She cocked her head and studied me. "You're Nissa Montgomery."

I blinked in surprise then narrowed my gaze as I tried to place her. "I'm sorry, have we met?"

I glanced around looking for Westin. "Relax, I'm not going to hurt you. My name is Amelia Jansen. I work for Interpol."

My stomach flipped. "What does Interpol want with me?"

"I want to cut to the chase because I don't have the luxury of time considering who your mate is."

"What do you know about Westin?"

"I know that he's a very good bodyguard. He will risk his life to protect you."

I scooted back, not trusting her at all. "What do you want?"

"It's not so much what I want. It's more about what I need. But I'm going to give you something that you need first. So, you know, you'll see that I'm helping in good faith."

"I don't know you. Why would I believe anything you tell me?"

She sighed. "You are smarter than most people give you credit for." Her smile was soft.

"What do you want?"

"You are looking for your sister, and you haven't any leads for a while now."

"What do you know about my sister?"

"Not a lot. But I have a lead for you." She slipped over a piece of paper. "You can go ahead and research that on your own."

"Why would I trust you to help me?"

Her chuckle was rich and throaty. "Because I want something from you."

"Of course."

"Everyone is looking for something."

"Well, I don't have what you need."

"Are you sure about that?"

"I don't know you. How could I possibly have anything you want?"

He was right. He'd been right all along. There were people looking for me.

"Okay, I'm going to give you something else too. Your sister used to write to you all the time. Lots of letters."

I shook my head. "She wrote three times, and then I never heard from her again. I think she was adopted and maybe couldn't write me anymore."

Amelia shook her head. "She wrote to you always. There is evidence in your house. You just have to find it."

"How do you know this?"

"We've been watching your father's correspondence for a very long time. But I'm not going to insist that you go ahead and trust me. Oh no. I'm going to let you find out for yourself. Look closely, and you'll be able to find what you're looking for. Your father's arrogance precedes him. I promise, he kept those letters."

"I don't believe you."

"Okay, that's up to you."

"I-I don't know what to tell you."

"Just have a look. If I'm telling the truth, and you find evidence that your sister wrote to you, great. You'll know your father has been lying to you this whole time. If you don't, you'll never have to hear from me again. But I know for a fact that your sister did write to you. And your father is just arrogant enough to hold on to those letters as a way to control you. You can see that, can't you?" She slipped off the stool then, flagging down our waitress.

You know it rings true. You need to look through that house.

She took a final sip of her tea. "Look, if worse comes to worst, I'm wrong. You'll never see me again. But if I'm right, maybe you'll agree to see me again. Maybe you'll want to call me. Maybe you'll want some revenge. My phone number is also on that piece of paper." And then she swiveled on her stool, put her mug down, and was gone.

I watched in confusion as she sashayed out of the café, leaving my turmoil in her wake.

I frowned. The truth wove through her words, and I just didn't know what to believe.

When Westin came back, he gave me a smile. "You all right?"

I nodded. "Yeah, I'm fine."

He frowned. "You look off. Did you order?"

I nodded. "I got you black coffee and a scone."

He nodded slowly. "Thanks. What else is going on? You don't look right."

"Oh no, I'm perfectly fine. You know me."

"That's bullshit. Something is up."

"Nope, nothing is up. Let's just enjoy our scones, yeah? Okay?"

"Are you sure you're good?

"Yeah, I'm all right." Except now, I needed to go home. I needed to see for myself.

Be careful what you wish for. You never know what you're going to find.

17

NISSA

I HADN'T BEEN able to get that woman out of my head. Amelia Jansen. She acted like she knew about my father. She had information on my sister. How did she know all that if she wasn't for real?

There's one way to find out.

Today was my scheduled torture session with my father. Dinner at the house followed by his attempts to pull me into business conversations. Which I would avoid. And then of course, there would be a fight.

Except tonight would be different. Tonight I was going to get some bloody answers. I was tired of being controlled.

On the drive to my father's, Westin kept staring at me. Or more specifically my hair. I'd worn it out and curly today.

"No, you can't touch it. Matter of fact, do you want to take a picture of it for later?"

He blinked rapidly before turning back to face out the window. "Sorry, I just haven't seen you wear it like that before."

"It's called hair."

He cleared his throat and directed his eyes back to the road as he navigated my father's Maserati Quattroporte over the slick London streets. "Yes. I'm aware. I'm just... It looks... pretty."

I had a retort cued up and ready to launch, but his murmured compliment froze me. I didn't know what to say.

I was already mugged-off about coming back to my father's house in Surrey. I hadn't planned on seeing him much after he'd refused to listen to me about the bodyguard situation.

Like usual, the drive to my father's filled me with immediate dread.

I did not want to do this.

All he would do was try and push me into a decision I didn't want. I really, really did not want to have the same conversation again.

Just keep fighting him. He can't force you.

He couldn't force me. But short of running away from home, I didn't exactly see a way out.

Well, you have a way out. It's just dangerous.

And I didn't like putting all my faith in someone. I was used to taking care of myself. Trusting that someone else had my best interest at heart was a difficult pill to swallow.

The tires crunched on the gravel as we parked, and I had to force a long, deep breath. I could do this. It wasn't the end of the world; it was just my father.

The main reason that you even need a bodyguard in the first place.

Yes, well, there was that. And I might even be able to get some damn answers.

We were met by Dennis in full livery as always.

I always wished he'd defy my father one day and run to the door in jeans. But he was always perfectly dressed.

We found Julian was in the sitting area.

"My darling daughter. How are things?"

I scowled over at my constant appendage. "They'd be greater if I didn't have leeches attached to me."

Westin smirked then. "I'm hardly a leech."

All I wanted to do was whack the smug look off his face. I could tell that playtime was over though, because my father didn't seem to appreciate our back-and-forth banter.

"So, you're well?"

I breathed a sigh. "Fine."

He rolled his eyes. "I see you're still in a snit?"

"I'm a broken record."

Westin shrugged. "I'm delighted by the assignment as always, sir."

I hated that. I hated the way he'd referred to my father in that loyal-soldier voice. I wanted to scream, 'That's not your real voice. Use the real one. The one that shows that you give two shits about something other than pleasing him.' But I knew that wasn't going to happen.

Besides, I had a job to do.

After dinner, Westin and my father headed for the library, and I knew what I needed to do.

Are you sure you can do this? What if he catches you?

If he caught me, I'd be in a world of trouble. But I didn't care. I needed answers. So, I'd do what I needed to do. It didn't matter what it would cost me.

The terrace next to the dining room was something out of a Cinderella story. Stone and ornate statues, vines cascading down the wall. I felt like I was transported to another world into a time of princes and princesses, fairy godmothers, and magic. I loved this terrace growing up. It looked straight down to the gardens where I spent a good deal of time when tutors weren't haranguing me.

As I looked out, I couldn't help but think of what a different life it would have been if Lenora had been here with me. I wouldn't have been so lonely, for starters, and I wouldn't have felt like I'd left her to the wolves. Julian Montgomery was no picnic, but I'd been well fed and taken care of. And while he was cruel and controlling, he hadn't physically harmed me. This must have been better than Lenora had it staying behind. I just hoped that someday I would find her and that she hadn't suffered too much, whatever her story was.

I made a point of walking by the library to make sure that Westin and my father were still engaged. If I wanted personal documents, I was going to have to go to the safe in my father's room.

That was the only place I could think of that he would hide something like my letters. Though why he would hide letters from my sister, I didn't know.

You know why. It's time to really face who he is and know for sure.

My father's bedroom was massive. There was a big, ornate bed, and the walls were a dark gray. I knew they were trendy, but ugh. His massive walk-in closet was like an explosion of wood and brass, very masculine. But to me, it was much too dark.

Julian's personal safe was hidden in the back of the wardrobe behind a fake Picasso. He'd shown me once when I was a teenager. He'd told me that if anything ever happened to him, I was to get my passport and instructions for the business from here.

I pressed the button behind my father's suits and the Picasso lifted up revealing the safe. It was exactly as I remembered it, but Christ, what was the combination?

He'd told me it was my birthday, but when I keyed the combination in nothing happened. I tried again, desperate for it to be right. But still, nothing. I blinked back the stinging tears. I was not going to lose it.

I didn't even know what I would find. Maybe it was better to let sleeping dogs lie. Even if I did know the combination and found something I didn't expect, then what? What was I going to do with that information?

So my father was a liar. So what? That changed nothing. I already knew that.

My nose still stinging from unshed tears, I turned to leave. I was asking for trouble and heartache. But then it occurred to me. Julian never celebrated my actual birthday. He always stubbornly ordered cake for the day I'd come to live with him.

Whirling around, I keyed in the date and I prayed harder than I'd ever prayed in my life. When the keypad flashed green and a click sounded, my heart started to race. Still unsure about what I was going to find, I reached for the lever with hope.

Inside were things I expected to find. Money, documents, passports. Why there were so many passports, I had no idea. But that wasn't why I was there. There was a box at the back of the safe that I had to reach for. When I pulled it forward, my mouth went dry. Oh God could I do this? Was this an answer I wanted to have?

Move your arse. Now is not the time to dawdle.

My hands shook as I lifted the lid. My mind ready to turn away from whatever I found. With the lid off, I swallowed hard.

Letters.

So. Many. Letters.

All addressed to me. From Lenora.

Bile started to rise in my throat. It was true. Amelia was right. My father had kept my sister from me. And lied to me all along.

I grabbed a few letters from the top then shoved the box back into the safe. I was easing back into the main room, when I heard footsteps.

Fuck me.

I couldn't hide in the wardrobe. There was nowhere to go. The bathroom? Under the bed? Oh, bloody hell, that would just be disturbing and awful.

I dove for the door to the right. His shoe wardrobe was my only option. I just prayed to God he didn't need anything in there. With a twist of the doorknob, I secreted myself away, and the only thing left to do was pray.

WESTIN

Nissa was up to something.

The entire drive over she'd been pensive, focused. I didn't know on what, but I'd seen it through dinner too. She'd been far too eager for her father to head for his study.

So were you.

Yes, but I had bugs to plant. What was her game? I'd been dragged into the library to talk to him. He wanted to discuss more men for Nissa. It seemed like overkill. Which was what I told him.

Montgomery had gotten the full debrief of Nissa's movements. He seemed satisfied and then excused himself to take a call, which left me free to do my real job. I'd already placed a bug in his office and one in the sunroom where I knew he liked to take coffee and calls in the morning. Just a few more to go and my team would have a live feed into the house.

I checked the security feed on my phone to make sure Montgomery wasn't coming back toward me in the living room, and I caught movement in the upstairs hallway. Nissa.

Bloody hell, what now?

She'd always had a knack for getting into trouble. How the hell was I supposed to keep her safe if at every turn there she was, doing something that was going to get her hurt... or worse?

You're too emotionally tied to her.

I swallowed hard, watching as she explored the house. Ultimately, no room was off-limits to her. After all, it was her house.

When I was a kid, the manor seemed like a castle. At the time, I'd been bitter that I couldn't live with my godfather. After all, my parents had just died. I needed him.

He told me, though, that he didn't have the time to spend with someone like me, but Mrs. Pembry would. And I couldn't deny it; she had.

Nissa had a different upbringing. She'd lived in this house, technically with access to my godfather, but ultimately, she was completely alone. She didn't have the kind of family that I had with the Pembrys. At least not until we'd become mates. But that was all so long ago.

I watched her make her way up the back stairs and toward Montgomery's room, and I frowned.

Nissa was going to get herself into trouble. What the fuck was she doing in his room?

My heart started to gallop when I watched Montgomery, still on the phone, heading for the front stairs. He had a second study upstairs, so maybe there was no problem. But when he didn't turn right toward the upstairs study or terrace, my heart attempted to leap out of my chest.

With a muttered curse, I slapped my laptop closed, ran into the kitchen, and yanked open the door for the butler's pantry. Once inside, I depressed the panel and the tunnel access door swung open.

Luckily, I knew exactly where I was going. Using my phone to light my way, I booked it upstairs along a narrow stairwell, hoping I wasn't too late.

Fucking hell, if he was going to his bedroom, she was going to be in trouble.

My brain tried to force my lungs to be calm, my heart to relax. At the top of the stairs, I popped out in the opposite hallway, dashing toward the master bedroom.

I made noise too. A lot of it. If she didn't find a hiding spot right now, fuck it, she could be caught in the act.

I could hear Montgomery's whistle coming down the corridor. As I let myself into his room, I glanced around for her. Where the fuck had she gone? She'd just been here a second ago.

I checked my phone and quickly rewound the scenes from the surveillance footage. Ah, the shoe cupboard. I could hear the jingle of keys coming my way. Fuck. Now *I* needed a fucking place to hide.

I didn't have any other choice, so I opened the shoe cupboard and stepped into the darkness.

There was a sharp intake of breath as she gasped. I could feel her heat in there. "Be quiet," I said, keeping my voice low.

Immediately I was surrounded by her scent. Vanilla and brown sugar. Not too sweet and overwhelming, but light and enticing, and I had to fight the urge to lean in and inhale.

Focus you twat. Julian finds you in here, and this ends badly.

The door to the main room opened, and she gasped again. But this time, I clamped a hand over her mouth. She struggled in my hold, and I growled in her ear. "If you don't shut the fuck up, you will be found out."

I could feel her pulse jumping in her slender throat. She still struggled, and I clamped my hand tighter. "I'm trying to bloody help you, so shut the fuck up and come along."

I eased back, giving her some room, and she whispered, "How do I know you're not here to kill me."

"Really? If I'm some kind of killer, you don't think I'd be more efficient?"

She stopped talking then, but mumbled something unintelligible, shifting her weight a little. The soft press of her body against mine sent blood rushing to my cock.

I forced myself to take long breaths. Distraction was going to get us both killed.

There were rows and rows of shoes in the cupboard, and at the very back of it, there was tunnel access on the wall that shared the side with the bathroom. I just had to find the latch. "Come on."

I kept my hand over her mouth but loosened my hold around her neck and gently pushed when she tried to fight me.

I finally had to rearrange her so that she stood in front of me with her back to my chest, and my arm around her waist. She tried to wiggle, but when I moved her forward, she walked obediently. "Be quiet."

At the panel, I leaned in closer. "I'm going to let go of you. You cannot scream. Do not make a sound."

This time she nodded vehemently against my hand, and I eased my hold. When I did, she dragged in a sharp breath, but she didn't say anything.

I groped around the wall and finally found what I was looking for. The panel gave way, and the secret passage was revealed.

When I was little and Julian had traveled, I would sometimes come to work with Mrs. Pembry. The old butler, Henry, had shown the secret passages to me, hoping to keep me out of trouble. I was only a boy back then, one who needed distractions and adventure and had no one to play with. So the staff had taken mercy on me. I didn't think Montgomery used them himself, but I'd always felt like I was in a castle, discovering all the ways to move in and out of the house.

As Nissa moved in front of me, she stumbled, and I paused. I didn't say anything, but I had to rotate our position, and in the tight passage, it forced her body to plaster against mine as we adjusted.

Her soft intake of breath as she no doubt felt my thickening erection sent a wave of lava through my veins.

I halted her movement and then rotated her body, and she whispered. "Shit."

Automatically my hands tightened on her hips and under oath I would have sworn that I heard her moan. In my front pocket, the light from my phone illuminated her face. Her eyes had gone wide and her lips were parted just so, and when her tongue slipped out to moisten her bottom lip, I bit back a groan of my own.

I was strong enough to resist the temptation. I had to be.

Are you sure about that?

Our bodies had to press up against each other, and I was more than well aware of her tits pushing against my chest. In the darkness, she sucked in a sharp breath, and her scent wrapped around me, assaulting me, infiltrating my senses, making sure she was all I was aware of. And all the work I'd done over the last two weeks to put her out of my head, to keep her at arm's length, nearly shattered at that moment.

When I shifted in front of her and then reached for her hand in the dark, she tugged it back, forcing me to grab her wrist. "Fucking come on, already."

I dragged her through, trying to visualize the map in my head. When we finally reached the outlet behind the stairwell, I took a sharp breath. I used the light on my phone to find the panel.

When I tugged her forward, she halted. "What are you doing?"

"Saving your arse." And then I released the panel, opened it, and shoved her out, depositing her at the very top of the stairs leading down to the servants' quarters. No one would ask her why she was there, and she would be safe.

I heard her mutter, "Who the hell have you become?"

18

NISSA

WESTIN'S GRIP on my elbow was sharp and tight as we left my father's house later that night. My heart was beating a rapid tattoo against my chest. He hadn't told my father, and how the hell had he known where I was going to be?

All I knew was he'd saved my arse. And I had no idea why.

"Could you let go, please?"

He gripped tighter and leaned over me. "No, I cannot fucking let go. You and I are going to talk."

The car was brought around, and the keys were tossed at Westin. He snatched them up and then opened the door for me to slide in. But before I could climb in, he leaned close, muttering, "Not until we get home. I haven't been in charge of the car, and it could be bugged."

Bugged? What the hell? It had never occurred to me all the different ways in which my father could surveil me. It never occurred to me all the different ways that I would need to pay attention and watch my behavior.

I was in a prison. For so long I thought that, but with where I was now, I could see the bars. They'd been invisible all this time. And now, they were crystal clear.

The drive home was terse. Westin checked the flat and then checked his phone before nodding. He waited until my coat was off, my shoes as well, before he turned to me. "Fucking explain."

"I don't know what you're talking about."

Isn't that a lie? I knew it was a bad lie. And I knew *he* knew it was a bad lie. But I still tried it.

"Bullshit."

He leaned in close to me then, and I swallowed hard as his scent wrapped around me. "I'm not scared of you."

"I don't want you to be scared of me, Nissa. I want you to fucking trust me and tell me what the hell is going on with you."

I lifted my gaze to meet his. "You want me to trust you? What the hell were you doing in my father's closet?"

"What was I doing? What were *you* doing?"

"For the record, I was getting my passport. As you know, I'm trying to interview."

He narrowed his gaze. "That's not it. I really wish you wouldn't fucking lie. You're making this difficult."

"I'm not lying."

"Yes, you are. I can see it right there. Did you forget, I know you inside and out? I know everything about you. So tell me the truth, and for fuck's sake, let me help you."

"I don't need your help." He had already saved me once today. If he was going to rat me out to my father, he would have done it by now.

From my back pocket, I pulled out a stack of letters. I was going to tell him the truth, but I was going to leave out the part about Interpol. At least until I knew what Interpol wanted from me. "I found these in my father's safe."

He frowned. "What are these?"

"Letters. From my sister. Julian had said that she stopped writing, that he didn't know what had happened to her, and that there wasn't much he could find out."

Westin's brow furrowed. "But all this time, she was writing to you?"

I nodded. The tears that I had previously kept at bay, were freely flowing now. "I-I found them in a box in the safe, and I took a few. I didn't think I'd get the rest. I didn't have time, and I couldn't hide the box and sneak out of the house."

"Fucking hell, Beauty." He reached for me, his thumbs gently swiping away the tears that were freely falling now. "That was dangerous. You shouldn't have done it."

"I heard the footsteps and then I panicked, and you were there, and I just... Why is he like this?"

His brow furrowed. "Sweetheart, I don't know."

"Why can't I have a father who actually cares about me?"

"I wish I had answers for you. I really don't, and I'm sorry. You don't deserve this."

I nodded, swiping away the tears on my face. He pulled me in close and inhaled me. "You have to be careful with your sister, Nissa. If Julian finds out that you're looking for her, there will be hell to pay. And she could be in danger. If he has done this, what else has he done?"

I pulled back. "You don't think he'd hurt her, do you?"

He swallowed hard. "I think your father is capable of anything. And anything that threatens him in any way is in danger. I don't want that to be you. Like I said, I will defend you with my life, but I need you to be careful with him, okay?"

I nodded. "So, are you going to tell me what the hell you were doing in the closet?"

He held up his phone then. "I saw you on the surveillance feed, going upstairs. When I didn't find you, I took a guess. I didn't expect to actually find you in there."

I cursed. "Fuck. There's a surveillance feed for the whole house?"

He nodded. "Everyone in security has access to it."

I ran my hands through my hair. "Oh my God, he's going to see. He's going to see. Oh my God."

The bile started to rise again, and this time it was from sheer fear of what my father was going to do to me.

Westin said, "Don't worry. I already wiped it. He won't know you were in there today. Unless he goes looking at that safe and notices the box. Did you put it back exactly where you found it?"

I nodded. "Yeah. I hope so."

"Yeah? Or do you hope so?"

"I don't know. I think so."

He nodded. "We're not going back in there to check. So right now, let's just hope that you did. Can I ask a question?"

"What?"

"Now that you have this information, what are you going to do with it?"

I lifted my chin. "I'm going to find my sister."

"Anything else you plan to do?"

I knew he wanted to help. I knew he wanted to keep me safe. But I couldn't tell him. All I managed was, "I'm going to make him pay for every single day he kept me away from her. I'm going to make him pay."

"I'm almost afraid to ask what you're planning."

"I haven't solidified it yet. The moment I do, you'll be the first to know."

He released me then, and I missed the warmth of his grasp.

"Westin?"

His voice was husky. "Yeah, Nissa?"

"Thank you for saving me."

"I keep telling you, Nissa. I'm here for you. It doesn't matter who's employing me. You are entirely my main focus."

My stomach flip-flopped, and I knew I couldn't trust those feelings. As beautiful as he was, that seemed like a recipe for disaster. I said good night and headed back to my bedroom. I could feel his gaze on me. Almost like he knew I was holding something back.

When I reached my room, I pulled my phone out of my pocket along with the letters. The letters I placed on the night-stand, then I pulled up the number I'd put in the other day on my phone and texted it.

We need to meet. You were right about my father. What do you want from me?

I may have told Westin I wasn't exactly sure of what I wanted to do, and I wasn't, really. I didn't have a definite plan yet. All I knew was that I wanted my father to pay.

19

NISSA

In the morning, my hands were still shaking. I'd slept like shit, imagining all the ways that last night could have gone wrong.

And all the ways that Westin could have had you.

Every time I'd closed my eyes last night, there he'd been. His hand over my mouth, telling me to be quiet. And then things had gotten significantly more R-rated from there.

In some dreams, he ripped my clothes off in the tunnel. Others, the car. Oddly the dirtiest ones were always after he'd admonished me in the flat.

You have got to get a grip love.

I truly did need to get a grip. At least I'd have a reprieve today as Westin was off. So my meeting with Interpol would be under the radar.

My new human tank wasn't familiar. This one didn't say much and stayed at the entrance of the Law Section of the library. Better he didn't see where I was headed and get too curious and ask questions.

Oh, I was nervous, but I was one hundred percent convinced he had lied to me for years. He'd kept her from me and then lied to my face about not being able to find her. All to control me and my movements, to keep me docile. Well, I was done being docile. I was done with him.

Maybe I would regret this. Maybe I would want to think twice about doing this, but right now, this was the right decision.

If you're so sure of that, why didn't you tell Westin about it last night?

I licked my lips as I sat at the corner table in the stacks, waiting for the text that let me know Amelia was nearby.

If you trust him then why not tell him?

It boiled down simply to the fact that I thought he would stop me. And I was done being patient. I was done waiting. I was done letting someone else control my movements, actions, my life.

But also, I didn't want blowback on him. If he didn't know, he couldn't be forced to tell anyone.

As I waited for Amelia in the library, I was still shaking. The nerves from last night hadn't dissipated yet. I'd taken one too many risks, and I'd almost been burned.

But it was worth it.

My phone chimed, and I breathed a sigh of relief.

Amelia: *Come to Listening room A.*

I gathered my things and headed back to the listening rooms.

Amelia was pacing the room when I entered. "Hello. Why are you pacing?"

"I'm glad you decided to come and talk to me."

"You knew what I would find."

Amelia's eyes went soft and sympathetic. "I had a feeling what you would find, yes."

"How did you know?"

"Your father has been a person of interest for a long time. We've been looking for a way into his organization. We've been unsuccessful thus far. Currently, you have been making moves to separate and distance yourself from him. Which makes you a good potential asset."

"So you want to use me."

"I want us to use each other." Her shrug was slight. "I won't pretend like I'm helping you to be altruistic. I want your assistance. I want your cooperation. Will I hurt you to get it? No. But I'm not above giving you what you've wanted in exchange to get what I want."

"What is it you want?"

"Your father's head on a pike. He's been doing business with some very nasty men. One in particular. His name is Antonio Igno. Your father took something from him. Or maybe it was an exchange, we don't know. All we know is he has something on Antonio Igno. Or has something that belongs to Igno. We don't know the whys or the hows, but we know it's the reason for the increased security on you. We need to listen in. And if possible, we need to catch your father and Igno in the same room. We don't need you to do anything dangerous, just plant a couple of bugs so we can listen in. That's all."

"Oh, that's all, is it? Do you understand that this man has been controlling every facet of my life since I was ten years old? I don't have any proof, but I think he sabotaged my interviews recently. You want me to help you spy on that kind of a person?"

"Yes. We know it's a great risk to you. But you're the only way in. Igno is the literal boogeyman. He's evil personified, and we need to catch him. But we recognize this is a great risk to you, so in return we want to help you find your sister. I have some leads in that respect. Not to mention we'd like to help you get your freedom. I understand you have great translation skills. If a job is what you want, we can make some calls, advance your resume in places that it couldn't be seen before."

I smoothed down the edges of my hair before crossing my arms. "Why should I trust you?"

"I'm with Interpol. We're the good guys. All I'm asking you to do is go home and plant some bugs. That's it. Nothing more. I don't want you getting fancy. I don't want you putting yourself in the line of danger. And I don't want you telling anyone. No friends, no one. This is delicate and extremely dangerous. If anyone finds out, he could harm them. Do you want that?"

And just like that, all ideas of telling Westin evaporated. If I agreed to do this, to go against my father like this, he would hurt him. After all, wasn't that why I hadn't told him last night where I was going today, what I was doing? "And if I help you, you'll put him in jail?"

"That's the plan. We want to take not just Igno off the board, but men like your father as well. Can you help us do that?"

It wasn't even a question. I knew what my father was like. As we sat across the small study table from each other, I nodded and whispered, "Yes, I can do that."

She pushed to her feet. "I have something for you." She slid a piece of paper over to me. "This is a lead on where your sister was sent after she left the group home you were in together. I know you've been trying to trace her without much luck."

I glanced at the sheet of paper. "Are you serious?"

"Yeah. I'm sorry it's not more, but at least it's a start. I can't guarantee you anything, but we'll keep on looking too."

Amelia didn't seem like a hugger, but that still didn't stop me from dropping my bag and wrapping my arms around her lean frame. "Thank you. Thank you. Thank you. Thank you so much."

She gave me a light squeeze back. "You're welcome. Hopefully, we'll be able to find her. I have to say, she's hard to track down. It's making me think maybe she doesn't want to be found."

I shook my head. "I don't believe that, and I know she'll be looking for me. Julian must have done something to scare her off."

"Well, hopefully, I've been able to help a little."

"This is perfect. Thank you."

"Be careful. You don't know what disturbed stones will unearth."

WESTIN

Nissa was hiding something. Of that, I was sure. She told me what she was doing last night, but she was holding something back. Like for example where she'd gotten the idea that Julian was hiding letters.

There was no way that information could have just fallen in her lap.

What had made her go looking? Had Julian said something? Slipped up somehow? I hated that she needed help and she wasn't coming to me.

I'd rotated off shift with one of Montgomery's guards. I was supposed to head back to Rogues, but something told me I should stay on Nissa. It was like a shadow snaking down my spine, and I couldn't shake the feeling.

But now I wasn't even following orders. Instead, I was following her.

She had been hiding something, and I most certainly didn't believe she wanted to go to the library at all. Was she meeting someone?

I could leave her be and pretend I hadn't seen anything. I could let her live her life.

But that's not the kind of person you are.

It didn't matter what sins I'd committed. It didn't matter what my mission was. I couldn't let it go, so I followed her.

I made all of the excuses. I wasn't being a creepy stalker. I wasn't doing the exact same thing that Julian did. I wasn't deliberately making her life difficult. No. I was *helping* her. I was keeping her safe.

She was wearing black leggings that hugged her arse. She had no business having curves like that. Curves meant to tempt me and make me forget the promises I'd made, the vows that couldn't be broken. Nissa Montgomery was off-limits. Not because of her father or what he'd said to me, but because of what I had done. So it was better if I didn't pay so much attention to her arse.

I kept to the shadows. Thanks to the backpack she carried, I at least knew her general vicinity and interactions from a distance, so I could stay in the dark and not have to follow her too closely.

But Nissa was good. I knew she could feel that something wasn't quite right because she paused right at the stairs of the library and turned, searching the darkness.

The library was open twenty-four hours, so students were allowed to burn the midnight oil. That was what happened when you went to a prestigious university. You had to be able to learn and study and grow. Sometimes I wondered what it would have been like to have this as my real life and not pretend. What if I'd gotten into one of these schools on my own?

You did get in.

Yes, I had gotten into Oxford as Westin St. James, but I hadn't been allowed to go, obviously. And when I created my new persona, a new version of me, it wouldn't have been smart to go to Oxford, so I sent myself to Cambridge instead.

That was a long time ago. Now focus.

When Nissa entered the library, I followed behind, keeping my distance but making sure that I had an eye on her. But the moment I checked my phone to ascertain her location, her phone vanished off my map.

Bollocks.

I quickly spun around, wondering if I was just in a Wi-Fi blind spot or something. No. I had full bars, just no tracking capabilities.

Fuck. Had she turned off her phone?

She was wearing her black leather jacket, and I'd slipped a tracking device under the collar, but I couldn't find it either.

I was going to have to do this the old-fashioned way.

Stack after stack I scanned, trying to look like a student who belonged there. And I *was* a student; I just wasn't there to study anything but Nissa.

I grabbed a book off one of the stacks to at least look like I had a plan going, and then I headed to the International Law section because I knew that was one of her classes. I couldn't find her, but there were a lot of places to hide. After searching for twenty minutes, there was still no sign of her. She wasn't fucking there. So where had she gone?

I'd just come back downstairs and deposited my cover book on one of the shelves when I saw her coming out of International Law.

Then suddenly my phone beeped. I had her jacket and her phone back online.

She stopped short when she saw me. "Jesus Christ, were you following me? You're not even on duty now."

"Yes. Frederick there called it in and said he couldn't find you." A lie, but Frederick didn't talk much. And truth be told, he hadn't noticed I'd come into the section as I'd snuck in with several blustery corporate law students. "What's your excuse?"

"Homework."

I could tell she was lying. "Where were you? I've been all over these stacks, and I haven't seen you."

"You know, I have my own little secret spots in the library."

I wondered why was she lying. "You can tell me. What are you working on?"

"A translation project for a consulting gig. You know since Julian killed my interview opportunities, I need to line up what I can." Again, there was a kernel of truth in what she was saying, but she was being deliberately evasive. "I'm going home."

"I'm walking you back." It was better if I personally kept an eye on her. Not that I had any other options.

She scoffed and tried to shove past me. "Wow, you're pretending chivalry now?"

"It's dangerous to walk the streets of London by yourself at night."

"I'm on campus! And Frederick is a human tank."

"LSE is in the middle of London. It might be campus, but it's still not safe."

"I promise you, I can take care of myself."

"You can pretend you don't know me if you want, but I'm walking with you."

She walked past me, and I took her elbow. When she shook me off, I let her. "Easy does it, Beauty. I'm trying to help you."

"Why don't you get that I don't need your help, or you interfering with my life, or your constant presence in it?"

Her scent wrapped around me just like it had earlier, drawing me in, threatening to fry every last brain cell I had, tempting me to just give in and taste her for once.

Maybe if you taste her just the one time, this will stop. The constant burning need will end.

That was a lie. That was the devil on my shoulder trying to get me to give in. And I was not going to do that.

She whirled on me and jabbed me on the shoulder. "What is your problem? Damn it Westin, you're driving me mad."

"Have you ever stopped to consider that maybe I bother you so much because you like me?"

"Leave it to a man to assume that when a woman is legitimately asking him to go away it's because she's overcome with feelings for him." Her voice dripped with sarcasm.

"So you're telling me you're not overcome with feelings for me?"

"Oh my God, I swear, I may be stuck with you as my bodyguard, but we're *not* mates."

"I'm hard to get rid of. I already told you that." I knew I shouldn't push her. This was a delicate situation, and Rogues needed her. But still, I took her elbow again and pulled her close to me. "I don't need us to be mates. I just need you to do what I tell you."

"Oh my God. You arrogant, mule-headed, persistent, jackass."

I was watching her lips as she spoke, the tip of her tongue peeking out as she insulted me. I leaned in, inhaling her scent, begging it to drive me mad slowly. "In your whole tirade just now, not once did you say I wasn't right." Then I released her. "Start walking. Otherwise, I'm going to find all kinds of ways to ask you exactly where you were hiding in the library and who you were hiding with."

20

NISSA

THE CONTACT NAME Amelia had given me had been burning a hole in my pocket all week, so there was no avoiding that. I needed to go and see if there were any leads on my sister. And in all honesty, it was nice not to have to do a task like that without someone there. But goddamn if I was going to tell him what I was doing.

After classes, he started to turn toward the library on the main street, but I shook my head and angled it toward the Tube. "I have an errand to run."

His brows dropped down. "I don't have an itinerary for this."

"It's just a quick errand. It won't take long."

"On the Tube?"

"On the Tube."

"We should drive instead."

I sighed in frustration. "Where we're going, we'll just be advertising that the car is great for parts. Before you even park it, it'll be stripped."

"That doesn't fill me with confidence about where the hell you're going."

"It'll be fast. Besides, aren't you my human shield?"

His aquamarine eyes narrowed on me, and I could feel the piercing heat of them straight through to my core, making me pulse all over. But like hell I was going to tell him that. I just cleared my throat and started walking. He didn't have much choice but to follow me.

"What's the problem? Where I go is where you go, right?"

"I like having advance notice. That way I can get a secondary guard if we need to."

"This isn't some dangerous place. I'm not walking into a brawl or anything."

"Right."

What I had miscalculated was just how close Westin would stay to me. Too close. Like, boyfriend close. He didn't touch me, but he was close enough that I could feel the heat of his body and his breath along my ear on occasion. And each time it sent a shiver through me.

When we switched trains, the crowd was packed and thick, and for a moment I thought I'd lost him. And that immediate loss of his heat sent a wave of panic over me. Shit. Where was he?

Shouldn't you be grateful that he's not plastered against you?

Fuck. Somewhere along the line, I'd gotten used to him being there. His ubiquitous presence was like a safety blanket I didn't know I wanted or needed.

You're starting to remember him the way it used to be.

No, I was not. He was just a constant now, so I was used to him being there.

The lies I told myself, really. Along with the immediate relief I felt when he took my elbow and didn't let go until we were on our next train. I told myself that relief was just in not being alone in a strange part of the city, but in reality, I knew it was about feeling his solid presence. I did feel safe when he was near. I also felt like throwing things, but that was neither here nor there.

When we arrived at the station for Angel, I pulled out the address from my pocket, and he glanced at it over my shoulder. "What's that?"

"It's where we're going."

"I don't like this. I should call it in."

"And say what? That I dared to go off script? That I went someplace other than campus, the library, the shops, Jamila's, and home?"

He pressed his lips together. The bottom one was fuller than the top, and I had the irrational urge to reach up and nip it with my teeth.

"Taxis are over there," I said. "I'm going to grab one."

He hesitated for a moment but then followed closely behind. "You won't tell me where we're going?"

"We're going to visit a social worker. She works at Bristles Home for Girls. It might be where my sister was sent after she aged out of the children's home."

His brow furrowed. "What?"

"My sister. This was a home she might have been in for a while."

The cab I'd hailed was a Prius, and Westin looked squished in the back seat. His legs were too long, knees were almost to his chest. His gaze flickered to the driver, who was clearly listening intently. "I wish you'd told me. We could have done some more research before we headed out."

"Yeah, but we haven't exactly been talking since... Well, you know."

His lips were still pressed firmly together, but his gaze flickered to me and held a light of mischief. "Oh, by all means, if you want to talk, let's talk."

I then looked at the driver, whose gaze stayed astutely on the road. "Nope, I don't feel like talking about anything."

"Excellent. Neither do I."

When the cabbie dropped us off at Bristles home, the outside of the building made my heart sink. While it looked decently maintained, it was a rough gray stone building. It looked dreary.

The neighborhood wasn't terrific. Across the street was an off-license, and there were some shops along the way. Up ahead were a block of flats that looked like they belonged to the Council. Instead of the usual buzz and energy of a high street, it had more of a dreary, downtrodden vibe. The whole place felt like where hope went to die.

I pressed the bell of Bristles Home for Girls, and we were led into the front vestibule and directed to wait by an elderly Black lady who wore her hair in a short afro peppered with gray. Within minutes, I was seated in front of the director, Christine Jones. Westin opted to stand by the door.

Christine lifted a brow at him and turned her attention to me. "Would your mate like a seat?"

I glowered at him. "I'm so sorry, my mate has no manners. He'll continue to stand. He's ornery like that."

She nodded slowly, and I could tell she was trying to ascertain if I was in any kind of danger.

"I assure you, we're not a thing. You don't have to worry about me."

She blinked rapidly and then set her gaze back to Westin, who just gave her a nod. His gaze was impassive. I couldn't read him, couldn't figure out what was in his head. But she didn't look like she liked it.

"So, Miss Jones, I appreciate you talking to me. I've been looking for my sister, Lenora Crane. She might have been sent here when she aged out of the younger girls' home."

"Yes, Lenora. Ah, poor lost soul."

"What do you mean by that?"

"Well, she left the children's home shortly after she turned thirteen. Bristles is a home for teenagers. We usually get them for about three years until they turn sixteen, and then we get them into a Council flat. Your sister seemed to do okay here. She wasn't exactly happy, but she always wanted to talk to you. I remember she used to write you letters."

I frowned. "I never received any letters from her after she left the children's home."

She frowned then. "No, she wrote religiously. All the time. She had a little notebook. I mailed her letters to you, myself."

I cleared my throat, emotion threatening to wash over me like a wave, taking me with it back into the sea. "I-I didn't know that until recently."

This all matched what Amelia had said. What I had found.

"Maybe your parents thought it best to sever contact, but I never thought it was a good idea to separate siblings. She had a difficult time. The longer you didn't write back, the more difficult she found it to cope. All we could do was forward on the mail. She grew quite despondent. When she turned sixteen, she tried hiring an advocate to help get in touch with you through proper channels. But still, nothing. And then she just became lost. Problems at school, drugs, the whole thing. And finally, she just wanted to be on her own. So, we arranged for her to have Council accommodations."

I swore under my breath. "Where?"

"Tower Hamlets had a place open, but she didn't want to live there."

"My parents left us money. She could have accessed her trust fund."

"No. Not by law at that age. And the trustees... Well, the

lawyers of the trust can determine if the heirs are competent to receive funds, and they can hold onto it longer if they aren't."

"But that's not fair."

"I didn't make the rules. And with all the trouble she was getting into, she didn't exactly show competency. But we did finally manage to find her a placement."

"Oh, okay. Do you have someone I can talk to there?"

Christine furrowed her brow. "It's been years. I'm not sure if she's still—"

I shook my head. "I'll take that name. I'm looking for my sister, and these are the only leads I have. So anything you can tell me would be great."

She sighed. "Right. I've got it somewhere." She tapped furiously on her laptop. "This is the name of the Council office and my contact there. If anyone knows where she is, it will be her. Hopefully, she stayed in the flat they got for her and was able to clean up."

The whole time she spoke, I just bit my bottom lip and blinked my eyes rapidly, trying to keep the tears at bay. And all the while I could feel the fluttering of my heart, the panic starting to take over.

When we left Bristles Home for Girls, I stood outside, dragging in deep breaths. I could feel the warm pressure of Westin's hand on my back, making circles, soothing me, calming me. He'd heard everything. I could take all these questions to my father, but I knew he wouldn't help me.

I *needed* to find her. And the only person right now who seemed to give a shit about how I was feeling about it was the man I'd vowed to hate.

It doesn't feel like he hates you.

He might not, but this wasn't what I wanted. All I wanted was my sister.

But everyone needs help. And right now, Westin St. James is offering his, so what are you going to do with it?

WESTIN

It was a mistake to touch her. I knew that, but she looked so shattered. Broken. In pain. And I wanted to make it easier. But once I touched her, all that emotion that I'd managed to keep bottled up for the last two weeks bubbled to the surface. I wanted to fix this. I wanted to make it better. I wanted to make her life easier.

That's not the job.

"Are you ready to go home," I asked?

Outside of Bristles Home for Girls, she finally wiped away her tears and nodded. "Yeah. I think there's a mini-cab place down the street. Actually, I'm tired. I'm just calling an Uber."

I glanced around. We had nowhere proper for the Uber to stop as there was a red line at the curb. "Do you want to walk down a little further?"

"Yeah, let's do it."

As we walked silently, I eyed the chip shop on the corner. "Are you hungry?"

Her nose wrinkled. "Yeah, I could do with some chips."

"Okay. Come on."

She slid me a glance. "You're being nice. Why are you being *nice*?"

"Contrary to what you think, I am a nice bloke."

"Yeah, sure you are. A nice bloke who doused me with water balloons."

"Yeah, that was me. I also remember keeping your secrets."

She ducked her head, her curls cascading over her cheeks to

mask any flush that would appear on them. Even with her brown skin, I could always tell when she was embarrassed.

"Do we have to talk about that? I feel like if we're going to talk about it, we might as well have drinks."

I chuckled. "Fair. How about you tell me over a pint what the hell you were doing?"

"And maybe you will tell me what the hell you were doing?"

With her face upturned, I could see mischief and a direct challenge in her eyes, and I couldn't help but smile at her. Really smile. She blinked at me rapidly and then shook her head as if trying to stop herself from saying something. "You know what, actually, I really want a meat pie."

I grinned at her. "All right, there's a kebab shop there. We'll see if they have some."

When I bought her a meat pie and a drink, I grabbed one myself. And it was delicious, the spicy, meaty goodness exploding on my tongue around the flaky pastry. But the look on her face, eyes rolled back as if she was having a mind-blowing orgasm right on the street, that was fucking picture perfect. Her lips were parted, the oil from the crust making them look moist. Supple. Lickable. *Fuck me.*

I didn't realize I'd said it out loud until she blinked at me, hazel eyes focused on mine. "What?"

I cleared my throat. "Nothing. You just looked like you're really happy with that fucking meat pie."

She nodded and took another bite, mumbling something about it being fucking heaven, and then she took a drink. As we waited on the corner for our car, I made the error of looking away just fucking once.

For a moment.

For a breath.

Just long enough that when I turned back, some geezer was dragging her back into the alley by her elbow.

Nissa's heeled boots made her tumble back and fall on her arse.

Three strides. Two and a half, maybe, and surprisingly, Nissa helped. With her free arm, she happily dropped her drink and used her elbows as she went down, not into the bloke's gut, but into his balls.

He cursed, losing his grip, and she continued to fall backward. I should have broken her fall, but I was more concerned if he had a gun. And I was right to be worried because he was already reaching inside his bloody coat.

I reached for his gun arm, and as he pulled it out, I grabbed it with both hands, did a quick twist and flick, sliding the gun off his hand and thrusting it to the side. As he howled, I gave him several jabs to the face with my free hand. And as his head snapped back, I adjusted my grip so that with my left hand, I held his right one far out to the side, gripping his shoulder hard enough that my fingers were pressing through the layers of his clothes to skin, and I dragged him forward, delivering several knees.

When he went down, I grabbed him from behind, wrapped an arm around him, and put him in a sleeper hold. As he passed out, Nissa was registering what the hell was happening. "Westin, you're going to kill him."

I lifted a brow as I gazed up at her, not sure of the monster she saw in front of her. "He was going to do far worse to you."

He still struggled in my arms, and he was reaching for something. Before I knew it, Nissa ran forward, coming within kicking distance. "Nissa, no."

But she didn't listen as she raised a booted foot, and then brought it down straight down on his balls. He howled. He dropped whatever was in his hand and cupped his balls. With the choke hold I had on him, he couldn't go forward, so instead, all he did was press his trachea harder against my arm. And three, two, one... He passed out.

I frowned up at her. "I told you not to come close. Why did you do that?"

"H-he—" Her hands were shaking, and she was staring at something on the ground. A goddamn syringe.

I kept hold of him and did the one thing that I knew I couldn't hide, knew I wouldn't be able to mask from her. I had to call it in. I needed a bloody clean-up crew.

I tapped in the code for clean-up and left his body there. I eyed the car at the other end of the alley and told Nissa to stay fucking put. Of course, she didn't listen, and I could hear the clomp of her heels right behind me as she followed me down the alley. At the car, I could see the keys were still inside, so I liberated them and then slashed his tires just to make sure no one could remove the vehicle for him. At least not quickly.

I also ran around and opened the bonnet. Lucky for me, it wasn't an electric car. Not that Igno or whoever else could be after her would exactly be environmentally conscious. I took the spark plugs easily enough and then grabbed her. "Nissa, listen to me. We have to go."

She kept staring back at the bloke on the ground about halfway down the alley. "He's not dead, is he?"

I shook my head. "No. There are more efficient ways to kill people. I don't want him dead; I want him incapacitated."

"Who was he?"

I shook my head. "I don't know. We have to go. Right now."

"I don't..."

She was shaking and going into shock. I needed to get her off the street in case there was another attacker close by. Fuck. I had the syringe in my pocket. Whatever they'd been about to inject her with, I needed it analyzed. I deliberately dropped it by one of the tires. Lock and the team would find it.

I wrapped her in my arms. "Hey, you're okay. I have you. I did my job today, okay? This is exactly what I'm supposed to do. Protect you. I don't know who he is, what he wants, or why he was after you, but we'll ask those questions later when you're safe. Do you understand me?"

She nodded against my shoulder. "I think so."

"Good. Now, come on, let's get you home."

We were all the way in fucking North London. We should have driven. I should have insisted.

Except you didn't know where she was going.

"We're going to take a taxi all the way home, okay?

For a moment, I thought she might argue with me, but she didn't. She nodded instead, so I hailed the first taxi I could find and shoved her inside. "I have you."

Once we were in the car and safely moving, I tucked her into me. She was still shaking. It was only then that I realized my heart had been hammering inside my chest. I hadn't been that worried about anyone in a long time. And just as I was about to remind her why the fuck she needed to trust me, my bloody phone rang.

21

WESTIN

"Wʜᴀᴛ ᴘᴀʀᴛ of *low profile* did you not get?" That was the first thing Gabe said when I picked up the line.

"Mate, I'll call you back," I mumbled.

"You left a mess, mate. I don't like cleaning up messes."

I hung up on him. I hadn't left a mess. The guy was knocked out. They should be able to handle that. Why the fuck was he calling me?

It took us nearly an hour to get back to Nissa's flat. And when we did, she was knackered. She headed straight for her room. But before she closed herself in, she turned and gave me a smile and a nod. "Thanks. I don't know what would have happened if you hadn't been there today."

I shrugged. "Just doing my job."

"Yeah, I know. But I'm still grateful. Even if I didn't particularly want you here."

I grinned. "Well, I have been kind of a twat."

She grinned at me. "So, you admit it."

"Only because you were being a brat."

She shrugged. "I may or may not resemble that remark, but still, thank you."

The smile she gave me was so vulnerable. All I wanted to do was protect her. What the hell was in that goddamn syringe? Was Igno after her?

It was only when I was sure she was in her room and locked in that I went to mine and used my code to call in. Lock answered immediately.

"Seriously, mate. Low profile. What the fuck, Westin?"

I blinked rapidly. He never used my name. He either called me kid or Rook, my call sign. "What are you talking about? I just knocked him out, that's it."

He was silent for a moment. "You knocked him out?"

"Yeah, with a choke hold. Standard protocol."

"Mate, he's got a bullet hole in his head."

I sat still for a long moment. "What the fuck?"

"Clean shot. Like a professional. I assumed you did it. You're the crack shot when it comes to these things."

I frowned. "I didn't shoot him, mate. I don't even have a gun on me. Montgomery wanted me to carry a gun, but I refused."

"Fucking hell."

"It wasn't me. But that means..." I let my voice trail.

Unfortunately, Lachlan finished my thoughts for me. "There was a redundancy. You got out of there just in time."

What the hell was going on here? And how much was Montgomery hiding? "Christ. Did you find the bloody syringe?"

"Yeah, by the tire? Nice drop. We got it. Saff's got the lab boys on it now, evaluating what it is."

"What the fuck have we walked into here, mate?"

"If Igno's involved, it's something bloody nasty. I guarantee that. Nissa Montgomery is lucky to be alive."

"Fucking hell."

"I do need to give you some shit about leaving the body in plain sight though."

"Hey, technically, it's not my body."

Somewhere in the distance, I could hear Saint chuckling. I knew it was Saint by the deep rumble of his laugh. Wanker.

Lock laughed too. "Yeah. Did you get anything off the body?"

"No." I paced as I answered because I was concerned that we had a real fucking problem. "There was nothing on him. He was clean. But as soon as you find out what was in that syringe, fucking tell me, because he nearly got me with it."

"Fucking hell."

"Yeah, exactly. Surprisingly, it was Nissa who saved me. She stomped on his balls."

Lock coughed at the words and then it sounded like he was full on choking. "Mate, are you serious?"

"Unfortunately, yes. Honestly, she saved my arse."

"Well, I guess she's not so innocent, after all."

"What do I say to Montgomery? I need to tell him something."

"Call it in. We didn't leave the body, so he can make his own determinations on that. We left the car though."

"In that neighborhood? It will be stripped for parts in no time."

"Exactly."

"All right, fair enough. I'll call it in."

Lock was silent for a moment. "Are you okay, though?"

"Yeah, I'm fine. I just want Igno's head on a pike."

"Join the fucking queue. I'm not sure if it's better or worse that Saff is the one at the head of the queue. She might not leave you anything to kill."

"You know what, if it's Saff who kills him, I could be happy about that. She'll at least make it hurt."

"Yeah, right on."

Saff was a force of nature. Hands down the best hand-to-hand specialist we had. Granted there was a reason she was called the Heir. Rogues Division would one day be hers. And she'd been training her whole damn life for it.

When she fought, she was deadly. I wasn't bad in hand-to-hand, but my specialty was tech, and I was a fair shot.

I hoped to God they figured out what the hell was in that syringe and what the hell we were dealing with.

I hung up with Lock and then made the call I was dreading.

When Montgomery answered, his voice was full of ice. "What?"

"Someone made an attempt on Nissa up at Angel."

"What the fuck was she doing in Angel?"

I should have been surprised that he was more concerned about *why* Nissa was in Angel than the fact that someone had been trying to take her out, but I knew better. This was Julian Montgomery after all.

"Research for a school project. I was with her the whole time. She didn't want the car. It was either let her take public transport or be messy, and you told me to be discreet as possible. I'm worried she might be tagged though. They definitely knew exactly where we would be, but I took care of it."

"Body?"

I cleared my throat. "No. I cleaned it up."

"Well done."

"In case you're wondering, she's okay."

Montgomery laughed low. "I have no concerns. The reason I picked you for this gig is that I know you have a soft spot for her. You always have. You always put her best interest above all. Which makes you the perfect one to protect her. Just as long as you know to keep your hands off."

With that, he hung up the phone. He was a fucking twat. But like him, and like Nissa today, I was glad I was the one who was here. I wasn't letting Igno's men anywhere near her again.

My phone vibrated and I glanced down at it. The name on the text message had my heart falling into my stomach.

Nissa

Fear. Worry. Disappointment. My emotions were chaotic.

The knock on my door startled me. When I peeled my eyes open, I snatched the duvet from over my head. I glanced up to find light streaming in from the hallway, and Westin was holding a tray.

"How long have I been asleep?" I asked.

"A couple of hours. I figured you could use some food. I would have pushed this on you sooner, but I thought maybe the rest was more important."

He'd brought me food. The sheer act made my heart squeeze. Not only was he terrifyingly dangerous, good-looking enough to make you lose your knickers, and knowing enough to make you want to shoot something; he was also genuinely kind.

"You don't have to do this. I'm sure it's not in your job description."

"It's not about the job description. I actually care. So come on, up you get. Let's get some food in you."

I was about to decline and lie that I didn't want any food, but my stomach grumbled. "Okay."

When I turned on the light, my gaze drank him in. It was as if I was even more aware of exactly how he moved his body. He was long and lean, and I could see those insane forearms and biceps. He had a tattoo winding around his right forearm, disappearing under his sleeve. I knew he had another one on his left pec, and no others as far as I had seen before. But who knew where else he was hiding ink?

He marched into the room, and I drank in the rest. His T-shirt pulled tight on his shoulders, and his jeans hung low on his hips. His feet were bare and enormous. The light dusting of blond hair on his toes made me smile.

"What are you smiling at?" he asked.

"Nothing. What do we have here?"

"Well, I called in an order from that pastry shop on the corner. They had some scones, and I made you an omelet and some tea. I figured you needed some protein. And there's juice there too, in case you need a fast sugar hit."

"You didn't have to—"

I closed my mouth when he pressed his lips into a firm line, scowling at me. I rolled my eyes. "You know, I don't trust your scowl anymore. I have seen your sensitive side. I know it's a front."

Except, maybe it wasn't. He did look downright dangerous. Annoyed, even. But there was a lilt in his eyes, like I could almost see the mischief dancing there. "Be quiet now and eat something."

He sat on the end of my bed and watched me as I picked up the fork. "Are you going to watch me eat?"

"I need to make sure you have some extra calories in you to counteract the shock. You'll feel worse in the morning if you don't eat and drink something."

"So now you're a doctor?"

He laughed. "Maybe in another life. I'm better with the computer though."

"Did you ever want to become a doctor?"

He shrugged. "If my life had been different, I would have had a lot more options, I suppose. But it wasn't different, so it is what it is."

I frowned at that. "How did you end up working for Julian?"

He shook his head. "That's not important."

"I'd love to know if you're willing to tell me. I kind of figured it's not the job you'd take if you had lots of options."

He licked his bottom lip as he casually rubbed along his jaw as if trying to decide what he could share with me.

"Please, I'd like to know. I don't know anything about you anymore. I have a lot of things maybe I *assumed* about you, but I'd like to know the facts. After all, you saved my life today. I should probably know something about you besides just your name."

"You want to know how I ended up here?"

"Well, for starters."

"Julian found me. Gave me a chance to come home and look out for you."

There was something he couldn't say. I could tell. "Okay. So you felt like you owed him?"

"Well, it's more like he called in a marker. Besides, I owed *you* for the way I left."

My heart squeezed as I considered. "I don't want an apology. It's been too long."

"But I owe you—"

I shook my head. "We can't go back."

"No I suppose we can't."

He pushed to his feet, shoving his hands in his pockets and pacing across my floor, stopping at one of the snow globes on top of the bookshelf in my room. "I see you still have the snow globes."

I shrugged. "Yeah." When we were younger, I'd told him that my parents and my sister and I used to travel a lot. And wherever we went, they'd get us these mini snow globes of the city. They were my memories of Lenora.

My nose started to sting, and I rapidly blinked my eyes as I spoke. "Sometimes I'll find something that I know that she would really, really love and I'll just buy it, you know? And save it for when I see her again one day."

His gaze met mine. "I'm sorry you still haven't found her. But if she hasn't been able to get in touch with you, I know it must be for a good reason."

"I refuse to give up though. I will find her."

"I believe you." He indicated the plate again. "Eat."

"I'm doing my best. Can we... Can we get out of here? I sort of don't want to be at home right now."

He frowned. "I don't think it's the best idea to go out."

"Oh, I'm not talking *out*, out. Just the campus pub. It's down the street. It's local and full of students. I just think it'll help stop me from feeling shaky, and I just don't want to be here right now."

He nodded slowly. "All right. Only for a little bit though. And we probably shouldn't drink."

"Okay, *Julian*."

He wrinkled his nose. "Please, are you one of those girls with a daddy fetish? I mean, you can call me daddy if you like, but I find it odd."

I started choking on the piece of egg that was in my mouth. "No. I'm not calling you daddy."

"You don't have a daddy thing?"

"I think it's clear I have daddy issues, but not in that way. And you are no one's daddy."

"No, clearly, I'm not. I'll give you a sec to freshen up and what not. Be ready in five, then we'll go."

When he reached the door, I stopped him. "Hey, Westin?"

"Yeah, what is it?"

"Thanks again."

He shrugged. "Sure thing. Mostly, I'm trying to butter you up so that you're ready to talk to me about that whole thing in the closet where you were giving me soft doe eyes and practically begging me to kiss you."

22

WESTIN

I was officially out of time. I needed Nissa to trust me, stat. If she was planning a stance against Julian, then I needed to know so I could give her better coverage.

And read her in on what you're doing.

As much as I could anyway.

She didn't trust me. If she didn't trust me, she wouldn't talk. And the longer she didn't talk, the longer she'd stay in the cross hairs.

You're going soft.

Maybe I was. It didn't change the fact that I knew what I was doing. I knew the position I was putting her in. And while there was a part of me that was helpless to stop it, I was still doing it, still deliberately hurting her.

Technically I had been off the clock since we got home from the pub last night. So this morning I went out early and picked up something special for her. I told myself it was merely a peace offering. That I wasn't giving into the churning feelings I had.

My pulse started to beat frantically when I heard the front door to the flat open. My stomach started to twist. I knew this all meant something more, and I didn't know if I was ready to walk off that precipice again.

It's a nice gesture, but are you doing this for the right reasons?

Who the hell knew. All I knew was that I'd heard her crying last night, and I'd felt like shit. I hadn't meant to be a complete arsehole. I had been furious with the whole situation we found ourselves stuck in again because of Julian's manipulation.

The constant need for her ate at my soul. Like an ache that begged to be relieved. It didn't matter how I tried to dance around it, how I tried to adjust it, how I tried to move away from it. The point was, it was there, and I was going to have to live with it.

Pushing her away was just making it more painful for both of us.

I tucked the little globe inside the gift bag and headed out into the living room. She was putting her groceries in the fridge when she looked up. "You're back on duty then?" I could tell from the expression on her face that she'd been stewing about something all day, even though we'd had a lovely evening together the night before.

I nodded and held up the bag before gently placing it on the counter. "I come in peace."

"Peace. Sure."

I narrowed my gaze. "I'm trying here."

She sighed. "Why didn't you tell him about me snooping in his room? Why are you really here?"

At least that part I could be truthful about. "He brought me back to look out for you. I'm meant to protect you. Sometimes that will mean *from* him. If he'd found you in there, I'm certain you wouldn't have liked the outcome."

"What aren't you telling me?"

I licked my lips. "Too much. Just know that I'm back for you. I want you to know I'm on your side."

Like it or not, Rogues needed her, and my mission was to make sure she stayed put. Didn't matter if it was Julian's directive or one from Rogues, my mission was to keep her safe. I wasn't lying about that. If either of them got an inkling of how I felt about her, who would protect her then?

I held up the bag. "I have something for you."

She frowned at the silver gift bag sitting on top of her marble countertop. "What is it?"

"Why don't you open it and find out."

Her hazel eyes narrowed at me. Her lush, thick lashes framed them like her eyes themselves were a present. I knew for a fact they weren't false. I'd seen her rubbing her eyes when she was tired. Anyone who had paid several hundred pounds to have their lashes done would not do that. No, those were natural. Besides, Nissa Montgomery had the same eyes the very first time I'd seen her by the brook.

Her teeth grazed her bottom lip. "I don't know what to say."

"I understand what you're going through. It's a blow when you realize the people who are supposed to love you are utter twats. I promise I'll ease up."

As I walked toward her, she squared her shoulders and tilted her chin up, but she didn't budge. And if that didn't make her something I coveted even more, I didn't know what would. I watched her swallow hard. I was unnerving her. Well, good. At least I was under her skin too.

You still can't have her.

I knew that, but it was nice to know I wasn't the only one who was hot and bothered.

She placed her tangerine juice on the counter and eased the gift bag closer, moving the tissue paper around to tentatively look inside. When she pulled out the small snow globe of the city of Cape Town, she gasped. "How did you—"

I smirked. "I remembered that one from when we were kids,

the one that broke. I saw this in a shop and couldn't help myself."

She nodded slowly. "Oh my God," she whispered breathlessly.

"I'm sorry I couldn't find the exact one, but this one has the city and a map as some background there."

She inhaled deeply. "Thank you." Her lip quivered and she bit at it. "It's perfect."

"I hope it's okay."

She nodded. "Cape Town was the last place my sister and I went with our parents before they died. You know, my memory of them is... fading a little. But I remember that day like it was yesterday. My sister was ten. I was eight. We had the time of our lives. My father was working, and Mum took us sightseeing. But then he joined us and that was the perfect vacation."

"That sounds nice." I nodded along because I'd had some memories like that too before my parents were gone too soon.

"That snow globe was my souvenir from that trip. Lenora picked out a pair of earrings."

The tears brimming in her eyes made me want to say something to soothe them away, to make it better.

Careful there. Do not touch her again.

"I'm sure she misses you every day."

She nodded, and the emotion in her gaze was too much for me, but I didn't want to run away from it back into my room. "Um, do you want to get out of here? Maybe grab a pint? You've had a long couple of days."

"Careful now, Westin St. James. Are you trying to be my mate now?"

I shrugged. "It's better than being enemies, yeah?"

She glanced down at the globe and then flickered her gaze back to meet mine. "Yeah, a drink actually sounds nice. But you're buying."

She set the globe on her bookshelf, and then we both grabbed jumpers to head out for a pint. That voice at the back of my head tried to warn me.

This is dangerous. You know better. This is not a road you can travel down. If you do, it's all going to blow up in your face.

I should have listened. But that voice was the harbinger of doom, and for a couple of hours tonight, I wanted to pretend doom was not impending.

23

NISSA

UP until this point I'd been able to convince myself that Westin was a stranger, that there hadn't been a point in my life where I had known him inside and out. That once, long ago, he hadn't been my everything.

But now, sitting across from him, looking him in the eyes, it was impossible to ignore. This was him. The man who had walked away from me four years ago. And the air was permeated with the things that we didn't say to each other then and the things that we *couldn't* say to each other now.

"It seems that neither of us knows what to say," he murmured quietly.

"That's the understatement of the century." But I couldn't resist. "Where did you go after you left four years ago?"

He shook his head. "I—" He sighed, his eyes grave, and his handsome face now a mask. "I wish I could tell you, but I can't."

The bite of disappointment stung. "Of course you can't."

He sat forward on his stool with a look of grim determination. "Just know that I thought about you all the time. And I wished I could come back, but I knew Julian would make it impossible. So I stayed away."

"You ended up right back here in the end though, didn't you?"

His gaze was hot on mine. As if trying to communicate something to me with just the gravity of his expression.

"No one's ever left and come back." It was true. I never saw anyone return to my father's employ. There were some old guys who had been with him since I was a girl, but I'd never seen anyone leave and come back.

Westin continued. "It wasn't planned. The mere fact that he found me and hasn't killed me yet tells me he needs me for something. Or maybe he knows I'm the only one he can trust when it comes to you. I will always do what's best for you."

"You can see how that's hard for me to believe, right?"

"Nissa, I—" He ran his hand through his hair. "I have no right to ask for your forgiveness. But please, know that if I could have, I would have come back for you."

The worst part about all of this was I *wanted* to believe him. Everything about him said I could trust him. That I *should* trust him.

But he abandoned you.

"I know we can't go back. But can we start over," he said hopefully. "Maybe I don't deserve that. And maybe until I can explain more, I have no right to ask. But right now, we both have to be here and I'd like to call a truce."

I could keep fighting him. I had a lot of pent-up anger, but I was tired. I'd already fought so hard, and I didn't want to keep fighting. And maybe, just maybe, he wasn't the enemy after all.

"Westin, I don't think we can pretend we don't have history. But maybe we can start fresh."

He nodded slowly. "Okay, in the interest of starting fresh, tell me, what have you been up to this last four years?"

"Oh you know, school, mates, being prepped to take over an international criminal organization." He winced and I had to laugh. "But I have no intention of going into the family business. What about you?"

He licked his lips as if trying to determine what he could tell me. "Julian made it clear that I was ruining your life. If I went near you again, he was going to put you somewhere very unpleasant to keep us apart. When I left, I had to hide. For your safety and my own. I needed to make sure your father never found me. But eventually, I made a mistake, and Julian found me and made me an offer I couldn't refuse. Come back and protect you."

"Is it that simple? Even after he threatened to kill you?"

He nodded. "Whatever he's gotten himself involved in has him worried enough to get me back. I would have come back sooner if I'd thought it wouldn't endanger you."

"I'm different person now, Westin."

"I look forward to figuring out who you are. Starting with the PlayStation. Don't think I didn't see it in the closet." He grinned. "I challenge you to a game when we get home."

And for the first time since he'd come back into my life, I felt a little bit more like my old self. "You're on. Just so we're clear, I'm not going to take it easy on you. I will make you cry like a teenage girl who just discovered Tom Hiddleston will never be her man."

He clutched a hand to his heart. "Still as ruthless as ever, I see. Good thing I can stop letting you win now."

I stared at him, agog. "*Letting* me win? What a pile of horse-shit. I always beat you fair and square."

"If that's what you need to tell yourself."

"You're on! To be fair, I always took it easy on you. I know how fragile the male ego is."

"Moi?" He mockingly placed a hand on his chest. His eyes danced and the mischief in them made my belly flip.

He's not dating material. He's here to protect you.

My libido didn't feel like listening though.

I chuckled. "Well, aren't we a pair?"

He raised his glass then. "Hopefully we can start fresh now."

I nodded, lifting my glass off the dark wood table. "To starting fresh."

When we left the Slug and Crow, I noticed just how careful he was with me. As we walked, he made me walk on the inside, and he was vigilant about walking me around anyone that looked even vaguely dodgy.

"So, what's your story anyway?" I asked. "Do you have a partner? In four years, you must have found a supermodel or two along the way."

He gave me a sly smirk "So, you're curious about who I'm dating?"

Yes, I was curious. No, it wasn't any of my business, and I absolutely understood I couldn't have him. Not after everything that happened between us.

Mates we could try for, but anything above and beyond that would be bad. It had taken me a year to even start to heal after he left. I wasn't going through that again.

He leaned forward met my gaze levelly. "Not dating right now. It's hard to date on assignment anyway. The nature of the job is already so intimate. It's hard to maintain another relationship when your focus is completely captured by what's right in front of you."

The current between us crackled, and I could almost feel it cocooning me into place. It was almost a touch as it hummed over my skin. But then he leaned back and the moment disappeared with his movement. "So, no. I'm not dating. What about you? Obviously, you're gorgeous. I've been here for a few weeks, but I haven't seen you with anyone. As part of the gig, I assumed I'd be beating down some jealous boyfriend."

I scrunched up my face. "Nope. No jealous boyfriend, or girlfriend, for that matter. I'm focused on school right now. Besides, with my father being who he is, I'm not exactly dying to drag someone else into his sphere. I can focus on all that stuff when I'm done with school."

"You don't date at all?"

I laughed then. "You know Julian. Can't you see why? The fact that I have made it out of the house and was allowed to stay in my own flat is shocking."

"Must be tough."

"Yeah. He really gets off on the control, you know. Every time he says jump, everyone around him stops, asks how high, and falls at his feet. I don't. I've never been like that, and it bothers him. You can tell he really hates the idea that I won't bend to his will."

"I think that's what makes you so fascinating."

"Careful now, I might almost think you like me."

He chuckled low, and my gaze fell on his lips. "Don't you worry, no danger of that happening here."

We walked and talked for another hour, meandering slowly through the campus before heading toward my flat, and I finally got comfortable enough to tell him a version of the truth. "You wanted to know why I was hiding in the shoe cupboard. I wasn't supposed to be there, but I was looking for information on my sister. I hoped I might be able to find something in his room, but I almost got caught for my efforts."

"Maybe I can help you."

"How?"

"I'm not just a bodyguard. I'm pretty handy with a computer. I can poke around."

That little flutter in heart was back again at his words. "You would do that?"

He narrowed his gaze at me as if I had asked something

stupid. "Of course. After all, we're mates now, and you're not going to kill me in my sleep."

I chuckled under my breath. "The jury is still out."

When we reached the flat, he took the keys from me to open the door. "You don't have to do that," I said.

"Part of the gig. But also, let me be a gentleman, would you? After the last few weeks being a complete twat, a part of me wants to show you that I'm not and make up for it."

He turned the lock and then stepped forward, hitting the light switch. I was right behind him, but as I attempted to step inside, I bumped into a brick wall of muscle. He immediately backed me up. "No, get out."

I frowned and shoved against his solid muscle. "What the hell are you doing? I'm exhausted, Westin. Come on, let me in."

I tried to move around him, but he stopped me, trying to shove me out of the flat. I ducked under his arm. "I don't know what the hell you're—"

I stopped short.

Someone had tossed my flat. Completely ransacked it. Several of my snow globes were broken.

"F-fuck me."

He tugged me back. "Let's go. We need to call the police. We can't stay here."

A few weeks ago, my life was neat and orderly. It made sense. But now, fucking hell, now my life was a wreck. In pieces. I had been cascading downward ever since he'd walked through my door.

Turning with tears of anger pouring down my face, I swung hard against Westin's chest and shouted, "This is all my father's fault. He did this."

"Nissa, stop. Listen to me. I'm here to protect you. We are leaving right now, and you can comply or I can toss you over my shoulder. Your choice sweetheart, but either way, we're leaving. So what will it be?"

24

WESTIN

"I'm in no mood for another one of your *I fucked up* phone calls Westin, especially at this hour." Gabe growled through the phone at me. For someone who was in charge of a whole division of spies, he could be a downright son of a bitch when woken up.

"That was damn out of order, especially when your guys made a mess of my knicker drawer. I thought you trusted me to get you information, not come in on the backside and try to find it yourself."

I could hear the fatigue in Gabe's voice and could almost picture him pinching the bridge of his nose. "Just what the fuck are you talking about?"

"Your team. I told you I would get you what you needed. There's no reason to take that route. I have to tell you, you're losing your touch, mate. The fuckers left a mess."

The phone went silent.

"Gabe, are you going to fucking pretend you don't know what the team did?"

Suddenly, Gabe's voice was more alert. "It wasn't Rouges, Rook. Intel report, now. How compromised are you?"

"Fuck. As far as I can tell, nothing was tripped in my room. I played it straight, and we went directly to a station to make a police report. Sorry Gabe, I really thought this was coming from you, so I punted back to the normal mission plan. Currently we are at the Mayfair safe house."

MY GAZE FLICKERED to the closed door of the loft bedroom where I'd put Nissa. When Lachlan and Saffron had gotten engaged, he'd bought her a house in Notting Hill, which made his loft in Mayfair empty and available. Rogues repurposed it for a safe house, and it was the first place I thought to bring Nissa.

All the progress we had made was shot to hell when Nissa hadn't said much on the drive over here. She just stared out the window. I'd put her straight to bed before coming down to raise hell in quiet whispers on the phone. Regardless of the secrets I was keeping, I needed this to at least appear on the up-and-up, so when we closed the door on the flat, we went right to the police to report the break-in. I had thought it was Gabe and a report was the best way to cover my arse to both Nissa and Julian.

I watched as Nissa spoke to the officers, giving them a basic inventory of anything valuable that was in her place and what we quickly had seen was broken. She hadn't been thrilled about me hauling her out so quickly, but the police had insisted that we did the right thing by leaving. Not that it cleared any of my guilt by having a break-in happen at all on my watch.

"Gabe, I need someone to collect my gear. I had a couple of sensors rigged, but nothing tripped. They were looking for something of hers and were really careful entering the flat. They tossed my room, but not in any real kind of way. It was the girl they were after." Even as I relayed the information, my brain tried to sift through Nissa's explanation for why she'd been in her father's room the other night. There had been truth in it, but there had been something else she was leaving out. Was that why she'd been targeted?

"Could it have been her father?"

"He's my next call. I assumed it was us because you couldn't be patient."

"You said you would get what we needed."

"But I hadn't yet. That's why I thought you did this."

"No, it's not us. I'll assign you an extra man. Saint just came off mission."

"No, I don't think that's necessary, and Nissa is being really cagey. It's almost like she's aware she's being watched. That will just make it worse."

"Do you think it's her father? Or worse, Igno?"

"I don't know what to think right now. I need to figure out who broke in and what they wanted, or if it was random, which is very unlikely."

"What about your security tapes?"

"They upload to my cloud, accessible only through my laptop, which I cannot access right now, thanks to the police."

He cursed low under his breath. "If anyone finds out who you really are..."

"I know, Gabe, I know. They won't be able to. Even if they take the laptop to their tech team, they'll have a difficult time getting through my firewalls. Rogues are protected."

"They better be. Maybe you might get your wish after all and you'll have to come in."

"If I came in, that would leave her in the wind on her own. Or worse, she'd be brought in and would hate me when she knew everything."

"That might not be necessary yet."

"I'm just trying to keep the girl safe."

"And I told you, sometimes we have split objectives, and

when that happens, what comes first?"

"Yeah, I hear you. Rogues. Rogues always comes first."

"Good. Then don't make it seem like you need a refresher."

"I don't. I just wanted to ask if you were the fucker who did this."

"I'm a twat and an arsehole. Occasionally, I've been called a dick. But I trust my agents. Despite what you think, I'm not actually the villain."

"Maybe, but you are controlling, and you do have a tendency to play both sides against the middle."

"I have one side. Rogues. It's all I ever care about. That is my sole focus. Besides, if I had sent a team there, you would never have known."

Deep down, I knew he was right. He would have found a different way to get what he wanted. And I never would have known.

"Where are we with the girl?" Gabe asked.

"She doesn't seem to know much. It's going to take more time to work her."

For the last year or so, I'd heard Saff call her brother an arse. Lock had called him a dick on several occasions. I'd heard Saint threaten to kill him once. But while Gabe was tough, I'd never experienced any of his finer points for myself until he said, "Maybe you don't get it, Rook. Your job is to get information. You know you're not actually her bodyguard, right?"

I frowned at that. "She still needs protection, though. Isn't that right?"

"Yes, but you do that as a means to get some fucking answers as to what Montgomery is doing with Igno. Did you get anything at the house?"

I knew I should tell him about Nissa's little adventure, but I held back. After all, who knew what the hell she was really looking for?

You know he's right. You do need to question her more.

She'd only just begun to trust me. There was no way I was pushing that hard.

"I didn't have much opportunity to dig around much more. Have we picked up anything from the bugs?"

"A little, but we need more."

"Yes, I know what my job is. I can do it."

"Let me be clear, Rook, you're not to get too close to her. That's not the gig. If you can't do the job, I'll have to bring her in forcibly."

My blood quickened at that. I was not having him bring her in. She'd had enough of being dragged around and controlled, given who her father was. Knowing now who he was in bed with, and his penchant for exposing her to the bastards, she would be terrified if she was dragged into Rogues. She already felt alone all the time as if she had no one in her corner. That would devastate her.

"Not bloody necessary. Give it a few more days. She'll talk to me."

"And if she doesn't, we'll need to accelerate. Don't make me take this over from you."

"I'll get the information you need. Just leave Nissa out of it."

Gabe chuckled low. "Already getting too close, I see. Maybe this was a mistake." He took a deep breath. "Rook, it seems I'm the one who has to tell you the truth of the way things are. We're not playing games here. You might look at Lock and Saff and Saint and Kaya and think we're running some sort of Tinder setup on these grounds. We're not. This mission is fucking life and death. You are a Rogues Agent. Do your job."

I bit my tongue. He had a point. Nissa was part of the job, and I was getting distracted.

You are beyond distracted. You want her just like you've always wanted her. And now that's getting in the way of you doing what you're supposed to do.

"I know, Gabe. I've got this."

"See that you do, or you'll be unhappy."

"There's no fucking need for all the bullshit threats. I told you. I fucking know what to do."

"All right. In that case, do it. And Rook?"

"Yeah?"

"Bring me the fucking ledger."

"I'll do my best."

I hung up with him then scrubbed a hand down my face. Fucking hell. I always knew that what we did at Rogues was important. The whys might not always be clear to me, and I might not agree with all the missions. But this shit with Nissa in the crosshairs made me start to wonder if I'd just jumped out of the frying pan into the fucking fire.

Then I took a deep breath and called Montgomery.

He answered on the second ring. "Why are you calling me?"

"You tell me. Someone tossed Nissa's place."

He was silent for a beat. "What the fuck are you on about?"

"Somebody tossed her flat."

"Where the fuck were you?"

"Doing my job. I was with Nissa. And that was a good thing because who knows what would have happened if she had been there."

He cursed under his breath. "You see, this is why you're needed. Where are you now? Bring her home right this minute."

Like hell I was doing that. "I have her somewhere safe. Bringing her home is only going to put more of a target on her. If she's in the crosshairs because of you, the last place she needs to be is standing right next to you."

He was silent for a breath and then asked, "Did they take anything?"

"Not to my knowledge. Is there something specific you need to know about?"

"Never mind, you just keep doing your job. I want you on her like glue. She never leaves your sight. I don't care what you have to do."

"What's going on, Montgomery?"

"What's going on is that I made a deal with the devil, and he's looking to collect. I thought you'd make a decent deterrent. But right now, it seems that Antonio Igno doesn't follow the rules of engagement. He wants something he thinks I have, or Nissa has, and if I don't hand it over, he's going to scare Nissa until I get it for him."

"What have you done, Julian?"

"You don't worry about what I've done. You worry about the job I hired you for, protecting my daughter."

After hanging up with him, I lightly knocked on the bedroom door, and Nissa answered with a soft, "Yeah." I poked my head in the doorway and saw her sitting up against the pillows at the headboard. She just seemed broken. So frail and fragile, but I knew she wasn't. Her brown skin looked sallow, her curls less shiny, like all the exuberance that normally glowed around her had dimmed to a dull hue. "Nissa, why don't we get you in the bath."

She shook her head. "I don't know what to do. All my stuff. They just destroyed everything."

I licked my bottom lip, hoping I didn't have to make her leave. "Just get in the bath. I'll take care of cleaning up when we go back in the morning to pack up a few things."

Shoulders slumped in defeat, she walked toward the ensuite bathroom. I watched her close the door and my heart just shattered, even though I knew it wasn't supposed to feel anything for Nissa.

Someone had stolen a bit of her shine today. And I wasn't

going to stop until I made them pay for taking that away
from her.

NISSA

I WAS FROZEN. Honestly, just frozen. All I could do was hold myself together from crying. Someone had done this to me. Rifled through my things, broken the snow globes, and the worst thing, they rummaged through all my notes on my sister. I couldn't even tell anyone what was gone. They'd been looking for something, and I didn't know what.

My mind flashed back to the mess of my flat as I sank into the tub, trying to ascertain what to do next. Was it even safe to return home in the morning? I didn't want someone to chase me away; it was my home. It was the only place I'd had since my parents died that felt entirely mine.

After my bath, I went downstairs in the loft. Westin was organizing a cleaning crew to go through my place. "You don't have to do that. I would have done it in the morning."

His gaze flickered up at me. "You need help. Let me help."

"I appreciate it, but you've done a lot for me tonight."

"Not nearly enough. I can however take care of at least the big stuff. You know what you're going to do? You're going to stay here and take the day off. Sleep it off or do whatever you want.

Anything, but don't go to Jamila's. It's better if no one goes looking for you there, too."

My heart twisted then. That was the first place I'd thought of going.

I eased down onto the couch, allowing myself to be sucked into the comfort. "I guess I've made your job a little difficult tonight. I wasn't much use."

"You don't have to apologize. Someone broke into your flat."

"I know, I'm just used to being independent."

"I said it's okay." He hung up the phone and crossed something off his list.

When I angled my body, I saw that it was a little to-do list of items to take care of me. Shopping, sending someone to pick up my clothes. Sending a cleaning crew. He was almost done. "Why are you doing this?"

"Doing what?"

"I can't figure you out. It's like you're my fairy godfather or something."

Westin laughed then. "Well, consider me an enigma then."

"An enigma, great. But truly, thank you. I appreciate it. And I'm sorry, very sorry, I brought this to your doorstep. All part of the charm of working for Julian. Do you know why my father brought you back in on this babysitting gig?"

"No, just that it was dire enough for him to put *me* on the job."

"Julian doesn't exactly have the cleanest track record. This isn't your average babysitting gig. You need to watch me because he fucked up and got in bed with the wrong people."

He frowned and crossed his arms as he watched me.

"He's been really pressuring me for ages to join the family business."

"You have no interest?"

I nodded. "Exactly. And now with this thing with the letters,

I've done something potentially dangerous that you should probably know about."

He lifted a brow. "What?"

"Interpol approached me and I've agreed to give them information on my father.

His eyes went wide. "What? When?"

"At the café when you went to the loo."

He stared at me blankly for a long moment before he ran his hands through his hair. "Fucking hell. Nissa, this is dangerous."

"I know. I know, and I just... My father is at the very least a manipulative narcissist. And while I don't think he would hurt me, he does hurt other people. The kind of people he wants to do business with are terrifying and scary, and I don't want any part of it. And he lied to me for years so he could control me. I'm not sitting back and taking it anymore."

"Bloody Interpol? You know they just have their own agenda."

"I had no choice. It's not exactly like I have anyone else to trust."

Westin cursed under his breath. "Bloody Christ. You have me. You have to stop, Nissa. This is a dangerous game you're playing. You cannot get any more involved. You have to let Interpol handle this."

"You think I don't know that? Especially now. This just got way more fucked up than I ever imagined. I never thought anyone would come into my home. And now... now... shit."

He scrubbed both hands over his face and then marched over to me, hands back on my shoulders again like I was a touchstone he needed in this moment of crisis, even though I was the one on the verge of angry tears.

Leaning forward, touching my forehead with his, he spoke so calmly to me. Not the yelling I was used to from Julian, but like I mattered, and he didn't want my tears to fall. "It's okay.

You're okay. I'll help you. It's going to be all right. We will figure this out. I'm not going to let anyone hurt you. I have some friends I can call in for favors. We will get your freedom."

"Is that really even possible? You got away once, but now you're back."

He tilted my chin up to meet my gaze. "I'm back by choice, Nissa. Julian didn't find me and drag me back. He only thinks he did. I'm exactly where I want to be. And you and I are going to make him pay."

Before I knew it, he wrapped me in his arms, holding me close to his chest. The steady beat of his heart soothed me. His heat helped me relax, seeping into my muscles, releasing the tension in them. Then there was his voice, so familiar, not terrifying, not scary. "I have you. I will protect you, okay? For now, let's get you to bed, and then we'll figure out just what the hell we're going to do in the morning."

It was so easy being in his arms. And for once I didn't feel all alone. "I'm not sure this is the best idea."

He stepped back, pinching my chin between his thumb and forefinger. "You have to trust someone at some point, Nissa."

"Everyone I trust either leaves me or is dead. So that does not bode well for you."

"You let me worry about myself. In the meantime, I'll stay with you until you fall asleep, okay? When you wake up in the morning, we'll come up with a plan. And that plan will focus on keeping you safe."

I wanted to believe him. But the truth of it was, I could see it was all a mirage. There was no security for me tomorrow or any day after that. There would be no safety for me, ever, not as long as my father was free.

Nissa

I WOKE up with a firm arm like a steel band around my middle.

When I gently tried to roll out of the way, the arm just tightened.

I blinked rapidly, trying to get my bearings. Not in my room, not in my bed, but I was clothed. So thank God for small favors.

As consciousness filtered in, I remembered what had happened. The break-in, the trashing of my flat, how I ended up here in a loft that Westin brought us to after the police station.

Westin.

Back in my life where I once swore he never would be again.

Being in his arms last night and falling asleep together was the best rest I'd gotten in a long time. His scent washed over me, and the light sound of his breathing lulled me into a place of comfort I didn't know could exist as an adult.

When I rolled over, I found his blue eyes blinking back at me.

"You're finally awake?" he asked.

"You're not asleep either."

"Well, every time I tried to leave and go to sleep on the couch, you held on to my arm pretty tight."

"I did not," I muttered.

"I'm the sole witness. Who wouldn't believe me?"

"You were the one holding onto me just now."

He shrugged. "You were sleeping a bit fitfully. Are you okay?"

I nodded. "I just... This is all a mess."

"I know. But you're okay. I have you and you're not alone."

"What time is it?" I asked.

"About four a.m."

I laughed. "You're so sure without looking at the clock?"

"I can tell."

I lifted my head to peer out the window. "It's still pitch-black outside."

"No, not quite pitch-black. Do you want to pinky-swear on it?"

I laughed. "Oh, we're making a bet?"

"Yes, we're making a bet. What do I get if I win?"

I bit my bottom lip, trying to think that through. "I don't know. What do you want?"

His gaze dipped to my lips. "It's probably best I don't say. Besides, you should probably pick since I know I'm right."

"You're so sure?"

"One hundred percent."

He was looking at me in a way that made my stomach knot and pull, and something lower than my belly began a tingly feeling. For weeks I had wondered what it would be like to be one of those women. The ones a man casually wrapped an arm around while walking around campus. They always looked happy to be in someone's arms. And at this moment, I knew the warmth Westin's arms gave.

What would one kiss be like? Just how I remembered?

I swallowed hard, unable to say it out loud. To give credence to that desire building in my mind.

"Nissa, I'm going to need you to stop looking at me like that."

"Like what?"

"Like you want to find out if we're still explosive together."

The hardness against my hip wasn't letting up. It was as if a steel rope had taken up residence along my hipbone, and it twitched as I just stared into Westin's eyes. I swallowed hard, and my gaze dipped to his lips.

"Westin? What if I *do* want to know?"

He groaned. "Fuuuuck, Nissa. I should go."

As he eased his arm from around my waist, I held onto it. My fingers barely managing to capture the muscle. "No. Don't leave me."

"If I stay, I'm afraid you'll regret it."

"I've never regretted you," I whispered softly.

His gaze searched mine for a long moment, and then in an instant, his lips were covering mine, hands in my hair, tugging on the curls and angling my head roughly as he dove in deeper. His tongue licked into my mouth, stroking against mine as he gathered me close.

All I could do was respond with gasps and moans. Even as I whispered his name and wrapped my arms around him, I was not in control here. I was not in charge of this machine of passion. This was all Westin. He was a hundred percent driving, and the man knew how to drive.

He quickly rolled us over, his big body covering mine. He placed a leg between mine, his knee wedging between my thighs and urging them open further.

When I adjusted my position, he laid between my legs, his hand fisting in my hair, turning my head to the side as he dragged his lips away from mine and along my jaw. When he nuzzled my neck, his hips rocked into me, making me cry out.

"Oh my God, Westin, please."

The exquisite tingle of his cock sliding against my clit made my breath hitch.

"Nissa, fucking hell," his voice rasped out. He didn't sound triumphant and strong, like a man who was in control of his emotions. Westin sounded just as desperate as me. A plea to make this moment never end.

I was not a hundred percent sure what I was doing. My body moved of its own volition as I rolled my hips upward, silently giving permission for more. Westin's heat and pressure caused me to stir like a boiling kettle. As he ground against me, his teeth nipped my neck, making me grasp at his shoulders, pulling him closer.

"Fucking hell, that's it, show me how you like it."

I didn't know what I was showing him exactly. I didn't know what I was telling him. All I knew were the sensations threatened to take over my life. My entire existence was at his mercy, for all I cared about in this moment was being in his arms.

His free hand cradled my face for a moment and then slid down, his thumb working over my lips as he pulled back. His gaze was hot, burning with an intensity I'd never seen before. His eyes going dark blue as his pupils dilated even further. His hips rocked against me, and that exquisite grind made everything at the apex of my thighs throb with desire I never knew possible.

When he slipped his hand down to stroke my throat, the gentle squeeze had me arching my head backward. My eyes fluttered closed, and all I could do was sigh with pleasure at the incredible sensation. I could hear Westin's breathing hitch, and he muttered, "Fuuuuuck."

Then his hands slid down further, palming my breasts, one hand stopping to stroke my nipple and squeeze. I snapped my eyes open, lifting my head to meet his gaze.

"You are so soft, Beauty."

His thumb on my nipples was like a straight connection to my clit. The gentle roll of his thumb combined with the stroke of his erection between my legs made me hitch my hips and wrap my legs around him. How could I pull him any closer? Whatever I had to do, I needed him so much closer.

He dropped his forehead to mine and kissed me gently, using his thumb and forefinger to tease my nipple as he rocked harder against me.

"Westin. Oh God, I need you."

My hands pulled at his back, sliding under his T-shirt, my

nails scouring his back. He dragged his lips from mine again and growled above me. "Ah fuck, Nissa."

His hips were moving faster now in a cadence that made my body sing.

His hand impatiently released my breast and slid back up under my top, yanking down the cup of my bra. Now we were skin against skin, his thumb, and forefinger playing and plucking.

He kissed me harshly before whispering against my lips. "You feel fucking incredible. Do you have any idea how long I've wanted to do this?"

His next pluck was harsher, making my entire body shake, and my legs tightened around his waist.

Then we were just a compilation of teeth and tongues and desperate roving hands, and his cock stroking against my clit. The cotton fabric of my knickers and his boxers keeping us from actual penetration. But it didn't matter. Sensation, and need, and desire, and...

Something snapped inside me.

I didn't realize the scream I heard was mine until he chuckled low and kissed me deeply again. His tongue mimicked the motion of his hips, the stroke, retreat, stroke, retreat, stroke, retreat. That lightning streak of desire that had just taken me on a ride was back for a second round. And this time, as he dragged his lips from mine, Westin watched me intently, his gaze dark now. Sweat was pouring off his brow. And as I broke in his arms, he gave me a satisfied smile before he cursed low, rocking his hips against me one more time, and then burying his face in my hair.

"Fuck, fuck, fuck, fuck. Oh my fucking God. Nissa." The sticky warmth between us was evidence of just how far we'd gone, but he didn't separate from me. He didn't pull away. He just held me tighter as he rolled us to our sides, holding me close. "Go to sleep, Nissa. When we wake up, we'll shower. But right now, I need to hold you."

And he wasn't wrong, because as much as maybe I thought I should shower, or process all of this, or be embarrassed, there was none of that. Just the heady bliss of being in his arms, feeling sated but still wanting more, followed by the distinct question of, *What the ever-living-fuck was that, and how do I get more of it?*

26

NISSA

Sometime during the early hours, we'd woken up and Westin had cleaned us both off and gotten me new sleep clothes. I'd expected him to leave but he'd crawled back into bed with me, cocooning me in his heat.

I was surprised to find myself alone when I woke again. Where was he?

When I tiptoed into the living room, I stopped short.

There was Westin, in the kitchen, cooking breakfast, shirtless.

I glanced at the clock. It was only 7:30. Had he even slept? I knew he must have at least briefly because I remembered being encased in his warmth while he snored lightly next to me. When had he woken up, much less prepared a whole English fry up?

I started down the stairs and he called up to me, "Oh, you're awake."

"Yeah. You weren't next to me, so I couldn't sleep."

The smile he gave me was sheepish and almost shy. When I joined him in the kitchen, he pulled out a chair for me. "Here, grab a plate and eat. Once you've eaten, we'll get ready for class and then make plans to go see the flat. Cleaners have already been there though."

"Already? When did you have time to do all that?"

"Let's just say I was up and staring at the ceiling hours ago. Thought I might as well make myself useful."

Something was up with him, but I couldn't put my finger on it. He wasn't avoiding me exactly, but there was distance in his movements.

Duh? Even if he doesn't regret last night, there could be repercussions. The biggest one is named Julian Montgomery.

Last night when I'd been burning, needing to feel Westin's touch, his hands in my hair, his fingertips on my skin, I hadn't exactly been thinking about the repercussions of what my father might do to him.

When he placed the massive plate in front of me, my stomach rumbled. I dipped my sliver of toast into the beans before taking a bite and moaning. "You made bloody curry beans? Where have you been all my life?"

His smile was soft as he brushed a hand over my hair. "For the most part, I've been right here."

But he hadn't been, had he?

"So, are we going to talk about it?" I wasn't good at beating around the bush.

He joined me at the table, straddling his chair backward as he nabbed a piece of bacon. "What do you want to talk about?"

"Last night, obviously."

His icy blue gaze focused intently on me. "What about last night?"

I licked my lips nervously. Last night had been incredible, a moment of spine-tingling weakness, and a really bad idea. I still wasn't entirely sure how I felt about him being back.

You're focusing on a lot of things here.

What had happened last night? Was that just a matter of

getting caught up in the moment? Hell, maybe he hadn't felt anything. Maybe hooking up with a client was a regular occurrence for him.

All I knew was I hadn't slept that well in months, and I had never experienced anything like that before in my life. And I wanted more.

Don't get ahead of yourself. It was just a one-night thing. And after everything you told him last night, there's no way he wants to be part of any of that.

"I think maybe it's better for me if we pull back a little."

Again, his icy blue gaze was steady, no avoidance, just steadily watching me. It was almost more unnerving that way.

"Whatever you need, Beauty," he said, his voice mellow and smooth.

I licked my lips nervously. "We just probably shouldn't complicate things. And honestly, I'm still not sure I can trust you."

He nodded slowly. "You can trust that I will do everything in my power to protect you." He said it so earnestly I had no choice but to believe him. I just wasn't sure I could trust him with my heart again.

The rest of breakfast was finished in companionable silence. Though every time I tried to stop eating, he'd shove another banger or more beans my way.

I finally had to beg off. "I swear I'm stuffed. I can't eat any more."

"Okay, let's get you to class and then we'll swing by the flat later."

Class? What bloody day was it? A quick glance down at his phone on the table and I realized it was Friday, which meant I still had classes today. My brain had just tried to go into shutdown mode and pretend I never had to go to class again.

Another glance at the clock had me groaning and running to

the shower. Last night had been something else. And maybe it was a mistake letting him anywhere near my heart again. Maybe it was a mistake playing with fire.

Later that morning, Jamila marched by my side as we headed toward the flat with Westin several paces behind.

"Are you sure you're okay? You don't want me to come up?"

I shook my head. "No, I'm fine, honestly. Westin had someone clean everything up, so there's nothing to do."

"There's always something to do. Besides, maybe you need me to sit with you. You don't have to do everything by yourself, you know?"

That smarted. "I don't do everything by myself."

"Yes, you do. You're forever Nissa the Conqueror. You never seem to need any help."

I stopped short and frowned. "Is that how you see me?"

She laughed and wrapped her arms around me. "I see you as a completely capable and wise independent woman. You, my darling, are a badarse. You never ask for help. And when something scary happens, you always want to protect other people before you protect yourself."

"I'm sorry that you see me that way."

She sighed. "My love, I just want you to know that *I'll* be there for *you* for once, okay? But I get it, if you're processing, that's okay. Just know that I am here for you, and I love you."

I gave her a squeeze back. "I do know you're here for me. Sometimes I just need time on my own to think about stuff. Anyway, how about tomorrow we do dinner? Your place. Right after I get out of class."

"Perfect. Lads or no lads?"

"What do you mean, lads or no lads? I mean, it's Adam's flat. He can be there."

Jamila rolled her eyes. "Oh, for the love of Christ, are you bringing Westin?"

I frowned. "He's my bodyguard. There's no getting around it."

"Isn't he *more* than that?"

I stuttered. "What are you talking about?"

She rolled her eyes. "Oh come on, I can see it. The tension. And the boy is cute. There's a reason bodyguards are a thing. You watched that Netflix show just like the rest of the world. Hot protectors. He's so sexy. No reason he can't be there as your date."

I open my mouth to say something. Anything. But I couldn't really get into it. There was so much she didn't know. There was so much I hadn't told anyone. "It's complicated."

"You are about to complicate yourself out of a really good shag."

"Jamila!"

"What? I'm just saying."

"Oh my God, it's a long, complicated story that is going to require many drinks."

"During these many drinks, are you going to tell me that you shagged him last night?"

I stopped in the middle of the pavement. "What?"

"Oh come on, you have that guilty face on. You have the *I shagged my bodyguard last night* face on."

"Fine. I threw myself at him last night, basically. And while I did get a very satisfying orgasm out of it, he didn't go any further. Someone who's into me would have totally gone all the way."

Jamila rolled her eyes. "He made a move. That's all that matters. He was probably just being respectful. Besides, dry humping is hot."

I flushed. "Okay, dry humping was hot, but that's not the point. What I'm trying to say is, I was the one who initiated what happened. Me, being the idiot that I am."

"I honestly think that's commendable. But we shall dissect more tomorrow. We'll get a guy's perspective."

"Oh my God, please don't tell Adam."

"What? We live *together*. What I know, he knows. Sorry, love."

"I don't need Adam knowing that I dry-humped my bodyguard."

"Trust me, he'll get it. And he'll give a good guy's perspective. I promise."

"Oh, for the love of God, I'll see you later."

She pecked me on the cheek and then jogged across the street to catch a bus, which came around the corner just in time. I waved her off just as she climbed on and flashed her Oyster card at the driver.

After seeing her off, I proceeded to go toward the elevators and up to my flat. I didn't know what I was going to find there. Westin was right behind me, silently offering me support.

My stomach was twisting and roiling as I did the death march to my door and inserted the key. But when I turned the lock, I was met with a tantalizing aroma of garlic and herbs. "What the—" Had someone else broken in to cook?

From behind me, Westin said, "I had food delivered. I figured we could have lunch here and remind you that this is still your home."

I rapidly blinked the tears out of my eyes. He was making it hard to keep him shut out.

I also noticed that the flat mostly looked back to normal. Some of my snow globes were missing, but for the most part you couldn't tell that anyone had broken in.

"Should be good as new."

His hand brushed my hip, and he gave me a warm smile. And just like that, as if last night he hadn't been murmuring dirty things in my ears about all the things he wanted to do with me, as if he hadn't come all over my stomach, now he was feeding me lunch. What the hell was going on here?

This is called having someone give a shit about you. Buckle in.

As I watched him grab two bowls and plate some pasta, I couldn't help but wonder again, if it was wise getting used to this.

27

WESTIN

I'd made a mistake last night. And she'd pulled back today. Getting involved was a mistake. This was not the mission.

It could be worse. You could have fully given in.

I needed my head on straight. How the hell did I keep my head on straight and keep on mission?

While Nissa packed a few things, I picked up my phone to text the one person who might have some insight. I could have blown it last night. I was losing my shit. I needed to figure out what the fuck to do. There were really no other options. Honestly, I needed the advice.

Advice, sure. You know you're fucked.

KING: *What's up?*

ROOK: *How bad of a fuck up is it if you hook up with a client? Technically not a client, but a witness, so to speak.*

King wasted no time because the next thing I knew the chat title said, *Rook got his dick wet*, and there was another person added, too. Fucking hell.

SAINT: *You got your dick wet, did you, mate?*

ROOK: *Shut the fuck up. Why did I even bother?*

KING: *Lol. Relax, kid. He's just giving you a hard time. It's not the end of the world. You just don't tell Gabe.*

ROOK: *Why the fuck would I tell Gabe? I'm talking to you two to figure out what to tell him.*

Saint sent a laughing emoji and replied.

SAINT: *Are you really asking what the fuck to do? Say nothing. None of this matters. Gabe doesn't need to know. Also, try not to fuck her again, would you?*

ROOK: *I didn't fuck her, I just crossed the line.*

King came to the rescue.

KING: *Ah, fuck it. I'm making a phone call, we gotta talk through this.*

It took another three minutes before we ran through all the specific protocols to get on a secure line, and they called me.

"What?"

Lock laughed. "Aw mate, you sound strung out. That bad?"

"Look, I shouldn't have called you. That was a mistake."

Lock laughed. "No, you should have called me. I'm like your big brother."

I rolled my eyes. "No. No you're not."

Saint laughed. "I'm like your big brother, too. The one whose girlfriend you tried to steal."

I sighed. "If you two can't be serious, there's no point in us talking."

Lock decided to be the voice of reason. "Okay, relax. Everybody chill. What's the problem? I assume it's the girl. The one that has you all fucked up in the head?"

I sighed. There was no point in hiding it. Saint knew everything now, too. "Yeah, it's her."

Saint sighed. "Look, at the end of the day, Gabe's not going to throw too much of a fit. As long as you stay on the mission."

"That's the problem. Staying on mission is going to be kind of hard now. I mean, I care about her. Which is a fucking issue."

"Yeah, maybe," Saint said. "But at the end of the day, you do have a job to do."

"Mate, was that how you got past everything with Kaya? Just doing your job?" I muttered.

Saint sighed. "That was different."

"Oh yeah? Explain to me how different it was. Because it sounds like it's the fucking same right now."

Lock intervened before the two of us could get into it. "Look, kid, I think the one safe thing to say is that you saw the mistakes we made. We fucked up. A lot. I fucked up with Saff. He fucked up with Kaya. Big time. Chances are you're going to fuck up. If you are at least as honest as you can be, you'll be all right. And if you can't be honest, which is going to be difficult in your case, then stay away. It'll just make your life easier. Look, how much does she know?"

I pinched the bridge of my nose as I paced back and forth downstairs in Lock's loft. "Nothing. She knows nothing. She went looking for answers at the wrong place at the wrong time. So, it's bullshit. She doesn't deserve this. She got caught up in the whole thing, and it's fucked."

Lock whistled under his breath. "So, you like her?"

I shrugged. "Too damn much."

"Just think about how she's going to feel when she finds out the truth. It's not going to be pretty. She'll never trust you again."

"Fucking hell." I scrubbed the pads of my fingers over my eyes. "I know. I fucking know. I crossed the line, and I couldn't stop myself."

Saint chuckled low. "We know the score, mate. Been there. Done that. But the difference is you have to do the job. Protect her now. She's all tied up with her father's business. You don't want that mess. When this is over and she's safe and we have Igno, then do this. It's the cleaner way to do it. If I had to do it over again, I wouldn't have fucking lied to Kaya. I would tell her the bloody truth. Let the chips fall where they may. But I wasn't thinking about that. I was trying to save my family while I was trying to save her. She sort of fell into my lap, and I got sucked into the slipstream. You have a chance here, an opportunity to stay focused. If I were you, I'd choose it."

"Even though you know you wouldn't have Kaya if you had chosen sanity?"

Lock laughed. "What Saint is trying to tell you is we didn't have a choice. We were so caught up in everything, there was no thinking. There was no stopping to breathe. Saff and Kaya were the hurricanes we got swept up into. If you've got a chance to back this thing off, then back off. You shagged her once, okay, but it's not the end of the world."

"But I didn't shag her."

Lock coughed. "What?"

"I didn't shag her. I don't know. I kissed her and made her come."

There was nothing more humiliating than two blokes who were basically your big brothers mocking you. "Aw mate, you couldn't get your dick off?"

"I swear to fucking God, I will kill you both."

I could hear the smile in Lock's voice as he spoke. "It happens to the best of us, mate."

"Shut it."

Lock snorted. "Did she ask you the dreaded *is it in yet* question?"

"No. For your fucking information, she—" I shut my mouth. They didn't need to know what she'd said. "You know what? Fuck you both."

Lock roared in laughter. "Apparently, you don't mean that."

Saint chortled on the phone alongside him.

"Why did I even bother?"

Lock stopped me then. "Because you're worried. If you

haven't done anything yet, don't worry about it. Just put the cork back in the bottle and back away slowly. Be the bodyguard she needs, because before the dust settles on this one, it's only going to get more dangerous. And she will be caught in the crossfire."

Nissa

MY STOMACH TWISTED in knots as I turned to Amelia and asked her, "Are we really doing this?" Knowing what the answer would be, yet still racked with anticipation.

After grabbing a few things from the flat, I'd come to the library. Westin hadn't liked what I was doing at all. He wanted to meet her, but I told him it wasn't the best idea. So instead, he stood guard at one of the music rooms while I paced around.

"You came to me. You wanted justice for what your father has done to you. This is part of that reckoning. All I'm asking you to do is to go to the event with your father and wear the glasses we provide. That's all. Nothing else. I will have agents there that will handle the dangerous things."

"From what you're telling me, just being there is dangerous."

She sighed then stepped in front of me, placing her hands on my shoulders. She was slightly taller than me with a lean athletic build and gentle curves. Her slim braids we're held back from her face in one massive braid.

She had the kind of bone structure that was reserved for models and completely poreless medium brown skin.

"I'm scared."

She nodded slowly. "You should be afraid. The people your father has dealings with are the stuff of nightmares, and we need to eradicate them for good."

I shuddered, but I attempted to look brave and meet her gaze. "Okay, so I need to go to the Bedford gala without my security detail."

She slowly nodded her head in agreement. "Your bodyguard won't be necessary. But don't worry, we have our people infiltrating the guest list, so you will be safe. All I need you to do is be our eyes and ears and identify anyone you recognize."

She moved over to the table and opened a folder. "Obviously, if you see this man, don't ask questions. Just confirm the sighting and move on. But otherwise, anyone you recognize from your father's circles, we need identified."

"It just seems a lot to go through to not have me do anything."

"You are doing something. You will stand and nod and smile and shake hands and air kiss. And you'll listen. Every little nuanced piece of conversation, you'll be there and record. That's all you have to do. Hell, maybe you'll even get a dance out of it."

"The last thing I want to do is dance. I just want my father behind bars."

"And we'll get there. First, we need you at the Bedford gala."

I could do this.

I stood there and nodded, but I was far from secure in that knowledge. The only thing keeping my grip on sanity in place was imagining the look on my father's face.

My mother used to say that the most powerful weapon of all was invisibility. "In that case, it looks like I'm going to need a dress. And please, tell me I'm going to get some super-secret *Mr. & Mrs. Smith* style weapons."

She rolled her eyes and shook her head. "Sorry to say, that's not real spy craft. Spy craft is boring. Spy craft is a lot of listening. And you might just be our most dangerous asset yet."

28

NISSA

BY THE TIME we returned from the library, I was knackered.

Westin had me pack my things and said for the time being we would be staying at the loft. The scene of the dry humping crime.

Okay, maybe he hadn't said that exactly.

I couldn't lie, I loved the loft. Hardwood floors, cozy atmosphere, art on the walls. Was this where he lived when he wasn't attached at the hip to me? I had no idea my father paid so well.

The thing was, there were no pictures. Not a single one of Westin. And I had snooped, looking for one. I figured there would be one of little Westin somewhere. But no, just the art and the exquisite furnishings, masculine but comfortable. It was well-decorated and beautiful, and it suited him in a way, almost in a way that said he was a chameleon. I don't know what it was, but something told me that he didn't live here all the time.

Of course, he doesn't. He goes where the assignments are. This is his crash pad.

Which was sad. Someone like him needed a home. Some-where to land that he belonged.

Like you? Don't you need a home?

I did, actually. I had my sister. And when I found her, I would be at home.

If you find her.

My gut twisted just thinking about it. I had failed her.

You should have kept looking.

I'd beat myself up about this for so long, I didn't know when I should stop. I should have been looking. I had trusted my father to do the looking for me, but this whole time, he hadn't been.

And now, I was in this trouble because I simply couldn't let it go. I was determined I'd find her on my own.

If he lets you.

I was pouring over my International Law books, my eyes blurring as I stared at the words. There was a knock at the door, and Westin frowned. "You didn't tell Jamila where we were, did you?"

"No, you said not to."

"Then who the hell is that?"

"Julian?"

He scowled at that. "He didn't come to the flat when it was ransacked, he wouldn't come here now."

"Well, I didn't tell anyone we were here."

Westin nodded and indicated that I should head up to the loft. And then he reached under the coffee table. Hold up. Jesus Christ, was that a gun? "Where did that come from?"

He gave me a wry look and nodded his head indicating he needed me to get my arse upstairs.

After what had happened, I was more inclined to listen and tucked myself upstairs behind the door. But just because I hid that didn't mean I wasn't curious. So I pressed my ear up against the door, straining for information. There was another voice.

Deep. Low. Westin sounded ticked off. "What the fuck are you doing here?"

"I can't come to see my little cousin?"

Cousin? He'd never said a word about a cousin. Finally, Westin called up to me. "Nissa, come on down."

With the sound of the way he said my name, my belly flipped. *Stop it.* I'd already made it clear that what happened was a mistake and it was not going to happen again, so I needed to let it go. Even though I'd had fevered dreams of him over me, drugging me with kisses, pulling at my lips, the length of his cock between my legs, hitting my clit just right in an excruciatingly slow grind that made me ache all over.

Yeah. I had completely forgotten all about it. Not.

I jogged down the stairs and halted midway down when I saw the gorgeous man with a three-day-old scruff of beard. He was dressed in dark jeans and a white pullover jumper. His hair was darker than Westin's, but much of their coloring was the same. A hint of an olive tone, but not quite. Other than that, their features weren't similar at all. The stranger's eyes were a piercing green. "Ahhh, who's this?"

I wish I had asked the question with a stronger voice. One that sounded less breathy and worried. But I didn't. The stranger grinned at me.

"Hey, are you all right?"

He put a hand out for me to shake, and I stared at it. "Do I know you?"

I didn't mean to be rude, but a crazy man tried to take me off the street, and then my flat had been ransacked. Then the concert. I wasn't inclined to meet strangers whether Westin knew them or not.

When my gaze met Westin's, he was scowling at the other man. "Nissa Montgomery, meet Gabe, my cousin."

"Your cousin? I didn't know you had a cousin."

"Yeah, well, I try not to think about it. You know how it is. Older cousins are the worst."

"Oh. You don't look anything alike."

Westin grinned. "You're right about that. All the looks obviously could only pass to one person. Me. He got all the attitude."

Gabe grinned, and I didn't care what Westin said, his cousin was beautiful to look at. His smile was so completely arresting that I had to blink several times to shake off the effects.

Even Westin was confused because he stared at his cousin for a long moment. "He heard I was in town, so he wanted to come and say hello."

Gabe nodded. "Yeah, just passing through. I just got back from Spain."

"What do you do?"

"Ops manager. It's boring stuff. But I do travel quite a fair bit."

"The travel part sounds interesting."

"Nah, it's a bit tedious after a while. I'm just here to follow up and make sure people do what they're supposed to do."

"Well, no one likes to babysit."

"Don't worry about it." He grinned at Westin. "And then my cousin here is being a bit cagey about his job now. I see there's lots he didn't tell me. One being that his flat mate was so beautiful."

I flushed at that. "Oh, um that's lovely of you to say, but—"

"It's true. I'm sure he's nervous."

I rolled my eyes then and smiled. "So anyway, can we get you a drink or something?"

"Yeah, sure. I'd fancy a pint. What do you have?"

Westin glowered at him. "Not much. The fridge is that way."

I laughed. "Westin, it's your cousin. He's a guest."

"Oh, don't mind Westin's attitude. I'm not really a guest. Besides, I know my way around the place."

"Oh, I don't know why I got the impression you hadn't been here before."

Gabe frowned at that and studied me. "Why do you say that?"

"I don't know. Because we're hanging out in the foyer area? If my sister were here, I'm sure she would have been sprawled all over the couch by now like she owned the place. And where are the pictures? Care to tell me? Because I'm dying to know what Westin was like as a kid before I met him."

Gabe laughed. "Oh, I have stories for days."

And he did have lots of stories of Westin and their family. And the whole time, Westin just sat there, jaw tight. And I had to say, Gabe was a master at never quite answering questions and turning them around on you. Before I knew it, I was answering lots of questions about my sister and my dad and how I came to live with him. It was so easy to just tell him everything about myself. Before I knew it, a couple of hours had passed, and Gabe was more than aware that I was looking for my sister.

"Ah, rough going, love. I hope you do find your sister."

"Thanks, that's sweet of you."

Then Gabe stood and said, "Well, I must be going. I've taken up your night. I hope you didn't have much to do. Westin, mate, I'm leaving tomorrow morning. Let's grab a quick coffee before I head out."

"I can't. Nissa and I have plans."

He nodded. "Oh well, I'm sure she can make it to class on her own, right? It's just a coffee with your cousin."

"Um, all I have is Marketing Dynamics. It's fine."

Westin frowned. "Like I said, I'm busy."

I rolled my eyes. "What Westin is not telling you is that he's my bodyguard. Dad hired him to watch my arse."

Gabe blinked rapidly. "Oh, did he now? Why? Is your dad someone really important?"

"Hardly. He only thinks he's important. But anyway, poor Westin here has been charged as my babysitter. He's worried I won't have coverage. There is a coffee stand right downstairs in the same building. You can meet there while I'm in class, okay?"

I could tell he didn't like it. His jaw was working, but he finally said, "Yeah, fine."

"Well, I'll let you two say goodbye. It was good to meet you, Gabe."

I excused myself, aware of their eyes on me as I headed up the stairs. I was given no reprieve upstairs though. Because the moment I stepped into the bedroom, a text chimed on my phone. When I picked it up, my stomach fell.

A text from Jamila flashed in the screen and all it said was 911.

Nissa

I'd stayed up way past my bedtime. Jamila's 911 message was a doozy. Adam had apparently been accepted into a grant program in Norway. And like a sometimes-clueless bloke, he'd accepted without talking to Jamila about it first.

Her emotions had run the gamut of from denial and her being pretty sure that he hadn't meant to say yes, to the two of us coming up with several ways to murder him in his sleep, to bargaining if there was some way to undo this, and finally to acceptance.

But I was drained. Truth be told, it was nice to focus on someone else's problems. At least I could pretend for a few hours that I wasn't scared or worried.

When I finally hung up with her, all I wanted to do was pass out in a coma.

That was an hour ago.

Apparently running away from my emotions only lasted so long. The moment I was off the phone, the anxiety crept back like rats in the darkness with its little *tick, tick, tick* sound going off in my head, reaching into those parts of my brain that would spin out.

Now it was bloody 2:00 a.m. and I hadn't slept a wink. And it wasn't just because I'd had Westin on the brain.

It was everything. The break-in, my father, exactly who he was in business with, what he was capable of... Okay, it was also Westin. But my point was that all of it was fucking with my sleep.

To be fair, someone did break into your house. Not to mention someone also tried to grab you off the street a few days ago.

I tossed again before dragging my pillow over my eyes, willing myself to fall asleep, trying not to picture Westin in my bed, holding me, the hard length of him pulsing against my hip, the way he'd tried to avoid taking advantage of that, and then the weight of him on top of me. The way his cock felt against my clit, my body arching into his, the way he kissed me hungrily, vibrantly, as if I was in fact, the prize. Not something to be owned or controlled, but more like someone to hold.

Just admit that you want him.

Yes, fine. I wanted him. Like I had never wanted anyone before. But this whole situation was fucked. I was pretty certain he wanted someone normal, not someone with a mountain full of baggage and a father like mine.

This whole situation was a lot, and he didn't even know half of it.

Not to mention he works for your father.

I wanted to trust him. He'd already proven that I might be able to, but I couldn't just ignore that he worked for the same man who'd lied and betrayed me. And Julian had done all of that under the guise of loving me.

When it became clear that I wasn't going to be able to sleep, I shoved the cover down and snatched off my satin bonnet.

I had been managing my class workload okay, but I didn't know how long that was going to hold if I kept this up.

It wasn't like I was making some accommodations for recent events. I didn't want to take advantage of that. I needed to get my shit together.

Gently, I eased my bedroom door open and padded out to the living room. The lights were off, and I hooked a left into the kitchen, opened the fridge, and grabbed the milk. I grabbed a mug and the cocoa I'd seen in the cupboard earlier to make myself a mug of hot chocolate when a voice from behind me murmured, "It's not hot chocolate unless you have the mini marshmallows."

With a squeak, I brought the mug around, intending to use it as a weapon. But Westin caught my hand easily in mid-air. I automatically tried to use the other arm to escape. But with another smack, he caught it. "Easy, it's me. You're okay. You're in the loft. It's just me, Westin. Bodyguard, remember?"

I blinked rapidly and nodded my head because I knew it was Westin. I did. Honestly. But the panic had set in, and I couldn't breathe.

His fingers soothed where he held my wrist. "You're okay. You're okay, Nissa."

I shook my head. "I am not okay, clearly."

He released me, his eyes sharp and intent. His voice was gravelly when he asked, "You needed something to put you to sleep?"

"Yep. I figured the hot chocolate was worth a try."

"I think there are some marshmallows in the pantry. Let me get them for you."

It wasn't what he said, but how he said it. His voice was already low, but fresh from sleep, it sounded like there was an added growl to it. The sound made me pulse in places I shouldn't be thinking about with him. "Y-you don't have to do that."

"Well, you're up and I'm up, so we both might as well have some hot chocolate together. Or are you trying to enjoy mini marshmallows without me?"

I bit my bottom lip. Despite my best efforts, he was actually pretty decent at making me smile.

When he turned back his gaze studied me. "You look flushed, Nissa."

I laughed under my breath as he placed the mini marshmallows on the counter. "I'm not flushed. Besides, you can't tell that. It's too dark."

"I can tell. Even here in just moonlight, I can tell your pupils are a bit dilated. You're panting softly. And while you're brown, I can tell from just touching your cheek." He raised a hand up and brushed his knuckles over my cheekbone. "You're warm. See? Flushed."

"That's cheating. You had to touch me to know for sure." Every word out of my mouth sounded breathy.

"Oh, trust me, I'm hyperaware of everything that you do. I *know*."

"Are you now?"

He nodded once. While he didn't move, I felt like he was suddenly closer, invading my space somehow. "I am indeed."

"And why is that?"

He chuckled under his breath and got two mugs from the cabinet. "Haven't you figured out by now? I'm aware of everything that you do. There isn't a move that you make that I'm not instantly aware of."

I cleared my throat. "I don't know what that means."

"What it means is the other night wasn't some fluke. But you and I, it's a bad idea. I have a job to do, and I need to do it well.

You are a complication I do not need, but I can feel the connection between us, and it is bloody impossible to ignore. I want you. I wish I didn't. I wish I could fall asleep without feeling you pulse against my cock."

I swallowed hard. "What am I supposed to do with that?"

"Why can't *you* sleep, Beauty?"

I swallowed hard. "I'm just thinking."

"You're thinking about me. I'm thinking about you. Let me be clear... All I do is think about you. The words I have to describe you are spunky, loudmouth, know-it-all, bloody pain in the arse. But guess what? *Because* of all those things I like you a whole hell of a lot. You keep me on my toes. But none of that changes how much I crave you. I have my orders, Nissa, and that makes these desires impossible to follow down the path I wish we could take."

Somehow in the time he said all of that he had moved closer. So close I felt the heat of his body. I could smell the sandalwood and spice fragrance that was him. A manly essence that made me want to lick him all over.

I swallowed hard and nodded. "I get it. I do. I don't want any complications. You work for my father."

"That I do. But Nissa, listen to me closely. Where the paycheck comes from doesn't change how I feel or how much I thirst for more of you."

My whole body hummed. I involuntarily swayed toward him. I knew what was good for me. I knew what the safer outcome was, but I still felt the pull and I couldn't ignore it. I wasn't strong enough to change trajectory off a collision course with Westin St. James.

He moved to stand directly in front of me and leaned in, bracketing his arms on either side, pushing me to rest farther into the counter. I just looked up at him, my body immediately relaxing in the cocooned safety of his arms.

"Tell me, Nissa. Tell me what you need. You want me to help you get to sleep tonight? Is that what you want, Beauty?"

My body knew what I wanted. My clit pulsed, begging for more contact, begging him to touch me again, anywhere.

"Westin..." Again, my voice was too breathy. "I need..." my voice trailed.

I couldn't even say what I needed. I just yearned for Westin's touch again. Needed him to make me fly. Help me forget even for a few moments.

"I know what you want. I know what I see in front of me."

I stared up at him, registering just how close he was, and it made my throat dry as I squeaked out, "What is it you see?"

"The woman I want so damn much to kiss. The beauty who's hiding from herself by denying exactly what she is desperate for, but won't say the words. But I'm not going to kiss her unless she asks."

When his tongue peeked out to moisten his bottom lip, I groaned low. "That's hardly fair."

"That's the way it goes. You need to say the words."

"Westin?"

"Yes, Nissa?"

"Kiss me, please."

His mouth was hot, insistent, commanding. His tongue slid into my mouth and over mine like its sole mission was to drive me mad. His body pinned mine against the counter, and I struggled to catch my breath.

His large hands fisted my hair, tugging enough to make me pant but not enough to hurt. Both hands dug in as he angled my head and pressed his body tighter against mine.

Westin dragged his lips off mine just enough to whisper against them, "Is this what you wanted? To drive me bloody mad? You want to feel my cock between your thighs again? You want me to make you come? Will that help you sleep?"

Oh God, he knew exactly what I wanted. What I needed. "Yes."

"Yes what, Beauty?"

I glowered up at him mutinously as he held his lips a hair's breadth away from mine. "Yes, I want all of what you say I need because I bloody well do." I ground out. I didn't just want it. I *needed* it. The phantom pulsing between my thighs had become like a daily torture.

"Good girl."

His lips were back with an onslaught against mine. Every slide and stroke of his tongue caused a shiver to tear up my back. My nails scored over the bare flesh of his back, and he hissed in my ear. "Somebody's impatient."

I *was* impatient. This was the restless feeling I'd been chasing since the first time I was in his arms. This high. This bliss couldn't be found anywhere else but with him. *My Westin.*

He nipped at my neck and I arched to give better access to his meanderings across my body. While he nipped at the sensitive flesh just below my ear, his hands snaked under my tank to stroke over my ribs with his thumb. Eventually he grazed the sensitive underside of my breast, and I tried to arch into him, showing my approval of his ministrations.

When is palm finally grasped tightly around my breast, thumb sliding over my nipple, I cried out. "Oh God."

I rocked my hips, trying to get leverage, and when my center lined up so his cock fit snugly between my lips, all I heard was his low murmured, "Fuuuuuuck."

But then he suddenly released me, and I whimpered my frustration. "Westin."

With a murmured hush he turned me around so I was facing the counter. He leaned down, his lips against the shell of my ear as he said, "Bend over."

I did as I was told, my breath coming in ragged pants now.

One hand slid up under my tank again, pumping my breast, and he whispered again, "You are so unbelievably beautiful from every angle."

His words were so soft I wasn't sure I'd heard them. His hold eased into something gentler, more seductive, less desperate. With his other hand he slid into the waistband of my pajamas, past my knickers. The moment his fingers met with my slick heat, he dropped his head and bit my shoulder.

"Fuck me Nissa. You're so goddamn wet."

Against my arse I could feel the steely length of his cock pulsing, begging for entry.

He slid the tip of one finger inside me, and I heard his breath catch. His hips rolled into my arse and I waited for him to tug down my pajamas and fuck me here against the counter.

Instead, he whispered against my skin how beautiful I was all while he teased my breast and then released it to paw the other one until that nipple was a beaded peak as well.

I kept pushing my hips back against him, rotating, begging him to hurry up already. But instead of fucking me, he drove me exhaustingly mad. Slowly he penetrated me with one finger, his thumb reaching to gently slide over my clit.

I bit my bottom lip to keep from crying out, but he knew what I was doing. "No, Nissa, I want to hear you. When I dip my finger inside you, I want you to pretend it's my tongue or my dick. When I slide two fingers inside you, I want you to know how I'm going to stretch you. I want you to know how good it's going to feel."

His dirty words against my skin were the added touch of desperation I needed. Electricity pulsed through my body, aiming directly to one location, my clit.

He slid his finger deeper and moaned. "I love how wet you are for me. Do you have any idea how mad you've been making me? How the fuck was I supposed to pretend none of it happened? I'm not supposed to touch you, though Christ help me, I can't stay away."

"I-I don't want you to stay away."

"It would be better for you if I did," he said cryptically even as he moved his finger faster in time with his thumb, finger fucking me, making me buck my hips backward sliding over the length of his cock.

"Fuck, fuck, fuck. Is my talking making you wetter?"

At that point, all I could manage was a low keening moan as I parted my thighs in an attempt to make more room for his big hands, He took the hint, eased out his finger, and slid two back inside.

The new fuller feeling had me gripping for purchase against the counter. He immediately slowed his penetration and shushed against my skin. "I'm sorry. I should have gone slower. I just want to make this good for you."

I was desperate. I nodded vehemently. "It's good. So good. I need more."

"That's my girl. You want my cock, don't you? Hitting you just right while I stroke your clit and play with your tits." He pinched a nipple as if to drive his point home, all the while increasing the pace of his fingers.

The bliss I was seeking stayed right out of range, just on the horizon, teasing me like Westin was. But then, he released my breast, slid his hand down my torso, to my belly, just above where his thumb was stroking me in time to his fingers, and he pressed down.

The crash of electricity hit me like a wave, and I screamed his name. "Westin!"

He buried his face in my hair, pressing hard on my clit now, his fingers driving in and out, the pace picking up. And then he hooked his fingers and rubbed short, tight circles over my clit again as my vision went white and my knees collapsed as I exploded around his fingers again.

Behind me, he ground against my arse, and I heard his hushed murmurs of, "Fuck this feels too good," and, "God I want to fuck you so bad," and, "You are so goddamn sexy," and, "I will burn for this." His words were almost lost on me in the bliss that held me in its chokehold even as he continued to press and hold me, his fingers forcing me to ride out that wave. Then he lightly released and pressed again, causing another wave to come over me.

When my knees gave out, he released the press on my belly and tightened his arm around my waist before crooning in my ear, "Good girl. This is the hardest thing I've ever done in my life."

I tried to turn in his arms to meet his gaze, but he held me in position before slowly easing his fingers out of me, pulling his hand free. When his hand was freed from my pajamas, I turned in his arms and watched wide-eyed as he lifted his fingers to his lips and licked them clean as he watched me.

His broken moan almost had me coming again as he met my gaze. "Go to bed now, Beauty. I'll see you in the morning."

29

WESTIN

My cock was harder than steel.

I still couldn't believe that I bloody sent her to bed. Who the hell turned down the most beautiful woman on the planet?

You do. Because you weren't supposed to touch her in the first place. You cheated.

Okay, I'd cheated. But at least I hadn't dragged her upstairs and sank into her like I wanted to. That would truly be the point of no return.

Nope, you can just smell and taste her on your fingers right now.

I drew my fingers up to my lips and licked off her essence, having to fight back a boner.

Fuck me. There was no way I was going to be able to sit through a meeting. It just wasn't possible, not while I was thinking about all the things that I wanted to do to her.

I checked my Piaget. I still had thirty seconds, so I ran to the loo and washed my hands, scrubbing them intensely. With a quick drag of the towel over my palms, I was back on my laptop in seconds. Just in time to see the debrief room.

Gabe was already scowling and pacing. Saff was there, and

so were Saint, Legend and Devlin, who had all been put on this assignment. But no Lock and no Tabatha.

"Where the hell are Lock and Tabs?"

That question earned me a growl from Gabe. "Not bloody here, are they?"

Was it unusual for Gabe to be in a shady mood? No. Was it unusual for him to be in a shit mood and taking it out on all the rest of us? Yes. He wasn't exactly warm and fuzzy, but you always knew you were respected. Something was up.

Finally, Lock and Tabs walked in with apologetic nods of acknowledgment. Lock open his mouth like he was going to talk, but it was Tabatha who spoke at first. "Apologies for our delay. Gennifer Goode from Oversight requested an audience with us. She wanted to know about the Igno situation."

I could practically see the lava escaping from Gabe's ears. But it was Saffron who was well and truly ticked off. "And why would she be getting information from you two?"

"We asked the same thing, as we are not primary or Ops Command," Lock said. "She fed us some bullshit about how Oversight from time to time wanted team insight."

"That's a load of shit. No one from Oversight has ever requested a meeting with me," Saff said.

I could see the tension in Gabe's shoulders. "I'll address her after this meeting. For now, let's focus on this Igno mission so we can brief Rook. We have word that he is going to be at a secret meeting at the Bedford Manor. We've got some players we haven't seen out in the wild in a bit. If we play our cards right, we'll be able to tag and trace several of them while also grabbing up Igno."

So we were just going to fucking ignore the fact that Oversight had just meddled with Rogues? I itched to ask, but something told me that was information I did not need to have.

"Rook, you're on assignment that night correct?"

I nodded. "Yep, I got the duty roster this morning. I'm not sure what Montgomery is playing at. He knows we've obviously got pressure on us. Nissa's flat was ransacked. Common Denominator is Igno. Our threat level is red right now for this gala."

"You'll be with the principal. Saff and Lock will be on the ground along with me and Saint. We'll send schematics to your tablet. But your job is simple; stay on Nissa. And get us visual confirmation as well as audio. Some of that will need to be done on-site after arrival. Saff will shadow Montgomery. All other eyes are on Igno."

"Copy. And if anything goes wrong? If I have the chance to take Igno?" I asked.

He shook his head. "You call for back up. Do you understand?"

I knew how important Igno was. He was the end game. If there was a chance to end this, to make Nissa safe, I didn't give a fuck what my orders were. I was going to take it.

Nissa

I tried to keep my posture straight and not peek back at Westin. I could sense his eyes lingering on me, and in spite of the fear that gripped me, it was a comforting feeling. I was surrounded by criminals and people that my father had wronged in some way. Knowing that Westin was here with me, watching my back, made me feel protected, but it terrified me to think of all the potential repercussions if Amelia's plan went wrong.

The waiter passed with glasses of champagne, and I selected one, my father giving me an admonishing glare as he talked to someone whose name I couldn't remember, which was probably for the best.

I was doing my best to do my job. Which was wear the glasses, stand dutifully by my father's side, and nod at the appropriate times.

Dad had been displeased by my eyewear. First thing he'd asked me when I came down the stairs in my dress was, "Why are you wearing glasses?"

I'd made the excuse about my contacts irritating my eyes, but I could tell he didn't like how I looked. Didn't matter. I didn't care.

Eyes on the prize.

Out of the corner of my eye, I caught a glimpse of Amelia. She had come to stun in a white and red open-backed dress. The gathered silk plunged off her shoulders and pooled at her waist, where it was tied with a belt of hand-woven rope. She also wore red high heels, and her long black hair was swept back from her forehead. She was stunning, but I quickly diverted my attention back to my father because that was the gig.

This is all you have to do. Do it well, and you'll be done.

As the minutes ticked by slowly, I wished that I could talk to Westin. At least a dance or something. But no, I stayed right next to Julian.

My father leaned over to me at one point and tapped my glass with his. "Look alive, Nissa. Maybe we should dance?"

I widened my eyes. "What?"

He rolled his. "Dance. The point is to mingle and look like you're enjoying yourself. You look miserable."

I sighed, placing my glass on the passing tray of a waiter. "I don't remember the last time we danced."

He smiled. "It was your 20th birthday. Remember?"

Oh yes, I did remember. Julian had insisted on a very boring stuck up affair when all I wanted to do was go to the clubs with my mates. I *had* been able to invite my friends from school. But even they had looked bored. Sure, they'd enjoyed the idea of going to a fancy ball, but they thought they'd get to hear Dua Lipa and Taylor Swift. They didn't think they'd be subjected to an orchestra that refused to play anything modern.

The night was a disaster. But yes, we had danced.

Julian held out his hand. "Come on, Nissa. You always have to be aware of how things look. How they're being perceived."

I frowned at him. "Of course, because that's the only thing that's important, right?"

When he took me in his arms, moving me easily through the crowd, I fell into step with him. I'd been taught to dance at school. I thought it was completely useless because it felt like one of those finishing school type activities and when I would much rather have been in my books, obviously. But as we danced, it afforded me the chance to check out the room properly. Westin was by the bar, in the corner. Looking like, well, like a bodyguard. Amelia was moving through the floor, looking every bit like the party goer. She was sipping champagne, talking animatedly. She looked so comfortable. How did she do that?

As my father spun me around and around, I felt something inside of me soften. For just a moment, I could almost imagine he was a real father, someone I could trust and turn to for advice. I was so wrapped up in the illusion, the fantasy of this moment, that I almost believed it.

But then, just as quickly as the dream had come, it was gone. Out of nowhere, a large man with a flat face and a sloping forehead stepped forward and whispered something into my father's ear, and suddenly the image faded away as quickly as it had come.

He stopped our dance and seized my hand, yanking me to his side. In a dangerous and bitter tone, he hissed, "Our presence is being requested. When we enter this room, say nothing. Do you understand?"

I nodded quickly, my mouth going dry. "What's happening?"

He remained silent as he cast a signal of acknowledgment over his shoulder. Westin fell into step behind us. With each step, I could feel my heart pounding, my pulse racing as I remembered the wire I wore beneath my clothes. Amelia must have heard it too, and she was warning her team about something going off script. This was definitely not part of the plan.

We were led up the ornate, winding staircase to the upstairs level. There were some guests mingling about, in and out of balconies, but not many. And then we were led down a hallway. It was just as beautifully decorated as it was downstairs, with art and beautiful decorations on the wall, and our shoes made a clopping sound on the marble floor.

At the end of the hall to the right, a mountain of a man opened the door and stepped aside to let us in.

Except he barricaded Westin's way. "Just those two."

Westin scowled, looking up as if assessing if he could take him.

I'd always known Westin was a bodyguard. But there was something about the intensity in his eyes that screamed, 'Oh no, he is *absolutely* dangerous.' It reminded me of that day up in Angel. He'd been all business, not the Westin I was used to seeing.

When we were led into the room, there were several men already there, and my heart stopped.

By the fire, sitting in one of the ornate high-backed chairs of red leather trimmed in gold weave, sat an all-too-familiar man.

Amelia had shown me how the glasses worked. In essence, I didn't have to do anything except turn them on and wear them. I knew they were getting this, and of course they were listening in. They were getting all of this on a recording, and they knew he was there.

"You brought a little girl to a meeting, Montgomery?"

My father remained unfazed. "Well, considering this little girl's life has been affected by your movements, yes, I brought her so you can see she's still alive despite your best attempts. You had your goons break into my daughter's flat. That's going too far. Families are untouchable."

Igno pushed up from his seat. "How dare you speak to me this way? I set the rules. And if one of you has transgressed, I can break any rule I see fit to rectify it."

I could tell that he was a man used to being in power. A man used to getting his way.

My father stood his ground, which surprised me. "You have no power here, Igno, unless you have that ledger in your hands. In which case, you know, I'll wait. If you can produce it, then by all means."

Igno lifted a brow. "You play a dangerous game, Julian."

"No. You crossed a line. My daughter is off-limits. Understand that. What you did means war. How do you think the Syndicate will feel?"

Igno stalked closer. The other men in the room exchanged glances as if concerned that the meeting would erupt into violence.

"You will watch your tongue with me, Montgomery. You think you can threaten me? The Syndicate knows I have their best interest at heart. I believe in business and money. Right now, you think I'm weak, but at some point, I shall be strong again and then you will regret your choice of words." Igno turned his attention on me. "If I were you, young lady, I would get as far away from your father as fast as possible. Because he is going to get you killed. Now, Julian, log your name in so that our friends know you were in attendance tonight."

My father marched me over to the massive desk in the corner, and he signed his name in something that looked like some kind of guest book. I didn't know what it was. But I made sure my glasses caught the list of names even as my father signed.

Another man with a thick shock of white hair and light brown skin stalked forward. "We do not have time for your petty squabbles."

Igno turned on him. "Petty? My ledger's gone missing. And Montgomery here is the last man to have seen it. We have unfinished business."

The other man shook his head. "Until you produce proof, we cannot interfere."

Igno laughed. "I don't need interference. I can handle Montgomery all by myself."

My father sneered at him. "You have no leverage here. You heard Sono."

Igno's gaze remained impassive. As they were arguing, I fiddled with my clutch, pulling out one of the bugs I'd been given by Amelia. She'd given them to me with the glasses saying if there was a chance for me to bug the conversation, I had to do it.

My heart felt like it was beating in my ears as I nervously glanced around the room. I dared not breathe, terrified of the consequences of my actions, yet I had to do it. Sweat prickled my skin as I plunged my hand into my purse and grabbed hold of a tissue, pretending to wipe away an imaginary tear. Digging further in, I manage to bury my fingertips deep enough to find the bugs, and with quiet precision, I peeled one off with my nails and released it from its prison before drawing my hand out, gripping the edge of the desk, and depositing the bug.

I was sweating. I had to be sweating, but no one seemed to notice.

Igno stepped to my father. "Where is my ledger?"

Julian shrugged. "I don't know. All of our necks are on the

line unless you find it, so I do hope you think of where you might have put it."

As Igno was talking and I was trying desperately to catch everything being said, an explosion rocked the house. Through the window across the courtyard, I could see it on the west wing. My heart almost stopped. What the hell was going on? Amelia had said nothing about explosions.

My father pointed a menacing finger at Igno. "You did this. There are people looking for you. And this is what you reap when you're careless."

Igno glowered at him. "This isn't me. If it's law enforcement, I think maybe Montgomery here has been talking a little too much... as he's known for doing."

My father shoved him just as another explosion hit. When he turned to me, his eyes were wild. And then it was as if he suddenly realized that I was there. "We're leaving, Nissa."

"What the hell's going on?"

"That man's enemies are coming for him. I don't intend to be here when they arrive." And then my father dragged me out behind him as another explosion rocked the building.

WESTIN

This was a mistake. I'd been uneasy all night. From the outside, this looked like a normal mission. My team was in place, I had everything I needed, and we were moving forward. The problem was I could *feel* that something wasn't right.

All night, I'd kept my gaze pinned to Nissa and Montgomery. Nissa looked miserable as Montgomery schmoozed and pressed palms. And while he might look comfortable to everyone else, I could see it just there in the tension of his jaw. Something was going on.

Even though I was working and not supposed to be drinking, I needed a way to cover up talking to my team. So I snagged a champagne glass from a passing waiter. Around the rim, I spoke. "Everyone, be on alert. Something's going on. I see a flurry of guards and Montgomery is tense."

Saff's voice was cool and calm. "Copy. All units prepare to move."

We had Interpol in play, but our goal was to get to Montgomery first because he would lead us to Igno. And if Igno was here, well, we would do whatever it took to bring him down.

As long as Nissa stays protected.

After all, she was my primary. If after all of this she was in even more danger, I planned to take her somewhere very far away. I knew how to hide. I could show her how. I had done it before, obviously.

Suddenly, Ivan Resnick, a known mercenary, was tapping Julian on the shoulder as he danced with Nissa. He led the way for them. They were headed toward the center staircase. Julian inclined his head for me to follow. We were on.

"Saff are you seeing this?" I muttered under my breath before falling in position.

"I see it. We have your six. King, Legend, Saint fall into position."

I followed tightly behind Nissa, Resnick on my tail. Whatever the hell was going to go down was going down right now. And I had no way to get Nissa out of the line of fire. At the top of the stairs, Resnick led the way down a long hallway. Our footsteps on the marble floor echoed off the art-lined walls.

At the end of the hall to the right stood an intricately carved wooden door. Resnick opened it, making way for us. Julian went first then Nissa. Before I could follow, Resnick barred my way. "Only them," he murmured.

I frowned down at his arm, assessing whether it was a smart

thing to fight with the door open or wait until it was closed. Either way, I would need to take out Resnick if I wanted to protect Nissa.

In the end, I had to take my team into account. They were on their way. I had tagged Nissa's phone with the listening device weeks ago. Kaya could hear everything in the room. If we got confirmation, they would move forward. And then I would get myself and Nissa out of there. Post haste.

As soon as the door closed, Resnick smirked at me. "You didn't think the help would be invited to the table did you?"

I grinned at him as I leaned against the door. "Oh, I don't need an invitation to the table. I already have a man inside."

Just as his brows furrowed in confusion, I shot him with the tranq gun. He'd been so excited about barring me from entry, he'd missed it when I had palmed my weapon. To be sure he stayed down, I fired three into him, one into his thigh to ensure fast absorption, two more into his chest.

That dumbfounded, confused look on his face remained as he lurched toward me, but he slumped, nonetheless.

I let him fall, letting his face hit the marble. Whoops. I grabbed his shoulders and dragged him across the hall to the other door as I spoke into my mic. "We have a go for number ten on our most-wanted list. Michael Garrett. I saw him through the door. Let me know what Nissa is picking up."

I dragged Resnick into the nearest room, which was back down the hall and to the left, and unceremoniously dropped him back on the floor, using the zip ties I had in my pocket to tie him to a massive conference table. Suddenly, something skipped up my spine. A warning, a feeling. I couldn't pinpoint it, but I had the heebie-jeebies and I couldn't shake it.

Saff, it seemed, had the same instinct. "Rook, what do you see?"

I ran to the window. "I see three guards on the balconies,

none in the hall we came down. And obviously the five rotating ones we saw downstairs at all the exits. We may have a tricky egress."

Gabe's voice was firm. "Don't worry about the exit. A-team, get to Igno right now. We have confirmation that Igno is in the room with primary and secondary."

My gut twisted. Fucking hell. She was in the room with that psychopath.

I eased out of the conference room, careful not to make a sound, and found Saff running up the stairs. As we ran down the hall, she leaned down to her garter and pulled out a weapon. I reached into my tux and pulled out mine. Then she gave me a nod. "You got this."

I grinned at her. "I was trained by the best, so of course I do."

She headed left to go around to the room from the balcony side. I headed right and prayed to fucking God Nissa knew what to do next. She had her orders from Interpol. Stay low, record only. I prayed to God she listened to them because the room she was in was about to become a hot zone.

A server room was near where the meeting was taking place, and my job was to pull all visual data from their system and access any data we couldn't get from the outside. These men weren't meeting in a public place, but people said all kinds of things when they thought they were alone. There were security cameras everywhere, and some details would be picked up.

I waited for all agents to call in their positions before taking a deep breath. This was almost over. In moments, I would have her safe. I had already set the algorithm on the cameras to loop, and Kaya had it under control from the van.

But still, I eased into the server room that I knew would give me security feed access. Morgan Bedford was very particular about his privacy and security. This party had a lot of high rollers, which he used as a reason for all the cameras.

What I needed was access to everyone's movements. On a lower monitor I got my wish and hit paydirt. "Upstairs, toward the back balcony at the back of the house. All agents, southwest corner. I repeat, southwest corner. We've got three guards coming up the stairs, one on the back stairs, two up the center stairs. Saff, stay in the shadows. One is heading toward you on the balcony."

Gabe's voice was clear. "Roger. Saint and Legend, outside. Heir, King, and Rook approach. I will handle clearing the egress."

We all had our assignments, and I eased out from the room, noticing King coming up the stairs as well. He wasn't even looking at me. His eyes were on the guard as he feigned drunkenness. He deliberately stumbled into the guard at the top of the stairs clutching onto him like a long-lost lover. From where I stood, I called out. "Oi, do you two need some privacy?"

With the guard momentarily distracted, King hit him with the Taser. We had military grade units that had been fashioned for close combat fights. The guard never had a chance, and he slumped into King's arms.

The problem was that the second guard who had been heading for the balcony saw his partner go down and came back out toward King. Lock was still supporting the weight of the other guy, so I had no choice but to take out my tranq gun and shoot him, the silencer barely making a sound.

I ran to deal with the second body and dragged him to the same room I'd dropped Resnick in. King's eyes went wide, and I turned, almost too late. But Lock had me. He aimed his Taser just over my shoulder and fired. All I heard was a slump several feet behind me.

When I chanced a look, I found the third guard on the ground. "Cheers, mate."

He gave me a nod. After we dealt with all three of them, King went to join Saff and I booked it down the hall toward Nissa and Montgomery.

And then we all heard Gabe's exit strategy. The rocking boom of the explosions. King and I stared at each other. It was unlike Gabe to be so conspicuous. We'd always been trained to make our exits quiet. After all, no one wanted a public firefight, so why the hell had he opted for explosions?

Another boom exploded across the courtyard, and suddenly, the hallway flooded with people, several of them naked.

King went to join Saff and I went for Nissa. But as it turned out, she was already running toward me, with Montgomery tugging her out of the room.

It was pandemonium. Chaos.

Gabe's voice was terse and clipped as he shouted orders. "All teams move in. Move in. The explosions weren't me. I repeat, explosions were not me. Get Igno and move to the egress point however you can."

Nissa's eyes were wide with fear, and that son of a bitch's hand was on her wrist, pulling her behind him as she tried to fight him. Seeing her distressed was the only thing that managed to get my feet moving. Unfortunately, I started moving in the wrong direction after her instead toward my team. She was already out of the danger zone, and Ingo wasn't chasing her. I should have gone after him.

I heard a gunshot and heat grazed my upper right shoulder. Fuck. Those public firefights were avoidable sometimes, and some motherfucker did not have a muzzle on.

My body automatically knew what to do. Duck, take cover, and fire my weapon at the nearest threat. But my brain wasn't where it was supposed to be and cost us seconds we didn't have to spare.

I had to fight not to run after Nissa. Montgomery would cover her. Interpol would cover her. My job was to go after Igno.

I knew that. I hurried and followed where Saff and King had gone, and both were on the balcony of the other room. King was fighting one of the guards. Saff was up and over on the balcony, falling.

Christ.

When I ran to the edge, she was already down and chasing Igno's men, but the crowd had already filled the courtyard with too many panicked people milling around for her to be successful nabbing the bastard. In mere seconds, we'd lost him again.

30

WESTIN

That had been a shit show. Bloody hell. I'd hesitated for just one minute and my team had paid the price. We'd lost Igno.

Not to mention Nissa had almost been caught in the cross-fire. Jesus Christ, Igno was playing to win.

But why blow up his own meeting?

Was there another player on the board? That didn't make sense though. From what we'd heard from Nissa's bug, everything was fine... until it wasn't. But so far none of us knew why.

I pinched the bridge of my nose as I watched Nissa pace back and forth in the loft's living room. She hadn't been able to settle since we'd come back.

Obviously. She almost got blown up tonight.

My stomach cramped at the thought. I hadn't been in the room with her. I'd been trying to fight my way in and save my team. A team she didn't even know I had. The weight of the secrets I was keeping from her were weighing me down. And all I wanted to do was hold her.

"We could have died tonight, Westin."

"I know, I know. But you're okay. We made it out. Julian's okay, too."

She turned on me. "I don't care about him."

I leaned against the door and gave her a tight smile. "Sure, you do. First of all, it's in your nature. Second of all, even though the two of you fight like cats and dogs, there's still a part of you that wishes he'd been the father you needed. There's a part of you that wanted to care about him. That wanted him to be everything he should have been. That part of you won't wish ill on him. That part of you loves him."

"He kept my sister from me. I hate him for that."

I shrugged. "Both things can be true. And you're relieved."

"I'm not. He belongs in jail."

My beautiful Nissa. Still hiding from all of her emotions. Burying them so deep that I was the only one who could excavate them. "You want him in jail, *not* dead. At your core, you believe he can change. You believe that you could be the one to change him. While you've been fighting him all this time that I've been back, you've been fighting him for your freedom. You've been fighting for him to see you as you are. You haven't been fighting him for greed or revenge or hate. You've been fighting him because you *want* to love him. You *want* him to be worthy of it. And even though he's not, you love him anyway."

She whirled on me, her bottom lip quivering. "Shut up."

Slowly I pushed away from the door, walking toward her. "The Nissa I know loves deeply. Once the roots take hold, that's it. The Nissa I know, despite anger or the need for vengeance or justice, doesn't wish death on anyone."

A tear ran down her cheek, and she swiped it away. "It would be easier if I could control how I felt. I don't want to feel like this. Out of control, like my life isn't my own. Why can't I just make my feelings do what I want them to do?"

When I reached her, I took her face in both my hands. "We're not talking about Julian anymore, are we?"

She shook her head, the tears flowing freely now. "I couldn't turn off how I felt about you. And seeing you on the ground tonight. I just—" She tried to shake herself loose from my hold, but I dropped my forehead to hers and forced her to keep looking at me. To speak the truth. "I was afraid I'd lose you forever."

I held her tight, wishing I could take away the pain, wishing that there was something I could say to make any of it remotely better. "I've got you. I'm going to hold you for as long as you need, okay?"

She nodded, lifting her head from my shoulder to glance up at me. "I know what I need."

"What? Your favorite takeout? Just name it."

"You were right before when you said I was the one holding off. The reason that we hadn't... You know..."

I frowned then. "Nissa, we can talk about this later. Right now, this is—"

She shook her head and placed her delicate fingers on my lips. "I really want to forget. I want to hold onto the one thing that's made me smile in the last couple of weeks, and that's you."

"You are holding onto me now."

"I have been hiding. I've been too scared to jump, and if anything, tonight taught me to take the happiness I can right away. Waiting is a waste of time."

"Nissa..."

"I know what I want, Westin, and it's always been you."

Nissa

All I wanted was him.

When he kissed me, an inferno erupted between us. He licked into my mouth and our tongues danced as they chased each other. We fought each other with urgent desperation as we tugged and pulled at our clothing, until we stood before each other in nothing but our heated skin. When he lowered us to the couch, his eyes glowed with a feral hunger as he stared at me. His lips scorched along my flesh as his hands explored me with a fierce hunger until I was trembling from head to toe. When he raised his eyes, the plea was almost tangible.

"Yes."

And then he was on me, kissing and licking and tasting, but there was no frenzied, pulling need. No. This was tender. Softer. Gentler. The soft tugging of his lips made my hips arch.

"Westin, please..."

Instead of hurrying, he pulled back and watched my breasts as I dragged in breath after breath. He kept his gaze on me, and I felt the heat of it washing over my body. My skin prickled in anticipation, and my nipples pebbled under his gaze.

"I want to taste you," he murmured, his voice low and raspy, making my heart skip a beat as he came closer and brushed his tongue along the edge of my nipple.

His mouth was warm against my sensitive skin, and when he suckled softly, I groaned with pleasure. His hands moved down my body to cup my hips as he explored every inch of me with his mouth, licking and nibbling until I was panting for more.

He finally arrived at my right nipple and locked eyes with me as he moved his thumb in circles around it. "I'm in love with your nipples," he said huskily. "They're so sensitive."

My eyes shut as I rolled my neck back and begged, "God, Westin. Please."

"I know, Beauty. And I'm going to give it to you. But first, I need to taste. The other night was just a tease. I've been thinking about your taste ever since. Sugar and sin."

He moved to the other breast, giving it equal attention before returning to the first one again. His hands were everywhere, and his mouth never stopped until both of my nipples were hard peaks begging for more of him. He finally pulled away, leaving me wanting more.

Breathless, I opened my eyes to find Westin watching me with an intensity that made my heart flutter wildly in my chest. He moved lower as he kissed down my stomach. Using his thumb, he traced over my clit softly, making me shiver. "It's not nice to tease," I pouted.

"Then by all means, let me not tease. It's been so long, Beauty. Don't hide from me.

Biting my bottom lip, I inhaled and parted my thighs.

"Wider," he growled through clenched teeth. "I want to see how wet your pussy is for me."

I obliged, but apparently it wasn't good enough, because he bracketed my thighs with his hands and splayed me out before him. "Just as I thought. Bloody perfect."

His fingertips glided over the skin between my legs before lightly tracing circles around my clit, making it swell in response. I gasped when one finger slowly slid through my slickness, then penetrated, fucking me gently until I started raising my hips, asking for more. My eyes widened in surprise at the intensity of pleasure that coursed through me as he moved his finger in a steady rhythm.

He removed his finger and replaced it with two more until I was panting from pleasure overload. His hand moved faster, and I couldn't take any more.

Then he tasted me in one long, slow stroke that sent electricity through every single nerve ending in my body. I clenched around him tightly as if begging for release from this sweet torture. But instead of giving into what I wanted desperately, he continued to tantalize me until I felt like I was going mad from wanting him, from needing him inside of me now, but still he drove me higher and higher.

With his free hand, he cupped my breast, rolling the nipple between his thumb and forefinger, tugging gently as he suckled on my clit.

His moan was low and throaty. "I've been waiting for weeks. No way am I rushing this. You and I, we're happening. And before *we* happen, I'm going to make you feel so good you will never question who you belong to."

I nodded up and down. I would have agreed to anything at that point. Anything at all. His thumb slid over my clit, and I yelled out. "Oh my God."

He did it again, slower this time, applying more pressure to my clit, and my hips bucked up off the couch. "More... please."

And then his mouth, oh God, his mouth. He planted it over my clit again as his fingers made shallow thrusts, sucking, teasing, pulling me deep down under the abyss. Oh fuck, I was going to die. I was going to die just like this. With him sucking, licking, taking me to the edge, making me feel alive. Begging me to fall, begging me to come apart and give him what he needed from me.

I was so close to the edge and Westin sensed it, pushing me closer and closer. His fingers were driving me mad with pleasure as they thrust in and out of my wet core. His mouth making its way up and down my body, licking and sucking at all the most sensitive spots.

Just when I felt like I couldn't take any more, he pressed his thumb onto my clit one last time sending me over the edge. A wave of pleasure crashed over me like an exploding star in the night sky as I screamed out his name.

Westin kept going, intensifying my orgasm until finally it passed and he released me from his grip. He smiled down at me with a satisfied look on his face as if he had accomplished exactly what he had set out to do.

My body still trembled from the intensity.

I couldn't move. I was broken. Death by orgasm. Surely, this was why they called it *la petite mort*.

Westin rolled back on his heels and pulled a condom for his wallet.

I wish I could say I was patient. I wasn't. I reached for him, and he groaned. "Beauty, we need the condom. Just a second."

I watched in wonder as he rolled the latex on and studied him in awe. His length and thickness made my mouth water.

"You keep watching me like that and I'm not sure I'll last very long. Now come here." He sat on the couch and pulled me down, so I straddled his lap.

Westin adjusted my body, and the tip of his erection nudged my pussy. He dug his fingers into my hair, gently tugging me down for a kiss.

He slowly lowered me onto his cock as our lips met, his thick head pushing past my swollen lips, parting them wide. The pressure was intense and delicious as he stretched me. I wrapped my fingers in his hair and raised myself to his mouth. My chest pressed against his face, the rough stubble of his beard abrading my skin as his mouth branded me with gentle sucking and biting. All the while, his hands gripped my hips tight, pulling me down onto his cock over and over, filling me up inch-by-inch until he had filled me completely.

Westin's hips moved slowly at first, then he picked up his pace, like a gymnast showing off his skills. His body was strong against mine, and I held on tightly as he drove me to the brink of pleasure. He thrust in and out and back in again, his erection sliding against my inner walls and tantalizing my g-spot. I arched my back, eager for release again as Westin reached between us, stroking my clit with his thumb.

Just when I felt like I couldn't take anymore, Westin grabbed both my hands tightly in one of his own, anchoring them behind me as he continued to drive into me with powerful strokes that sent shockwaves of pleasure through every part of me. His grip on my hands was fierce as he pushed me closer and closer to the edge.

"Come for me love. Let me see it." His deep voice was a soft growl in my ear, sending chills down my spine. I could feel the delicious pressure building and then suddenly it burst forth in a wave of heat that left me trembling and gasping for air. Westin followed shortly after, his hips jerking against mine as his orgasm crashed into him.

"Holy hell," I murmured as my body sagged against his.

"You, my love, will be the death of me. And I cannot wait," he murmured against my skin.

After easing out of me and heading to the loo to dispose of the condom, he came back, picking me up and taking me upstairs to bed. Pulling the sheets back, I slid in, and he followed, tucking the duvet around us. "Get some rest, Beauty. I think we have some making up to do when we wake up."

31

WESTIN

Nissa turned in my arms as sunlight streamed into the bedroom windows of the loft.

I couldn't think about her beauty or the love she poured forth to me last night. All I could think of was how I'd royally fucked this up.

But do you actually care?

Nope. Not one damn bit. I was fucking keeping her. Gabe, the team, hell, even Julian, would just have to deal with it.

Yeah, he'll deal all right.

And when she found out the truth? The whole charade was going to blow up in my face, and I didn't know if we would be left standing together when it was all said and done.

I was here to protect her.

She would understand.

I'd tried to fight it, but staying away from her was too diffi-cult. Besides, we were inevitable. Maybe a part of me had always known that. But it was done now. Now that I had her in my arms, I couldn't let her go.

She turned in my arms. "You're up early."

"Yeah. Well, you can see why."

She giggled as she lifted the duvet and noted my erection against my stomach.

"See? He misses you already."

She giggled and ducked her head under the covers. "God, you are insatiable."

"Well, I think you have something to do with that as you are the one in my bed."

She lifted her gaze to mine. "This is going to get complicated, isn't it?"

I shook my head. "No. It'll probably get easier now that we're not fighting it."

"Just like that?"

I shrugged. "Maybe not. But I'm hopeful."

"Westin, I—"

I kissed her to keep her from talking.

I didn't want her running or trying to get out of this until we talked. I knew there were going to be tough moments ahead, but I wanted one more kiss before she said something that made the regrets come to light.

One more kiss and then I tried to bring reality slowly back into our lives.

"I need to ask you to do me a favor, please. In light of last night, promise me that you won't go running off on your own. If you're doing anymore sleuthing, I'm doing it with you. I lost years off my life when you were in danger."

She chewed her bottom lip, and my attention wavered slightly, but I dragged it back and put a leash on it. We had to talk about this. "I can do that. I feel like I'm in over my head."

"You're not alone. Okay?"

"And you were right. I didn't want Julian to die last night, even after everything he's done to me."

"You're human. And you care about people whether or not they deserve it."

"Why are you so wise?"

"Well, I made a lot of mistakes. At least that's what my mates will tell you."

"I doubt that." She bit her lip. "Can I meet them?"

I ran a hand through my hair. How was I going to manage that? She thought Gabe was my cousin. He had pushed me to bug her, and he still wasn't convinced she didn't know where the ledger was. He would sell her out to get her father because it would put him a step closer to Igno. And she wanted to meet my fucking mates.

She can meet your mates. She just can't know what they actually do for a living.

That was true. Lachlan and Saint were technically businessmen. They had a real presence in the real world. She wouldn't think anything was amiss.

"You know what? I think that can be arranged."

"Really?" She sat up giddily, pulling the duvet to her chest, which I tugged down. Perhaps a mistake because I immediately became distracted by the view.

"Yes, but first..."

"No, Westin, not now. You said I can meet your friends, and I want to do that soon. I'm dying to know what they are like."

"Yeah, okay, fine. We can make that happen."

"And maybe we can invite them over for dinner. Wouldn't that be nice?"

I lifted a brow. "Um, I'm not sure about that."

It would be awkward as hell having Lachlan and Saffron here, in Lock's flat, pretending it was my flat. Jasper and Kaya would be merciless in their teasing. But she looked so excited about it.

"Okay, I'll make a call and see if I can get everyone together."

"Excellent. What are we going to say? You know... how my

father hired you to be my bodyguard. This is going to be completely awkward, right?"

I winced. But honestly, it was no more awkward than anything else I'd had to do in this farce of a double-cross.

"Okay, okay, okay. Let's do it. Let's have a dinner party."

She laughed and launched herself at me. And as I tugged her down back under the duvet, our lips fusing together before my fingers found her slick wetness and delved inside of her warmth, I knew I didn't want to leave this. I wanted this to be real and for a long time.

Nissa

"You slag."

I glanced around to make sure that Charlie, Westin's relief guard, hadn't heard Jamila.

"Would you keep your voice down?"

"Sorry, sorry. But still, you are sly. Tell me, how was it?"

I glanced around the class, but no one was minding us. Our Law Arguments class was so busy with everyone discussing their papers that were due today.

"What do you mean?"

"Please, I can see it on your face. You totally shagged him."

"Be quiet, Jamila," I hissed.

She giggled and then glanced around. "Sorry. Listen, I'm still not speaking to Adam, so your love life is the only entertainment I have right now."

"How exactly is it working with you living with him and not speaking with him?"

"Well, we derived a very handy way of communicating things in the flat using the blank board on the fridge. Like, 'take out trash' or 'call your mum,' just the basics, you know."

I groaned. "Oh my God, you guys have to work this out. You're my favorite couple. You can't break up."

"Honestly, I don't know what's happening, but I don't want to talk about that. I want to talk about *this*. My sheer and utter joy in you getting dicked down. Let's discuss details. Out with it woman!"

I laughed and covered my face with my hands. "I don't know. We had this thing with my dad. And something went down, and as usual my dad was at the center of it. So I was in my feelings. And for the first time since he's come back, we talked, really talked. Feelings I'd buried came to the surface. One thing led to another and…" I let my voice trail off as I shrugged. "So I kissed him, again."

"Again?"

"Yes. You know, after the break-in, we made out."

"Yes, but has there been more? You are making it sound like more. Are you holding out on me?"

I hadn't told her. "We have kissed a few more times."

"Oh my God, Nissa, this is news I needed to know!"

"I just… I didn't know what to make of it, what we were doing, but I had a bad dream, and you know, one thing led to another, and then we were totally hooking up in the kitchen."

She laughed and took a sip of her latte. "Oh my gosh, please remind me not to eat from your countertops."

I laughed. "Actually, I was thinking of having some people over."

"Oh, to the new fancy flat?"

"Yeah. I want to meet his friends and see who his people are. I met his cousin, Gabe. But he has friends; I just never see them. I don't know where he goes when he's not on duty."

She lifted a brow. "Uh-oh, does he require investigation? Because you know I stay ready to cyber-stalk guys at the drop of a hat."

"Your skills are admirable, but he knows his way around a computer."

"I doubt he can out hack me. I can find out everything about him."

"Maybe we put that on the back burner that for now. I'll try and, you know, get him to talk to me like normal adults."

She sighed and opened her notebook as our professor walked in. "God, if you're going to insist on being mature about it..."

"What am I going to do with you?"

"I don't know. Love and adore me? But it wouldn't hurt you to know something about him, because right now, all you know is that he works for your dad, and that's not exactly a glowing endorsement."

She was right. She was very, *very* right.

"Thanks for the offer. Seriously though, I don't need to access his past. I don't care about that."

And I meant it. Really. I didn't want to know his backstory. What I did care about was if he was lying to me now or not.

"I don't want to go behind his back. I just... I want to know him, and he keeps so much locked in, you know?"

"You know I get it. My boyfriend is heading off to Norway. I'm convinced he has another girlfriend."

I rolled my eyes. "Please, Adam adores you. You can tell by the way he stares at you like you walk on water. He just fucked up. Talk to him. Cold shoulders aren't going to fix it."

She sniffed. "It might make me feel better though. Being petty does have its purpose."

"If it's actually making you feel better, then I endorse it. But I don't think it is."

She rolled her eyes. "Fine, there you go being mature again."

"Speaking of mature, I have a dinner party this weekend

with his friends. Maybe I can pump his friends for information. I just want to know something about him, okay?"

"I will help you come up with probing questions."

"Of course, I would expect nothing less."

Just as our professor instructed everyone to open up our notes from last week's class on compliance, a text came in.

AMELIA: *We need to meet.*

32

WESTIN

IF I WAS the prince of hacking, then Phineas Devlin was its god.

I sat back and listened as Phineas described how he was able to clean the security footage from the mansion where the gala was held.

"So you'll see here, we've got cameras in that room."

My stomach roiled watching Montgomery hold Nissa tightly in place as she struggled. Igno tracked interest in her. There was no sound, but we could tell when the chaos ensued. There was a bright flashing pop outside, then everything went south.

I leaned forward as I watched the playback.

Holy shit.

I almost didn't see it, but Nissa had put something under the table.

What the hell was that?

"Rewind that again please. What the hell did she just do?"

Phineas nodded, his eerie silvery gray gaze landed on mine. "You caught that too? Likely planting a bug."

I cursed under my breath. I was slipping. Why hadn't she told me what she was doing? Had she done this for her father?

For Interpol? She promised me she wouldn't go running off half-cocked. This was worse. It was downright dangerous.

Gabe smirked at me, and I wanted to slap the expression off his face. "You have something to say?"

"Nope. Just surprised at you getting bested by an asset."

"I didn't get bested."

He smirked again and shrugged. "If you say so."

When Gabe and I finished our exchange, Phineas continued his presentation, and it was the last frame that we all focused on. Nissa wasn't the only Montgomery up to something in that meeting.

When all the men in the room panicked and tried to get Igno out, Julian, did something with his phone. It was right next to Igno's. And something flashed on the screen.

"What the fuck was that?" I asked

Lock chimed in. "It looks like some kind of download or something."

I leaned in close to Devlin. "Can you pull in tighter? As soon as Montgomery walks in?"

He did, but I didn't see anything. "Nothing."

"Okay, fast forward. That part where he approaches. What's happening there?" There had to be something.

Devlin leaned forward, cleaned up the video, then whistled low. "Holy shit, do you see that?" He pointed at the screen, and we all had to squint.

I saw it next, Montgomery's hands in his pockets, then a light. It was the accompanying light on Igno's phone that tipped me off. "Holy shit, he's cloning it."

Gabe cursed under his breath. "How much you want to bet the cipher to decode the ledger is on his phone?"

"That means Montgomery has both. He's making a play for Igno's seat.

Saff nodded. "No way Igno let's that happen without

bloodshed."

Gabe nodded. "Your girlfriend is in a heap of trouble, and she has no idea she's walked into a power play."

We needed our hands on that ledger. Igno thought Montgomery had put it away for safe keeping with Nissa, but I knew him better than that. He'd want to look at it every day. "I need to get it back in the house."

Nissa

I rushed to the library that afternoon with my shadow in tow, happy that this guard kept a good distance, didn't bother me, didn't ask questions, and provided no disturbances.

Immediately, I missed Westin. Having someone there to confide in would have made all of this easier to deal with, no matter what Amelia had to say.

When I reached the assignment room, as I'd come to think of it, Amelia nodded at me in greeting as I asked, "What's the emergency?"

"Have a seat."

The hairs at the back of my neck stood at attention. *Was this it? Were they finally going after my father?*

"Amelia, you're freaking me out."

She pulled up her phone and shoved it toward me. "Have you ever seen this?"

I frowned. "No, should I have?"

"This is a ledger. It belongs to Antonio Igno."

"Okay, what's that got to do with me?"

"Your father stole it from him."

"What?"

"Yes. Apparently, this is what Igno has been looking for. We weren't able to capture much from the bug you placed, but we have a few things."

"So he doesn't know I captured any part of the meeting with them?"

"Doesn't look that way. He's preoccupied with your father. Believes he hid the ledger with you."

"What? Why?"

"My guess is your father tipped his hand that he has the ledger, and Igno is taking a guess."

"So it's at the house," I murmured.

"Likely. Your father will want to keep it close."

"If he took the book, it is in his safe. That's where he'd keep it. God can he even read the ledger? Don't these things have like a decoder or something?"

"Are you certain it would be in his safe? Are there any other locations you can think of where he'd stash something?"

"A hundred percent certain. He's so paranoid I'm sure that's the only place he'd stash it."

"I've got the schematics here of your house, I'll send it to you to double-check other options."

"Why do you have schematics of my house?"

" Julian Montgomery amassed a fortune after two of his friends died, and they just happened to be your bodyguard's parents. A massive fortune that seemingly appeared out of nowhere. We've had him on our radar for years."

"And still somehow you haven't managed to put him away until I came along."

"You've been very helpful, Nissa, but I don't want you to do anything dangerous. I'm worried about you now. This could get really messy."

"Wait. You knew he was dangerous and had a child in his care, but you didn't worry about my safety until I'm about to give you all the evidence to capture him? Seems like the time for worry should have been back then."

"That was unfortunate."

"Unfortunate? That's the word you are using?"

"You have to trust someone at some point in time."

She had a point there. I didn't trust anyone. People leave you, lie to you, steal from you. Why should I be in a hurry to trust anyone?

You trust Westin.

But that was different. He literally put his body between danger and myself to keep me safe. Of course, I trusted him.

"I have a dinner scheduled with him. I'll look for it then."

"This is dangerous, Nissa."

"Of course, it is."

Amelia pursed her lips together. "I can't stop you, can I?"

"No, you can't. And I gather that this ledger is extremely important?"

"Yes, it is.

"Then I'll do what I need to do."

33

WESTIN

I FELT like I was having an out of body experience. I was standing in Lock's kitchen, pretending it was mine, making dinner and drinks like these were my best mates. The way Lock and Saint were busting my balls, they definitely talked as if we were friends.

"You're really in this shit now, aren't you?" Saint asked as I carved off an orange peel and put it in Saff's drink. Then I added a lemon peel for Kaya's lemon drop and poured an uncorked chardonnay for Nissa.

Saff and Kaya were keeping Nissa busy in the living room as they chatted.

"I didn't exactly expect this to happen," I sparred back as I finished the drinks and set them on the counter for a moment.

Saint chuckled. "Yeah, well, best-laid plans and all that."

"So do either one of you have advice or not?" I asked Lock as I handed a sample of the chicken marsala over to Saint to taste test.

Lock chuckled. "Fuck, I have zero advice for you. Matter of fact, I think you're toast."

I sighed. "That's not helpful."

"Well, what was I supposed to say? Either way, she's going to be pissed the fuck off when she finds out you are a lying bastard."

"I'm doing my best to make it right, guys."

"My only advice is to be ready to say something. Obviously, you didn't mean to fall in love with her. And she's not going to take it well when she finds out you work for Rogues."

I shook my head as I placed the drinks on the wooden serving tray to carry into the living room. "I'm not talking about Rogues. A part of me thinks that she'll probably understand that. I'm talking about the fact that I have worked for her father for a lot longer than she thinks."

Saint whistled low, grabbed Kaya's drink, and took a sip. "Chivalry is fucked, but this is delicious."

I frowned at him. "Kaya is going to have your balls for stealing some of her drink."

He shrugged. "Actually, you're more afraid of her than I am."

I laughed. "She's coming along with the training, I'm telling you. I'd sleep with one eye open if I were you."

Saint shrugged as his gaze slid over Kaya, the love clear in his eyes. It was funny how easily I could recognize love now.

I was going to have so much explaining to do.

"I'm just trying to get Nissa out of this alive, in one piece, with her father and Igno behind bars and her safe. Anything else is a bonus."

"Are you anticipating problems from Montgomery?" Saint asked as his gaze lingered on Kaya.

As I cleaned up my workspace, I kept an eye on the women, making sure that Nissa handled everything in stride.

"He is focused on Igno and has no idea Nissa has talked to Interpol and she's the one he should really be worrying about."

"Yeah, Gabe had her handler checked out by Interpol. Amelia Jansen. She's so good she's been put in charge of their investigation of Igno. If she gets a whiff that we're involved, this whole thing will come crashing down."

"Are we stepping on toes?"

Saint shrugged. "I can't tell. Gabe is pretty cagey, but the Rogues aren't known for playing nice with our other government teammates."

Lock popped an olive in his mouth. "More and more other departments don't want to play along with us. We're their best kept secret. Everyone likes to quietly fund us on the side, but we only get called in when someone doesn't want to get their hands dirty. So likely, Interpol is going to be the one wanting to keep us very far away from this. If we want to be the one to bring in Igno, we need to keep Nissa out of any plans. She can't know what you're up to."

I frowned at him. "Sure. All I care about is protecting her. As long as she's safe, mate, I'm all good. If I had it my way, I would keep her far away from her father too."

"Easier said than done."

"There will be a lot of explaining to do, but I'm not worried about it. My concern is getting all of us out of there in one piece. Nissa too."

"We have you, mate, there's no doubt you'll get the job done."

Turning into the living room, the ladies were setting up to play Catchphrase, and Nissa seemed to be fitting in very well with Saff and Kaya. She and Kaya looked like they could have been sisters. Their skin a similar hue, and while Kaya wore her hair blown out, Nissa had her curly hair in its natural afro. Nissa reached for her wine, moaning the moment she took her first sip. "Just the way I like it. Tart with a hint of kick."

"I aim to please."

I handed Saff her drink, and she winked her thanks. Kaya looked up from her glass and then scowled at her husband. "Where is the other half of my drink?"

Saint shrugged. "Talk to Roo— uh, Westin. He made it."

It amused me that he'd stopped himself from using my call sign.

Funny, I hadn't been Rook in weeks now. I didn't think I'd feel good taking back my old name, but it didn't make my skin crawl like I thought it would.

If I did keep my name, could I go back to my family's legacy? Would I still want to be part of the Rogues team when Montgomery was behind bars along with Igno?

And what about Nissa?

The twist in my gut told me there were too many questions to be answered tonight. Instead of focusing on all those swirling thoughts I needed to concentrate. This gathering with friends was all that mattered right now. I needed to have fun and enjoy what time I had with Nissa.

What was really fun was watching her with my mates. I watched Saint as he tried to explain the Catchphrase to Kaya. Her guesses weren't bad given that Saint's descriptions were akin to a giraffe trying to play charades.

When the buzzer went off, he groaned and then gave her the answer. She frowned at him. "How was anything you just described even close to wicked witch?"

"I said sinful and supernatural."

"I said 'witch.'"

"But you didn't say 'wicked.'"

Saff leaned in and whispered something to Nissa, who clinked her glass to Saff's. Saint pointed at the two and yelled good naturedly, "Don't you two get too comfortable. It's your turn next."

Nissa laughed as she took another sip of her drink. I warmed as I watched her with my mates.

As they all jeered and cheered over each other, I laughed. Yes, Nissa would fit right in. If she wanted any part of this, that is. I'd told her I wouldn't lie to her anymore, and I wasn't. Well, that's if you didn't count lies of omission. I wanted to be able to tell her what was going down tomorrow, but I couldn't.

First, by telling her I'd only put her in danger. And second, I couldn't risk her warning her father, even though I knew how she felt about him. Things always got complicated with family.

As Lock stood up, bunched up his hands, and attempted to give Saff enough clues for her guess, my phone buzzed in my pocket. The message on the screen made my heart leap.

———

Nissa

"Who's that?"

I hadn't meant to pry. I wasn't snooping. The moment his phone lit up he'd looked down. He had facial recognition which immediately unlocked his phone and the message appeared boldly on the screen. "Confirmed for tomorrow."

What the hell was that? What was confirmed? I grinned at him, expecting him to explain something, but he didn't. Instead, he leaned forward and kissed me on the nose.

"It's nothing."

I hated that.

He was so used to holding back. So used to keeping things close to his chest. I just wanted to get to know him, fill in some details about who he was and what we were doing. Be on the inside of his life instead of dangling on the precipice of the wall he created around himself.

Nissa, be happy that you are getting this, I chided myself inwardly.

He probably meant more to his friends than anyone else.

That was obviously true based on the easy way they sat together tonight. Sure, they were ridiculously good-looking. But they all had that same ease of motion, the same ability to adapt to their surroundings like chameleons.

Of course, I knew who Lachlan King was. The heir apparent to King Media. And a billionaire. Westin said they'd met at a club, but Westin didn't really seem like the club-going type to me. We hadn't gone to a club once. And to be fair, Lachlan King hadn't been in the tabloids for well over a year. Almost as though the moment he'd met his gorgeous fiancée he'd given up that party boy lifestyle.

And as for Jasper Saint, he was a tech mogul. It made sense why he and Lock were friends. But there were moments when it seemed as if he didn't even like Westin. Like now, while Kaya and Westin high-fived each other after she answered one of Westin's clues. Jasper's eyes narrowed just a tad, or enough for me to feel the tension there. Which told me maybe there had been something with Westin and Kaya?

And then there was Saffron. Possibly the most beautiful woman I'd ever seen in my life. Gorgeous dark skin, beautifully done braids. I needed to ask her where she'd gotten them done. I really wanted to change up my look. It had been years since I'd had braids. Julian hadn't liked them.

When I was fourteen and he'd traveled, I begged my nanny to take me to get it done. When he returned, he told me I looked common and made me take them out. He didn't exactly like my natural curls either. He always insisted I needed to straighten my hair to look appropriate for his endless functions and school. That was until I'd turned sixteen and told him that if he didn't want his daughter to look Black, he shouldn't have slept with a Black woman. If he was embarrassed, I couldn't tell, as it still didn't stop his commentary on my hair.

Saff was watchful. Oh, but she was fun. Chatty. Amiable. But it was as if she was constantly processing information. She seemed unsure of me, Westin, and our relationship.

Westin wrapped an arm around my shoulders, and I gave him a small smile. Unfortunately, between Saff's inquisitive gaze and Westin lying about the phone call, my easygoing demeanor from earlier had disappeared. I had a lot on my mind, and the distraction seemed to be showing.

When my phone went off, I groaned and looked at it, wishing I had shut it off.

ARSEHOLE: *Make sure you're on time tomorrow.*

I groaned, and Westin hugged me tighter. "What's wrong?"

"It's Julian, reminding us that we've been summoned to the house tomorrow and we are not to be late."

Westin groaned. "You'll be okay. You won't be alone."

"I know. But it doesn't stop me from being worried though."

Antonio Igno wanted something bad enough to send people after me. I was afraid of what lengths he would go to get it.

"Are you sure you want to do this?"

I slid my gaze to Westin. "Do I have a choice?"

He shrugged. "Not really. Your father is adamant that you return for these dinners, so let's do this. Remember, I'm right by your side. Nothing bad is going to happen to you while I'm around, okay?"

I knew I could trust him. I'd always known I could trust him. It was my father I didn't trust. My father was unpredictable, at best.

He lifted a brow, watching me as I took his hand and marched up the stairs to the front door. "No surprises, right?"

"No surprises." The lie felt bitter on my tongue, but I couldn't tell him. For a start, I wasn't a hundred percent sure if the plan was going ahead. And even if I was, I couldn't risk it.

Dennis answered the door with a flourish. He took our coats, leaving Westin looking dashing in his navy-blue pinstripe suit and me in a strapless, sequined rose-gold gown. Then Dennis ushered us to the study.

It was hard enough to pretend not to watch Westin with one person. It was nearly impossible to pretend in a room full of people. It was easy to sneak sidelong glances. To watch for him. To feel his gaze on me.

I was ready for this. My necklace had a camera in it, and all the while it was taking pictures of everyone who attended. Pictures of the layout of the house I had grown up in. Pictures of all the bodyguards. I was getting it all.

Anything and everything required to take down my father. To my chagrin, Westin was right. I didn't want Julian hurt. I just wanted him to pay. And the easiest way to do that for me was to send his arse to jail. Amelia had assured me that would be the outcome. This wasn't a hit job. Interpol wanted him in *custody*. They had many questions for him. And he was a valuable asset to them if they could get their hands on him.

At one point I was at the bar, getting a glass of champagne, and the shiver of cold skipping up my spine was my only warning before somebody leaned in. A part of me hoped it would be Antonio Igno so that I could say the phrase, and Amelia and her men would come rushing in. It wasn't Igno, but this man had also been at the meeting. What was his name? Terrence something or other.

"You look beautiful as always." He traced a clammy palm down my exposed spine in my backless dress, and I shuddered.

Deftly, I stepped out of touching distance using my glass of champagne and an arm as a distance maker. "We've only met once. What was your name again?"

"You wound me. But that's all right. If a beautiful woman doesn't hurt your feelings at least once, you're not doing something right."

I furrowed my brow. "That statement is actually quite disturbing."

"What's disturbing is that you and I have yet to dance."

"She's occupied." Westin's voice was low and menacing

behind me. I could hear the light growl in it, and it made me shiver in a good way.

Terrence didn't like being thwarted. "Does Montgomery know the help is talking to his guests?"

Westin smiled. As beautiful as he was with those sparkling, Mediterranean blue eyes and the frame and elegance of a gentleman, there was an edge to that smile that should have warned Terrence off.

But it seemed Terrence was a complete git. "Now sod off, I'm talking to the young lady."

But when he tried to take a step toward me, Westin stepped between us. "I might only be the help, but my sole job is to keep offensive, sweaty, paunchy geezers like yourself from bothering Miss Montgomery, and I take my job very, *very* seriously."

Terrence glanced around then, looking for help. But anyone within earshot had already skittered away, leaving him to his own devices. And everything about Westin's stance said that his protection detail happily came with bloodshed.

When Terrence finally skulked away, Westin inclined his head politely to anyone watching, as merely my bodyguard letting me know that now all was well, and I could resume my duties. Anyone else would have missed the wink entirely.

Later that night, I entered my old bedroom and waited for Westin to knock on the door. Nervous excitement made my stomach flip. I knew he should stay away. It would be safer if he stayed away. At the same time, I knew he wouldn't be able to. Nor did I want him to. The idea of sleeping in this house by myself, made me uneasy.

Who are you kidding? You want him. His little aggressive display downstairs made your insides melt and your mouth drier than the Sahara.

I didn't make the rules. His little show of possession had made me weak.

While I was expecting his knock on the door, I squeaked in panic as one of the hidden panels slid aside. And in walked Westin wearing a pair of gray joggers and a T-shirt.

"Holy shit. You scared me."

"Sorry. For obvious reasons, I couldn't come in from the hallway." His shrewd gaze studied me. "Are you okay? You look on edge."

I shook my head. How did I explain it? The zinging energy, the need to be near him, the adrenaline flooding my veins. "Yeah, I'm fine."

He smirked as his gaze narrowed on mine. "Oh. You're not edgy because of what happened downstairs with that Terrence bloke. You're edgy because you want me."

I bit my bottom lip to keep the smile from peeking out. "Cockiness is not a good look on you."

He very deliberately looked down at his joggers. "I don't know. I feel like I have an excellent imprint here. These are just the right thickness, enough to give you a tease but not overwhelm you."

He said it was such a straight face that I almost thought he was serious, but then I could see the mirth in his eyes. The giggle escaped before I could stop it as I launched myself into his arms.

"Shut up and kiss me. Also, if you could get all growly like you did with the bloke downstairs, that would be excellent."

"You like me growly do you?"

"Oh, very much."

"Bend over on your hands and knees on the bed."

WESTIN

I watched as she licked her lips nervously. "What, are you going to spank me?"

"Do you want to be spanked?" His voice sounded like gravel. "Do you understand that you distract me when I'm supposed to be focused? All I can think about is touching you again. I'm not supposed to be here."

I unsnapped the buttons along her spine in a swift motion, my eyes on her arse. I wanted to bite it. And spank it. And Christ, I wanted to fuck it. Would she let me?

I needed her too damn much. And now here she was, offering herself up to me. My cock twitched painfully in my joggers, and I tried to rationalize with my inner demons. Telling them that they didn't want out.

Shaking with anticipation, I looped my hands in the waistband of her leggings and yanked them down her legs.

Her gasp was sharp, but she didn't protest.

In the darkness, I could just make out the sweet lips of her pussy, and I wanted to bury myself inside her deep and never come up for air. Her scent surrounded me even as I fought for some measure of control. But it was no use around her.

With her knees apart, I helped her tug the leggings and her thong all the way off her legs.

When her legs were bare, I repositioned her so that her legs were parted, bracing her on the bed properly in the perfect position for me to slide home.

But as her scent wrapped around me, driving the need that took over my body, I knelt behind her. "So fucking pretty."

The first taste of her on my tongue was better than anything I could think of eating. She was sweet and spicy, and I lapped at her swollen lips like a starving man. *Please, God, please let me die like this. Let this be my final resting place.*

Her breathy moans spurred me on, and I spread her lips with

my fingers, exploring every inch of her. Unable to leave any part of her unexplored. When I wrapped my lips over her clit, she moaned my name and scored her nails on the bed linens. That's what I was looking for from her. Something deep and primal drove me on. I had to mark her as mine. I flicked my tongue against her clit, and she moaned. And when I slid a finger into her, pressing the raised flesh at the front of her tight, silken walls and stroking her G-spot, she came around me with a tight grip on my finger.

Watching her come, knowing I'd taken her there, should have calmed me a little, but it didn't. It just drove me harder. I wanted *more*. Wanted to make her beg to come again and again and again.

I kissed her inner thighs before standing behind her. I quickly shed my clothes and grabbed a condom out of my wallet. Her smooth, wet lips beckoned me, and I couldn't resist sliding the bare tip of my cock through her folds.

"Oh my God," she ground out.

When I aligned the tip to her sweet opening, I could still feel the tremors of her around the head of my cock. I stood perfectly still, letting her convulse around me, before I pulled back with a growl.

Sliding the condom on, I aligned myself back to her slick core.

Nissa canted her hips backward, and I bit my bottom lip. *Go slow, go slow, go slow.* But I was too far gone to listen to my meddling brain. She was so wet, and I slid all the way in with no resistance. Like she was made for me.

She gasped and dropped her head as I drove into her again and again. Her inner walls stroked me, massaging steadily. My blood boiled, and I gritted my teeth against the impending orgasm, the feeling of freedom within reach. But it didn't come. Focusing all my attention on her and the sensation around my dick, I gripped her hips tighter, my fingers pressing into her soft flesh.

The sweat dripped off my brow as I filled her, so high on the feeling of being inside her that I never wanted to be anywhere else.

As I fucked her from behind, Nissa cupped her breasts and moaned as I thrust in and out of her, my grip on her hips steely. Her eyes were half-closed, mouth slightly open as if in a trance. I leaned into her neck, my chest against her back, nipping at the soft flesh there and breathing heavily as our bodies slid together in rhythm.

Wrapping my hand around her throat, I squeezed slightly, eliciting a gasp from her. The feeling of control was almost too much for me, but it felt so good at the same time, as if all the power in this moment was concentrated between us two and we were one unstoppable force of passion and lust. "Play with yourself," I growled, feeling her inner walls quivering around me. "I want to feel you coming around my cock."

She obliged, slipping one hand down her belly and teasing her clit. With each rub of her finger against that sensitive bud, she chanted my name like a prayer, sending sparks of pleasure throughout my body.

With a snarl, I released one hand and joined it to hers, sliding over her clit. I tried to rub faster, but she slowed me down. I tried to control it, but she intertwined our fingers, making me take my time.

I ground into her from behind as we moved together, her tight walls gripping me like a vice as my hips crashed against hers. As she dragged out each moan and gasp of pleasure, I felt myself getting closer and closer to release. Our breathing grew ragged and our movements desperate as if trying to capture a feeling too fleeting for words.

But it stayed just out of reach. I needed to see her face. I pulled back, sliding from her, and turning her over. Our eyes locked for a moment, and I saw the heat and desire in them. She was just as addicted to me as I was to her.

I settled between her thighs, and my gaze slid down her body. I swallowed thickly, homing in on her wet lips where I wanted to bury myself again. My hands found purchase around her hips, my thumbs brushing circles against her skin.

I leaned down and kissed her. All it took was her tongue sliding over mine, and the promise of bliss was back. I started to spiral out of control again, but in a good way.

Nissa anchored me.

She took my hand and slid it to her breast, and I relished the softness of her skin. "Nissa," I breathed. She arched into my caress, seeking more of my touch.

The emotion welled inside me until I thought my heart might burst with it. I wanted time to stop, to savor the moment forever, but that wasn't going to happen as her smooth, soft thighs squeezed my hips while she rose to meet me. My thumb traced over a nipple, rolling it between my fingers, and she threw her head back, gasping my name.

Slowly, I pushed inside of her again, inch-by-inch, until I was fully sheathed within her tight walls. I paused there for a beat as we both savored the feeling of being so connected. Then I moved slowly at first, gradually picking up speed as our bodies welcomed the pleasure that only we could give each other.

Nissa's moans grew louder with each thrust, and she grabbed onto my shoulders tightly as if trying to hold us together forever. Her long legs wrapped around my waist, pulling me closer while our skin slapped together with each stroke. With her body tightening around me, squeezing me like a velvet fist,

I watched her. The unabashed way she responded brought a smile to my face.

The tremors from her body and the tightening around mine were enough to set me off. I felt myself quickly building as I moved faster, our skin slapping together with each thrust. Even with my eyes closed, I could still see her beautiful face in my mind, in the throes of pleasure.

With a loud gasp, she started to come around my cock again, her tiny convulsions gripping me like a vise. I was right behind her, but before the white-hot flash of heat took me, she fisted her delicate hands in my hair and pulled me down to her neck. And then it was upon me.

My orgasm slammed through me like lightning and I threw back my head in blissful agony. With each spasm of pleasure, I got closer and closer to a kind of relief that words couldn't describe. Unable to keep anything from her any longer, I poured everything I had inside her until we were both trembling and exhausted.

I stayed deep within her for a few moments longer before rolling over onto my back and pulling Nissa next to me in bed. Our bodies were slick with sweat as our breathing evened out and we curled up against each other like two pieces of one puzzle.

35

NISSA

In the morning I racked my brain trying to think of where my father might have hidden the ledger. I hadn't found anything last night. I'd left the party twice, once to search his office safe, and once to search the study. I'd tried the most obvious spots already.

I needed to search his bedroom today.

Behind me, I could hear Westin's footsteps on the marble. I still grinned as I thought of all the places he'd left little bite marks. I glanced back at him as he marched stoically behind me, doing his full bodyguard routine. Stern face, stiff shoulders. Always aware.

But when I glanced behind myself I noticed that his gaze was on my arse. When I lifted a brow, he just winked and then refocused his gaze directly ahead of us.

Careful now, you're getting attached.

I was getting attached. It was so easy to slip back in time and let myself be loved. To let myself believe that I was free. That I could do what I wanted. Be who I wanted. Live how I wanted.

I eased down the wide marble staircase, my fingers delicately tracing down the banister, my flats making little light tapping sounds with each step, and my dress fluttering around my knees and flouncing as I descended.

At the bottom of the stairs I froze, and Westin almost walked right into me.

My one nightmare was standing in front of me in living color. The one thing I didn't want to happen ever again. But there he was like the devil himself come to taunt me. My father was in there with Antonio Igno. He was seated with six other men who'd been at the party last night.

Holy Christ.

Westin tensed next to me.

Igno stood. "Ah, the guest of honor. I have to say, Nissa, you're just as stunning now as when I first met you."

I gave him a wide smile. "Mr. Igno. What an unexpected surprise. I trust my father is showing you hospitality." I'd said it. The phrase. Amelia had to be listening. Would her men barge in? How long would it take?

His gaze shifted to Westin by my side.

A deep frown formed between his eyes. "And who's the young man?"

Oddly, before I could say anything, it was my father who answered. "That's her boyfriend."

It caught me off guard, but Westin went with it straight away.

Igno's brows rose. "I was unaware that Nissa had a young man. This is interesting."

My father shrugged. "Why is it interesting? She's a young lady. I might not like it, but she goes on dates no matter what I think." He gave Westin and I a pointed look, then turned to Igno. "Come, we'll all have breakfast in the sunroom and talk."

I felt like my father was trying to tell me something, but I wasn't sure what it was. He didn't know that Westin and I were together.

Or does he?

What in the hell was going on with him? I didn't know how I was going to get through this now that the ultimate surprise was standing before us.

Breakfast was uncomfortable, to say the least. As we struggled to make small talk my father kept looking up at Westin as if trying to communicate something with him.

Even with Westin at my side, I was hyper-vigilant, all my senses on alert as I tried to keep an eye on the guests as well as my father's business associates.

Throughout breakfast, my father kept watching me. When I walked toward the powder room in the far-left corner of the room, he grabbed me and dragged me down the hall. "What the hell are you doing?" I hissed.

Westin was hot on our heels. "What's going on?"

"You need to get Nissa out of here."

I frowned up at my father. "What are you talking about?"

"Igno, he wants you, Nissa."

My stomach roiled. "What the hell are you talking about, Julian?"

"Somehow he thinks you would be the perfect trophy to taunt me. He wants you. Westin, you know what to do."

Westin was already dragging me toward the door. My heart raced with adrenaline but not nearly as much as it did when we ran straight into the man of the hour.

"Nissa, darling." His voice dripped with mock sweetness. "You're not leaving, are you, sweetness?"

Westin threw an arm casually over my shoulders. "Nissa is not feeling well. We were just going to get some fresh air."

"Oh no, I can't have that. Beautiful girl, if you're not well, why don't you go lie down?"

Westin pulled me into his side. "I'll take her to her room."

Igno smiled that leering, sadistic smile. "Oh, I don't think so.

I'm sure your father has told you I prize loyalty to me above all else."

My father said, "Antonio, this is unnecessary. Any slight you believe my daughter has committed, I will address."

Antonio laughed. "Oh yes, the doting father. But you brought her into our business, so this is your doing. You have no one to blame but yourself. So your daughter stays until I get my ledger back."

"I don't know what you're talking about," I spat back.

He grinned down at me. "Ah yes, this is the part of the conversation where you deny everything, and then you start pleading for your life. And your father's. And this... this so-called boyfriend. I know he's a bodyguard."

Westin shook his head. "No. She's *mine*."

Igno laughed. "If you insist. Then you'll be locked in with her." He turned to Julian. "I assume the ledger is somewhere on the property."

My stomach suddenly became encased in ice as my father sputtered, "I don't know what you're talking about. I do not have your ledger."

"I don't believe a single word you say, Julian. You have until noon to return my ledger to me... and save your daughter's life."

Westin angled his body so it was directly in front of mine. "Over my dead body."

Igno laughed. "I have to say, Julian, your daughter's life is on the line and yet you are preoccupied with matters that aren't nearly as important. I'd think you'd be begging to spare her."

Antonio nodded at one of his security men. "Lock them in her room."

As the security guard grabbed me, Westin immediately placed a hand on his wrist, twisting his arm back. The guard yelped and Westin delivered an elbow to his face. Cold steel pressed to the back of my neck as another guard came at us more prepared

Igno tsked. "You don't make a very good bodyguard. I'd hate to hurt such a pretty girl."

Westin's eyes flicked to mine, an apology and more swirling in their depths. He immediately released the other guard and put his hands up. "Fine, we're moving."

As I rapidly blinked back tears, I turned to the man I now hated more than my own father. "I hate you. I'll make you pay."

"I've heard it all before, love." Antonio stroked my arm, and Westin lunged forward. The click of the safety releasing had Westin freezing in his tracks.

"Stop, stop!" I cried. "All of you stop this. We're going. We'll do what you ask. Just don't hurt him, please."

36

WESTIN

ARSEHOLE: *Are we a go?*

I had missed my check-in time, and now Gabe was trying to figure out what the hell was happening. It had been a long damn day. Twelve hours we'd been locked in with not a word from Julian or Igno.

Thankfully, I could access my messages and the cameras from my watch even though they'd taken my phone. Luckily those twats wouldn't be able to read my messages.

I glanced over at Nissa, who had finally fallen asleep after being a knot of tension all damn day. I jotted a quick note letting her know I was trying to find a way out through the secret passages and not to move.

I hated to leave her, but I had a mission to complete, and this was the only opportunity I was going to get.

How do you think she's going to feel if she wakes up and you're gone?

She would worry.

My gut twisted thinking about it, but this was the only way I was going to be able to keep her safe from her father and Igno.

That is the last time you'll touch her.

I hated to think about it, but it was the truth. Even if she didn't wake up while I was gone, I would have to explain that Gabe wasn't my cousin. Saint and King weren't just my mates. The problem was there was no way on earth she was going to understand. She would feel hurt, betrayed even.

If you pull this off, she'll be hurt... but at least she'll be alive.

I dragged down my boxers and pulled off my shirt. Our bags had been searched and brought back to the room before we'd been shoved in here. Luckily, I hadn't been hiding anything in the bags. I threw on my cargoes and my long-sleeved black shirt, slipped into the corridor behind the panel, and then hustled down the hall, making a right to the stairs where I retrieved my kit that I'd stored the last time I was here with everything I needed in it. I grabbed the flashlight then bent down and grabbed the rest of my gear. Night vision goggles. Check. Ultrathin vest. Check. And most importantly, my weapons. A switchblade, my Taser, and an ankle holster and my gun.

Once I was armed, I headed downstairs to the study. I needed to confirm the ledger wasn't in that safe. Had he already retrieved it for Igno? I didn't think so. Igno had been a complete arsehole this morning, determined to torture everyone there.

I had very little time, and I needed to get my team ready. Even though Nissa had complicated feelings about her father, she still cared about him enough to not want him to die.

I knew she was worried. I knew she didn't want any of this. And I didn't know how to fix it for her.

Do your job. Worry about this later.

I continued down the stairs, my weapon up, I followed the path down to the study, checking the map on my watch, making a right at the end of the hall, and then pausing. Inside the study, I peered through the night vision lenses and saw nothing. It was completely black in the room. I had no way of knowing if Igno had placed cameras in here or if he was aware of what was going on in the house at all. I could only pray that he wasn't.

I moved quickly and efficiently. Behind the desk, I moved the massive Rembrandt aside and placed the decoder I'd programmed myself next to the number pad. I kept my eyes on the door while I waited for the safe to unlock.

Since this required quiet work, I had my Taser at the ready. Probably should have had my gun instead, but I didn't know who would be walking through that door. The decoder beeped at me, and the lights all turned green. I removed it, pocketed it, and swung the safe open. Papers, files, money, a couple of passports, but that was it. *Fuck.* No ledger, which meant it was likely in his office, clear across the house.

I took the passports and put everything else back right where it was. I shoved the passports into my pack so that there would be no escape for Montgomery. He might not be the primary, but he'd mentally tortured Nissa by not letting her know about her sister. He'd hurt her in ways she didn't even know about yet. He wasn't escaping if I had a way to stop him.

Once the painting was back in place, I made my way across the room and slid into the secret hallway. I started running, hitting a right, another right then a short left. Once I reached the door to the office I sent a coded text to the team. Weapon at the ready, I pressed the panel, grateful it didn't make a sound.

I paused when I saw a short shadowy figure standing in front of the safe with a light illuminating the contents, allowing them to retrieve a folder with ease.

The thief leafed through the contents of the file then dropped the folder, the contents spilling on the floor. Surprised, I stared at the photo of me and Montgomery the night he'd sent me running away.

He'd been recording me. *Fuck.*

The thief picked up a flash drive that had fallen out with the rest of the papers and went straight to the computer. Something in my gut told me this was not going to end well. A couple of clicks and Julian's voice came over the speaker. "If you want to live, all you have to do is eliminate her sister, Lenora. It's really very simple. Your life, and let's face it Mrs. Pembry's life, for one girl. You kill her, you get to come back home."

And what was worse was what I said next.

"Okay, I'll do it. But you can never tell Nissa."

"It'll be our little secret."

Sweat popped on my brow. No, no, no. That was all out of context.

Context or not, that conversation did happen. How long had he been keeping that recording a secret? And when was he going to use it against me with Nissa?

A light blinded me as the perpetrator shone his flashlight in my face. I reached for my Taser, but he crouched and launched at me.

This was no man, it was a woman. My heart tried to burst out of my chest and my stomach cramped. "Oh fuck, Nissa? Nissa, stop."

But she didn't stop. Punches were aimed at my face. One of them landed, clipping my cheekbone as I tried to block her shots.

I tried to gain a hold on her without hurting her, but her knee came up, getting me square in the gut. A grunt escaped my lips and I rolled over. When she tried to drop down for an elbow at the back of my neck, I twirled around and caught her by the waist as she flailed, her legs kicking out.

"Nissa, listen to me, whatever you think—"

She managed to jab her elbow between us, creating a space that allowed her an open-palmed shot straight to my dick. I coughed and immediately released her. "Fuck."

She ripped off the mask she had over her head. "I fucking

trusted you, and you killed her. All this time you've been pretending. You're worse than my fucking father. Luckily for me, he keeps meticulous records. What did you do to her?"

I cupped my groin, face planted in the carpet as I waited out the wave of nausea. "It's not what you think, Nissa. I wouldn't—"

"She was my sister, you piece of shit."

And suddenly, from behind her back, I heard the unmistakable click of a safety. I turned around to see Nissa pointing a gun at me. "Nissa, you'd fucking shoot me?"

Nissa

He studied me closely. "What are you doing, Nissa?"

"I asked first, Westin. You promised there would be no more secrets."

His gaze flickered to the window. "Nissa, we don't have time for this. Igno is going to notice that neither one of us is in bed any moment, and he's going to come looking. And then he's going to do something to your father, so let's just go."

"We're not going anywhere until I have answers." I steadied my grip on the gun, and he swallowed hard, hands up.

"Okay, okay, I hear you. We don't have to move. Listen, I'll do what you want, okay? Just relax."

"You are a liar."

"Yes, I am. I'm a trained liar. I had to be. It's called survival. But there are things I haven't lied to you about. One of them being that I love you, and you know that."

"How am I supposed to believe you when you say that?"

"Because it's true. And you can feel it. I know you can."

I shook my head. "I don't know what I feel anymore."

"Nissa, listen to me, I get it. You don't trust what you're feeling, and you're upset. I understand. But listen to your heart, okay? Just listen to your fucking heart."

I shook my head. "I know what you're telling me, and I want to believe you, but now I discover you knew what happened to my sister all along."

"Nissa, look at me, we don't have time for this. Igno is coming. He wants the ledger, and we have to make sure he doesn't get it."

"I don't believe you."

"You know it's true. He's got your father right now."

"I don't care."

"Yes, you do. Because you're still you, Nissa. You can pretend you don't care about him all you want, but he's still your father."

"And he kept my sister from me, and you helped him do that."

"I know, okay? Look, you can be mad at me all you want. I get it. I really do. But in a minute, my whole team is going to come in here, and we need to be gone when they do. I can protect you, I just—"

"Your whole team? You mean my father's people?"

He swallowed hard then. "No. I work for someone else."

I choked out a laugh. "Oh, right. Remember that time you and I looked at each other and we said no more lies?"

"Nissa..."

"No, this is illuminating. I can't wait to figure out what else was fucked up between us."

"Listen to me."

"No, I don't think I will."

I knew what I needed to do, except this was going to hurt. "That ledger, Nissa—"

"It's not here." I lied smoothly. I'd already tucked it into the back of my trousers.

He looked confused. "What do you mean it's not here? I have to find it. Besides, it's no good to you without the cipher."

My brow furrowed. "The cipher? Where did you put it?"

"Your father took it off Igno's phone at the gala. It's likely stashed somewhere in the passages of this house."

"You're lying."

"The point is you will never find it, and the ledger is useless without it."

"I don't believe you," I whisper screamed.

"It looks like we have a trust issue, don't we? Look, I know you won't believe me, but I never hurt your sister. I gave her money. Helped her disappear."

Whispers of the truth tickled my clammy skin. *No. Don't buy it. He's a trained liar.* "I guess we do," I agreed.

"Give me the ledger, Nissa. I can get you out of here safely. We can reunite you with your sister."

The way he said it was like he meant it. Like he loved me. Like he cared about me. But I knew I couldn't trust him, so I fired.

***

Westin

I wheezed at the pain in my left side. I couldn't fucking breathe. Jesus Christ, she'd fucking shot me.

She was furious.

God, this shit hurt. I'd lifted my head to evaluate the damage, but the sheer act of looking up was too much and I laid back down. I pressed my hand against my side to ease the pain but when warmth gushed between my fingers, I pulled back my hands to see... Oh, what do you know? Red. I was fucking bleeding.

Gray started to edge in my vision, but there was movement

in the room, and I tried to lift my head again. This time I managed and saw a shadow in the corner. I didn't have much energy. The exhaustion was pulling me down, telling me it would be easier if I just closed my eyes, but I knew better. I had to stay alert and awake. My team was coming. I just had to fucking stay alert until they got here.

And even though my hand shook, I leveled the tranq at the figure in the corner. Just because I was laying there bleeding didn't mean I had to ditch protocol. The protocol was tranq first, and always shoot only when absolutely necessary.

My eyes felt so heavy, my lids pulling down, down, down. I just wanted to fucking sleep.

But as I forced my eyes to open, and saw a familiar face. And then I bloody wished I *had* shot him.

"Not a fucking word, Gabe."

"You're bleeding all over my shoes, kid."

"Fuck you."

He grinned. "Who shot you?"

"Nissa Montgomery. Apparently, she doesn't like being lied to."

Gabe's brows rose. "Nissa shot you? Shooting you over a lie seems rather extreme."

"She's pissed because she found out I paid her sister to disappear and stay away from her. Hell, maybe she even still believes what her father suggested, that I killed her."

Gabe whistled low even as he bent down to lift my arm and wrap it around his shoulders. "Fucking hell. Do you have the ledger?"

I shook my head. "She does. But I have the cipher. It's in the house in the hidden passages. Nissa took the ledger."

When Tabatha came in through the window, she winced when she saw me. "Oh no, pretty boy, she didn't shoot you in the face, did she?"

I coughed, the pain flaming at my left side. "Fuck, Tabs, don't make me laugh."

"Well, I mean honestly, that face, that body, that's the reason you're here running around looking like a young Brad Pitt." She turned her attention to Gabe. "Do we have what we need?"

He shrugged. "Only part of it. Tell her where the cipher is."

I directed Tabs to the cipher, and she helped Gabe get me on two feet. I wasn't steady, but I could shuffle. I heard shouting, and then... gunfire.

"I can't believe she fucking shot me."

Gabe chuckled. "Well, hell hath no fury and all that."

"Fuck you."

He chuckled again. "I tried to warn you. Focus on the task at hand. Mixing business and pleasure always ends badly."

"Like you fucking know."

I couldn't be sure, because my head wasn't exactly level, but I could have sworn he glanced back toward the tunnel where I'd sent Tabatha. Once we were outside, he handed me off to Tweedle Dee and Tweedle Dum. For once, King and Saint looked concerned. "Fuck, he's bleeding on my shoes."

Gabe shrugged. "He did the same to me."

Saint hauled me up against his body, and I coughed in pain. "Ugh, God only knows what Kaya sees in you. You're not exactly a gentle touch."

"Hey, you're lucky I'm holding you up, man."

On my other side, King held on tight. "Mate, getting shot doesn't seem very bright of you."

"Are you two taking a piss while I'm bleeding, or are we in a cuddle session and going to start making out now?"

King laughed. "Well, I'm actually into Black women with really fine asses, so you don't exactly fit the bill, but I could try anything once."

Over the comm unit, Saff's voice was chiding. "You idiots are on an open line, for fuck's sake."

I smiled when I heard her voice. "Ah, an angel, at last. Why aren't you out here saving my arse? I think you'd have a better bedside manner."

"Someone has to make sure shit gets done. All agents, roll call to egress."

As we all sounded off to make sure we had everyone, I heard gunshots to the west. I glanced over, worried about Nissa. "Does anyone have eyes on Nissa?"

My teammates all replied negatively. A flash of movement had Gabe turning toward the east, and he fired his tranq.

The person went down quick, and he frowned. "They were in tech gear."

We hustled to the far garden. There was a cart waiting that would take us to the servant's exit from the property. I lolled my head back and called out, "To your north."

Gabe whirled, aimed again, and fired. Another man in tech gear.

Saint said, "Those aren't Igno's men. Montgomery's either. That's another party."

Gabe cursed under his breath. "For fuck's sake, why are things so goddamn complicated?"

When the lads had me loaded on the cart, everyone climbed on and Tabatha sprinted to the grass with the speed of a cheetah, lunged on to the back, her foot on the platform that was probably used for golf clubs or some such shit, and hung on for dear life. "I've got the cipher. I tried to find the secondary target, but she's not there."

I winced. "I don't know where she is. Everything went hazy after she shot me."

I could almost hear Tabatha's low growl. "I can't believe she shot you."

I winced. "Well, to be fair, I deserved it. She understands who I am now."

"Ugh, for fuck's sake, you shagged her? Can any of you lot go on a goddamn mission without shagging someone? I go on missions all the time. I shag no one."

The whole cart went silent. The lot of us were basically waiting for Tabs and Gabe to fuck like bunnies. But Gabe was very much all about the rules, and he would never go there with Tabatha. Eventually, Tabatha was going to replace his arse. But still, he made not a single move. All I knew was that it wasn't going to be pretty when she finally got tired of waiting for him.

As we drove out, I heard more gunshots toward the east, and then Saff cursed on the line. "Motherfucker. I see secondary on the cameras."

Gabe cursed under his breath. "What's happening?"

"Our friends in the tech gear, they've just shoved her in a van."

I immediately tried to sit up to get Gabe to turn this cart around and go back for her. She was in trouble. But the edges of my vision faded then turned black. I couldn't save Nissa.

37

NISSA

Westin St. James was a goddamn liar.

As I sat in the back of the van with Amelia, her partner, Nyla Hale, and several other agents, I leaned my head back and willed the tears not to fall. I was not going to cry in front of these people. I was not going to cry period. Not because of him, or the lies he'd told, or what I'd wanted to believe. It was almost easy to believe after last night when he'd looked at me with what could only be described as love.

Fuck him.

God, I hoped he was fucking okay.

Nyla leaned forward. "You did good, Nissa. You did really, really good."

"I don't feel like I did."

I pulled the ledger out from under my shirt and handed it over. "All that trouble for this. And apparently, there's a cipher you need to decode it."

Nyla and Amelia immediately snapped it open. After looking at several pages, they frowned, and Nyla cursed under her breath. One of the other agents, a younger bloke who looked like he was in his mid twenties, took the book from her, took a couple of photos with his phone, and then put it on some machine kind of thing. "We'll send this to headquarters. Have them evaluate it. They'll have something before we pull in."

Nyla nodded. "We heard the gunshot. That's why we came in. What happened?"

"One of my father's men found me in the office grabbing the ledger. He tried to stop me, so I shot him. I think it was just a flesh wound. I'm sure he's fine."

"Which one of your father's men? We want to account for everyone."

"It doesn't matter who. Besides, I don't care about any of them. What about my father?"

Amelia looked at Nyla, and Nyla shook her head. "I'm sorry. We didn't get him."

I banged my head against the side of the van. "Are you kidding me? All of that and you still didn't get him?"

"Not yet, but we will. With this evidence, we're going to get Igno too."

I opened my eyes. "Well, I hope you're happy. I hope you two got everything that you needed because my life is in complete shambles."

Amelia placed a hand on my knee. "Don't say that. You came out on the other side of this. You can go back to your life."

"Can I? Can I just go back to school next week as if none of this ever happened?"

"Igno is on the run. Your father is on the run. There's no reason for them to come for you. And you'll be protected. We wouldn't just put you back out in the wild without someone watching over you. You'll be fine."

I lifted my head and then shook it. "I am anything but fine."

For the next two hours, I closed my eyes and tried not to worry about Westin. I tried not to wonder if he'd gotten help or if he had a way out. I just couldn't get past the look on his face when he caught me in my father's office.

The dread and emptiness threatened to consume me. All along. He'd been the thing to fear.

I couldn't believe how things had gone down. All I had to do was get the damn ledger and give it to Amelia. That was it. One ledger, one last task, and I was home free to be with Westin, and my father could go to jail. Dangerous but simple. Instead, Igno had shoved Westin and I between a rock and a hard place.

Once we reached one of the bland stone buildings in Central London that could have easily been a bank, or a prison, or a school, for all I knew, we climbed out of the van, and Amelia and Nyla lead me to the equivalent of what looked like a small conference room, or maybe an interrogation room. "Have a seat. We'll get you something to eat."

I shook my head. "I'm not hungry."

Amelia sighed and sat opposite me. "Can you tell us anything else about what happened today?"

"No. Like I said, I don't know anything. I didn't know Igno was even going to be there until he showed up at breakfast this morning. The moment I saw him, that's when you got my SOS prompt. Then he threatened to kill me unless Julian delivered the ledger. Westin and I were locked in my room for hours."

Nyla nodded and looked down at her pen. "Right, Westin St. James. He has worked for your father for a long time."

"I guess so. It turns out I didn't really know much about him."

Nyla lifted a brow. "Okay, but didn't you two grow up together?"

I shrugged. "He lived with our housekeeper on the edge of the grounds. We saw each other sometimes, and he became my bodyguard a few years ago. But that didn't last long. He abandoned me. He only came back a few weeks ago."

"Where did he go when he left?"

"I don't know." *To kill your sister.* Or...Maybe he just made her disappear like he said. Either way. He made sure I never saw her again.

Fuck my life. How had I fallen for it all again? Believing that Westin cared about me. Believing that I was not completely alone in this world. I'd trusted Westin, opened up my heart like a fool. He made sure I would never see her again.

That's not him. You know it's not. He wouldn't. You know him.

I shoved those thoughts away. The truth was I wanted to believe him. I wanted to believe *in* him. But that wasn't the true Westin.

As much as I wanted to believe he wasn't the one pulling the strings, I couldn't. All this time he'd known I was looking for her, and he'd said nothing. I couldn't forgive that.

As much as Nyla and Amelia wanted me to believe that I could just go back to my life, I couldn't. Because now my life would be something completely different. The moment Westin came back, he'd changed me. For better or worse, I was a completely different person. I couldn't go back to the ignorance. I couldn't go back to pretending I was fine, not when I was really searching for something meaningful, for family. I thought I had found it. But clearly, I was wrong. He'd cost me all the family I'd ever known. My sister, my father, and I hoped to God I never saw him again.

WESTIN

I woke up in bed, groggy and tired, with a dull ache in my side.

"How long have I been out?"

"A few hours. The doc said it was through and through."

I nodded and tried to sit up. I winced when steel bit into my wrists. "What the fuck?"

Saint grinned. "Oh, our arsehole leader assumed that you'd try some dumb shit like trying to get up."

"I'm fine. You said it was through and through, right?"

Saint shrugged. "Yeah, mate, but you've been shot. So Kaya and Saff made us promise we wouldn't let you die. If you make a liar out of me, my wife will kill me. And I am more afraid of her than I am of you. So do us a favor and stay down."

"That's bullshit."

"You're in no shape to go after her anyway."

While that might be true, he didn't need to say it like that. "I've never liked you."

He grinned and gave me his usual cheeky wink. He was back in twenty minutes with our broody leader in tow. Gabe greeted me by saying, "Ah, there's the idiot now. You going to try and get yourself killed again?"

"I need to find her. Whatever Interpol has her messed up in, it's dangerous."

Gabe sat in front of me. "I'm inclined to agree." He turned his tablet to face me. "But we have a leg up since you got us the cipher for the ledger."

"What about Interpol. Did they get anything?"

Gabe pressed his lips together. "They have the ledger."

"Fuck me."

"Maybe when you're feeling better. Right now, you need to rest up. I have feelers out to Interpol. They have something we want, and we have something they need."

"Do I sense a team-up in the works?"

Gabe laughed. "It's almost as if you haven't been paying attention at all. While Rogues have the same directives for king and country and all that, we also have different ideas about how that should be done. As well as different ideas about the usefulness of our enemies once we capture them."

"So, in essence, we want to be the ones to capture them, not Interpol."

Gabe nodded. "So, we have a couple of options. Go in, ask them nicely, and retrieve the ledger. In essence... play nice. "

I laughed. "There's no way in hell Nissa's giving up that ledger. Not if she thinks they can put her father away. Which is all she wants."

Gabe nodded. "Well, I was afraid you were going to say that. The other option is we can go in and take her. And then we'll take the ledger. But it will be a fight."

"You don't honestly mean to go in and take her from Interpol? We would lose men."

"Right. Which is why it's not ideal."

I had a feeling there was going to be a catch and I wasn't going to like it. "Fuck. I just came in from undercover."

"I'm not asking you to go back, I'm merely laying our options before you. We have the cipher, they have the ledger. We'll work together. But I promise they won't talk to us unless your girlfriend says so. So you're going to have to go and say sorry for whatever you did to tick her off."

That was never going to work. "Fuck that shit. Besides, I don't have a girlfriend."

Gabe laughed. "Have a look around, mate. She's in this up to her eyeballs. And isn't she the one who snatched the ledger out right from under you? She's involved. So we can do this the easy way, or we can do this the hard way. When it comes to Nissa Montgomery, my feeling is, you probably want to do this easy."

I sighed. "When do we leave?"

"As soon as you're dressed."

"Well, I suppose I should be happy you waited until I was awake. How do you think this is going to go?"

"In an ideal world, you'll walk out of there with the ledger and the cipher. They see sense. They back off. We grab Igno."

I laughed. "You can't be that naive."

Gabe chuckled again. "Oh, I promise you, I'm not. I said in an ideal world. The most likely scenario is they'll want us all to go after Igno together. And you and your girlfriend are going to play nice."

I frowned. "She's not going to want anything to do with me."

He laughed. "Don't sell yourself short. I'm sure you can be very convincing if you need to be."

WESTIN

Gabe checked my vest. "Are you sure you can do this?"

"Yeah. I've got this." It was a lie. Just the pain meds talking.

"Are you sure she's going to be there?"

I rolled my eyes. "She'll be there. We have history. Just make sure that we're clear. No one else goes in or out."

Gabe shrugged. "Your funeral."

"Hopefully, it doesn't come to that."

I didn't know what kind of contacts he'd had to pull to let us have access to the library, but it was a nice neutral spot with plenty of exit points. Tonight, was about reaching a truce. We both wanted the same thing... to bring Antonio Igno down. When I passed Saint and Lock, they both gave me a nod and then grinned.

"Stop looking at me like I'm on my way to my funeral, team. I got this."

Saff frowned. "You seem sure, but don't forget she's unpredictable."

"To you, maybe, but I know her. She's mad, but she's not capable of hurting me."

Saint just rolled his eyes. "Mate, have you forgotten she already shot you once? I'm sure she'd be more than happy to do it again. But I'll let you figure it out for yourself."

At the entrance of the library, I put my earpiece in and walked in the front door.

I found Nissa right at the center, near the librarian's desk, and I raised my hands above my head. "See? I'm unarmed."

She grinned. "I see you have a vest on though. That means you think I might hurt you."

I shrugged. "It wouldn't be the first time, would it?" My gaze raked over her hungrily. "You're wearing a vest yourself?"

She grinned then, her thick hair cascading down her back when she laughed. "Oh yes, trust but verify. When someone already proves to be a liar, one has to act accordingly."

"How did we get here?"

She shrugged. "You told me you were back to protect me and to help me. I believed you. I trusted you when you said you cared about me. I shouldn't have done that."

"It was the truth, Nissa."

She sucked in a deep breath. "Maybe, maybe not. But the point is, we've got a situation on our hands that we need to resolve."

"That we do. We both hold half of the puzzle. And as my commander said on the phone, he's willing for us to work together."

She cocked her head. "A commander. You know what, it's becoming more and more clear that I didn't even know who you are, at all."

"I'm still me."

She frowned when she stood up. "Oh, yeah? Who's that?"

"Do you care to know? Can't you get me out of your mind?"

She slapped her hands on the desk. "You don't get to ask me those kinds of questions."

"So how does this work anyway? We'll bring Interpol in, but Rogues are on point."

She laughed. "There's no fucking way. Interpol is in charge."

I shook my head. "Pleasure doing business with you."

I turned to stalk out, and I thought she was going to let me. It wasn't until I hit the landing on the second floor that she called out. "Fine. Rogues takes point."

"Good. We'll need to work together. Determine who's going after him."

She laughed. "Obviously, I'm going."

I shook my head. "The fuck you are. You're just here to negotiate. You're not trained."

"You know, it's fascinating how little you think of me."

My gut was churning with raw emotion as I watched her. My beautiful Nissa, a completely different person than I'd known. A completely different woman. One who couldn't trust me.

Whose fault is that?

"I didn't need you saving me. I never have."

"Nissa, is that what you think this is? I know you don't need to be *saved*. I know you don't need *me* to save you most of all. But I know your feelings about your father are complicated. You love him, and that's okay. You're supposed to. But you want vengeance too. And that's a dangerous road."

"I may not want him to die, but I do want him in prison. And right now, this is the only way to do that. So like it or not, I'm coming."

I ground my jaw so hard I could feel the pain radiating into my skull. "Be careful what you wish for, Beauty, because you're right, I'm not exactly the man you think I am."

WESTIN

Two days later, Rogues paid a visit to Interpol's London offices. I wasn't sure what I expected. There were certain connotations that came with the image of Interpol. But this looked like an office building where people made decisions about who lived and who died, depending on the agenda.

Nissa walked next to a brunette who led the way for me and Gabe, and no one spoke as we walked. She wouldn't even look me in the eye. And maybe that was for the best, because Gabe was already suspicious of what happened in the library. But all he knew was that we were mission go, and now we needed some details.

Nyla had us take a seat, and Amelia came in with some sodas and snacks.

I sat back watching the whole room. "So, what are we doing?"

I thought Nyla would lead the way, but it was Amelia who spoke. "We appreciate your willingness to work with us as a team."

My gaze lifted to Nissa as she kept her eyes resolutely on Amelia. "We all want this done."

She nodded. "Understood. We only need a small team. Obviously, Montgomery wants Nissa and Westin. We're not going to give them to him, but we need to at least, make the appearance of an effort."

"Rook."

Amelia frowned. "What?"

"His call sign is Rook," Gabe stated matter-of-factly.

Amelia's gaze met mine. Her eyes were intelligent, curious, with a slight hint of mischief. "Rook. Fair enough."

Nissa kept her gaze fixed straight ahead.

Amelia continued. "When we raided Montgomery manor, Montgomery and Igno scattered like the roaches they are. They headed to Igno's compound in Greece. Montgomery has reached out to Nissa to bring him the ledger. Nissa and Rook will go in with the appearance of being alone. Our teams will go dark. We won't be sending a battalion. Interpol only wants Montgomery at this point."

"You can have Montgomery. All we want is Igno," Gabe said through gritted teeth.

"Of course, you do. The only person that would be able to tell if the ledger is a forgery is Igno. But Montgomery's not likely to be with Igno when Nissa hands it over. So we've got our counterfeit team working on making a copy now."

Gabe crossed his arms. "I don't like it."

"It's the best weapon we have. We are open to hearing some other solution if you have it. We certainly can't give them the real one. Not to mention we're having the pages tagged."

I grinned. "You're using isotopes?"

Amelia blinked in surprise. "Oh, you're aware of the process?"

I nodded. "Yeah. It's the latest in tracking software. Those isotopes can enter your skin and can track anyone anywhere. Whoever touches those pages won't be able to hide."

"Exactly."

This time, I could feel Nissa's gaze on me. Intent. Curious.

Fuck. I missed her. And that was the problem with Nissa being on the team. I was already distracted, and Gabe would have my head if anything went wrong.

Gabe laughed. "You'll forgive me if I don't trust Interpol, right?" He shook his head. "We'll take care of the logistics. Your team is just here as backup. And I will have my own backup, you know, just in case Interpol doesn't want to play fair. Our deal is you'll get Montgomery, and we'll get Igno. We have no interest in anything else."

"If you think you can get Igno, by all means, go for it."

Gabe chuckled low. "We can get Montgomery too. Don't fuck it up, or we will take him."

Nyla cleared her throat. "Easy does it. We're on the same team here."

Gabe eyed her up and down, and there was an electric charge in the air which made me terribly uncomfortable as I realized he was sizing her up. She gave as good as she got with what could only be described as a flirtatious smile. And then she very deliberately ran her hands through her hair, showing the enormous diamond on her left hand. Gabe shrugged then and turned his attention back to Amelia.

Nissa crossed her arms. "So, *Rook* and I are going to be locked in the house until my father arrives, making sure the coast is clear, right?" My call sign sounded an epithet on her tongue.

Amelia nodded. "You father will want to verify his own safety, so he'll be cautious. It'll be just overnight. But after everything that happened with Igno, he likely won't be taking any chances."

"I don't want to see him again."

Nyla watched her carefully. "He's your father and Rook's godfather. Likely, he has some things he needs to say to the two of you."

"If he suspects a fake, he'll shoot first and ask questions later," I said. "We don't want to take chances."

"You're going to be armed with what you'll need," Nyla said. "He'll have metal detectors in place, so we're going with some different options for weapons, and 3D printers are making them now."

Gabe's brows lifted. "Oh, you've got the budget all of a sudden."

Amelia shrugged. "We need to catch Montgomery."

Gabe tipped his chair back, and I almost wished it would fall over, just to watch him scramble back up. "Why do you have such a hard-on for him?"

"Guns, trafficking, drugs, you name it," Amelia said. "Why wouldn't *you* want him?"

He shrugged and said, "Montgomery is small time."

"And you? Why do you want Igno?" Nyla asked.

He frowned. "Besides the fact that he's a known terrorist and at the top of the ten-most-wanted list for over a decade? It's personal."

She cocked her head. "Fair enough."

As they discussed the details of travel and transportation, something caught my eye in the hallway. Or rather, someone with a familiar gait. The hairs at the back of my neck stood up. Who the hell was that?

I pushed my chair back. "Excuse me for a moment."

I ran down the hall, following a hunch. Up ahead, he started moving faster. Why was he so familiar? Was he one of Montgomery's men? This was Interpol and spies were everywhere, so why was this one setting me on edge?

I followed him into the stairwell, but he'd vanished. As I stood inside scanning around, I cursed under my breath. "Fuck me."

A hand clamped over my mouth, and an arm pressed around

my throat. I drove back my elbow, and the fucker didn't even move. "Easy does it. Don't go asking questions you don't want answers to."

A blow to the head had me dazed for a nanosecond before I whipped around to see his face, but he was already through the open door and into the hall as I struggled to stay alert.

Nissa

I HADN'T EXPECTED him to come looking for me.

Yes, you did. There is too much between you.

When I headed to get coffee at the break room down the way, he pulled me into one of the offices. "Westin, let go of me. I really don't want to have anything to do with you once we take care of my father."

"Nissa, I just need three minutes, okay?"

"There's nothing you can tell me in three minutes that makes up for what you've done to my life."

He ran his hands through his hair. It had been getting longer for weeks now, but it looked like he'd trimmed the sides recently. Maybe someone had done it wherever the hell he went after the raid.

You're not supposed to be focusing on how good he looks.

"I know what you heard, but you have to believe I didn't kill your sister. Do you think I'm capable of that?"

"She's gone, *Rook*. What the hell happened to her then? I heard you say you were going to do it. And then he let you come back."

"I came back for the undercover mission. That's all. I didn't touch your sister. I did help her get the fuck away from your father. I tucked her somewhere very far away where he was never going to find her again. I helped her hide. But I didn't hurt her. I would never have hurt her. I knew what she meant to you."

My heart was squeezing like it was actually breaking. "I can't do this." I tried to shove past him, but he blocked me. His fingers holding my elbow gently.

"If you want to hate me, hate me for a real reason. I lied. I didn't tell you who I really was, that I was on an undercover mission. Even though everything I told you as your bodyguard was the truth. I was there to protect you. That's been one of my primary directives ever since I took the mission. But you cannot hate me for something I didn't do."

"Oh, yeah? Then where the fuck is my sister?" I hated that there was a part of me that wanted to believe him despite hearing the evidence for myself. I wanted to believe that he wouldn't do that to me. That he wasn't that person. That the boy I had loved was still there inside him somewhere.

But it was folly. Pure folly. Because he had already proven what an excellent liar he was.

"Look, like I said and like you heard, your father gave me the ultimatum. Remove Lenora permanently, or he was going to hurt me and Mrs. Pembry. And he told me the caveat for me coming back was pulling the trigger. And I knew that night when I left that I couldn't go back to you, anyway. I had to walk away forever. And I knew he wasn't going to let me just get away with not doing as I was directed."

"So you just left?"

"Yeah. I grabbed my gear from the house, and he had one of his men escort me off the premises. And I did try to come for you. Two weeks later when you went back to school, I tried to get on campus. But his men were fucking everywhere. When I didn't return from 'eliminating' Lenora, he knew I'd try to come for you."

My brow furrowed. "Wait? You came to school?"

He nodded. "Yeah. You were with your mates after field hockey practice. Your one mate, I don't know her name, she was on crutches, and you were walking behind a larger pack of friends with her."

My stomach flipped. I remembered that day. Our captain had broken her bloody toe, and the fracture had gone all the way into her foot. So she'd been benched, and she was giving me pointers for my game. He was telling the truth.

"When I knew I couldn't get to you safely, I thought it was better to leave you be. I knew it would be safer for both you and for Mrs. Pembry. But I knew that if I didn't do the job he gave me, he would send someone else. So I had to take care of Lenora."

I could practically feel the hint of truth in what he was saying. But I didn't want to. I wanted to hold it at bay. Because I was terrified of what I would find at the end of this story.

"I tracked her down with the information Julian had given me. She was living in Council housing and was afraid to come with me at first until I showed her a photo of you and me and the snow globe I gave you for your birthday. That was how I got her to trust me."

Tears stung my eyes, but I tried to blink to keep them at bay. "Was she okay? Did she miss me?"

"Once she believed who I was and that I was there to help her, she had so many questions about you. I spent that first meeting with her just telling her every little Nissa story I could think of."

"What was she like? Did she have friends?"

He hesitated before answering. "She said she was fine, but that nothing was holding her there."

"Where is she now?"

He shook his head. "I haven't looked in a while. But when I

helped her and taught her how to hide, we spent about two weeks together. I got her some fake documents. I showed her how to stay under the radar and made her vanish. I gave her a drop location and a burner phone so she could reach out to me whenever she needed money or anything."

"You give her money?"

"I try. She never uses it though. Maybe she worries the money came from illegal means. I don't know. But through the years when she moves to a new location she sometimes lets me know. Last I heard from her she was in Barcelona."

"Barcelona," I breathed. "That was mum's favorite city. She probably feels at home there."

His eyes searched mine. "You believe me?"

My nose was stinging now from the unshed tears. "I wasn't sure until you said she was in Barcelona. We always talked about going back, maybe living there together when we were grownups."

He nodded slowly. "I knew you were looking for her, and I knew it hurt you not to have her in your life. But I couldn't tell you what I knew for fear that Julian would kill her."

My brows furrowed as I thought of something else. "If you didn't kill her, why did Julian let you come back?"

His eyes shone with tears. "I came back for you. When Gabe called me into his office and told me about the assignment, I could have refused. I could have said no. I could have used any excuse not to go back under. Julian thought I'd returned under duress, but essentially, I let him capture me. He thought he was following clues about my whereabouts, because as it turned out, he'd been looking for me ever since I left. His own hubris brought me back. I was very relieved to see Mrs. Pembry intact."

"So Lenora is alive, just living her life somewhere and she's okay?"

"She's fine. I taught her well. Turns out she's not half bad with computers. Every time she moves, she gets a job. Finds a life. Makes friends."

The tears were falling freely now, and I wiped them away with the back of my hand. "Thank you for not killing my sister."

"I was never capable of something like that. I could never do something that would hurt you that profoundly. Believe me or not, I have loved you ever since I met you by that brook. And I'm sorry that my leaving hurt you, but the alternative was something I just couldn't do."

I lifted my gaze to his. "I shot you."

His response was a low chuckle. "You did. Still hurts to breathe, but I'm okay." He pulled out a phone that was different from the one he normally used. "I wasn't allowed to have this one on the mission. But this is a photo she sent me from outside an Adele concert last year."

Lenora was grinning at the camera. A peppy looking brunette was leaning on her shoulder grinning like a loon as well. Behind them was the Adele marquis. And off to the right, was a sign announcing vendors for Oktoberfest last year.

"She sends you pictures?" my voice broke as I asked.

"Sometimes. She calls them her proof-of-life pics. I got worried two years ago when she vanished for three months and I couldn't find her. She didn't pick up her drops or anything. As it turned out, some boyfriend had dumped her and she'd gotten depressed." He put his phone away. "We'll get past this Julian thing, Interpol will arrest him, and I'll bring her to you. I swear it on my life."

He was telling the truth. He hadn't killed her.

"That's it. That's the story. I know I lied to you. I know that this whole time I haven't been honest about who I was. And truth is I would do it again. The truth would have been dangerous for you. And I would do anything to keep you safe."

His fingers traced up my arm, and I could feel the coldness

melting off my skin as the warmth of love seeped back in. Before I knew it, I was back in his arms and he was clutching me tightly. The last few days of uncertainty and guilt and pain melted away, and I felt how I always did in his arms. *Safe.*

Now all we had to do was survive this mission.

39

NISSA

Leave it to me that the first time I got to go to Greece it was under these circumstances.

It was just like everyone said. The water was such a crystal-clear blue it looked like you could dip a glass in and pull out blue water to drink. Of course that was all an illusion from the clear skies making it look like clean water, but I didn't care. It was beautiful.

All the stark white buildings surrounded us. I knew my father loved Athens, but I'd never actually come on his trips here. But I was not here for enjoyment. I was going to finally close the chapter with my father and after all this time, it would finally be over.

The kicker was, I didn't know how I felt about it.

"Are you okay?" The deep voice behind me had my blood humming.

Why did his voice always do that to me? Just hearing it was enough to make my libido stand up and purr.

I shook my head. "No. I'm not sure if I'll ever be okay."

"It's almost over, Nissa."

"Yeah, but at what cost? The plan we came up with involves me stopping my life until you can catch Igno. I hate that."

"Gabe already worked it out with your professors. As long as you finish the coursework, you'll be fine. And I promise you, my team is good. We will bring Igno down forever."

"I trust you, I guess. I just... I wanted something different, you know?"

He smiled at me then and sat down next to me. "What does Nissa Montgomery want to be when she grows up?"

I shrugged. "That's easy. Happy. I thought I wanted to do, you know, the translation thing. But once my father is behind bars, I can find a job here in London. Three months ago, I would have told you that I was going to find my sister. I was going to be a lawyer. I was going to do all these things. And now I don't know."

"You look really happy kicking arse. I just want to point that out."

"This is interesting, for sure. It requires a lot more training than I have, so I'd have to do that."

"I think you'd be good at it."

The heat crept up my neck and into my face. "Thanks."

"It's true."

We sat in silence for a moment, and the words *I missed you, please hold me* were on the tip of my tongue. Instead, I just nodded and looked back at the water.

It was his deep voice that brought me out of my reverie. "Nissa?"

I turned to face him, and he said, "Just so you know, I meant every word I said to you when we were talking about Lenora. Maybe you think that I was faking it or something, but I wasn't. I don't know what you're going to do with your life, but I'm going to clear the playing field for you so you don't have miles to climb to get to the top. You get to pick your path. I want to give that to you."

The tears were coming, no matter how hard I tried to blink them away. "Why do you have to be like this?"

"Like what?"

"Sweet. You're doing that thing that make me want to believe you, want to be loved by you."

His voice was soft when he asked. "If I said it over and over again, would you believe me?"

I lifted my gaze to meet his. His blue eyes were intent on mine and a lock of hair fell over his brow. "Are you saying it?"

As I waited for him to answer, I put my hand against my ribs and held my breath. I held it for so long I started to feel slightly dizzy, as he slowly nodded. "Nissa Montgomery, I have loved you, body, mind, and spirit since the day we met at the creek. You were trying to be so brave. I loved you when you punched Alistair Cooper on behalf of your mate, Emmy. I was so horrified that I had to let you in the car with Frank Michelin, but then you handled him, and I loved you for that. I didn't leave because I didn't love you. I left because I *did*. I knew I couldn't contain my feelings for you anymore, and your father knew. He threatened to hurt you, and I couldn't watch that. I knew if I wasn't there, you'd be safe. So, I left."

"I know you said something like that before, but—"

"Let me be clear, I have always and will always protect you with my life. My life is forfeit without you because I love you. I wish I could have told you about Rogues. If I could have shoved the assignment away, I would have. Anything to keep you safe, because my coming back only endangered you more."

"No, it didn't. I endangered myself. Fucking with things I didn't understand. Fucking with things I have no business poking around in. I did this."

"You were looking for your sister. That's all." He sighed and ran his hands through his hair. "You did everything you could do to stay out of this. You were just searching for a connection, for a family. There's nothing wrong with that. I'm proud of what you've done, every step of the way. And to say you got one over me... It's hard to do, so well done."

"I missed you so much."

"I missed you too, Nissa. More than I can ever say. All I've ever wanted is you."

"And all I've ever wanted was to be loved."

"Well, mission accomplished. Here we are."

Yes, I was hurt that he'd lied. Yes, it was all confusing. But I'd always wanted him. I turned to him, and he asked, "What's it going to be, Nissa? Are you mine?"

"Always."

WESTIN

In the morning, I caressed Nissa's arm as she lay awake staring at the ceiling. "I see you're up."

"Yeah. I see that you're up too."

She rolled over in my arms, and I pulled her tighter. "Is it okay that I'm worried?"

"You know this plan is how it needs to be."

"Forgive me, but I've spent half of my adult life trying to make sure that you're safe. So, putting you in harm's way is going to be a problem for me. How am I supposed to not worry?"

"Fucking hell. When I think of everything my father has done, everything he's put us through, I want to kill him myself."

"Believe me, I understand the sentiment. He kept us apart for so long, he kept you from your sister for so long, but we're going to put a stop to this. Put an end to him."

"It's hard to believe he's such a monster. Sometimes I actually felt love from him. But I think that was the point, to show us just enough love so that we'd do as we were told. In the end, he's about to reap the benefits of fucking with us."

From the moment we left the villa, we knew we were being watched. We walked along the streets of Athens, winding around the cobblestone streets like tourists. When we got the all-clear from Saff and Lock, we headed on down to the pier. We were being watched by Interpol and Rogues alike. Just as we'd said, everyone working together. I was worried that Gabe had some plan up his sleeve because we could never be sure with him. But as of that moment, everyone was playing nice.

When we got to the marina, I took the boat out nice and easy, and Nissa and I laid it on thick, kissing, holding each other, making sure that anyone watching could see that we were a couple in love. Absolutely in love. No question. And then, as we got further up to our marked point on the map, I put the anchor down. We'd already tagged Montgomery's location. He had men on us from one of the seaside houses. Nissa was sunbathing, and I had to swallow the instant surge of lust as my gaze ran over her.

"You do like to tempt me."

"Hey, it's not my fault you're tempted."

My gut twisted and knotted. "Nissa, I really wish we didn't have to do this."

"Me to, but we do, so get on board."

She strolled up to me, and then I picked up her bag and made sure that Montgomery's man could see it. In case they had someone videotaping to try and read our lips, we went through the script. "What the fuck is this, Nissa?"

She frowned and threw up her hands. "I don't know what you're talking about."

I opened the bag, making a huge production of it, arms flailing. Then I pulled out the one thing Montgomery wanted more than anything. The ledger. When I waved it in front of her face,

Nissa just tilted her chin up. "So what? I figured it was better in my purse than where you hid it."

"We agreed we'd keep it safe. Hidden. You have exposed us."

"Have I? Or are you just too paranoid?"

"And you're not paranoid enough."

"Relax. Besides, I have my own plans for the ledger. Sure, we told the old man that we were going to turn it over, but I don't want to."

"Are you mad?"

"No, I'm perfectly sane."

"You're one hundred percent mad if you think I'm going back on that deal. I'm not. I want this over."

She reached for the book, and I shoved her back.

My instinct wanted me to reach for her, but I stopped myself.

She laughed and launched herself at me. Again, I stopped her as easily and gently as I could. But with enough force to make it look real.

And then came the choreography. I blocked her attack above, dropped the bag and the fake ledger and wrapped my hand around her neck. I pulled her close, her eyes wide but completely trusting as she whispered, "Come on, get it done. I'll see you on the other side."

I knew that she was in no danger, but still, just the idea of it made me sick. I almost couldn't do it.

I telegraphed my punch on purpose, making it look like I hit her in the gut. And then in a choreographed move to make it look like I was hitting her in the face, I threw a punch. She deliberately collapsed and went limp in my arms. Her lips twitched, and I had to shove down a laugh. Now was not the time. I managed to look around, and then I lifted her body up and tipped her over. And just like that, she was in the water. There was no splashing. No moving about. I knew Lock, who was our strongest diver, was underwater watching her body as it floated to the top, and then he wrapped a hand around her ankle and pulled her down. The key to selling it was for her not to thrash around, not to flail, but to stay completely still. And she did. I knew he was releasing air bubbles underneath the water to make it look like she was drowning. And I prayed to God this worked. Then that was it. I knew for a fact she had breathing apparatus on. It was simple. And then I followed the script. I scrubbed a hand over my face and pulled anchor, just like we planned. I knew for a fact that Montgomery would be paying me a visit shortly.

It was time for the real game to begin.

40

NISSA

My HANDS WERE slick with sweat as I geared up.

Saffron eyed me up and down. "Are you sure you want to do this?

"Yeah. I'm sure. My father was going to hand me off to that psychopath, so I'm one hundred percent sure."

Saff gave me a sharp nod then handed me the butt of a gun. "This one's pretty easy. It's lightweight, not too heavy."

I took it gratefully and shoved it in the holster.

Kaya adjusted my vest for me. "This is the underlayer. You want to make sure that's pulling up over the top."

"I've never heard of this before."

"New tech. Ultrathin. I love the tech of it all."

"Okay. You look so young. How long have you been part of Rogues?"

"Well, it's a long story, but technically, I've been a Rogue since I was born. My mother was a Rogue before she disappeared."

I frowned. "I'm sorry."

"Oh, don't be. She's fine. Much to everyone's shock."

I found that curious, but now was probably not the time for questions.

"But I've only been training for about six months," Kaya said.

"Oh, so you're fresh like me."

"Yes, so as a training mission for me, I will be inside the van."

Saff nodded. "Damn straight you will be. I will not have your husband threatening me with certain death because you left the van."

She grinned. "He is a right pain in the arse."

I laughed. "Aren't all men?"

"Yes, actually, I've found that to be true."

I looked at Saff. "How long have you been in Rogues?"

"Literally all my life. My grandfather founded the Rogues."

I lifted my brows. "Oh, damn."

She shrugged. "It's kind of in the blood. But it's not all fun and games."

"I don't imagine it would be."

"No. Antonio Igno, he's been enemy number one for a long time."

I frowned as she glanced outside.

"When this is all over," Saff said, "you're going to tell us all about you and Rook over a drink."

I had to laugh at that. "It's a story that's been written for years."

"Aren't all the best stories like that?"

"Actually, yes. Okay, I'm ready."

When we were all geared up in black head to toe, Saff handed out masks, and then Gabe stepped out of the van. His gaze met mine. "I'm only allowing you to do this because Rook owes you something. Otherwise, you wouldn't be here. Do you understand me?"

I nodded. "Yeah, I get you."

"Make sure you understand. You are here by invitation, so

stay focused and don't get dead. I can't have Rook in my face if something happens to you."

I nodded. "Who gets in your face if something happens to him?"

He sighed. "By the looks of it, you."

I shrugged. "Accurate."

We all had our positions. I went with Saint and Saffron as Lachlan and Gabe headed to the north side.

Saint was behind me, and Saff was in front of me. And when we pushed to the house, Saff waited as we listened in on Westin's conversation. We heard a man's voice say, "I don't think you understand, you were meant to bring her with you."

"There has been a complication," my father said. "Nissa and Westin had a slight misunderstanding."

There was silence for a moment, and then Igno's voice was low and icy. "You killed her?"

"Yes, it was expeditious. She was holding on to the ledger. And I know Montgomery well. There was no way he planned on me living. Lo and behold, I was right."

Saff gave me the hold command and I tried to be still.

Igno's voice was terse. "That was the deal. No girl, no deal. What's to keep me from killing you, St. James?"

Westin's voice was clear. "Oh, nothing. Except I didn't bring it with me. I know better. This is a live feed of exactly where it is. As you can see on my phone screen, right there is the ledger, and there's a time stamp."

Igno laughed. "Well, well. You have outsmarted us all, haven't you? Except, you see, I seem to be without my cash."

Westin's voice was firm. "In that case, I guess this is a stalemate."

Those six words were our cue. We were going in.

The fear erupted through me as Saint and Saffron went forward. I knew exactly what my job was. Hang back, stay close.

And when my father, being the weasel that he was, invariably tried to sneak off, my face alone would stop him.

We marched in, gunfire already exploding around me. It was complete chaos. This was what it meant, staying cool under fire.

Saff gave me a signal on my shoulder, and I drew my gun. Point and shoot. I'd been shooting before, and I was okay at it. But I'd been taking judo since I was a child. So if push came to shove, I knew how to handle myself.

What I wanted to do was go to Westin and confirm that he was okay, but it was impossible.

All I could do was play my part and hope to Christ that he played his and this would all be right in the end.

I followed the figure sneaking out the back along the side of the house. I met him in the backyard, weapon drawn. "Where are you going, Dad?"

He whipped around. "No."

"Yes. I know you're confused. Shocked, even."

"So, it was ruse?"

"Does it matter? All you need to know is I'm here, and you're not getting away."

"Nissa, this is ridiculous. You know that. It doesn't have to be like this."

"In fact, Dad, it does."

He sighed and lifted his phone to his ear. "On my mark, take the shot."

I looked down and saw the red dot on my chest. He had a backup plan. "Well then, I guess this is it. I knew you never loved me."

"You're a means to an end, Nissa."

And then the crack of gunfire filled the air.

41

WESTIN

In the chaos that ensued, the gunfire, the smoke, and the stench of seared flesh, I ran after Igno.

Fire blazed through my right arm where a bullet had grazed me, but I didn't let up. Igno was running, and I had my sights on him.

In my ear, Saff was shouting orders. "Rook, confirm sighting. Come in, Rook."

"Yes, I have him. North side, headed toward downtown. In pursuit."

Saff's voice was clear. "Roger. We've taken care of contingencies."

For someone older, he was quick. I was faster, but I also had to be smarter. He knew exactly where he was going, which meant I had to anticipate his movements.

We'd studied the map of this area during planning, and knew he had three possible routes. One down by the water, which meant a waiting boat. We had men down there, but I didn't think that boat was the way he was going to go. Open water was going to be a problem for him. He would need a port. A car was the other way out. Entirely possible. We might not be able to follow him in traffic as he'd be going to a more heavily populated area. And then there was the helipad. So, was it the car or the helipad?

He ran into a crowd ahead, celebrating the Apokries Festival. It was harder to pick him out in the crowd.

"Fuck, anyone have eyes?"

Saff's voice was winded. "No, no eyes. King?"

"No, no eyes."

Saint huffed. "No eyes, but we have Montgomery."

I had to know. "Secondary Montgomery?"

Her voice sounded like the sweetest nectar. "Alive and kicking. Please go get that arsehole, Rook."

"On it."

Gabe's voice was the one that came through. "I see him in the crowd. He made a left up ahead. I'll head him off."

"Where do you think he's going?"

Gabe's voice was clear. "He's going for the car."

That made sense. Outside with the crowd, he'd be easy to lose. Except I had a nagging feeling. "I'm playing a hunch."

Instead of going right, like Gabe instructed, I went left, heading up the stairs onto one of the taller residences. The network connections between the houses and rooftops made it easy to leap from building to building. I hoped the fuck I was right. The helipad was four buildings southeast.

I slammed through the door of the roof, going full tilt, thankful for the ledge at the top and my experience doing some long jumps.

Lungs burning, legs feeling like lead, I waited at the rooftop. Had I been right or had Gabe been right? "Gabe, report."

"I lost him in the crowd. I'm still searching."

In the distance, I saw a helicopter coming in. But was it coming for him? Oh fuck.

Blood hummed in my veins, and I tried to take control of my

breathing. But nothing worked until I knew for sure. I could hear stomping feet coming up the stairwell of the building. And when the rooftop door slammed open, I stepped out of the shadows and grabbed the man that came through in a chokehold.

A deadly calm settled over my body once I finally had my target. "I've got him. Target acquired. I have Antonio Igno."

He threw back an elbow. I took the hit and tightened my hold. With his free arm he clawed at his neck, trying to reach back for me, but I held on tight. And when he tried to slam me backward, all I did was wrap my legs around him in a jujitsu hold. Holding on. "You'll never hurt her again."

I held on until he tired and finally fell to his knees and onto his side.

And as I sank down, I finally released him. I drew my gun and turned to aim at the door just in case anyone was coming. Igno always had a plan B. Always. But no one came.

The helicopter hovered two buildings away, then it suddenly banked left and flew off. He had no other resources. He was down. I had bagged Rogues' number-one target. He was going to pay for everything he'd done.

He moaned on the ground, and I held my gun steady. "Uh-uh, you're not getting up.

He frowned up at me. "You can have all of it. All of the money."

"Would it surprise you to know that I don't want the money? I have family. Money is irrelevant."

"Money is never irrelevant. Go on, take me in, if you think you can make charges stick."

"Oh, that's interesting that you think you're going to be charged. You are going into a very deep dark hole. And no one is ever coming to get you."

Nissa

Westin held my hand as I asked, "Have you been back here recently?"

He shook his head. "No. Not since... you know."

We stood in front of the house in Surrey. One that apparently had been meticulously maintained.

I absently rubbed at my rib where my father had shot me, though the Kevlar I'd been wearing saved my life.

A part of me couldn't believe he'd actually fired. But then a part of me could believe it. I'd been worried about saving his life. And all the while, I was completely expendable to him. But out in the field, I had back up that I didn't know about. He'd shot me after my shot had gone just wide. But behind me, Kaya Reynolds had been there. And she hit her mark right dead center in the chest. Three shots. And my father had fallen.

"It's beautiful."

"You know," he said, "there were times that I wondered if I'd made this place up."

"Well, clearly not."

"Yeah." He slid the key inside the lock and turned it, gingerly stepping inside and then pausing. "God, it smells the same. Like cookies and perfume, I think. It smells of my mother."

"Well, now it gives you a good memory."

"Yeah, it does."

As we walked into the room, there were all these photos of the young Westin. I could see glimpses of the boy I knew. The little chubby face, the gap-toothed grin, the unruly hair. But it was the eyes. It was always the eyes. Ice-blue and slightly mischievous, framed by thick dark lashes despite the blond hair. "You were cute."

"You still think I'm cute."

I rolled my eyes. "Jesus. Of course. I see you're so humble."

He laughed. "Well, no one's ever accused me of that."

I laughed. "I can see why."

As he walked down memory lane, my heart squeezed. I was young when my parents died. I had only flickers of memories of that house, but not much information. And someone else lived in it now.

Saff had done some digging for us. It turned out Westin's father, Royce St. James, and my father, Ebert Crane had started an investment firm together. And what happened was basically an elaborate Ponzi scheme with Julian Montgomery at the helm. From what the Rogues had been able to pull together, my father and Royce hadn't known until it was far too late. After they both died under very suspicious circumstances, Julian had then realized that the money he'd thought to siphon from his business partners had been left to their children. So then he'd worked to get us under his care, even going so far as to fake a paternity test and claim to be my biological father. My feelings for him were complicated now. He'd robbed me of my entire childhood. He'd robbed me and my sister, someone who actually loved me. But there had been times when I would have sworn that he'd cared, and I was handling some shit that I was going to have to pay a lot of money to a therapist to deal with.

Westin took my hand. "I see you working it all out in your head."

"I mean, it's hard not to."

"I know. It's hard for me too, especially being here. But at least we know we were both loved. Our parents didn't abandon us. They were taken from us."

"I know. I just... It's hard to reconcile it all."

"I know. And I know it will take time. But at least we have each other."

He pulled me to him, and his woodsy, spicy scent wrapped

around me, comforting me. I inhaled deeply and a sliver of desire wove through me like a shadow. Soft and tempting. "Westin?"

He nuzzled me. "Yes, love?"

"Are those your hands on my arse?"

"Yes. Sorry, but what's a man to do? His sexy girlfriend smells good and looks good."

"You are incorrigible."

"I mean, you do smell good."

I lifted my head, looping my arm around his neck. "You smell good too. Since this is your house, where would you like to christen first?"

His gaze immediately dipped to my lips, and he bit his bottom one. "Ugh, of course, you would tempt me now."

"I tempt you always. But what's the problem with that?"

"The problem is we don't have time for that."

"Why? Where are we going?"

"We're not going anywhere. But we have to finish the tour."

"We can't make the tour wait a few minutes? I was going to give you a pretty amazing blow job."

That stopped him in his tracks. "Fuck me."

"Yeah, that's the idea."

He laughed and scooped me up, twirling me. "God, I fucking love you."

"I love you too. We survived."

He nodded once. "We survived." He slid me down his body and tentatively started kissing my lips. "But I'm hoping to do a lot more than survive. Come here."

He took my hand, pulling me through the massive kitchen and out into the sunroom. My feet faltered when I saw that there was someone in there. "Who's that?"

"Oh, you'll see."

And as he tugged me forward, my stomach started doing that flippity-floppity thing, and I knew exactly who it was.

"Lenora?"

She looked up from her phone and gave me a tremulous smile. "Hey, Nissa."

My gaze bounced back and forth between Westin and Lenora and back again. "What? How?"

She said, "I thought you two were never going to arrive."

Westin shrugged. "I got distracted."

My eyes filled with tears, and I blinked them rapidly. "You did this?"

"I did this."

The tears started falling now, freely at their own will, making my face a slippery wet mess. Lenora stepped forward, arms outstretched. "Hi, stranger."

I shook my head, weeping now. "I have been looking for you my whole life."

"And I've known exactly where you were all along. I knew every math competition you had, every debate. If I could go, I did. I got into a lot of trouble in the group homes for sneaking out, but I never, *never* forgot you, Nissa. I love you so much."

I was a weeping, blubbering mess by the time she wrapped her arms around me. She smelled like sweet brown sugar and love. And for the first time, in a long time, I let myself revel in the feeling of being whole at last.

EPILOGUE

TABITHA

He closed the door and watched me pull out of his driveway. The Hennessey Venom tires scrunched on the gravel drive. And watching him in the rearview, I knew what needed to happen next.

I opened the car up and peeled down the drive to my location point. Once I reached it, I threw the car into park, reached into my glove box, grabbed my weapon, my com unit, and the change of clothes. The leggings were easy to put on. The rest was difficult. I just gave up, ripped the dress off, tits flying in the wind, and put on my special Kevlar black tank and then the accompanying jacket.

Once I was fully dressed in tactical gear, I followed the direction of the route back toward Gabe's house. I knew I was being watched every step as I approached. I slipped into the shadows and finally eased myself into the backdoor, hoping that the people paying attention could see. When I slipped into Gabe's living area, he smirked at me from the couch.

"Hello, Tabs. Is this the part where I look surprised?"

I pulled my weapon and smiled back at him. "You're coming with me, Gabe."

"Wow, this is awkward. And here I thought you came back for round two."

I flushed thinking about his fingertips on my skin. "Nope. Don't make this difficult, or I will tranq you."

He lifted a brow. That was adlib. Not part of the script. And he knew full well I wasn't going to tranq him. I would have to drag him out of here. He was enormous and weighed a ton. He smirked at me. "Okay, I'm not one to argue with a lady. But just so you know, you'll never get away with this. My team will come for me."

And then I said the words that I worried might be true. "You'll be dead long before anyone ever comes for you."

To be continued in *The Spy*

As a special gift to my readers, I have a special bonus for you of Rook and Nissa. Click here to get your exclusive bonus epilogue for The Rook! And if you like your Epilogues on the spicy side, click here!

THANK you for reading *THE ROOK*, book 4 in the Gentlemen Rogues Series. I hope you're ready for a wild ride, the Rogues just get sexier from here!

FIRST RULE OF BEING A SPY, hide in plain sight. Second rule of being a Rogue, never get involved, the mission above all.

But I'm being tempted. I've managed to keep my hands off of my sister's best friend for years.

But one slip, one mistake, one taste and I'm obsessed. I will burn the world down for her, but first, I'll need to give up everything that I am.

Read about Gabe and Tabitha in ———>THE SPY!

WHILE YOU WAIT, dive in to another house pending heart thrumming story with Liv and Ben in **The See No Evil Trilogy:**

It began with a stolen **almost-kiss**.
And ended in **revenge**.

She was never supposed to cross my path.
She was never supposed to know about the oaths I swore or the secrets I keep.

But like a thief in the night, she **took my heart and ran...** even if she wasn't mine to possess.

➔ Yes, you can pick up **Big Ben, The Benefactor** and **For Her Benefit** now!

"...a **dramatic, suspenseful and amazing read** that you just can't put down. I loved it!"———*Goodreads Reviewer*

Love royals? Meet a cocky, billionaire prince that goes under-cover in **Cheeky Royal!**

He's a prince with a secret to protect. The last distraction he can afford is his gorgeous as sin new neighbor.

His secrets could get them killed, but still, he can't stay away...
Read Cheeky Royal Now!

Turn the page for an excerpt from Cheeky Royal...

UPCOMING BOOKS

THE ROOK
THE SPY
THE VILLAIN

"You make a really good model. I'm sure dozens of artists have volunteered to paint you before."

He shook his head. "Not that I can recall. Why? Are you offering?"

I grinned. "I usually do nudes." Why did I say that? It wasn't true. Because you're hoping he'll volunteer as tribute.

He shrugged then reached behind his back and pulled his shirt up, tugged it free, and tossed it aside. "How is this for nude?"

Fuck. Me. I stared for a moment, mouth open and looking like an idiot. Then, well, I snapped a picture. Okay fine, I snapped several. "Uh, that's a start."

He ran a hand through his hair and tussled it, so I snapped several of that. These were romance-cover gold. Getting into it, he started posing for me, making silly faces. I got closer to him, snapping more close-ups of his face. That incredible face.

Then suddenly he went deadly serious again, the intensity in his eyes going harder somehow, sharper. Like a razor. "You look nervous. I thought you said you were used to nudes."

I swallowed around the lump in my throat. "Yeah, at school whenever we had a model, they were always nude. I got used to it."

He narrowed his gaze. "Are you sure about that?"
Shit. He could tell. "Yeah, I am. It's just a human form. Male. Female. No big deal."

His lopsided grin flashed, and my stomach flipped. Stupid traitorous body...and damn him for being so damn good looking. I tried to keep the lens centered on his face, but I had to get several of his abs, for you know...research.
But when his hand rubbed over his stomach and then slid to the button on his jeans, I gasped, "What are you doing?"
"Well, you said you were used doing nudes. Will that make you more comfortable as a photographer?"

I swallowed again, unable to answer, wanting to know what he was doing, how far he would go. And how far would I go?

The button popped, and I swallowed the sawdust in my mouth. I snapped a picture of his hands.

Well yeah, and his abs. So sue me. He popped another button, giving me a hint of the forbidden thing I couldn't have. I kept snapping away. We were locked in this odd, intimate game of chicken. I swung the lens up to capture his face. His gaze was slightly hooded. His lips parted... turned on. I stepped back a step to capture all of him. His jeans loose, his feet bare. Sitting on the stool, leaning back slightly and giving me the sex face, because that's what it was—God's honest truth—the sex face. And I was a total goner.

"You're not taking pictures, Len." His voice was barely above a whisper.

"Oh, sorry." I snapped several in succession. Full body shots, face shots, torso shots. There were several torso shots. I wanted to fully capture what was happening.

He unbuttoned another button, taunting me, tantalizing me. Then he reached into his jeans, and my gaze snapped to meet his. I wanted to say something. Intervene in some way...help maybe...ask him what he was doing. But I couldn't. We were locked in a game that I couldn't break free from. Now I wanted more. I wanted to know just how far he would go.

Would he go nude? Or would he stay in this half-undressed state, teasing me, tempting me to do the thing that I shouldn't do?

I snapped more photos, but this time I was close. I was looking down on him with the camera, angling so I could see his perfectly sculpted abs as they flexed. His hand was inside his jeans. From the bulge, I knew he was touching himself. And then I snapped my gaze up to his face.

Sebastian licked his lip, and I captured the moment that tongue met flesh.

Heat flooded my body, and I pressed my thighs together to abate the ache. At that point, I was just snapping photos, completely in the zone, wanting to see what he might do next.

"Len..."

"Sebastian." My voice was so breathy I could barely get it past my lips.

"Do you want to come closer?"

"I--I think maybe I'm close enough?"

His teeth grazed his bottom lip. "Are you sure about that? I have another question for you."

I snapped several more images, ranging from face shots to shoulders, to torso. Yeah, I also went back to the hand-around-his-dick thing because...wow. "Yeah? Go ahead."
"Why didn't you tell me about your boyfriend 'til now?"
Oh shit. "I—I'm not sure. I didn't think it mattered. It sort of feels like we're supposed to be friends." Lies all lies.
He stood, his big body crowding me. "Yeah, friends..."
I swallowed hard. I couldn't bloody think with him so close. His scent assaulted me, sandalwood and something that was pure Sebastian wrapped around me, making me weak. Making me tingle as I inhaled his scent. Heat throbbed between my thighs, even as my knees went weak. "Sebastian, wh—what are you doing?"
"

Proving to you that we're not friends. Will you let me?"
He was asking my permission. I knew what I wanted to say. I understood what was at stake. But then he raised his hand and traced his knuckles over my cheek, and a whimper escaped.

His voice went softer, so low when he spoke, his words were more like a rumble than anything intelligible. "Is that you telling me to stop?"

Seriously, there were supposed to be words. There were. But somehow I couldn't manage them, so like an idiot I shook my head.

His hand slid into my curls as he gently angled my head. When he leaned down, his lips a whisper from mine, he whispered, "This is all I've been thinking about."
Read Cheeky Royal Now!

FREE READ

DOWNLOAD a **_complimentary_** copy of the USA Today Bestseller, SEXY IN STILETTOS? Just head to www. nanamalone.com and sign up!

NANA MALONE READING LIST

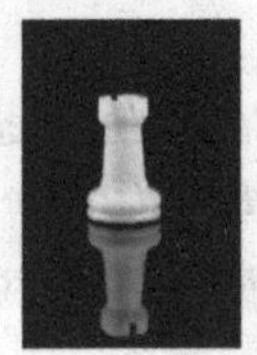

Looking for a few Good Books? Look no Further

FREE

Cheeky Royal
Protecting the Heiress
Big Ben
The Heir

Gentlemen Rogues
The Heir
The King
The Saint
The Rook
The Spy
The Villain

Royals
Royals Undercover

Cheeky Royal
Cheeky King

<u>Royals Undone</u>
Royal Bastard
Bastard Prince

<u>Royals United</u>
Royal Tease
Teasing the Princess

<u>Royal Elite</u>

The Heiress Duet

Protecting the Heiress
Tempting the Heiress

The Prince Duet
Return of the Prince
To Love a Prince

The Bodyguard Duet
Bodyguard to the Billionaire
The Billionaire's Secret

<u>London Royals</u>

London Royal Duet
London Royal
London Soul

Playboy Royal Duet

Royal Playboy
Playboy's Heart

London Lords
<u>See No Evil</u>
Big Ben
The Benefactor
For Her Benefit

<u>Hear No Evil</u>
East End
East Bound
Fall of East

To Catch a Thief

<u>Speak No Evil</u>
London Bridge
Bridge of Lies
Broken Bridge

The Donovans Series
<u>*Come Home Again (Nate & Delilah)*</u>
<u>*Love Reality (Ryan & Mia)*</u>
<u>*Race For Love (Derek & Kisima)*</u>
<u>*Love in Plain Sight (Dylan and Serafina)*</u>
<u>*Eye of the Beholder – (Logan & Jezzie)*</u>
<u>*Love Struck (Zephyr & Malia)*</u>

London Billionaires Standalones
Mr. Trouble (Jarred & Kinsley)
Mr. Big (Zach & Emma)
Mr. Dirty(Nathan & Sophie)

The Player
Bryce
Dax
Echo
Fox
Ransom
Gage

The In Stilettos Series
Sexy in Stilettos (Alec & Jaya)
Sultry in Stilettos (Beckett & Ricca)
Sassy in Stilettos (Caleb & Micha)
Strollers & Stilettos (Alec & Jaya & Alexa)
Seductive in Stilettos (Shane & Tristia)
Stunning in Stilettos (Bryan & Kyra)
~~~
***In Stilettos Spin off***
*Tempting in Stilettos (Serena & Tyson)*
*Teasing in Stilettos (Cara & Tate)*
*Tantalizing in Stilettos (Jaggar & Griffin)*


***Love Match Series***
*\*Game Set Match (Jason & Izzy)*
*Mismatch (Eli & Jessica)*


**Don't want to miss a single release? Click here!**
~~~